William Hussey is the critically acclaimed author of over a dozen novels. Winner of the Genre Busting Book of the Year Fingerprint Award for *Killing Jericho*, he has also been shortlisted for the Theakston's Old Peculier Crime Novel of the Year, the CrimeFest Award and the Polari Prize.

Born the son of a travelling showman, he has spent a lifetime absorbing the history, folklore and culture of fairground people, knowledge he has now put to work in his Scott Jericho thrillers. William lives in Dumfries with his partner Chris and their criminally adorable cat Harry.

Also by William Hussey
Killing Jericho
Jericho's Dead

BURYING JERICHO

WILLIAM HUSSEY

ZAFFRE

First published in the UK in 2025 by
ZAFFRE
An imprint of Bonnier Books UK
5th Floor, HYLO, 103–105 Bunhill Row, London, EC1Y 8LZ
Owned by Bonnier Books
Sveavägen 56, Stockholm, Sweden

Copyright © William Hussey, 2025

All rights reserved.
No part of this publication may be reproduced,
stored or transmitted in any form by any means, electronic,
mechanical, photocopying or otherwise, without the
prior written permission of the publisher.

The right of William Hussey to be identified as Author of this
work has been asserted by him in accordance with the
Copyright, Designs and Patents Act, 1988.

This is a work of fiction. Names, places, events and
incidents are either the products of the author's
imagination or used fictitiously. Any resemblance to
actual persons, living or dead, or actual
events is purely coincidental.

A CIP catalogue record for this book is
available from the British Library.

Hardback ISBN: 978-1-80418-166-9
Trade paperback ISBN: 978-1-80418-167-6

Also available as an ebook and an audiobook

1 3 5 7 9 10 8 6 4 2

Typeset by IDSUK (Data Connection) Ltd
Printed and bound in Great Britain by Clays Ltd, Elcograf S.p.A.

www.bonnierbooks.co.uk

*For Veronique Baxter and Ben Willis.
Agent and editor extraordinaire, without whom Scott Jericho
would never have left his trailer.*

Chapter One

HARRY TRIED TO PASS ME the walking stick and I wrenched it roughly from his grasp, throwing it onto the back seat of the Merc and slamming the door. Then my gaze swept that peaceful suburban crescent, hunting out potential threats behind lace-curtained windows, anxious as a condemned man who'd just been handed his death sentence.

'What the hell do you think you're doing, you rank joskin?' I hissed at him. 'Do you want to get us both killed?'

Swaddled in my long trench coat, a thick minder's scarf wound around my throat, still I shivered. And not just through the cold. The coat felt two sizes too big for me, like I was a little chavvy all dressed up in his father's duds. Harry stood at my side in his canary-yellow cagoule, those gentle jade eyes crinkled with concern. He looked seasonally elfish with his green beanie hat and the pink tip of his nose. Altogether too innocent for a job like this.

'I'm sorry, but we can't risk it,' I told him, moderating my tone. 'Not here. We show any sign of weakness to these people, it'll be like throwing Chum to a school of sharks. Sharks with knuckledusters and Beretta pistols.'

'But you can hardly walk without it,' Harry objected. 'You've only been in physio a couple of weeks, and admit it, Scott, you're crap at keeping up with your exercises. You're not strong enough for this. Not yet.'

I stole a glance at myself in the Merc's driver-side window. He's right. Who was this wiry-framed stranger, his strong-featured face thin and pinched; whose were those hollowed-out eyes staring from behind a curtain of dishevelled blue-black curls?

I've lived what some might call a hardscrabble existence, born in my parents' trailer on a travelling fair; moving from place to place, building up and pulling down rides and stalls, working ever since I could hold a spanner. The kind of life that tempers a boy into a man early on, forging him hard and flinty. It was also a life I'd longed to escape. And I had, for a time. My head full of romance and books, in my late teens I'd waved farewell to the fair and run away to university. The only good thing I'd found among those dreaming spires was the man standing next to me. Harry Moorhouse. My love, my conscience, my lodestar in the darkness.

When I had lost him for a decade, to his own guilt and despair following the death of his father, the physical strength I'd built in my travelling days had served me well. In the misery of those lonely years, when I'd wanted nothing more than to forget the man I'd loved, I had become a thug for hire, collecting the debts and repaying the grievances of gangsters. Actions that chipped away at my soul, until finally a man named Peter Garris entered my life. A mentor and a monster who had drawn me over that thin blue line. I had flourished working in CID, but again only for a time. My attack on a far-right lunatic and suspected child-murderer had been rewarded with imprisonment and disgrace, following which my fairground family had, without question, taken me back. All that was six months ago, and since then I had reforged something of a reputation as a detective, albeit now in a private capacity.

Cases had come my way, strange and harrowing mysteries which called to that darkness that seemed to move inside me like a shadow self. And so yes, a hard, eventful life. Until recently, however, it seemed to have taken little out of me. I had never once looked my thirty-one years.

Now I looked it, and more. The best part of six weeks in a coma will do that to you I suppose.

'You're not strong enough for this,' Harry repeated, his gaze on one of those nondescript terraced houses across the street. Again he pulled open the rear door and offered me the walking stick, again I ordered him to put it back.

'Then I'd better learn to fake it,' I said. 'And quickly. Or else neither of us might be getting out of here alive.'

'Scott, please—'

'Come on,' I said, leading the way. 'A favour is owed, and we've left Mark Noonan waiting long enough.'

A hard frost glinted across the roofs and bonnets of the cars lining that charming west London crescent, landscaping windscreens into miniature tundras and laying thick cataracts over mirrors and headlights. Above us, a nothing December sky capped the borough of Hounslow. It was freezing, the pavements death traps, the paths up to the houses a fractured hip waiting to happen. Still, at our approach to number 56 Sanford Crescent, doors were opened and neighbours gathered on those lethal steps, cardiganed arms folded, snorting steam and monitoring us with fixed smiles. These were the mobster's watchdogs. Mark Noonan owned all the houses on this street and let them rent-free to a select club of pensioners who kept their eyes open and their mouths shut. It was the perfect camouflage for the headquarters of that wily old cockney gangster, in whose service I had once forfeited my conscience.

The gate squeaked on its frosted hinge as we stepped into the front garden of number 56. The neatly ordered flowerbeds, tended in spring and summer by those old dears who stood sentinel on their doorsteps, now lay dead or dormant. We were halfway along the path when I grasped at the fence for support, the coma-wasted muscles of my left leg almost giving way. Harry made a grab for me, but a word was enough to usher him back. I glared at my gloved hand planted on the fencepost. Under the leather, this was no longer a strong showman's hand, bunched with muscle. What lay beneath was now more like a withered claw.

'Compliments of the season, stranger,' an age-cracked voice called out. I turned my head and the pensioners waved in unison, like festive figures in some automated shopping centre tableau. *Stranger?* I'd been here before, many times, but perhaps I could forgive them for not recognising me now.

'And to you,' I called back. 'Merry Christmas.'

A holly wreath hung from the letterbox of number 56. Plastic blood-red berries among sprigs of artificial ivy, as synthetic as the street behind me. I rang the doorbell and a burst of *Good King Wenceslas* trilled out.

'I must be mad, letting you come here,' I murmured to Harry.

'You didn't let me,' he said. 'It was my decision. We're a team now, remember?'

I shivered and he rubbed a little warmth into my arm. I never used to feel the cold. Travellers never do. We stand out in all seasons, face every element to earn our living. It inures us to the chill.

'Here, let me, it's slipped a bit.' Harry reached up, pulling aside the scarf and adjusting the collar of my polo neck just at the point where my burns became visible. The puckered pathways of flame, a memento from my last case. 'There.' He smiled. 'Like I said, a team.'

'We are,' I agreed. 'God forgive me.'

I thumbed the bell again and this time we're treated to 'O Little Town of Bethlehem.' Harry grimaced. I could tell the off-key jangle offended his musician's sensibilities. I stamped my feet, blew out a frustrated breath, rapped my knuckles on the door. It juddered in response, a little loose in its frame. I glanced over my shoulder to see the Stepford Geriatrics still watching from their perches. Fuck it. I pushed open the door. The short hallway beyond stood empty. My eyes followed a flight of ceramic ducks up the stairs to the vacant landing.

'Mark? You here … ? Noonan, it's Scott Jericho. If you or your hubbies are about, don't fucking shoot us. We're coming in, all right?'

I opened the door to the dining room, kitchen, downstairs toilet and finally the sitting room at the back of the house. A hideous gold and brown hexagonal-patterned carpet, two bow-seated armchairs and a violently green settee, the arms worn to the stuffing by generations of overflowing ashtrays and the tap of nervous fingers. I glanced up at the painting that hung over the electric fire, a strand of tinsel draped around the frame. Dear old Nana Noonan seemed to return my gaze. This pug-faced gorgon had raised her grandson faithfully in the family business, introduced him to a dozen pimps and drug traffickers before the age of ten, then taken him along to the Mecca Bingo Hall every Friday night with her best friend Mabel Goodman. A beloved matriarch of the underworld who could turn children into psychopaths, make hardened criminals beg for mercy, and run a score of bingo cards simultaneously.

'Shit decorations,' Harry murmured.

'They were hers,' I said, nodding at the picture. 'Noonan is sentimental about stuff like that.'

I took a turn of the room, pulling aside stray sofa cushions as if they might conceal a rogue gangster. Where was he? And where were the husbands – those young men who courted the middle-aged mobster and played up to his vanities? The house breathed an unnatural kind of stillness.

It was as I drew the coffee-coloured curtains that covered the French window that I noticed movement at the far end of the garden, right where the fence ran up against the railway tracks. A large block of a boy, all steroid-enhanced biceps with the stick-thin legs that often goes along with such a physique, was holding something sharp and shiny at Mark Noonan's throat. Even from this distance and with the windows closed, I could hear the mobster's squeal.

I limped over to the artificial fireplace and plucked up a poker. Straight away I could tell it was hollow, ornamental, no weight to it at all. Noonan had money, not as much as he used to, admittedly, but he was still rolling in the posh. He could afford a real poker, but instead he insisted on keeping Nana's house pretty much as she had furnished it in the fifties, in memory of that moustachioed queen-pin. If only she'd known her beloved boy might one day be panting at the business end of a switchblade, she might have invested in the genuine article.

'Go back to the car and get my stick,' I whispered to Harry.

'Oh, so you want it now?' he asked, his eyes wide as he followed my gaze.

'Just go.'

He didn't need telling twice.

I moved back into the hall, looked about again, called upstairs, hoping Charlie or one of the old timers might be on hand. The house continued to breathe that uncharacteristic emptiness. I studied the vintage Bakelite on the table by the door, wondering if I should put through an anonymous call to the gavvers. I wasn't sure Noonan would thank me for such an act, and anyway, by the time they arrived the godfather of Sanford Cresent might well be rolled up, snug as a bug in a knock-off Persian rug, awaiting disposal.

The house was so still that I couldn't help flinching as Harry stepped back inside, my rubber-handled, height-adjustable, NHS-issued walking stick in hand. When I told him to return to the car and wait for me there, he shook his head. And so I reluctantly led the way to the kitchen and the side door.

'Now listen, Timmo, I'll get you whatever you want, baby doll,' Noonan blubbered. 'Always been a good hubby to you, haven't I? Always looked after you like the precious boy you—' He blinked those piggy eyes in wonder as he caught sight of us over Timmo's shoulder, moving as noiselessly as we could down the garden path. *Yes, it's me, you psychotic fuck.* I made a rolling gesture with my hand: *keep him talking.*

'You want some ket? I'll get you some ket.' Noonan swallowed and the blade surfed the wave of his Adam's apple. 'All the ket my kitty can take. You don't even have to blow me for it. Just calm down and let's talk this through.'

'Talk it through, you ugly piece of shit?' Timmo shouted in his dear old hubby's face. 'You keep making promises but you never keep none of 'em. If I slit you open, right here and now, then I get to take what I want anyway. I know where you keep it, stored up like a fucking squirrel in the attic. And if I did saw through that fat throat of yours, I'd only be doing you a favour. Your time is done, old man.'

Focused on the need that burned through his veins, Timmo didn't hear the crack of my tread on the frozen ground behind him, didn't see my shadow fall at his victim's feet. I pulled the walking stick over my shoulder and took my swing. I'm a practised hand at such things and so calibrated the blow, enough to drop the kid without doing any permanent damage. Timmo went down like a swooning damsel in a Victorian novel. In the next instant, Noonan was busy laying in the boot, a dozen vicious kicks to the groaning boy's midriff, red-faced and screaming, jowls jangling away like cheap earrings.

'Take it easy,' I said, pulling the mobster off the kid.

'Don't you dare interfere with my . . .' Noonan took a breath, then smiled and shook his head. 'Nah, you're right. I'll deal with him properly later. It happens from time to time with these young 'uns, you know?'

'It will,' I said. 'If you keep them hopped up twenty-four-seven.'

A shout from the kitchen doorway as a host of husbands appeared, all loud voices and botoxed brows in search of an expression. They dropped their shopping bags and came running, clustering about their beloved boss like chemically inflated hens around a middle-aged chick.

'Where the hell have you useless bastards been?' Noonan demanded. 'Out spending my money again while I'm stuck here with a blade riding my carotid. If it hadn't been for Scott and his handsome friend, I'd be a corpse right about now, ready to be dumped in the nearest landfill.'

For the first time, I glanced at Harry. In all the excitement I had forgotten him. A hard thing to admit, troubling yet true nonetheless. He seemed a little shaken but I was proud to see he didn't show it. You'd have to know him like I did to pick up on the signs.

Looking back at the crowd of husbands, I scanned them for a familiar face but there was no sign of the man I most wanted to see among their number. Meanwhile, Noonan continued to berate his men while laying in a final kick to the gasping Timmo. His voice had always been high and piping, but I'd never heard it crack before. I looked at that grey flesh dangling from his jaw, creased as rhino hide, the designer tracksuit grubby and unwashed, those sausage fingers sporting fewer diamond rings than before. His outrage sated, the mobster turned back to us.

'Let's get up to the house,' he said. 'I'll have one of these useless bitches stick the kettle on. Then we can talk about that favour you owe me.'

Chapter Two

CHINTZY DOILIES, A PLATE OF Hobnobs, teacups and saucers with cats on for Christ's sake. Never mind the drug dealing and smuggling rackets, his flatware alone should have seen Mark Noonan serving a ten-year stretch.

'My, but aren't you a pretty one?' he cooed over Harry. 'Then again, Scottster here always could pull the most gorgeous boys. It was keeping them that seemed to baffle him.'

I looked at the pudgy, past-his-prime gangster and wondered: why had I come back here at all? I supposed the answer was obvious. When you owe Mark Noonan a favour and he calls it in, you better pay him court. If you want to keep the standard set of bollocks, that is. And after all, some old beasts are at their most dangerous when they sense the end is near.

'Cut to the chase, Mark,' I said. 'You called me, I'm here. What do you want?'

Noonan luxuriated in his armchair, one outsized leg thrown, coquettishly so he imagined, over the arm, teacup balanced on the slab of his knee. 'Yes you are, here at long fucking last. The Great Showman Detective returns, back from the dead and twice as ugly. I've been keeping all your press clippings, you know. Get the youngsters to print them off the net for me, can't stand looking at things on a screen. You were big news after that spook show business up north.' Panting a little, he swung his leg off the sofa arm and, reaching down, delved a hand into the kind of bag in which Nana might have kept her coke wraps and knitting patterns. Finding what he wanted among a jumble of papers, he threw half a dozen printouts onto the coffee table in front of us. '"Police Forced to Admit: Showman Sleuth Solved Celebrity Murder." "Who is Scott Jericho? What We Know About the Talented Traveller 'Tec". "Detective Jericho Slips into Coma – Potentially Fatal Injuries Sustained in Case of Slaughtered Psychics that Shocked Britain. Full Story of Modern-Day Showman Sherlock, Pages 3, 4 and 5".' A photograph of the old me stared back from among the collection; a powerful young man, thick shining curls and a face that would make Caravaggio swoon. 'But you had to play the hero and almost got yourself burned alive, so these vultures told it,' Noonan continued. 'Was touch and go there for a while, eh? I even heard they were getting ready to measure you up for your box a time or two. That right, pretty boy?'

At his words, I saw again the fire that had engulfed me and which had claimed the lives of two others I'd tried to save. I felt the kiss of flame, intimate as a lover's caress on my hands, my chest, my throat. Only I had made it out of that inferno alive, waking for a brief period in hospital before the medics realised my injuries were triggering a massive septic infection. An induced coma followed, all in an effort to stabilise my condition. A blessed blankness, no dreams, no nightmares of the people I'd failed, nothing to disturb the darkness. Finally, after six weeks unconscious, I had woken to Harry at my bedside and twenty missed calls from Mark Noonan.

Now my eye played over the cuttings. The press interest had continued for a few days after I came round. Requests for interviews, even letters and emails asking me to investigate cases. Harry had dealt with them all. *Mr Jericho will respond once he is fully recovered.*

'What're you hiding under those gloves and that supermarket-brand polo neck?' Noonan pouted. 'Is it possible, Scott Jericho? Are you losing that fair mask and starting to look like what you really are? You know what he is, don't you, pretty one?' he said, turning to Harry. 'What he did for me back in the day?'

Without hesitation, Harry reached over and took my hand. 'Yes, I know what he is. I know everything.'

And he did. Up to a point. After I'd woken from the coma, Harry and I had talked. Talked for days, it seemed, me lying prone in the hospital bed, gingerly trying out atrophied muscles that screamed at the slightest exertion. We had agreed: no more secrets between us. Harry had always avoided upsetting truths, but he was now determined to face my world as it was. He wanted to support me, as my partner, in everything. And so, I at last revealed what DCI Peter Garris had done to save me from myself following my imprisonment and disgrace. The people he had murdered in order to provide a puzzle that might reawaken my interest in the world. I also disclosed to Harry his own unwitting role in that blood-soaked drama, and how I had abandoned the fascist child-killer Lenny Kerrigan to his fate as Garris's final victim. 'He pleaded with me to save him, but I couldn't,' I told Harry in the curtained-off confessional of my hospital room. 'Kerrigan had hurt so many people. He'd killed little kids, for Christ's sake. And so I left him to Garris and his blade.'

Harry had comforted me, saying Garris's plot to save me was not my responsibility. As for Lenny Kerrigan? He was a monster and probably beyond any physical help at the point I'd found him. Even if I'd tried to intervene, it wouldn't have done any good. But had I detected a trace of doubt in his voice? Afterwards, when I confessed to being drawn to that darkness and violence that Mark Noonan now claimed was part of my nature, Harry had disagreed. 'That's just a by-product of you wanting to help people in terrible situations, Scott. It's not you.'

Harry was the smartest person I'd ever known, but he wasn't always right.

In any case, Noonan looked annoyed that he hadn't got under Harry's skin.

'I ain't got all day to reminisce,' he muttered. 'Deals need doing and my time's precious. When you were here last, I asked you to look into a family matter for me. Since then, it's only got more serious. Anyhow, I bet you're just itching for another puzzle to get your teeth into.'

I shook my head. Since coming out of the coma, I'd barely felt those old urges of mine – to unpick a mystery and to make bad men pay for the harm they inflicted. My concern instead centred on Peter Garris's whereabouts. After visiting me at the hospital, no trace could be found of my former mentor. Still, at Noonan's words, neglected instincts began to stir.

'What's the job?' I asked. 'I'll maybe look into it.'

'Oh, you'll look into it,' Noonan said. 'You owe me, remember.'

'I remember you threatening to eunuchise me with a gun in that very chair. I don't owe you a thing. The clue you offered on my last case turned out to be so much bullshit. You got the information wrong, and a man died. Plus, I just saved your sorry, scraggy old neck. If you want me to work for you, Noonan, you'll have to offer up something else. *Someone* else.'

'You mean our Benny boy?' Mark pulled at his blubbery bottom lip, pretending to consider for a couple of seconds before waving a dismissive hand. 'Have him. He's fucked anyway. Been a miserable, limp-dicked, useless little turd ever since he got back here.' He winked and I felt the gorge rise in my throat. 'And I have younger and prettier toys now. Prettier even than this one.'

My old friend Ben Halliday had taken Mark's offer of husband status to save himself from being implicated in a murder I'd been investigating. Total subservience to the has-been mobster was the price of Noonan's protection. But now here was a chance to get Ben out of this chintzy hell hole.

'Give me the facts,' I said. 'And then I want to see him.'

'Well, it might not be the biggest mystery after all,' Mark sighed. 'But it's causing me a massive headache. It's my nephew. Seems he up and vanished six weeks ago, following the funeral of some friend of his. The boy's mother thinks someone might've hurt him.'

'Badly?'

'Killed maybe, I don't know.' Noonan spoke airily, as if this mother thought her son might have been stung by a wasp. 'She's frantic, phoning all the time, asking me to help find the kid, or at least his corpse. It's beginning to piss me off.'

'What's the boy's name?' Harry asked.

Noonan blinked at him. 'Who are you, Columbo's secretary?'

'Columbo didn't have a secretary,' Harry said. 'What's his name?'

'First off, he's not a boy,' Noonan yawned. 'Not really, and he's not a nephew either. Wesley Sayers is a distant cousin. His father drank himself to death when the kid wasn't much more than a babe in arms. The father was Nana's sister's boy. Family being family, we looked out for them ever since the dad started pushing daisies. Couple of grand a year, school clothes, little holidays here and there, nothing extravagant. Butlin's at Bognor, that sort of thing. Kid even came down here about six months ago, trying to play the hard man and get a job with me. He was too soft by half. Too nice. Nice ain't a quality that gets you far in this trade. You were a smidge too nice, I remember, Scotty. Didn't stop you cracking a few skulls though, did it?' I saw Harry flinch despite himself and the mobster practically purred. 'Plus, Wesley was one of those.'

'Straight?'

Noonan shuddered. 'Imagine. I'm all for non-discrimination in the workplace, but even I have my limits.'

'Tell me more about him,' I said.

'Don't know much more to be honest. I've only ever really seen him and his mum at family weddings and funerals. Quiet lad, paid attention when you spoke to him, showed proper respect. Not with his head in his phone and his brain in his boxers like most kids nowadays. Might have made a good lookout or eavesdropper, if he'd had the spine. He lives with the mother up north.'

'Where exactly?' I asked. '"Up north" to you is anywhere beyond South Mimms services.'

'More up north than that,' Noonan insisted. 'Actually, it's not all that far from where you recently flambéed yourself alive. Fenchurch-on-Sea.' He clicked his fingers and looked at us in triumph. 'Some old holiday resort dump like Scarborough or Skeg-fucking-ness. Camp as Christmas and homophobic to the core would be my guess.'

'Fenchurch,' I murmured to myself. The name rang a bell.

Harry looked up from his phone. 'Fenchurch-on-Sea, only about forty miles from Aumbry on the Norfolk coast. And he vanished after a friend's funeral, you say?'

'According to the mother. He left a note saying he was going away for a bit, but she doesn't seem satisfied and thinks something's happened to him. She won't say what exactly but hints at violence. You know I don't do hints, Scott, especially where violence is concerned. Give it to me straight and with none of the trigger warnings. Stephanie Westmacott, she went back to her maiden name after divorcing Wesley's dad. Woman always struck Nana as a bit highly strung, even a fantasist. Definitely scared of that husband of hers and of our lot to boot.' Noonan laughed. 'No idea why, we're a soft-hearted bunch, ain't we? But they're still family, so I want it looked into.'

'Have you done anything so far?' I asked.

'Couple of the hubbies ran up there and made some enquiries, but they didn't come back with much.'

I took Harry's phone and cast my eye over his Google search. 'You sent your velvet mafia to this place? Steroid boys in tight shorts with lip filler and biceps as big as Bournemouth asking questions on the prom? That must have been quite a sight.'

'Some of the kid's stuff was missing apparently,' Noonan said. 'Bit of cash too.'

'But his mother doesn't buy the note saying he'd gone away?' Harry asked. 'Does she think it was forged then?'

'I don't know what the silly mare thinks,' Noonan grunted. 'She's a turd-brain, maybe even got a touch of the early onset. But she's convinced he's in trouble. I suppose with the best friend having died recently, he might have wanted some space away from all her crazy. Soft kid, like I said. *Nice*. She begged me to come up myself, but I've been dealing with my own shit down here. Hostile takeover, you know how it goes.' I nodded. Blood was in the water on Sanford Crescent. Old blood, thin and full of cholesterol. Young sharks in the neighbourhood would soon be circling. 'But look, if by some chance the silly bitch is right and something really has happened to Wes, I want the fuck that did it dealt with. You bring him to me, no questions asked, understood?'

I said nothing, only exchanged a glance with Harry. If I found someone had harmed Wesley Sayers, I would use my judgement as to that person's punishment. 'Put me on the books and you've got a deal,' I said. 'Old rate of pay will be just fine.'

'You're asking a lot, you pikey cunt,' Noonan roared. Then muttered, 'Oh, all right. And don't forget to take that pansy upstairs with you. He probably didn't hear when you came in. Mostly just lies there with his headphones on listening to self-fucking-help podcasts. Jesus wept. If you hadn't turned up, I might've taken him down the canal and put him out of his misery myself.'

Chapter Three

WE HEADED BACK TO THE car to wait for Ben. Easing myself behind the wheel, I turned the key in the ignition and the engine spluttered into life, heaters chuntering away. At the sound, curtains twitched all along the street, Noonan's fossilised foot soldiers back at their posts. I wondered what would become of them when the new sharks swam in, and found I didn't much care. Their souls were theirs to barter away but for a mortgage-free retirement, their pact had been Mephistophelean.

'What do you think?' Harry asked.

'I think I have a new case,' I sighed. 'Though it doesn't sound like much of one. I'll go up to Fenchurch, nose around, probably be back in time for drag bingo at the Swan on Thursday. What do you think of it?'

Harry cupped the side of his face with his hand, an old contemplative habit. 'I don't know. Why doesn't the mother pester the police? Why involve Noonan if she's so nervous of him?'

I shrugged. 'He gets things done. Or he did, back in his prime. If the police are satisfied that the note Wesley left is genuine and that he took sufficient funds for a month or two? Well, he's a grown man and they barely have the budget to investigate actual murders with honest-to-God corpses these days. Anyway.' I reached across the central console and took his hand. 'How're you doing? That was something of a baptism of fire back there with Timmo.'

Harry shifted in his seat. 'What do you think will happen to him?'

I was saved from providing a truthful answer by the arrival of Ben Halliday, tapping at my window. When I whirred down the glass, Ben's double take was practically cartoonish. 'It's been a rough couple of weeks,' I explained, shaking his hand.

That warm East Yorkshire rumble almost filled the street. 'You're as handsome as ever, Scott.'

'Always the charmer. Now get in, Ben, it's bloody freezing out there.'

Considering he was still trying to shake off the clutches of whatever Noonan had been feeding him these past weeks, I thought Ben looked reasonably OK. Denim-blue eyes, bright as the frosted air that sparkled around the headlights, that shock of red hair, now cropped close to his head, pale skin the colour of fresh fallen snow. He was wearing his trademark black tee and, although he'd lost a little weight, the material still had its work cut out accommodating that big barrel chest and blue-veined biceps.

'From Mark, with love.' Taking up most of the back seat, Ben reached forward and placed a bulging envelope on the dashboard. Expenses and a week's pay upfront. I didn't like to think where the money had come from, but the bitter truth was, winter had arrived and we needed the cash. Travelling fairs never do great business during the off months, and Harry and I were long overdue a chat about our future. Working the circuit was only ever supposed to be a stopgap measure. Anyway, this private gig for Noonan would tide us over for a time.

As we pulled away from the crescent, I noticed the ageing gangster had stepped outside to wave us off. In my rearview, I saw Ben scoot down in his seat like a child hiding from an abusive parent. Which was exactly the role Noonan played for many of his 'husbands'. Ben had been brought up by a fisherman father, a drunk who, railing against the death of his industry and the infidelity of his wife, had taken his fury out on the boy. Once grown, Ben had promptly swapped one psychotic tyrant for another. Now he was trying to escape the violence of his past – I only hoped he'd have the chance.

'Thanks, Scott,' he murmured as we left number 56 behind. 'I knew you'd come back for me.'

'I'm only sorry it took so long,' I said. 'I had a bit of an enforced nap after that business in Aumbry. By the way, this is my partner, Harry.'

The introductions should have felt awkward. After all, I'd once had something of a relationship with Ben, though it had mostly consisted of sex, shallow and functionary. Back then, I'd thought that was what I was best suited for, the odd casual fumble and fuck, nothing too demanding. Now I no longer believed that this was so.

Introductions over, Ben remained quiet until we turned onto the M25 and hit the motorway's almost eternal gridlock.

'Can I ask,' he said, 'what happened after I went back to Mark? You see, I've tried to keep away from the news this past month. It's always bad shit anyway – war, famine, murder. Not helpful when you're going through cold turkey. But it's been preying on my mind, all that stuff back in Aumbry. The killings and what might have happened after I ran away.'

It took some time to bring him up to speed about my last case, one in which Ben had played a pivotal role. A man had died, a celebrity Ben had been tasked with keeping safe in his role as bodyguard.

'It was my job to protect him,' he said now, in a small voice.

'You couldn't.' I shook my head. 'No one could.'

'But you caught the killer?' He nodded to himself. 'Of course you did, Mark told me that much. And I heard you suffered for it.'

'He always suffers for it,' Harry murmured.

Ben's great slab of a hand reached forward and gripped Harry's shoulder. 'Then it's lucky he has you. You're both lucky.' He settled back into his seat, arms folded. 'So, tell me, where are we going?'

Spotting a gap opening up in front of us, I began to weave a route through the gridlock. 'First,' I said, 'we're off to wonderland.'

We pulled into the vast empty car park and I hauled myself out of the driver's seat. Lifting my face to the sky, I winced against the twinge of my hip as Harry hurried around the Merc and placed the walking stick in my hand. I listened to him scold me, saying I should've let him drive the last few miles and that I was an obstinate dinlo. That bit of showman slang made me smile, despite the pain. Glancing over at the mathematical miracle of a fairground rising into being, my smile only broadened.

Huge rides and prestige stalls were being erected in one of the big parks situated just outside north London. Behind towering barriers, those familiar silhouettes soared and took shape while a billboard overlooking the site proclaimed:

'THE CAPITAL'S BEST WINTER WONDERLAND! OPEN FROM 14th DECEMBER. Brought to you by Global Boss Entertainment and Jericho Fairs'. I noted the smaller font of 'Jericho Fairs' and my smile fell. I could almost hear my late mother's voice inside my head: *What a pack of saucy, liberty-taking merchants!*

Ben and Harry paced slowly behind me as I limped across the uneven ground towards the gate, Harry giving the nod to Little Sam Urnshaw who, at just thirteen, was standing self-importantly beside a Global Boss security guard in puffer jacket and dark glasses. We gave our names to this Navy SEAL lookalike, me vouching for Ben, and then wandered together along the fair's main drag.

Raw-handed showmen were hard at work, assembling the complex skeletons of their rides – ghost train, helter-skelter, Miami Trip, dodgems, the whole shebang. Other people, not showmen, flounced around them with cappuccinos and weightless cardboard cutouts, debating where to erect two-dimensional Christmas scenes and deciding nothing at all. We were approaching my dad's half-built Waltzer when Sal Myers and her daughter Jodie spotted us. They'd been standing in a huddle with Big Sam Urnshaw, throwing dirty looks at the interlopers. Dressed in a pixie costume of fern green with a cute hand-knitted bobble hat, Jodie darted over and commenced skipping around Harry – her favourite adopted uncle – talking nineteen to the dozen. Harry grinned and looped an arm around her shoulder. Meanwhile Big Sam and Sal gave the 'corporate cappuccino divs' a final withering glare and came striding to meet us.

'What have we come to, eh?' Big Sam muttered. 'Sharing our sites with no-knowing gorger-breds.'

'Needs must, I suppose,' I said.

'Needs must,' Sam echoed bitterly. 'Your old man must be out of his box to do business with these leeches. You know they've started taking over fairground sites in towns and cities where our lot have staked a claim for generations? Big business conglomerates or hedge-funders or whatever they call themselves, seeing an opportunity and buying up flash rides from the Far East, squeezing real showpeople with proper heritage out of our own bloody living. And the punters don't know the difference, o' course. They just see it as a day at the fair, never guessing that real fairground folk, those of us with travelling in our veins, have all been thrown onto the bloody scrapheap. Soon enough our kind of fair'll exist in name only. And your old man's going right along with it, lending them his brand, providing our rides and joints to sit right alongside their glitzy machines. Filling up the gaps they haven't yet claimed for themselves.'

'Maybe you're right, Sam.' I nodded. 'But Dad's only doing what he thinks is best to keep bread on everyone's table. If he hadn't got us pitches as part of this show, we'd all be back at the yard, eking out our earnings until spring rolled around. At least here we can make a little extra to see us through.'

Sam muttered something about 'collaboration' under his breath and stormed off in search of a more sympathetic ear. I sighed. Part of me agreed with everything he'd said, but as head of the fair, my dad had to operate in the world as it was, not as others might wish it to be. Perhaps we were colluding in the death of our kind, only time would tell.

During Big Sam's rant, Sal had been giving Ben an unimpressed up-and-down. 'And who's this?' she asked. 'Bringing home waifs and strays now, Scott? Here, moosh, you look like you could do with some scran. Follow me if you're hungry.'

'I'd do as she says,' Harry advised. 'She's tougher than she looks.'

'She looks plenty tough,' Ben said meekly, and followed my oldest childhood friend towards Layla Jafford's hot dog stall. Meanwhile, Harry insisted I took a seat on the step of my dad's Waltzer.

'I can come with you to Fenchurch, help you look into this missing joskin,' he suggested.

I glanced over at Ben, already chowing down on a chilli dog while Jodie playfully poked his biceps. Ben smiled at her, though his free hand was shaking badly. 'I think he needs you more than I do,' I told Harry. 'He's still coming off the shit by the look of it.'

'*You* need me,' Harry said.

'I'm fine,' I insisted, then promptly stumbled trying to get to my feet. 'This fucking thing!' I shook the walking stick like I was trying to throttle it. 'I swear it unbalances me.'

'Don't be silly,' Harry said, helping me right myself.

'So it's just me, then?' I muttered. 'I'm fucked, end of.'

'It won't be forever,' he soothed. 'Remember what the physio said. You've been comatose for weeks, fed through a tube. All that time in bed, muscle wastage is normal. You'll be strong again, *if* you do your exercises properly.'

'Yes, Matron.'

'But you're not strong yet, Scott Jericho. Not enough to take on a new case all by yourself, anyway.'

'It's a misper, Harry.' He looked at me, baffled. 'Missing person. I won't be hobbling into anything I can't handle.'

'Famous last words.'

'It's probably a fuss over nothing,' I said. 'I'll find the bloke and be back before you know it.'

'Well, while you're gone, I'll continue looking into Peter Garris like we agreed. You won't have time to do that now. Not until this favour for Mark Noonan is over anyway. And I have the skills – I was a research librarian in a former life, remember. Digging up facts is my forte, and I've already made a decent start.'

It was true. Harry's preliminary enquiries had revealed that, following his final visit to me at the hospital, Garris had completely vanished. Phone disconnected, car off the road, bills paid up to next summer, even his library books returned. He had made preparations for this, I vaguely remembered him saying so in the hospital before the sepsis took hold, though little else of that conversation remained intact. Only fragments and tantalising hints, flitting at the edges of my memory. For how long had he made these preparations? I wondered. Perhaps ever since those early kills, before he had joined the police and learned his trade.

'I can do the background,' Harry continued. 'Go to his hometown, look into old army and police buddies. Scott, this could be important. We know he left no evidence of his crimes in Bradbury End. As you said, he was an experienced CID detective and too knowledgeable in forensics and crime scene investigation by that point. But those first murders, you told me he claimed to have kept trophies.'

Yes, I'd considered that possibility once – a garage lockup somewhere containing all the evidence I'd need to nail him. But back then, Garris's threat to expose Harry's own secret had kept me from investigating his past. Now though? I couldn't take Garris's word that the urge to kill had left him for good, and he needed to be brought to justice for his crimes. But to go up against a retired senior officer, especially one of Peter Garris's reputation? We needed evidence first.

Still, I shook my head. 'It's too dangerous.'

Harry sighed. 'We talked about this. We're a team now, right? You have to trust me.'

I looked into his eyes, saw the need there. After I'd revealed to Harry his own innocent collusion in the Bradbury End murders, I had tried my best to comfort him. He didn't know the full horror of Garris's plan, hadn't realised lives were at stake. Garris had used Harry's mercy killing of his father to blackmail him into playing his part. Much as I'd attempted to reassure him, however, I now saw that, in discovering and exposing the monster's past, Harry might be trying to make amends. Could I deny him that? What would I do to make up for the death of even so vile a creature as Lenny Kerrigan?

'All right,' I said. 'Go ahead with your research, but please be careful.'

Harry beamed at me. 'I will. Only listen, are you sure you can't remember anything else Garris said when he visited you at the hospital? Any little detail could help.'

'I'm not sure. I think …' It scratched at the back of my mind, an itch I couldn't quite reach. 'He told me something important.' I shook my head, gave it up. The sepsis had hit immediately after Garris's visit and the induced coma seemed to have scrubbed that part of my memory clean.

'Don't force it,' Harry said. 'It'll come in time. Just be ready when—'

'You're looking into someone dangerous?'

Startled, we both turned to find Ben looming behind us, lips smeared with ketchup and a second half-demolished hot dog on the go. He grinned and I puffed out my cheeks. 'Jesus Christ. I forgot how catlike you can be, or perhaps I'm losing my touch. How long have you been standing there?'

'Long enough,' he said, swallowing the last bite. 'So how's this for an idea: I volunteer to act as Harry's bodyguard while you're gone, a thank you for getting me away from Noonan. I'll keep an eagle eye, make sure he comes to no harm.'

I looked at the giant before me, recalling my own wasted reflection in the Mercedes window. Much as I hated to admit it, Ben could protect Harry much better than I could right now.

'All right,' I said. 'If Haz agrees, I think that makes sense. But before you two head off to play detective, there's one little job I need to attend to first. And if it works out as I think it might, your research could be unnecessary.' I looked up as a gleam of golden winter sunlight struck the pinnacle of the helter-skelter. 'You see, there's a secret Peter Garris has been hiding away, and it's high time that I dug it up.'

Chapter Four

STREETLIGHTS FLASHED PAST, THEIR ORANGE glow smoked by a freezing fog. Occasionally a smudge of carnival colour blared out of the gloom, but only from those homes that could still afford the frivolity of outdoor Christmas lights. For the most part, the mist wreathed only darkness. It was nearly midnight after all.

As we drove, Ben continued to question us about Garris. 'You had him under surveillance with private detectives, so how did he escape? An accomplice helping him out, maybe? Giving him a bolthole?'

'Possibly,' I said, my gaze flicking from Ben in the rearview to the shifting glimpses of road ahead. 'Although Garris wasn't a man for confederates.'

'He had you,' Harry observed. 'That was one connection we know he made.'

I nodded. 'And regretted. Regretted so much he engineered a way to get me out of the force before I could cotton on to who he really was. *What* he was.'

'But before that you were close?' Ben asked.

'I wouldn't say close. We shared our thoughts, our ideas. At least I thought that's what we were doing.'

'And perhaps that wasn't the first time,' Harry suggested. 'Maybe there's a version of you out there from his past. A darker version that he's kept in touch with and who might feel like they owe Peter Garris a good turn. He brought on a promising young detective in his role as DCI, could he also have taken an apprentice killer under his wing? Someone who once looked to him for guidance, much as you did, Scott?'

I couldn't help but shudder at the idea. It wasn't one I felt comfortable considering. 'We're here,' I said, grateful for the diversion as I eased the car into that unremarkable cul-de-sac. 'No talking from this point until we reach the back of the house, understood?'

I parked up and turned off the engine, once again cursing myself for agreeing to Harry's demand that he be part of this little adventure. It felt like I was drawing him further into my world, yet as he continued to insist, we were a team now. For good or ill, there was no going back. We all got out of the Merc, closing the doors behind us as softly as possible. I watched Ben go to the boot and retrieve the spades from their hiding place under a scrap of fairground tarp. His hands were shaking again, and I reflected that I could use a good dose of benzos and booze myself. The pain in my hip was already gnawing at me.

Shovels in hand, we moved down the street towards that inconspicuous little two-up two-down. Garris's house – suburban, anonymous, empty – much like the monster that had, until his recent vanishing, occupied it. Ben eased aside the wheelie bins that blocked the path to the back garden while I took the opportunity to give Harry's shoulder a quick squeeze. A gesture of reassurance for us both. The most frightening secret I'd shared with him after I woke from my coma was how

Garris had mutilated Lenny Kerrigan, and how I, in turn, had walked away from the pleading man, abandoning him to his fate. I wasn't certain in that moment that Harry could ever forgive such an act. When he surprised me by absolving me of the sin, I'd argued that he would never have made such a choice himself. 'Don't be so sure,' he'd murmured in response. 'None of us know what we might do, given the right circumstances.'

A motion sensor tripped, briefly setting a dog barking and splashing a hard glare on the marigold patch in the far corner of the garden. Its blaze of autumn colour had faded long ago, its stalks standing naked and frostbitten. If, as I suspected, Lenny Kerrigan's corpse remained buried here, we could then hand over the case to the police and let them run Peter Garris to ground. Yet before tackling the burial site, I first wanted to take a look inside the house.

Leaving our spades propped against the shed, Ben gave his expert attention to the patio door. He had it sliding open in under a minute. My heart missed a beat as I stepped over the threshold. It felt reckless to be guiding them into this place, my lover and my friend, like taking a pair of children on an inflatable dinghy and rowing them out into a hurricane. In the kitchen, knives and pans gleamed dully on their hooks. Letters were piled up at the front door, circulars, takeaway menus, a bill marked 'paid'. I doubted Peter Garris had ever left a bill unpaid in his life. To do so would attract attention and he had always lived his life under the radar. I made a quick search of the rooms, upstairs and down, but there was nothing. No trace of my old mentor, only his emptiness lingering among vacated wardrobes and in the dense, unmoving shadows that seemed to haunt every doorway.

Back in the garden again, we began to dig. The earth was hard as concrete, the bite of our spades treacherous in the stillness. We were a foot deep when my hip cried out and I careered sideways, dropping the spade and almost faceplanting the dirt. Ben caught me, his grip like iron.

'We can manage,' he said. 'Take a breath.'

And so I watched as they toiled away at the grave of a child-killer, feeling the scrape of Harry's shovel like an excavation of my heart. This was not a task for the Harrys of this world, but he would have it no other way. Not now he had made up his mind to share my reality. I looked at the marigold patch, remembering the riotous marmalade hue of October. How Garris had said, 'Give 'em a patch of blue sky and a drop of sunlight, these beauties will flower whatever the month.' If they're tended and cared for, perhaps. I shook my head, disgusted at another memory: how some remorseless part of myself had hated the beauty of Lenny Kerrigan's grave. How even now I resented it, dead and overgrown as it was. What sort of resting place would I approve for this hateful destroyer of children? Wasn't his own murder and mutilation punishment enough?

After twenty minutes of digging, Ben looked up and wiped the sweat from his brow. 'Nothing could have been buried deeper than this,' he said.

'How do you know?' Harry asked.

Ben passed him a bottle of water from the pocket of the old donkey jacket I'd loaned him. While Harry took a grateful sip, the former thug-for-hire treated him to a mischievous smile. 'I know, believe me.' Then he laughed at Harry's troubled expression. 'My uncle was a gravedigger up in Hull. I'd help him out for a bit of pocket money during the summer holidays. I've shovelled my share of plots, and you can always tell when earth has been recently dug up and tamped down. There's been no body buried here. Not in recent years anyway.'

Harry looked over to where I stood, my back planted against the French windows. 'What do you think? He told you Kerrigan was here, didn't he? After he killed him in Bradbury End, this was where Garris laid him to rest. Scott, are you listening?'

'He said something before I passed out in the hospital,' I murmured to myself, clutching at a memory that refused to be drawn. I shook my head, defeated. 'I guess he must have buried him elsewhere, simply taunting me with the suggestion Kerrigan was here. He likes his games, old Pete.'

'Mr Garris? Is that you, sir?' A voice came from behind the neighbouring fence and we all instinctively ducked down, like schoolboys caught out in a prank. 'Back from your wanderings, are you? Most mysterious, you didn't even say goodbye. We have some mail for you. I know it's rather late, but if you'd like me to pop it round, it'd be no trouble. Mr Garris? It is you, isn't it?'

Ben jerked his thumb over his shoulder and we collected our shovels, skulking around the side of the house, breaking cover only when we were sure the coast was clear. Back in the car, I flipped the ignition and nosed us as noiselessly as I could out of the cul-de-sac.

It was as we emerged from Garris's street that I glimpsed a figure caught in the wash of my headlights. A dark, thin, bow-backed silhouette, head hunched forward as if intently examining the pavement between his feet, the face cowled inside some kind of hood. Illuminated for a moment and then reclaimed by the night. I shuddered despite myself. In that momentary snatch of light, it appeared as if the man rested upon four spindly, spider-like legs.

The cocoon pulsated, a steady rhythmic beat. The figure encased within appeared dead, desiccated, drained of all life. A human mummy fixed at the centre of an intricate web. I crossed a room filled with instruments of slaughter – a tenderising hammer, a kitchen knife, a mortar – each slick with some syrupy substance that gleamed like molasses in the dark. The web was strung across the width of a patio door, yet there was no sense of scale to it. At once, the billowing white weave seemed to dwarf me and then immediately appeared fragile and tiny as I reached for it. A sensor light flicked on in the garden beyond the patio door, backlighting the web and caging me in a matrix of shadow. Then the light changed, softened and warmed, dyed the gossamer strands a marigold hue.

The cocoon at the web's heart suddenly twitched. I caught my breath and backed away. Stretching slowly against its bandage-like confinement, a human limb was slowly breaking the surface. Then another, and another, and another – an arm, a leg, a second arm, a third, a fourth, shattered and disjointed, mangled fingers clawing at the air like lips desperate for oxygen. Fingernails filthy with grave dirt scraped away a swatch of web and a single blood-soaked eye, hateful and accusing, stared out at me from its prison.

Juh–i–co. Huh–elp. Muh–ee.

I reached for the creature.

For the fascist child-killer.

I reached and—

I woke screaming, Harry sitting bolt upright in bed, holding me close.

'It's all right, Scott. It's all right,' he comforted. 'What was it? Bradbury End? Aunt Tilda again? One of the others?'

'No.' I pulled away from him. 'It was nothing. Haz, I don't ... I don't remember. I just need to ...'

I got up and edged my way around the trailer, moving over to the sink where I washed my face in the bitterly cold water from a canister. A pyjama jacket Harry had bought while I was still in hospital, correct for my old dimensions, billowed about me while the bottoms hung from the blades of my hips. My bare feet looked almost blue in the early morning light.

I glanced back at the bed.

'You'd tell me?' Harry asked.

'I would. No secrets now.'

I turned to the tiny window that sat above the sink, staring out across my father's yard. The place where Jericho's Fair and its people traditionally sat out the winter. In the corral of trailers space was tight but, as ever, the laying out of the site had been orchestrated by generations of master Travellers. A lesson in geometric perfection, not a scrap of ground wasted. Ben had been put up in one of the spare chaps' trailers near the back of the yard and, after we'd shown him where everything was, had passed out within seconds. Now I towelled the water from my chin and limped back to bed. Harry rolled against my chest and found my lips in the darkness.

'We'll be all right,' I promised, consoling myself as much as him. 'We will. I won't let anyone hurt us.'

Chapter Five

WE LAY TOGETHER FOR ANOTHER hour as the shadows softened around us. Then, at Harry's request, I was pulling on jeans and boots, a fresh polo neck, my thick minder's scarf wrapped around my throat to be extra sure. Even I still hadn't got used to my burns and I didn't want to upset the kid. With Harry up and dressed, we found Sal and Jodie sitting on the step of their trailer, already in their work dungarees, cups of hot chocolate cradled in fingerless gloves. Jodie leapt to her feet as she saw Harry and, cheeks flushed, they both scurried away to plot.

'Do you know what that's all about?' I asked. 'Haz said we needed to come over first thing. That he and Jodie had "plans".'

'I'm saying nothing.' Sal patted the vacated spot beside her. 'You look happy. Should I be worried?'

'I have a case.'

'Oh dear God,' she groaned. 'Just please try not to get burned alive this time. I'm serious.' She took my hand, pulled back my sleeve and rubbed the pad of her thumb gently across a blaze of scarred flesh. 'I'm glad you're happy, Scott.'

*

Before heading to Fenchurch, there was someone I needed to see. It was a short drive from the yard to the Winter Wonderland and I found Old Man Jericho exactly where I thought I would. By the guardrail of his Waltzer, looking out over a fairground that, for the first time in his life, was not entirely his own. I joined my dad at the rail and he gave me one of his trademark penetrating glares.

'What's in the offing?'

'Missing person case,' I told him. 'Said I'd look into it.'

'You're fit enough?' He played a callused forefinger across that salt and pepper moustache; more salt than pepper these days.

'I'll get by.'

We lapsed into silence for a time, observing the practised labour of showmen building up their rides, and the clumsy imitation of those working for the interlopers.

'They only wanted our biggest, shiniest, glitziest offerings,' Dad grunted. 'None of the old-fashioned rides and joints that make up the soul of a fair. I had to pick my battles, son. Get as many of our people into the gig as I could. I'm sorry that couldn't include yours and Harry's little juvenile.'

He sighed. He seemed diminished here, less sure of his footing somehow. No longer the master of his domain.

'Sam Urnshaw isn't happy about it,' I said.

'And he thinks I am?' George Jericho gripped the rail with hands weathered by six decades of hard graft. 'If we're to survive we need to adapt. Maybe even cut away a few bits of dead wood, and even that might not be enough. These joskins.' He looked up at the billboard, the name of 'Global Boss' dwarfing his own. 'It's doing a deal with the devil, I know that. These winter wonderlands are all being taken over by non-Travellers.

Huge hedge funds that can pony up enough cash for the kind of rides we could never afford, taking hits on ticket prices to drive us out of business, undercutting us at every turn. But we have no God-given right to survive, Scott. That's what the others don't understand. Anyway.' He tried out a smile that didn't quite take. 'How are you and the boy doing? If you need any extra work after this case of yours is done, I can put a bit your way. Security here, if nothing else.'

'You really think I'm up to that?'

'You will be, given time. You got better again after coming out of prison, didn't you?' We had never spoken much about what I'd suffered behind bars. The beatings and worse. But my old man was as much a detective as I was. Most Travellers are – an inbuilt talent for keen observation, the gift of the gab, the ability to win a stranger's confidence and that deep knowledge of human nature that comes naturally from running a fair. 'Anyhow,' he went on, 'what's the job?'

'A favour for a friend,' I said. 'A relative of his has gone missing in some old seaside resort called Fenchurch.'

'Up on the Norfolk coast?' My dad peered at me. 'I know it. An old pal of your mother's settled up that way.'

'A Traveller?'

'Tom Makepeace. Oh, he didn't become a joskin in a bungalow or nothing like that. He runs a permanent fair on the seafront at Fenchurch. The boy Makepeace.' Dad shook his head nostalgically. It was a Traveller eccentricity, especially among men of a certain generation. Tom Makepeace could be ninety, but he would always be referred to by people like Sam Urnshaw and my father as 'the boy Makepeace', just as others would speak of my old man as 'the boy Jericho'.

'Tom Makepeace, of course,' I said. 'That's why Fenchurch rang a bell. A friend of Mum's. I remember her speaking about him. Why did he leave the life?'

Dad looked away. 'Times were different back then, son. We all were, I'm ashamed to say.'

I nodded, taking his meaning. 'Times weren't so different when I was a chavvy. This isn't the distant past you're talking about, Dad. I lived it too. Why do you think I left?'

Dad told me that he had sold Tom Makepeace a couple of rides to get him established up at Fenchurch. 'I liked him a lot. He was a rare scholar. That's how they bonded, him and your mum, over their books and stories. Say hello from me, won't you, if your paths cross.'

I stepped inside the draughty hall and immediately spied Harry tucked away in a corner, beaming as he conducted his new choir. He had become a member of St John's only a fortnight ago and was already a favourite among the congregation. Set up in a defunct community centre, the place had foldaway chairs instead of pews, no pulpit, no altar, no damning verses or forbidding stained glass. Just a tea urn belching away in a friendly fashion at the back of the room and a pride flag hung over the door. These worshippers believed in a Jesus of tolerance and humanity, a saviour shunned and despised by so many of their fellow 'Christians'.

Harry caught my eye and threw me a wave. I threw him one in return and he went back to instructing his singers. Our partnership now included me supporting Harry in his beliefs, even if I didn't share them. Not completely anyway. After my last case,

I was perhaps less inclined to doubt. Those strange events in Aumbry, the mediumistic predictions of my late aunt; they might have given even the most logical mind reason to pause.

I moved over to the catering table where a young woman stood fussing with the urn. She blew out her cheeks in exasperation and fiddled distractedly with the small golden cross around her neck. And suddenly I was picturing another shining trinket, one I hadn't thought about in years. Perhaps discussing her today in association with Tom Makepeace had brought it to mind. Her cross was the only thing they hadn't found after the hit-and-run that killed my mother. Now I raised my hand, unconsciously touching my throat. We'd had so much in common, my mum and me. Dual souls that warred between practical hard-headedness and an inclination for the romantic. It was only in her faith that we differed. Her belief was something she may have shared with Harry, if only she'd lived another year or two and had had the chance to meet him. But some maniac behind the wheel of a car had made that dream an impossible one.

I had searched all along that country road after the police were done with it, scurrying down sidings and into ditches, wading through the ponds and dykes that ran for miles either side, even taking my old fishing net to dredge for clues. In my clumsy way, I'd tried to investigate my mother's death – my first case, if you will – but there was no CCTV on that lonely stretch, no neighbouring houses, no witnesses. She had gone off for a couple days after another blazing row with my dad. Not an unusual occurrence; their marriage had never been an easy one. She'd set herself up in a local hotel not a mile from where the fair was open. She'd read her books, ordered room service, gone for walks in the surrounding countryside, took time to cool down. Her temper had always been a sight to behold and I often wondered if my own rage might spring more from her than from my father. She'd always felt any injustice very keenly. But the storm of her anger was usually fleeting. She always came back after a day or two, right as rain. Or as right as she ever was, as my dad often observed.

In the end, I never found the cross that I remembered her wearing from my earliest childhood. The police said that sometimes happened. That a hat or a shoe or even a ring might be dislodged after such an impact and never be found again. People pick things up, animals and birds steal to make their nests.

I was still lost among memories when Harry touched my arm.

'How goes it?' I asked.

'They need some loosening up but we're getting there,' he said. 'It feels good to be conducting again.' Music was life to Harry, his meat and drink, his oxygen. 'Although it seems strange to be doing an Easter piece at Christmastime. The pastor here wants it included in our concert to remind everyone that Christ's birth was his ultimate gift. Resurrection, new life, forgiveness.'

I lifted Harry's chin and kissed him. 'Forgiveness is important. What was it that you were practising, by the way?'

'*Und hier der Stein; Der solche zugedeckt; Wo aber wird mein Heiland sein? Er ist vom Tode auferweckt!*' Harry spoke-sang the lyrics, his voice as lilting and beautiful as ever. '*And here is the stone which covered it; But where will my saviour be? He has risen from the dead!* From Bach's *Easter Oratorio*, where Mary and the disciples found the empty tomb in which Christ had been buried.'

'It's lovely.' I sighed. 'And I should be making tracks.'

He accompanied me to the small car park at the rear of the hall. We found Ben there, waiting beside my Merc. At our approach, he held out his hand and we shook.

'I'll look after him,' the man-mountain promised. 'You don't have to worry.'

Harry and I exchanged a final kiss, and then I dragged my already aching carcass behind the wheel.

'All right, Wesley Sayers,' I muttered to myself. 'Let's find out where you've disappeared to.'

Chapter Six

BEFORE LEAVING FOR FENCHURCH, I had picked up Webster from the yard. Dear Webster, best of fairground guard dogs, now too long in the canine to be among the chaos of something like the Winter Wonderland, yet I knew he hated being left alone in his juk box back at Old Harness Lane. Never the most sociable of animals, he was nonetheless like many old timers who grow gregarious in their waning years. Perhaps sensing the approaching darkness, they seek out company to make the end a little more bearable. In any case, I felt I could do with some company on my long drive north.

Webster had struggled to get up into the back seat and, truth be told, I'd struggled to lift him. We were both far from the pups we'd been fourteen years ago when my mother had first brought him home and named this devourer of fairground rats 'John Webster' after her favourite bloodthirsty Jacobean playwright. Now he dozed on the back seat, one hind leg twitching, lost in dreams of distant glory days.

Leaving the Home Counties behind, I was soon rolling with the thread of traffic along the A505 towards the fen country of East Anglia. All the while I fretted about Harry. I knew I could trust Ben to protect him from Peter Garris, not only because of Ben's loyalty to me but due to his need to make amends for past failures. Anyway, on balance I believed Harry was safe from the snares of that murderous old devil. Garris had felt real remorse when he'd handed over the recorder containing the truth about Harry's mercy killing of his father. A revelation that Garris had used to blackmail us both, holding the threat of Harry's exposure over our heads in order to protect himself. In fact, this remained my last clear memory of him before his vanishing. Standing there at my hospital bedside, confused by this new emotion that had prompted him to surrender his leverage. The recorder itself was now safely stowed away, the incriminating file wiped.

I thought back to that troubled expression on Garris's face, like a child trying to process some complex new idea about the world. In using my love for Harry against me, he had experienced regret for perhaps the first time. The memory gave me some comfort. In that act of surrender, Garris had shown us a courtesy. Although going after him now, delving into his past? If he caught wind that Ben and Harry were on his trail, could I really be sure he wouldn't act against them?

Almost two hours later, I found that I had the road to myself. The light was beginning to fail in the west while to the east a few early stars cracked the canvas of the night. Webster gave a full-bodied whine from the back seat and I pulled onto a siding. The juk flopped to the roadside, sniffed unenthusiastically at a frost-jewelled signpost, an act more ritual now than anything else. His roving days were behind him. I glanced up at the sign – WELCOME TO SUNNY FENCHURCH-ON-SEA – THE PLACE TO BE!

Not if you're Wesley Sayers, apparently.

A bitter wind whipped up and cut right through me, keen as a knife and salted with the scent of the sea. Below the rise on which I stood, the town of Fenchurch rolled out to meet the coast. A large leafless wood fringed the town to the north and west, holding it in a loose skeletal pinch. From my vantage point it appeared that nobody moved in those distant streets, and I got the vague impression of boarded shopfronts, lighted only here and there by the glimmer of an open doorway. A Norman church with an unusually high bell-tower brooded over the town. Grey, stolid, weather-worn and crenellated like a castle, the fen church from which this place obviously took its name had faced its perilous shoreline for centuries, challenging invader and heretic alike.

The church crowned the only elevation beyond the ridge on which I stood. From what I could make out, this was a high scrubby hill, overgrown, dotted with lopsided graves and bald of the trees that bustled around its base like a monk's tonsure. The rest was fen country, flat as a ledger-stone and splintered here and there with dykes and waterways that gleamed like silver thread.

The town itself appeared to be a muddle of post-war bungalows and Victorian boarding houses. A modern estate sprouted like a superfluous limb from the southern tip where a straight new road met undisciplined country lanes. Then, just before a pencil stroke of yellow shore and the slate grey of the sea sat the fair, a rectangle of rides taking up a good portion of the promenade. The climb and plummet of a boneshaker rollercoaster and the orb of a Ferris wheel stared back across the town towards that disapproving, blank-faced church.

Shivering against another icy blast, I hefted Webster back

into the car. Then, just I was about to start the engine, my phone bleeped: *If my calculations are right, you should almost be at Fenchurch by now. Check your glove compartment. A little gift. Love Haz x* I flicked on the inside light and snapped open the glove box. Inside a slim file awaited me. Pulling it open, I smiled. I had to hand it to Harry, he was a damn good researcher. The information he'd compiled was mostly online stuff – public records, local newspaper articles and, by some dark art, bits and pieces of data plucked from government archives.

Wesley Joshua Matthew Sayers had been twenty-four years old at the date of his disappearance. He had lived with his mother at 3 Cloister Cottages, Fenchurch-on-Sea, and had worked part-time at a local pub, The Six Ravens. Born at the nearby Norfolk and Norwich Hospital, his mother and father had divorced when he was still very young, the father dying of alcoholism less than a month later. Wes had attended Fenchurch's Elizabeth Fry Grammar School after scraping his 11+, had later won a team debating trophy, took part in some youth theatre productions, mainly in chorus roles, had a summer job aged sixteen at the local fair, left school with mediocre A levels in English, Psychology and Geography, had been a volunteer member of the RNLI and otherwise left barely any impression at all on the world.

The friend whose funeral he'd attended around the time of his disappearance (he was last seen on Friday 30th October) was a Miss Katrina Allingham, known at Kat to her friends. The same age as Wes, they had both attended Elizabeth Fry. But here was one new piece of information Mark Noonan hadn't told us, perhaps because he was unaware of it: Katrina Allingham had committed suicide.

Harry had included a photo from a local press report – a group of mourners accompanying a coffin up the hill to that high-towered church. I picked out Wes among the pallbearers, his nondescript face screwed up in grief, his left cheek kissing the side of the casket as he bore his childhood friend to her final resting place. I sat back, the photograph in my lap. *Why would regional press be interested in some poor girl's funeral? I hear you ask*, Harry had written on a note paperclipped to the picture. *Patience, my child! All will be revealed.* I glanced again at the funeral party. It was a surprisingly small group for a life cut so tragically short. But then perhaps I am too used to Traveller funerals, where the largest churches struggle to accommodate the town's worth of people that habitually attend any showman's passing.

By the look of it, including Wesley, three young men and four young women made up the bulk of the mourners. They all looked to be around the same age. I turned the page and continued reading. No note had been left by Katrina, at least none had been found, but it was clearly a case of suicide. The girl had taken her life in the same place that her little brother, Jamie, had died ten years earlier. She'd hanged herself from a tree that spread its giant limbs almost directly over the spot where he had drowned. A dramatic backstory, hence the ghouls of the fourth estate snapping their funeral photos. Harry had even got hold of a record of the inquest containing some of the autopsy results. No bruising to the deceased's arms or legs, no signs of a struggle or defensive wounds, no drugs or alcohol in her system. It had rained in the days before the tragedy and only Katrina's footprints had been found in the wet ground, just a single set approaching the tree, none returning. Loved ones reported that she had always been deeply affected by the death of her little brother. The child had drowned after a birthday outing with his sister and her friends to the local funfair. It appeared that Jamie Allingham, exactly seven years old on the day he died, had been disturbed by their visit to the fair's waxworks exhibit, and that Katrina had grown increasingly tired of his 'babyish blubbering'. The friends – almost all of whom had summer jobs at the fair alongside Katrina – had grown tired of it too and, having left the amusements to take a walk in Chattox Wood, had all gradually peeled away and gone home.

I glanced up from the file and looked again towards the distant fairground. Only Katrina, Jamie and Wesley Sayers remained in the woods that hot summer afternoon. Enraged and embarrassed by his infantile behaviour in front of her friends, Kat had eventually snapped and pushed the child into the Old Demdike, a river that cut through the forest. The boy immediately began to get into difficulties and, by her own admission, Kat had simply frozen. Thankfully, Wes was already in training to join the RNLI and had tried to save the boy, diving into the river and almost drowning himself in the process. Afterwards, he'd spent a couple of nights in hospital recovering from a gastrointestinal infection picked up from contaminated river water. His efforts were in vain, however, and Jamie drowned at around one thirty in the afternoon. The boy's body was recovered later that day, snagged downstream in a briar of deadfall that had partially dammed the river.

Sometime later, Wesley had been rewarded for his heroics. Harry was still looking into the specifics of this, but it seemed a substantial sum of money had come his way. I guessed that, since leaving school six years ago, our local boy made good must have dipped into this fund from time to time. According to Harry's online witchcraft, the only employment Wes maintained was his barman position at The Six Ravens. More recently, of course, he'd tried his luck with dear old Uncle Mark in London, perhaps drawn by the phoney glamour of the mobster life. Once he cottoned on to the set-up at number 56, a country kid like Wesley Sayers would have soon run, wee-wee-wee all the way home. But why had he tried his luck there in the first place? Had the reward money for attempting to save little Jamie Allingham finally run out? If he'd lived off it for eight years or more, that was entirely possible. Or had Wesley simply become dissatisfied with life in this run-down seaside town? In any case, he seemed to be a boy of little ambition.

And what of Katrina? It appeared that she too had felt no desire to leave Fenchurch. Perhaps the memory of what she had done rooted her here, unable to move on until, finally, the guilt had become too great for her to bear.

'But why wait ten long years?' I murmured to myself.

I turned back to the photo of the pallbearers and the other mourners. Seven of similar age. Could these be the friends that had been with Wesley and Katrina on the day of the boy's drowning? The co-workers who'd been employed alongside them at the fair that fateful summer?

I moved on. Always the completist, Harry had included a bit on Fenchurch itself: a line in the Domesday Book; the site of a minor battle in the Civil War; the birthplace of a radical Puritan sect that had exported both itself and its intolerance to the New World in the early sixteen hundreds, dispossessing native tribes and burning their own people as witches within a year of their arrival. These dramatics aside, Fenchurch had steered a sedate course through the past millennia as a small fishing town, unchanging, unremarkable, unnoticed. In the early nineteenth century, some lord of the manor had enacted a bold plan, following the trend of places like Cleethorpes and Skegness up the coast, by evicting the fishing folk from their cottages and transforming the place into a gentrified watering hole for upper-middle-class Victorians. This model of seaside gentility had endured until the turn of the last century when the town's clientele had largely changed to holidaymakers from the industrial north. Miners mostly, taking a week's break away from the lung-scarring, back-breaking toil of the coalpits of Sheffield and Derby. This had proved to be Fenchurch's boom time, all kiss-me-quick hats and bingo on the esplanade, right up until the post-war explosion in cheap package holidays abroad. The town had been dying a slow death ever since.

The only thing that seemed to mark this place out from dozens of similar resorts was its own peculiar brand of superstition. These customs, eccentric and numerous, had existed ever since the days of the old fisherfolk, beliefs and practices that had been predictably suppressed in the time of those witch-burning Puritans. But such things are hard to kill, and remnants live on. They found their most notable example in the ravens that claimed the fen church of St Peter as their home. Six birds known for some reason as the 'Cain Ravens'. All Harry was able to find at short notice was an obscure legend that, as with their more famous cousins at the Tower of London, should the resident ravens ever leave the town, then bloodshed and disaster must surely follow. A scribbled note in the margin here: *Sounds right up your street!*

Almost as if choreographed, I looked up at the church just in time to spy a host of black specks circling the tower. A good omen, no doubt. Enough history. It was time to check in to Fenchurch-on-Sea.

Chapter Seven

THE NARROW ROAD LEADING INTO town was soon overshadowed by the trees of Chattox Wood. Lean arms arcing overhead made a dreary sort of tunnel. My headlights flashed between gnarled trunks, spilling light into inky gaps and provoking the imagination to conjure faces where none existed. I toed the brake. The road jagged sharply to the left, a crazy dogleg. Thank Christ I had slowed on the approach.

As I came around the corner, a woman exploded from the treeline and careered wildly into the middle of the road. I slammed down my foot, feeling a thunderous ache pulse along the shank of my hip. The cost of a recent coma patient neglecting his exercises. The car came to a halt a foot short of the woman, who now stared back at me, eyes like peeled eggs in the gloom, frantic and somehow imploring. She had something white clasped in both hands, bunches of pale things which she held out to me like an offering. It took a moment for me to realise what they were: scraps of paper, not torn but fashioned in some way I couldn't quite make out.

'Welcome to Fenchurch,' I whispered to myself.

The woman continued to stare back as I hit the hazards and pulled myself from the car. Webster had lumbered to his feet, a growl puttering like an outboard motor at the back of his throat. I told him to stay put as I retrieved the hated stick from the passenger footwell.

'Are you all right? Can I help?' I kept my distance, didn't make any sudden moves. Common sense training from my days in uniform. Don't invade her territory, give her the impression of control. Suddenly withdrawing her paper offering, the woman hugged the scraps to her chest.

'My boys. My boys,' she whispered.

Webster growled again and I growled right back at him. 'Hush that juk. Hush.'

Her hair was wild, her eyes darting from the car to me to the treeline. She was dressed in a floral cardigan buttoned up to the chin, slightly stained jogging bottoms, scuffed Adidas trainers and a big, unzipped parka jacket with the hood thrown back. Apart from her modern clothes, it struck me that there was something anachronistic about her, like a relic of a different age when wise women might have roamed these woods. She made a beckoning gesture and moved off the road towards the trees.

'You want me to follow?' I asked. 'All right, just wait a moment.'

I slipped as quickly as I could back into the car, pulling the Merc onto a siding. Then I was out again and following her through a gap in the undergrowth. The day was fading fast and I used the torch on my phone to light our way, making sure not to focus its beam directly on the woman herself. We didn't go far. Just a short distance into the sleeping forest, our feet crunching across the discarded bones of autumn. In a small clearing still in sight of the road, she spun on her heel, arms outstretched.

At first, I believed that I was seeing the impossible. The trees all around us had defied the season and sprouted fresh new leaves. Fragile, fluttering shapes that whispered in the breeze. And then my eyes adjusted to the half-light and I recognised them as the same kind of pale offerings still clasped in the woman's hands. A host of cut-out paper men suspended by string from the branches, dancing on the freezing air. Looking closer, I realised that they weren't quite white but had all been stained, probably with some kind of wax, weatherproofed so that they might dance on even the stormiest night. Some were cut from plain foolscap, some from printed pamphlets, some with scribbled handwriting on them. Dozens, hundreds, all kinds of discarded scraps but all originally white and all in the semblance of a human form.

I turned back to the woman, who looked suddenly rapturous. I asked if she was all right.

'Who you looking for?' she wondered. 'What's your name? Tell me quick and be respectful.'

It was difficult to put an age on her, though if I had to guess I'd have said early sixties. Her voice though was surprisingly youthful. Direct and challenging too, like an old-fashioned schoolmarm.

'My name's Scott. I just wanted to check you weren't hurt. You surprised me, coming out of the trees like that.'

I held out my hand and she looked at it, studying the scars there, the touch of flame. Then she drew back with a gasp. 'That's an ugly hand. Ill-omened.'

'Fair point,' I admitted.

'You was looking for them birds, weren't ya?' she said almost slyly. 'I saw you up on the ridge there, snooping. You shouldn't be frightened of them birds, mister. Not unless you have murder in mind. They can't abide a murderer, them old birds.'

'Is that why they're known as the Cain Ravens?' I asked. 'After the first murderer? Cain from the Bible who killed his brother Abel because God loved Abel's offerings best?'

She shook her head almost ferociously. 'The first wasn't a murder. Nor the second yet. But the third ... ? Them Cain Ravens do kill killers, mister.' She put her fingers to her eyes. 'Ain't I seen it? Hex – hex ...' She coughed, a ragged croaking sort of sound. 'Ads. See my meaning?'

'Hex?' I shook my head. 'You mean like a curse? Who was cursed? Who was killed?'

She placed her hand across her mouth and stared at me as if appalled. The paper men spilled from her grasp and scattered at her feet. 'No, no, no,' she mumbled between her fingers. 'Don't say such wicked things, my darlin'. Not unless you want them to hear. They might, you know. They might.'

I tried a different tack. 'Do you make these?' I gestured at the forms in the trees. 'They're very beautiful.'

The fear appeared to leave her as quickly as it had arrived and she smiled now, almost bashfully. 'They're my fancy. My way of keeping him close. Of paying my respects.'

'To who?'

She frowned. 'The first, naturally.'

'My name's Scott,' I reminded her. 'Can you tell me yours?'

She glanced over my head, her gaze penetrating some point beyond the trees. Following her sight-line, I made out what I believed to be the blunt grey stonework of the church tower. At that moment, a harsh cawing cut through the stillness and seemed to silence the whisper of the paper men.

'Thems looking for treasures,' the woman said confidingly. 'The ravens do come here sometimes, greedy creatures. They fly down from their tower and peck at men.' She suddenly slapped her hand to the back of her head and laughed. It wasn't a sound anyone would care to hear in those woods with the light fading fast. 'Peck hard, them do, like Cain hisself. They call them an unkindness, you know? An unkindness of ravens. Sometimes them six bring white treasure in them talons for old Muriel, though they don't know I keeps it. Make my boys with it. They leaves it to rot in the hollow place, but it makes good boys to remember him by, my darlin'.'

She stepped towards me, as if to share a confidence. 'Them spoiled my birds that night. *My* birds. Not the greedy ravens in their tower. Them only want meat, sweet and bloody. No, I mean my little robin birds. Them didn't want them's dinner afterwards. Not after they ate their fill. My seeds and berries weren't good enough for them then.'

'Why didn't your birds want their dinner, Muriel?' I asked. 'What happened that night?'

'Aunt Muriel!' A voice echoed around the clearing, shrill as the ravens' shriek.

Glancing fretfully in the direction of the newcomer, the woman reached out to me, an intensified imploring in her eyes. 'Not a curse. Not a hex. You must *listen*, my darlin'. They pecks hard. They bring treasure. Understand?'

I shook my head apologetically and the old woman screamed in my face, striking out at me in her fury, drawing blood from my lip before fleeing into the embrace of the trees. I had dropped my walking stick in shock. From behind me, a rustling figure emerged into the clearing. Small, delicate fingers closed around the handle of the stick before I could reach for it.

'I'm sorry,' said the newcomer, handing me the stick. 'She didn't mean to hurt you. She doesn't know what she's doing or saying anymore. Here, please take this.'

I accepted the handkerchief and dabbed at my lip, all the while feeling ridiculous. 'Thank you. I'm fine, really,' I said. 'She ran out in front of my car and I followed her in here. I wanted to check that she was OK. She's your aunt?'

I took my first proper look at the girl. Woman really, but she looked younger somehow. Not physically, she was actually rather drawn and tired, the dark rings under her eyes ageing her beyond her years. But in her speech, how she held herself, she appeared like a child on the first day of school, cowed and a little too keen to please. She was dressed not unlike her aunt in a floral-print frock, the hem flowing out from under her thick winter coat. Her hair was russet-coloured and might have been fitting if it had been the previous season when these trees, aflame with reds and golds, might have complemented the shade. Now she seemed to burn here, in the cold, in the dark.

'It's a shame,' she said, apparently in no hurry to chase after her aunt. 'She was a clever woman once. I look after her when I can. Try to, anyway. But you can't tie her down to her bed and she's sneaky with locks and windows. So I spend half my nights chasing her through the woods.'

'I'm sorry,' I said. 'That sounds exhausting. What happened to her?'

'What happens to all of us?' she answered vaguely. 'Life. The weight of it.'

The young woman's face suddenly stirred a memory. It was a face from the funeral photo, one of the four female mourners following Katrina Allingham's coffin up to that hillside churchyard.

'I'm sorry, but do you live around here?' I asked.

'I do, yes. Why do you—?'

'Perhaps you might know a relation of mine. I'm looking for him.'

'What's the name?'

'Wesley Sayers. He seems to have gone missing and the family's worried.'

'I know Wes, yes,' she answered sharply. 'He's gone away, I think. His mother said so anyway.'

'Yes, we know. He left a note after your friend's funeral. I'm sorry, by the way. About Katrina.'

She stared at me. 'You knew Kat, too?'

'I barely knew Wes,' I admitted. 'I'm up here because his mother's worried, like I said. I promised I'd try to find him for her. He hasn't been in touch with you at all?'

'No. Not since the funeral.'

'And he didn't say anything at the time, about going off somewhere?'

She shook her head and looked in the direction of the vanished woman. 'I should really be getting after her. It's very dark.'

She made to move away when I asked, 'Was he badly affected by Katrina's death?'

With her back to me, she murmured: 'Wesley was devastated. Just devastated beyond belief. We all were.' When she turned to me again there were tears on her cheeks. 'I'd best be going. She needs me.'

'Of course. But maybe we can talk again? I'll be staying in town for a few days. Miss?'

She seemed reluctant to answer, parcelling out her name in snatches, like a confession coaxed from a reluctant perp. 'Row. Rowan. Rowan Chesterton.'

'Scott Jericho.'

She flinched at the name. 'Weren't you on the news? Something a couple of months ago.' She blinked, drawing out the memory. 'The Showman Detective. But in the pictures they showed, you looked different.'

'Age doth wither and custom stale my infinite variety, I'm afraid.' It sounded pompous. I could hear Harry laughing at me.

'Shakespeare.' She nodded. '*Anthony and Cleopatra.*'

I looked closely at her again. She had a lanyard around her neck, though I could only make out a portion of the print '... Norfolk County Coun ...'. 'You're a librarian?' She looked startled and I pointed to the lanyard. 'Local government employee, a knowledge of literature.' She's wrongfooted, I could feel it, and so before she could respond I asked, 'What was he like? Wesley? It's important I know.'

'But didn't you know him? He was your relation, wasn't he?' She looked at me earnestly, as if expecting something.

'I'm afraid I didn't know him well. Please, any information might be useful.'

'He was the best of us,' she said. 'The very best.'

'Was?'

'Is. Then and now. Ever since we were children. Look, I have to go. She needs me.'

And with that Rowan Chesterton followed her aunt into the woods.

Chapter Eight

She's frightened, I thought as I returned to the car. But was it a recent fear or simply the weary anxiety of looking after her aunt? I chided myself. Peter Garris had always warned me about a tendency to start speculating on a case too early. Facts first, theories later. He was a monster but a wise one.

Following the address from Harry's file, I took a left at the church and pulled into an avenue just wide enough to accommodate the Merc. Here stood a congregation of monastic cottages, their faces turned to the church at the top of the hill, as if in prayerful homage. Again, I told Webster to stay put. This suited the old juk just fine, his coat being threadbare and the night bitterly cold. Apparently, the weather had been like this throughout my cosy coma – the Great Freeze, the news was calling it. No fucking kidding.

I got out of the car and approached number 3 Cloister Cottages. No lights at the downstairs windows, curtains firmly drawn. I rang the bell and waited, clapped my hands, whistled part of the tune I'd heard Harry and his choir practising earlier. No one home, yet she knew I was coming. I thought about Miss Westmacott's repeated phone calls to Mark Noonan, the anxiety that something bad had happened to her son and her insistence on an investigation. So why wasn't she here to greet me? I glanced up and down the lane. The other cottages were in darkness too, the only light coming from a large house at the end of the road. I could just make out the sign on the gate – 'Fenchurch Vicarage. Meetings by appointment only.'

I turned back to Miss Westmacott's and noted the wodges of newspaper stuffed into gaps in the worm-eaten windows to keep out the chill. I considered calling Mark, getting him to chase down his recalcitrant relation, but I didn't want to start the case on any awkward footing. I'd come back in the morning.

My left leg groaned at me as I tried to get back in the driver's seat. I'd been a very naughty boy, as my physio Gloria often told me, and not done my exercises today. I really ought to stretch it out. And so I left Webster in the car with the window cracked and took a walk through Fenchurch.

My impression from the ridge had been almost spot on. A town gone to seed. The main high street was made up of a parade of once grand Victorian shopfronts and boutiques, boarding houses and villas, all steep-gabled roofs and rounded tower rooms perched at one corner. Half of the windows were soaped over or else boarded up, piles of rubbish heaped against doorways, men and women in sleeping bags protected from the damp by strips of torn cardboard. No one stirred as I passed, my stick tapping out a lonely tattoo on the pavement. A few faded signs could still be seen above some of the empty premises, the ghosts of glory days long gone: PILKINGTON'S FAMOUS TREATS – the best ice cream in Fenchurch!; JACKSON'S NOVELTY EMPORIUM – beach balls, inflatables, toys to treasure; THE LITTLE ROBIN CAFÉ – teas, cakes, breakfasts and luncheons to order. The phantom tracing of a red-breasted bird could just be made out, putting me in mind of Muriel's robins. Why hadn't they wanted their dinner? I wondered absently.

On a hoarding nearby, the corners of a poster for a 'Winter Wonderland Extravaganza – Come one, come all to Makepeace Funfair this weekend! In aid of the restoration of St Peter's church' flapped in the breeze. I recognised the font from some of the paper boys Muriel had hung in the clearing. Her white treasure. I smiled a little. Here at least was a funfair the hedge fund managers hadn't yet got their greedy claws into. Perhaps they'd have no interest in such a tired seaside attraction, but still I thought my dad would cherish a visit to this, one of the last showman holdouts against the modern world.

I had reached the end of the high street and stood now at the junction with the promenade, a mile long and dotted with beautiful antique lampposts, all unlit, most with their glass lanterns broken. And here stood the fair itself, surrounded by a high wall topped with a coil of barbed wire, the name 'MAKEPEACE' spelled out in concrete block letters over a shuttered gate. In all honesty it looked more like a prison camp than a fairground.

I wasn't entirely sure why I crossed the road to stand before that towering gate. Except an unfamiliar fair always calls to a showman. We are drawn like a specialist surgeon spectating at a colleague's operation – there is a science and an art to the life, and each Traveller has his own way of executing a fair. Beyond the barred gate, I could see the main drag. They did indeed look to be setting up for their own winter wonderland experience, but it was a poor version of the one I'd left behind in London. Spectacle on a shoestring. I spied Christmas decorations a decade out of date, tired-looking rides, paint scrubbed to a pale finish by that scouring North Sea wind. I jangled the padlock, all the while thinking of Wesley Sayers, Katrina Allingham, Rowan Chesterton and their friends. Hard to picture now, but this was the scene of that long-ago summer day when their lives had changed forever.

Although my dad employs chaps – those who work and travel with the fair but are not themselves showpeople – we don't take on teenagers. As a travelling outfit, touring from place to place, it would be impractical. But local static fairs often use sixteen-year-olds for cheap summer labour.

I jangled the padlock again and thought back to an old adage of Peter Garris's: know your victim's environment, his past and his present, it will tell you who he is, and who he is will often tell you who his killer might be. My thoughts tripped on that word. Killer. Other than Miss Westmacott's vague foreboding that some harm had come to her son, there was no evidence that any crime had taken place in Fenchurch, let alone murder. Why then had my mind gone directly to that possibility? *Because you desire it*, a voice like Garris's whispered in my ear. In response, I gripped the padlock until my fist ached.

Leaving the gate and turning with the sweep of the wall, I was again faced by the sea and a blast of bone-chilling air, a gale that seemed to rob the entire town of any odour, except of course that salty sting. At a smaller side gate near the rear of the fairground, I noticed a single camera perched high up on a swaying stalk, like some strange bird. There was no blinking light, no triggered motion sensor as I paced back and forth. Like much else here, the camera was just for show. What is there to steal anyway? No cash would be left on the premises out of season and the rides were both too bulky and outdated to tempt any thief.

Through the bars, I spied the frontage of the ghost train. Horror icons from eighties movies were painted on the outside while a huge fibreglass demon sprang like a jack-in-the-box from the roof of the ride, a medieval ball and chain clasped in one mighty claw. Like many sited on static fairgrounds, the ghost train sat with its back to the outer wall. And I knew why. Taking a fresh grip on my stick, I leaned back into the gale and slogged my way further towards the rear of Makepeace's ground.

Nothing is more predictable on a fair than the unreliability of a ghost train car. You only have to give them a sideways look and they break down. Makepeace's spook house was no different. That was why a single rail ran onto the land directly outside the wall, a place where knackered cars could be shoved out of the way to await repair. And if I knew chaps, this was my way in. Approaching a lone car that sat with its tail hard against the back access door of the ride, I reached under the bonnet and flicked the brake switch. It was a neglected old rust bucket and took a great deal of shoving before I could roll it off down the track.

Straightening up, I could easily picture the chap at the end of a long summer season, the fair closing down around him. He's anxious to get home or else eager to spend his end-of-year bonus at the nearest pub. If he goes back inside, some last-minute job will be found for him. And so he pushes the broken-down carriage hard up to the door, applies the brake and scoots on his merry way. If anyone bothered to check from inside, they'd find the door apparently secure. So it proved to be. I only had to give the thing the slightest tug and I was admitted.

A dormant ghost train is the least eerie of places. Its mechanical secrets were revealed by the flash of my phone torch – the trapdoor for the skeleton plunge, the spring-loaded coffin lid, the trip-activated bat-on-a-wire. Nothing here to chill the blood. I paced along the track and, to the surprise of no showman, found the key to my escape hanging on a hook right beside the exit door.

Out on the drag, I'd taken only a few steps when I came across the waxworks exhibit. To my knowledge, this kind of attraction hadn't been a regular feature on fairgrounds for at least fifty years. My dad remembered the best of them from his youth, collections of notable European royals, politicians of the day, stars of stage and screen and always the most notorious of murderers; Dr Crippen, Reginald Christie, some approximation of Jack the Ripper. In most cases, entire exhibitions were bought wholesale from defunct seaside waxworks and then toured around the country. From the look of it, Makepeace had bought his decades ago. The show still had what looked like its original advertising placards: *Come See the Astonishing Likeness of the Little Tramp! Gasp in Wonder at the Living Embodiment of Greta Garbo!*

Before I stepped up to the entrance, the gleam of a plaque caught my eye. 'This attraction is dedicated to the memory of Jamie Reese Allingham and to the heroism of Wesley Joshua Sayers.' Short and sweet and something I'd never seen before on a fairground. Wes was a local legend indeed.

The lock on the waxworks was child's play. Within seconds, I was inside and wandering among the exhibits. It was a relatively cramped space, a narrow walkway weaving around dusty mannequins with vaguely recognisable faces. I picked out a young Russell Crowe in gladiator gear, a cone-brassiered Madonna, a seventies-era Elton John – although Elton John might have been Margaret Thatcher in a sparkly Dodgers strip. Glass eyes followed my progress, shadows playing games with painted smiles. Ghost trains might not hold any terror for the showman, but waxworks never fail to cast an uneasy spell. I suppose it's that way with everything. No fictional monster can compete with the unsettling creak of an unused staircase or the unhappy arrangement of a dressing gown on the back of a bedroom door.

This idea was brought home when I discovered the storeroom towards the rear of the chamber. Marked 'MAKEPEACE EMPLOYEES ONLY – NO TRESPASSING', I pulled open the unlocked door to reveal a sizeable space, large enough for about a dozen people and containing a host of naked limbs, torsos and unscrewed heads. The disjecta membra of old exhibits. I gripped the doorframe and took a breath. For a moment, the scene had reminded me of another storeroom in another town: the back office of Bradbury End library in which I had last seen Lenny Kerrigan as he pleaded with me to save him from Peter Garris's blade. In his last moments, he too had appeared broken and disjointed. I shook my head, trying to dislodge the image, and focused again on the room.

The artificial body parts looked as if they'd been here a long time, all dusty and swagged with webs. They reminded me a little of Muriel's paper men – *paper boys*, I corrected myself. Was that significant? A tribute to the boy who died in the Old Demdike river and who, before drowning, had been brought to this waxworks by his sister and her friends. What had Muriel said of her paper tributes? *My boys, my boys. They're my fancy. My way of keeping him close. Of paying my respects . . .*

I glanced again at the room. Had little Jamie Allingham been brought here specifically, to this somewhat eerie and unnerving space? A nasty teenagers' trick to scare the child? Is that what had frightened him so, this room of pantomime butchery? In that moment, my eye alighted on the gleam of a bottle and two glasses standing on a shelf by the door. They had been tucked away, almost hidden behind a bald, featureless head that had rolled onto its side. I placed my hands into my pockets, that old bit of CID training coming back to me. Free hands are apt to wander and leave prints, and who knows yet what might become a crime scene?

Crouching a little, my left hip complaining all the while, I could make out the stain of bourbon at the bottom of both glasses and a smudge of bright red lipstick around the rim of one. Two people had been here and the disturbed dust on the shelf suggested that it hadn't been all that long ago. Perhaps a month. Perhaps six weeks. Friends toasting the memory of a little boy? Or perhaps fortifying themselves after some shared ordeal? Of course, it might have nothing to do with Jamie Allingham's long-ago drowning, and yet . . . I gave the disassembled bodies one last sweeping glance before closing the door.

Just to confirm that the head of Wesley Sayers wasn't among them.

Chapter Nine

I PARKED UP IN THE FAG-STREWN forecourt of The Six Ravens and wrestled both my bag and my juk out of the car. Webster grumbled as I placed him on the ground, glancing up at me with big wet eyes.

'Forget it, buddy. I'm not carrying you inside.'

He tilted his head, as if considering, then trotted dolefully after me.

Fenchurch's oldest pub was what you might expect. An aroma of spilled lager and old chip fat, a greasy sheen glimmering on the bar and the brasses that hung from the walls. A sad-looking Christmas tree was propped in one corner, decorated with tinsel and coloured lights that looked as if they'd been thrown, more with hope than design, in the tree's general direction. Cliff Richard preached a mawkish message of goodwill from a CD player next to the till while a plaque over the black-beamed bar proclaimed, 'Eat, Drink, be Merry, for Tomorrow we Die!' Some of The Ravens' patrons looked like they'd taken this advice to heart, all except the merry part, and were only a pork scratching or two away from fulfilling the motto's ultimate promise.

A landlord with the nose of a prize fighter at the end of his career asked my poison. I said I'd like a room for a night or two.

He looked as if he might advise me against such a rash decision, but then his good lady appeared from behind a pair of batwing doors and, having launched a plate of fish and chips at a startled punter, caught my eye. She beckoned me through to the 'parlour'.

The gloominess of this low-slung room was relieved a little by a Persian cat moulting before the electric fire and by pictures of the landlord in fishing gear, holding up a variety of catches.

'I have a dog with me,' I said. 'Will that be a problem? He's old enough to have chased that kitty's great-grandmother, so I wouldn't worry too much about her safety.'

A painted-on eyebrow was arched, but when I took Mark Noonan's wad of cash from my back pocket, the brow slid right back down again.

'Bill to be paid up front,' she sniffed, her eyes never leaving the wad. 'Call it a hundred for two nights. It's nothing fancy and we're out of season, so there's a bargain for you. I suppose you'll be wanting breakfast in with it?'

'I assumed that's what one of the Bs in your B&B stood for? Unless your good man is offering back rubs?'

'That way, is it?' she said, as I counted out the cash. 'Well, I'm not prejudicial, no one could accuse me of it. But Mr Berkeley don't swing that way, so you're out of luck there, dearie.'

'I'll try to get over the disappointment. Any chance of some food for my old boy, by the way? He's not fussy, as long as it's not too hard on his gums.'

Mrs Berkeley sucked her teeth. Then, in a voice that could strip paint, called her beloved from the bar. The poor man's face lit up when he spied Webster and, after a good deal of petting and meaningful glances in the direction of the malevolent-looking cat, he led the juk off to the kitchen.

'Be wanting anything yourself?' Mrs Berkeley asked.

I shook my head. I'd seen the fish and chips. 'Just a moment of your time. Can I buy you a drink?'

A long scarlet talon scratched the skin behind her hooped earring. 'Well, I wouldn't say no to a Drambuie and Coke. And for yourself?'

'A pint please, anything wet.'

She returned a minute or two later and we took our drinks to the armchairs by the fire. 'I've opened a tab,' she said, and raised her glass. 'In your eye. So, what would you like to chat about? I'm not a gossip, before we even start.'

'Never crossed my mind,' I said. 'I just heard that my cousin used to work here. Wesley Sayers?'

A little colour burrowed its way under those powdered cheeks. 'Wesley? Oh yes.' She seemed to channel the cat with her purr. 'A sweet lad, absolute charmer with the customers. A good listening ear, which is half the job description for a decent barman. You're comforter, confessor, bloody marriage counsellor half the time. Oh yes, young Wesley was liked by all. Not bad-looking neither.' She laughed. At least I thought that was the noise that bubbled at the back of her throat.

'How long had he worked for you?'

'Who are you, anyway?' she said, eyes narrowing. 'A cousin of Wesley's? You don't look a bit like him.'

'He got the family looks,' I said, and she nodded, as if this made sense. 'My name's Scott Jericho. His mother's worried about him and asked me to come up and check that everything's all right.'

'That old maid.' Mrs Berkeley took another long sip of her drink. 'She was lucky to have Wes at her beck and call. That's my opinion and I don't mind you knowing it, family or no family. I'd have brained her long ago if she was any mother of mine, but Wesley was so patient with her. Patience of a saint, that boy.'

'His mother was possessive, then?'

'Couldn't do without him. Always making up excuses to get him to stay home with her of an evening when really he was in the prime of his life. Ought to have been out raving it up with the right girl, not stuck inside watching *Coronation Street* with mumsie.' I could tell that Mrs Berkeley, fifty if she was a day, might consider herself the 'right girl'. 'Not that Wes ever complained. Wasn't in his nature. He even came back from London when she called and started making a fuss. That was his chance, so he told me. Had an uncle down that way that was some kind of big shot. Probably a relation of your'n, but of course she had to go and spoil it.'

I nodded. I could understand a proud young man not wanting to admit that he hadn't been able to cut it in the murky world of Uncle Mark. That he was too 'nice'.

'He weren't even flash with the money they gave him after he tried to save that poor wee boy from drowning,' Mrs Berkeley continued. Bending down, she plucked up the Persian from the rug and sat the lazy creature on her lap. 'You must've been proud of Wesley for that, him being family and all.' Arched eyebrow again, this time accompanied by the tip of a very red tongue licking a trace of Drambuie from her teeth.

'Oh yes, we were all very proud. Sent him a cake and everything,' I said. 'But remind me, how did he get it? The reward money I mean?'

'You don't know? Well, there's some as gossiped about that, though it ain't for me to say.' I thought the landlady might go on, but she glanced again at the bulge of Noonan's money in my pocket, and I stubbornly decided to leave her unsatisfied. I'd find out myself soon enough.

'But you say Wes was liked by all. That's a rare thing.'

'Well, he weren't like some of those kids brought up around here. Those who can't wait to shake the dust of the place from their heels, naming no names. But those Marsh kids, for s'ample. That pair always thought they were too good for Fenchurch. Uppity little shites.'

'They were friends of Wes?'

'He was too free with his friendship, that's my opinion,' she said. 'Gave it away to folk who didn't deserve it. Well ... they all came back for the funeral, I'll give them that.'

'Katrina Allingham's?'

'Silly girl. There was no need to do what she did, hanging herself like that. It hurt poor Wes very bad.'

'They were close?' I asked.

'Wes looked after her all right. Stood up for her like no one else after what happened to the little brother. Some people round here can't let a soul forget anything. We all have our faults.' I wondered what faults Mrs Berkeley's neighbours found with her. 'Couple of years ago, Wes was working the Saturday evening shift. It can get rowdy in here them nights, I won't deny it. Fishing boys all get their wage packets that day and the silly sods do love a session. Anyway, this one night, Kat was sitting up at the bar, sharing a drink with Wes. He just had a Coke, never drank on the job. He'd called her to come on over because he knew she'd be lonely and brooding. Looking out for her, like I say. Anyway, this young lad recognised her from school and started in about her brother. Calling her an evil slut and worse. In the next second, Wes was up and over the bar, laying into the man. Took my husband and three others to pull him off. "She's my girl," he shouted while pummelling the boy. "No one says a word about her." And then he grabbed Kat and held her tight, like his life depended on it.'

'My girl?' I echoed. 'Were they a couple then?'

She waved the suggestion away. 'More like brother and sister. But he was devoted to her.'

'So devoted he couldn't bear to live in the town without her?' I asked.

Mrs Berkeley sniffed. 'Not like Wesley to up and leave us without a word. It surprised us all.'

'And you haven't heard anything from him these past six weeks?'

'Not a dicky bird.'

'Where do you think he might have gone, Mrs Berkeley?'

She shrugged. 'Wherever he is, I hope he's enjoying himself. He gave his whole life to others – Katrina and that sourpuss mother of his. I think he just decided he needed to be young while he could, and good luck to him.' Her gaze flickered to the corridor where her husband passed by, a lip-smacking Webster at his heels. 'We all get saddled down soon enough.'

Chapter Ten

I CARRIED MY PINT TO THE main bar. It was practically empty and so I took a turn of the room, examining photos of the town from years ago – beaming crowds surging along the promenade, prim Edwardians emerging from bathing machines on the beach, a view of Makepeace's fair in its heyday, all life and bustle. I was turning away from this last print when the door swung open and a man who might have dwarfed Ben Halliday entered the room. Six foot seven and built like the proverbial, I recognised him at once as one of the pallbearers from Katrina Allingham's funeral. It's a night for chance meetings, I thought. Old friends coming together. First Rowan Chesterton and now—

'Evening, Stuart, what'll it be?' asked the landlord.

'Guinness.'

Stuart McDonald seemed to fill the bar. A rangy man with fair hair already receding to a widow's peak, an uneven slash of a mouth forested by an untidy beard, yet his hands, though powerfully made, were surprisingly elegant and beautiful. He looked like a wild woodsman who could live off the land and still make a small fortune modelling Rolex watches on the side. I stepped up beside him, resting my own pint next to his. He cast me a bleary glance.

'Do anything for you?'

Like Rowan, he looked desperately tired. When he spoke, the words came in a slur, like the slushy tread of a heavy truck on a winter road. He was dressed in a thick cable-knit jumper under a long old-fashioned yellow jacket, a bit like a cowboy's duster. Faded jeans so worn that the hairy knuckles of both knees protruded. He swayed as he stood there, as if buffeted by an invisible wind, and I could tell he'd already loaded up on a few before reaching The Ravens.

'This is a cousin of Wesley's, Stu,' Mrs Berkeley helpfully contributed, en route to the kitchen. 'Come down to see if the family can figure out where he's skedaddled off to.'

'Oh yeah?' Stuart took his time straightening the beer mats in front of him. 'But Wes left a note, didn't he?'

'He did. Not packed with detail, unfortunately,' I said. 'And his mother hasn't heard from him in weeks.'

I'm treated to another unfocused glare. 'Never met any cousin of Wes's before, and I've known him most of my life.'

'I'm from the black sheep side of the flock.' I smiled. 'Come up all the way from London. His Uncle Mark is worried.'

Stuart blinked at me. 'The mythical Uncle Mark? You're not telling me all that talk about a gangster uncle down in the big city was true? I mean, Wes was a good lad but we all thought he was spinning a tale with that one.'

I shrugged. Meanwhile, Stuart continued to arrange the beer mats, and I noticed a few flecks of bright magenta staining his sleeve. When he went to pick up his pint again the telltale callus halfway along his middle finger was plain to see. 'Another Guinness for my cousin's mate,' I said, as Stuart drained his drink in one go.

'Thanks, 'preciate it. Gotta pee, back in a sec.'

Mrs Berkeley reappeared, as if on cue, at my elbow as Stuart vanished behind a door marked 'Little Boys Room'. 'An old hanger-on, that one. Right from their school days. You didn't hear it from me, but Wesley should have chosen his friends more carefully. Stuart McDonald's been nothing but trouble these past weeks.'

'In what way?'

'Nothing in particular, I suppose,' she admitted. 'Just an atmosphere hanging about him, if you know what I mean? A feeling that he could burst into tears at any minute. Either that or break a skull or two.'

'Is he usually a violent person?'

'No.' Again she conceded a point grudgingly. 'I can't honestly say that. Always been a bit of a moody bugger, but then he probably gets that off his old man. I don't think I've ever seen the reverend crack so much as a grin, and I've lived here since I was a girl myself. But just lately, that boy gives me the heebies. Something in the way he looks at you.' She shuddered, as if to prove her case.

'How long's he been that way?' I asked.

She considered for a moment. 'Since the funeral. Then or thereabouts. It was a shock to all of them, I suppose.' She came around the bar and took over from her husband, topping off the Guinness and holding out her hand. 'That'll be £6.50.'

'Put it on the tab.'

When he returned from the toilet, Stuart seemed almost startled to see me, as if he'd forgotten I existed. 'Let's go outside,' he grunted, looking pointedly at Mrs Berkeley. 'I need a smoke. Clear my lungs of this delightful eau de chip fat.'

I followed him into the arctic chill of the night and we settled on a bench in that stub-littered forecourt.

'Here's to her majesty and all who sail in her,' Stuart muttered, holding up his pint in a mock salute to the landlady of The Six Ravens. 'You know she tried it on with Wes one Christmas Eve? Cornered him in the beer cellar and shoved her greasy fingers down his pants. He was seventeen, for fuck's sake.'

'Yet he kept working here for another six years,' I said.

'Yeah, well, he never had much get up and go. Not in the usual sense anyway.' Stuart wiped his palm down the length of his face. 'Jesus, I'm sorry, that's not fair. Wes was the best of us, always has been. It's not a crime to be content, is it?'

'Not the last time I looked.'

'Anyway, thanks. For the drink. Decent of you.'

'You're an artist, Mr McDonald?' I said.

'Stuart. And I am. How did you know? Did Wes tell you?' I pointed to the splatters of magenta on his sleeve. 'That doesn't mean a thing. I could be a painter and decorator for all you know.'

'Not with so little paint on you,' I said. 'And there's the callus on your middle finger too, the anchor point from holding an artist's brush for hours on end. It would take you a while to paint an entire house with a brush of that size.'

There's a spirituality about the face too, I thought. Something faraway in those eyes . . . I could almost hear my dad laughing at me. *What a load of poncy, middle-class joskin bollocks. Can't house painters be poets and artists too?*

Stuart sat back, a half-amused look on his face. 'You're a clever fucker, aren't you? What's the day job, some kind of mind-reader?'

'Some kind.' I reeled out the story about coming up here at Miss Westmacott's request and Stuart nodded and threw back half his pint. Then he took out a tobacco tin, rolled a fag with unsteady fingers, coughed and shivered a little.

'I don't blame her for missing him,' he said. 'There's none better than our Wes. A saint of a man, if you wanna know. We all loved Wesley. I loved him. He tried to save a little boy once, you know?'

'I heard about that. And did you know the boy's sister as well, the girl who died recently?'

'Kat.' He licked the fag paper and kept his eyes downcast. 'Yes. She was one of the gang. All pals together, right the way up from year seven.'

'You were one of the kids who worked at the fair that summer?' I asked. 'Part of the group who was with Wesley and Kat when her brother died?'

'Not me. My dad wouldn't have it. Blasphemous to work on Sundays, but then everything's blasphemous according to the good Reverend McDonald. But yes, I was one of them. The Sanctuarists.'

'Sanctuarists?'

'Dad's name for us, because that's what we did whenever we got into trouble, which was a fair amount. It was our safe haven, the keeper of our secrets.' He laughed and swilled the last mouthful of Guinness around the bottom of the glass. 'Where we sought sanctuary.' He glanced up, twisting his head at an awkward angle towards the seafront and the dark hulk of the fair. 'Down there, I mean.'

'So you weren't with the rest of them when Jamie died?' I asked.

'I'd been with them that day, but none of us were there when Jamie died. We'd all gone home by that point. All except Wes and Kat, poor sods. Anyway, why'd you want to know all this? It's ancient history. Nothing to do with wherever Wes . . .' He chucked back the last mouthful. 'Wherever Wes has ended up.'

I tried a new tack. 'I think I met another of your club earlier tonight. Rowan Chesterton?'

'Rowan's good.' He nodded. 'Like Wes. She looks after her aunt. Even when we were kids, she'd take care of the old girl. Tried to, anyway. She'd get up early and go round to Muriel's before school, just to make sure her aunt was washed and dressed, had something to eat. That was until social services were informed what was going on and Muriel was taken away. They said Rowan couldn't cope, that she was only a kid.'

'What about Rowan's parents, didn't they get involved with Muriel's care?'

'Not interested. Only Row looked out for Muriel. They put her in a facility, you know? Got her hooked on drugs, fried her brain with electric shock therapy. She'd have been all right if she stayed with Rowan, but it's too late now. Everything was spoiled. All because of nasty whispers. If we'd known then . . .' He trailed off, his gaze fixed on his empty glass.

'She sounds like a caring person,' I said. 'Like how Wes used to look out for Kat after her brother died.'

Stuart looked up, his features tight. 'He cared about Katrina very much. Like I told you, Wes didn't have much ambition, though he could have got out of this dump if he really wanted. He had the brains. Instead, he stayed here, with her, while we all ran away to seek our fame and fortune. Worked out for some of us better than others, but we went just the same. Only Wes gave up his life to always stay close by.'

'You all left Fenchurch? You, Rowan, the Marshes?'

He stared at me, those beautiful hands clasped around his glass. 'You know Maddox and Ryan?' I thought again of that churchyard photograph. I had now met two of the seven Sanctuarists who had mourned that day, Rowan Chesterton and Stuart McDonald. Another pair of women remained unidentified, but Maddox and Ryan Marsh? There had been a male and female who resembled each other quite strongly in the photo, and of course if they were all the same age ...

'The twins.' I nodded. 'I've heard of them. And of course, Wes mentioned his other friends too.'

'Indira and Lorelei,' Stuart murmured. Bingo. The full set. 'Have you been to see Ind and Lor as well, then? What did they tell you?' He glanced around, as if expecting his fellow Sanctuarists to jump out of the bushes.

'Indira and Lorelei are back in town too?' I asked.

'It draws us back, this place,' Stuart muttered. 'Like a bad enchantment. Not surprising really, this town is steeped in old magic. Right from the days of those old fisherfolk that were chucked off their land when they wanted to turn Fenchurch into a fancy seaside getaway for rich Victorians. They did rituals out in the woods, you know? The original Fenchurchians. Sacred rites to placate the dead. Muriel told us about it when we were little'uns. If you're born and raised in these parts, you can't resist the lure of Fenchurch. It's in your blood, it pulls you back. Unless you're Maddox and Ryan Marsh of course, they've managed to stay away. For now, at least.'

'Maybe it isn't magic,' I suggested. 'Maybe it's the tragedy you all shared that draws you back? Something like that experienced in childhood, it can form strong bonds of loyalty, to people, to places. Can turn you into a pilgrim of sorts.'

Is that what will happen to me, I wondered: would I make pilgrimages to the sites of my past tragedies? To Bradbury End, to Aumbry? To that little Polish food store where three innocent children had died at the hands of Lenny Kerrigan? Perhaps I would revisit those places. All except one. I felt no urge to return to the stretch of lonely country road where my mother had died. After my fruitless search for her crucifix, I'd avoided that hateful place. Shunned it and shut it out of my dreams.

I suddenly realised that Stuart was speaking again. In his half-drunk state, he had taken the bait and circled back to the decade-old tragedy that had shattered the lives of his friends.

'Kat didn't want to take him, but Jamie kept on and on at her. Said he wanted to go to the fair for his birthday. We said we'd go with her, she was so miserable about it. It was their day off, you see? The last place they wanted to be after working there all week – the smell of hot dogs and doughnut oil, the noise, the mindless chatter of the holidaymakers.' I nodded, understanding all too well. 'But we did it for Kat because we loved her.' He paused for a second and wiped his eyes. 'Then Jamie, he started going on and on about that bloody waxwork place. Kat knew he wouldn't be able to handle it, he was such a little wuss. Cried at cartoons, for fuck's sake.' Stuart planted his hand over his mouth, tears starting. 'Christ, forgive me.'

'What happened there to frighten him?' I asked gently.

'Just . . . the exhibits. The statues or whatever you call them. Like people but not. They're spooky enough for grown-ups, let alone little kids. Jesus, we thought we were grown-ups then. Sixteen and all the arrogance and blindness of youth. All the bright ideas that seem so funny at the time. Anyway, Jamie ... after he got the wind up in the waxworks, there was no reasoning with him. He was crying, hysterical. We eventually managed to get him out of the place and up into Chattox Wood. It's restful there, peaceful, we thought it might calm him down. But the kid, he seemed to get more and more out of control, crying and pushing us away whenever the girls tried to comfort him. He even shoved Wes, and Wes was his hero. In the end, the rest of us had enough and went home. Couldn't stand the bloody bawling anymore. I remember, it went right through me, and I thought, if I stay here one more minute, I'm gonna wring that fucking kid's neck.' He slumped forward, elbows planted on the table, the heels of his hands pressed into his eyes. 'We weren't there when it happened. When she pushed him. It was a momentary thing, a split-fucking-second of a good person losing their self-control. The tiniest fraction of her life, and it dominated everything afterwards. For Kat, for her family, for everyone. It ruined her and it ruined Wes. If he'd saved the kid that day, then Kat might still be with us now. Wes too. He wouldn't have had to go away.'

I placed my hand against Stuart's heaving back. 'Do you know where he is?'

He looked up at me, confused. 'Jamie? He's buried up there, in the churchyard. With her now.'

'No, I mean Wesley. He's not—'

'Who are you?' His tone became accusatory. 'Why are you asking all these questions?'

'I told you, I'm his cousin. His mum's very worried.'

'I'm sorry for that,' he said, his voice softening again. 'If I could . . .' He suddenly dropped his hands and gave me a curious look. Then, leaning in as if making up his mind to share a secret, he whispered: 'He passes by the gate of the hill and into the evil field beyond.' And all at once he was laughing, huge belly laughs, throwing back his head and roaring like a madman at the stars. It went on for what seemed like minutes but was probably less than ten seconds. Then he stopped just as suddenly and used those incongruously beautiful fingers to wipe a fleck of spittle from his beard. 'Do you understand? Do you get it? He passes by the gate of the—'

'Stuart? Stu, what are you doing here?'

Rowan Chesterton, appearing out of the night as if conjured. She stood at the entrance to the forecourt, the town lights misty behind her. As she hurried over to the table, placing her hand on Stuart's shoulder, I noticed again those dark rings under her eyes. It's been a trying time for these childhood friends. Her autumn-coloured hair flashed behind her in the breeze as she leaned in and murmured, 'Let me take you home. You've had enough.'

Stuart smiled and patted her hand. 'Good old Rowan. I need a piss first and then I'll come, quiet as a mouse. Promise.'

He staggered to his feet and we watched him go, shoulder bouncing off the door as he re-entered the pub.

'You're a good friend,' I said, getting up and leaning on my stick. My sodding hip was throbbing like a bastard. 'A good niece too, looking after your aunt. Is she OK, by the way?'

Rowan nodded distractedly. 'She's settled at home now, thanks. She remembered you, said to tell you sorry for the scare.'

I laughed. 'It was a memorable introduction to Fenchurch. So is that what drew you back here? Caring for your aunt? Stuart was just talking about the lure of this place.'

She shrugged. 'A job came up at the local library. I knew the area, the people, it was an advantage in the interview.'

'My partner's a librarian too,' I told her. 'Librarians are heroes in my book. And is that what you've always done?'

'Pretty much. I used to work at one of the Cambridge colleges, head librarian in the law department.'

'Coming back to a rural library must have been a bit of a sacrifice in career terms?'

'I got my aunt out of that awful place they put her in,' she said vehemently. 'In the end I did, anyway. Maybe I should have come back earlier but . . .'

'You had a life you wanted to live, I can understand that. Can I ask one more thing? The paper figures your aunt makes and hangs in the trees. She said they were her boys. Her way of keeping him close, of paying her respects. They're supposed to represent Jamie Allingham, aren't they? The boy who died in the river, in the woods. Was she greatly attached to Kat's little brother?'

Rowan's eyes flickered to the pub door and remained fixed there. 'She doesn't know anything. She's crazy, can't you see that?'

'Has anyone been back to the waxworks, Rowan?' I asked gently. 'Sometime around the funeral maybe? To pay their own respects, just like your aunt does with her paper boys? To toast the memory of Jamie? Two of the Sanctuarists who perhaps felt—'

She looked at me. 'Who told you that's what we called ourselves?'

A creaking door and Stuart was lumbering back towards us.

'Here's my number,' I said, taking out my old Moleskine notebook, scribbling the digits and tearing off a sheet. 'Please call me if anything occurs to you regarding Wes.'

Neither of them said goodnight. They just weaved off together into the dark, arm in arm. I watched them go and wondered about paper boys drifting among the trees where a guilt-ridden girl had hanged herself. Had they fluttered around Katrina in those final moments, filling her darkening vision and whispering away like spirits come to guide her to her rest?

Chapter Eleven

My room at The Six Ravens was as depressing as the bar downstairs. Threadbare towels thrown onto the bed, a minuscule en suite, all peach and plastic, like a nightmare plucked out of an eighties bathroom brochure. A TV with actual rabbit ear antenna sprouting from its backside stood on a battered chest of drawers. I chucked my bag onto the bed, the mattress slowly engulfing it like some strange tropical plant absorbing an insect. I sighed. I missed the homely little Eccles trailer that Harry had made so comfortable for us.

The window curtains were a shade of green unknown to nature. I pulled them back and looked out onto the street. A poster for Makepeace's Winter Wonderland was plastered onto the side of an old red phone box which someone had repurposed as a kind of community library. I wondered if that someone was Rowan Chesterton. I saw her again now as she helped Stuart along the frost-slick street, shouldering him in the direction of the cottages that surrounded the church. She was stronger than she looked.

I glanced back at the bed distrustfully. Now only the handles of my bag could be seen, arcing above the embrace of the prawn-coloured duvet. I chose the armchair instead. It at least held my weight without trying to consume me. Realising I was still gripping the hated stick, I threw it aside.

He passes by the gate of the hill and into the evil field beyond. Where had I heard something like that before? Was it a quote? If it was, I didn't immediately recognise it. At least, it rang a partial bell. I suddenly had a memory of myself as a child, lying snug on the locker bed in our old trailer, my head buried in some library book that I'd stolen from one of the towns we'd passed through. In those days, Traveller kids with no fixed address weren't allowed to borrow books and my parents hadn't been able to afford all those that I devoured. And so, needs must. By the light of the fair, I had read something concerning Greek or Roman history, a terrifying ritual practised by some holy order ... And then the memory shifted involuntarily, and I thought of my mother sitting in the chair opposite my bed, smiling at me over her own book. Finger twisting through the chain of that gleaming cross around her neck.

I stirred myself and took out my phone, tapping Stuart's phrase into a search engine. Results came back with references to Milton's *Paradise Lost*, *Childe Harold's Pilgrimage* by Byron and Bunyan's *The Pilgrim's Progress*. Had Stuart been referencing these works, the idea of Wes as some kind of traveller en route to a place of special significance? His ultimate destination beyond a gate and into an evil field? What kind of gate? What manner of field? Literal or symbolic? Perhaps he meant the gateway to Makepeace's funfair, but then how did the image of an evil field fit in with the fair itself? Hadn't Stuart instead indicated, with his pointed gaze, that the fair had been the friends' sanctuary? A place of safety and the keeper of their secrets. Was Wesley there somewhere, hidden away like those discarded waxworks, abandoned in a web-strewn storeroom? Perhaps even alive, kept captive. But why and by whom? And what of the reference to a hill? The only raised area of land in Fenchurch's boundaries was around the church, and surely the term 'sanctuary' was more associated with churches than with fairgrounds. Although the fair had offered me a kind of sanctuary after my imprisonment and disgrace.

I tapped my fingers against the armrest. The literary references didn't fit. It had been me, not Stuart, who had suggested the drawing back of the friends to Fenchurch in terms of a pilgrimage. Had he run with that idea or was it already planted in his mind? And did all this mean that he knew where Wesley had disappeared to?

'He passes by the gate of the hill and into the evil field beyond,' I repeated. Why did I keep coming back to that image of myself as a child, absorbed in the mysteries of ancient rites?

My phone buzzed and I dragged it from my pocket.

'Hello you,' said Harry. 'How are things going up there?' I smiled, grateful for another perspective. And so I walked him through my progress thus far. 'You're behaving with more than your usual tact and diplomacy.' I could hear the amused frown in his voice. 'Maybe being in a coma has mellowed you.'

'It's definitely fucked my hip, I know that,' I groaned, massaging the aching joint.

'Take it slowly. Do your exercises. Here endeth the lesson.'

I asked Harry for his thoughts on Stuart's cryptic words regarding Wesley's whereabouts. He agreed it sounded like a quote but not from anything he could automatically bring to mind. He said he'd look into it, and I asked how Ben was getting on.

'Still a bit wobbly but enjoying all the attention from Jodie. This afternoon it was a tea party up at Sal's trailer.' I pictured the former thug-turned-bodyguard sipping imaginary tea from a plastic cup, pinkie extended. 'I think she's hopeful that another gay uncle might be in play.'

'No one will ever replace her favourite,' I said. 'That's you, by the way. I think she's given me up as a lost cause. She always was a smart cookie.'

'In other news, we're all packed and ready for the off tomorrow,' Harry said. 'First stop, Bolesworth, a charming little industrial town in Lancashire, noted for its steelworks and pork pie factory. Also, the birthplace of one Peter Garris. I'm excited, my first solo case!'

I stopped myself from saying, 'I wish you wouldn't' and instead advised him to be careful. 'And phone me if anything worries you. I can be up there in a couple of hours.'

We said our goodnights, and I was just contemplating the challenges of getting in and out of that Venus flytrap of a bed, or else sleeping in the armchair, when my phone rang again. Assuming it was Harry having forgotten something, I answered without looking at the caller ID. 'Hey love, what's up?'

No answer, only the sound of the wind and a thin, reedy sort of breathing.

'Hello? I'm sorry, I thought you were someone else.' I pulled the phone away from my ear and glanced at the screen. Caller Unknown. 'Who is this?' At that moment, the church clock tolled the hour and I could hear its faint echo on the line. 'Rowan? Is that you?' She was the only person in Fenchurch to have my number, unless she'd passed it on to Stuart. Or perhaps Mark Noonan had given it to Wesley's mother. He said she was scatty, perhaps coming home she'd remembered our appointment. 'Miss Westmacott?'

And then I heard another sound on the line. The distant shriek of Mrs Berkeley calling last orders. The same caterwaul that came up through the floorboards of my room. I wrestled my way out of the chair and, bending low with a grunt, collected my stick from where I'd thrown it. Then, phone still planted to my ear, I went to the window.

'Who is this?'

A figure was standing inside the old phone box across the street. He appeared to be slouched against the door, some kind of stick in his own hand, as if in mockery of me. There was no streetlight on that side of the road and his face was drenched in shadow. Still, I got the impression of a raggedy, loose-limbed frame, almost emaciated, like a scarecrow cut down from its pole.

'Garris?'

No answer, only the sigh of the wind and the wheeze of what I took to be cigarette-scarred lungs.

'What do you want? What are you doing here?'

That silent, watchful presence remained unmoving.

I shoved my mobile into my pocket and lunged towards the door, clattering down the stairs, through the bar where Mrs Berkeley was collecting glasses and berating her husband and out onto the forecourt. I was breathless by the time I reached the road, wheezing as heavily as the man in the phone box.

Except there was no man.

I suddenly became conscious of Webster at my side as I tapped my way across the road and opened the booth's heavy iron door. The old juk whimpered and I told him to hush his noise. No one in the box, no one in the street. A couple of narrow shelves held the books that furnished this converted space. Without thinking, I stooped and picked up a volume that had fallen to the floor. It lay open at a page and, before replacing it, I scanned the text. A book of popular poetry, familiar lines I'd read as a child, ones that had inspired the odd nightmare.

Yesterday, upon the stair,
I met a man who wasn't there
He wasn't there again today
I wish, I wish he'd go away . . .

I looked down the empty road. 'Are you here? What do you want?'

Then, pulling out my phone, I called Ben. I told him to take extra special care of Harry. He asked if anything was wrong. I said no, not a thing, and then Webster and I retreated to The Six Ravens.

Chapter Twelve

I THOUGHT I'D DREAM OF GARRIS and perhaps Lenny Kerrigan. Of the raggedy scarecrow murderer and his shattered victim. Instead, my sleep was mercifully dreamless and I woke refreshed. I'd been having more of these empty nights lately, perhaps a side effect of the coma. If so, I was thankful. Oblivion beat the spectres that usually haunted me.

After a prompting text from Harry – *Rise and shine and do your bloody exercises!* – I left my room, ravenous, and so willingly submitted to The Six Ravens' breakfast. A mistake. Even Webster turned his nose up at the offer of a congealed sausage from my plate.

'Please don't feed that beast from the table, Mr Jericho,' the landlady scolded. 'We have our standards here, you know.'

'Don't worry, Mrs Berkeley,' I said, throwing a napkin over the culinary horror before me. 'I think we've both learned our lesson.'

'What are you about today?' she asked, obliviously flitting around the breakfast room with a duster.

'Off to see Wesley's mother, if I can find her in.'

This prompted a contemptuous sniff. 'She could be anywhere. The woman's a hard worker, I'll give her that. Juggles a few different part-time jobs, cleaning at the church and what have you.' Mrs Berkeley seemed to parcel out her praise like a miser dispensing coins at an orphanage. 'And it was hard on her after that husband of hers drank himself to death.'

I left Webster with Mr Berkeley, who seemed grateful for the company, and stepped out into another freezing Fenchurch day. Passing the old phone box, I couldn't help taking out my mobile and checking its log for the fortieth time. Caller Unknown. If I hadn't the evidence of the call received, I might think I'd imagined the gaunt form of my old mentor. It must have been him, mustn't it, playing his games? Well, at least if he was here in Norfolk his attention was focused on me. I might provide a distraction from Harry and Ben's investigations in Bolesworth. Only I had to wonder, what did Garris want? And why the silent pantomime of last night?

Back at number 3 Cloister Cottages, I rang the bell and blew into my hands. After a series of bumps and crashes from the hall, the door was finally opened by a harassed-looking woman with flyway grey hair, which she parted from her face like a wary pensioner peeking through her curtains. Except she wasn't a pensioner. Despite a heavily lined face and rounded shoulders, I knew Stephanie Westmacott was still a year shy of her fiftieth birthday. Again, like with Rowan and Stuart, tiredness seemed to weigh the woman down.

'Mr Jericho?' she asked, her tone at once hopeful and apologetic.

'Miss Westmacott, glad to have caught you in.'

'Yes, thank you. I'm so grateful you're here. Please do step inside.'

She guided me into a hall that was more steeplechase than corridor. Cardboard boxes everywhere, some open, some taped shut, old shoes and sandals stuffed into one, photo albums piled into another, a crate of tottering crockery that looked like it had been bought in a job lot from a car boot sale. Still, the place smelled relatively fresh and clean.

'I came last night,' I told her as we passed into the back kitchen, a small space as overstuffed with bric-a-brac as the hall. 'I thought Mark Noonan told you I would be here.'

'Yes, I'm sorry. I had an emergency call from Lorelei last night and your arriving slipped my mind. I'm a bit of a scatterbrain, I'm afraid. Hence all this.' She spread her hands in a despairing gesture. 'I keep intending to tidy things away but then something distracts me and I find myself immersed in another project altogether. But I was saying, dear Lorelei. She had a big order come in last minute and so I popped over to help out. I do now and then. Tea?'

She started opening cupboards, pulling out a cup from a dresser, a mug from a china hutch, finding the milk under the sink. She was such a tiny, frail-looking thing that everything in the kitchen seemed outsized in comparison. As she darted about, she picked up stray bits and pieces apparently at random – a chewed biro, a book of stamps, a used soup spoon – dropping them into the commodious pocket of her apron. Not even fifty and her hands were raw and chapped, a gold ring embedded in the swollen flesh of her third finger. It must cause her pain. She'd divorced Wesley's father a quarter of a century ago; I wondered why she still wore it. As well as her hoarder's apron, she was dressed in a plaid housecoat with matching slippers. Scratches of makeup, her mouth bracketed with lines, stray grips serving no obvious purpose lost in her hair. It was like the 1950s had reached out and claimed Miss Westmacott as one of its own. And she looked so very tired. I'm not sure I'd ever met anyone so tired, not even Rowan and Stuart. Exhaustion seemed to weep out of her like an infection.

Finally, the tea was made and a chocolate cake produced from the vegetable rack. She cut a slice and offered it to me reluctantly, as if she might be handing over a slab of arsenic.

'Bought from the local supermarket, I'm afraid. So sorry.'

'Thank you,' I said. 'It looks delicious.'

'Not up to my standards,' she sighed, 'but I don't bake. Not these days.'

'Please sit down, Miss Westmacott,' I said. 'Now, did Mark Noonan tell you who I am?'

She nodded slowly. 'You're the detective. He said you'd help us. He said you were the cleverest man he'd ever met.'

'I wouldn't take that as much of an endorsement,' I said. Although that wasn't strictly true; Noonan himself was as wily as they came, he had to be to have kept out of prison for so long. 'What exactly do you want me to do for you, Miss Westmacott? Find Wesley?'

'No.' She paused. 'I mean, yes. You see, I don't think my son is with us anymore.'

'You think he's dead?' I asked gently.

She took her time answering. 'A mother knows,' she said at last. 'You carry a child for nine months, you feed him, clothe him, try your best to make him into a good man. And I did. And he was. And when you do all those things, you know.' She tapped her chest with her palm. 'You know when they aren't in the world anymore. And I'm frightened, Mr Jericho, because who would take him from me?'

'But he left you a note, didn't he, saying he was going away?' She shook her head, and I sighed. 'Why don't you take me through his movements on the day of the funeral?'

'It was the Friday,' she said confidently. 'Last week of October. Only a fortnight or so after the poor child died. They all came back for the funeral.'

'The Sanctuarists?'

'You've heard of that?'

'I met Rowan and Stuart last night.'

'Reverend McDonald's son.' Her face brightened. 'Such a clever boy and a great friend of Wesley's. Yes, they all came back. They were always like that, right from getting their first summer jobs at the fair together. They'd known each other at school, of course, but that summer was when they really bonded. It's what happens when you're sixteen, isn't it? You never have friendships like that ever again. Wesley, Stuart, Rowan Chesterton, the twins Maddox and Ryan Marsh, Indira Bakshi and Lorelei Tey. And of course Katrina. Poor dear girl. Do you know, I think from the first time I saw her, I felt she was fated to live a short life. Some people have that look about them, don't they? Mayflies. The victims of this world. Victims of fate, of other people, of themselves sometimes.'

'But she had a good friend too, didn't she? Your son?'

Miss Westmacott wiped her eyes, a bit of white stuff clinging to her little nail as she pulled her hand away. I felt for this woman, but it turned my stomach to see that strand hanging there, like a grave worm from her finger. 'My Wesley and Katrina. Close as siblings they were. Especially after what happened with little Jamie. But then all eight of them had a special connection.'

'Including Lorelei Tey?' I asked. 'That's who you were helping out last night, wasn't it? With an order?'

'I help a bit at Lorelei's place.' She nodded. 'Sometimes I take the stuff home to organise, but last night she wanted me at the shop. They had a wedding, you see? All hands on deck. Then I babysat for her and Indira.' She beamed. 'Their little Grace is a sweet child. They adopted her quite recently.' She leaned forward conspiratorially. 'You know, I always suspected there might be something between those two girls, even when they were teenagers. Oh, I know what the Bible says, even what Reverend McDonald might say, but where's the harm? Love is love, isn't that the phrase?'

I smiled at her. 'So I've heard. You're a churchgoer yourself, Miss Westmacott?'

'Ever since I lost my husband. I'm not talking about his death, you understand. I mean our divorce. Wesley was just a baby back then, but I was left feeling very low after the separation. That's why I'd never condemn what poor Katrina ended up doing to herself. I've been to that dark place, too. Joining the church, finding my faith, it saved me. I only wish I'd known what Kat was going through, I might have guided her to the light before it was too late. But I expect you're a scoffer, Mr Jericho. Coming from London and ... everything.'

She let the implication hang for a moment.

'Not at all,' I said. 'And I don't work for Mark Noonan. I'm not part of his world. Not anymore.'

'I'm glad to hear that,' she said. 'He's a relation on my husband's side, of course. That whole set-up he operates down in London, the stories my Patrick used to tell, it scares me very much. I didn't like it when Wesley went down there to join him. Providence sent my boy back to me.' She took a sip of her tea while I tasted the chalky supermarket chocolate cake. Miss Westmacott winced as I chewed. 'Wesley was wild with rage, you know?'

'About what happened to Katrina?' I asked.

She frowned at me. 'Sorry, no. My mind tends to wander. I was thinking about Lorelei and Indira again. Someone told the teachers at school about them. Some sneak who spied on the girls in Chattox Wood, caught them kissing. Caused a fair stink at the time ... But where was I? Oh yes, the funeral.' I blinked. This conversation was giving me whiplash. 'They always came back to Fenchurch, for birthdays and special occasions, like Lorelei and Indira's engagement party, their baby's christening and then poor Katrina's funeral. They were the best of friends, always.'

'It must have been a big shock to Wesley, the suicide?' I said.

'Yes, I suppose it was,' Miss Westmacott pondered. 'Although she was never really happy. Not after what happened with little Jamie. Her parents moved away a few years later. I don't think they ever forgave her. She pushed him, you see? An accident, she was never prosecuted. I suppose the authorities thought she'd suffered enough, but I don't think her parents looked at her in the same way ever again. Maybe that's why there's no proper stone up there in the churchyard ...'

'And your son, what did Katrina's parents think of him?'

'Oh, Wesley was their hero.' Miss Westmacott beamed. 'Everyone's hero.'

'That must have given him a lot of confidence in himself. But like Katrina, he always stayed here, in Fenchurch?'

'He was a homebody, this was where he felt most comfortable. Not that he couldn't have been whatever he wanted. He was clever, Mr Jericho. And of course, he felt someone should stay and look after Katrina, especially when all the rest of them left to pursue their careers and whatnot. Then months turn into years, of course.'

'A good friend.'

She blinked back tears. 'He loved her very much.'

'What happened after the funeral?' I asked. 'I understand Wesley left town that very night? Because he loved her? Because the memories were too painful?'

Miss Westmacott shook her head and poured more tea. 'He stayed on for drinks with the others after the wake. Hung around The Six Ravens until close to chucking-out time, I believe.'

I nodded. 'As I said, I've already met two of them. They had only warm words for your son.'

'Rowan is a local librarian now. Runs the knit and natter group I go to every Friday afternoon,' said Miss Westmacott. 'A dear girl, she looks after her poor aunt. She had to come back, of course. It was either that or Muriel would stay in that home forever.'

'And Stuart?'

'A talented painter and architect. He went away to uni, you know? He's only back here until he can fund the next stage of his architectural education. He had to take a break midway through. Such a long course, his father tells me.'

'He seemed very upset last night,' I said.

'Who wouldn't be?' she asked plainly. 'One of his best friends commits suicide and the other goes missing.'

'Yes, of course. But going back to that night.'

'The last we heard from him was when Wesley called Mr McDonald around midnight,' Miss Westmacott said.

'He phoned the vicar?' I stared at her. 'Why?'

'He was trying to get hold of me. Mr McDonald lives at the vicarage at the end of the street.'

'But why not call here?'

She looked uncomfortable. 'We'd been having money trouble. I didn't like to ask Mr Noonan for any more help. As I said, he scares me.' I thought many things scared Miss Westmacott, but in Noonan's case, it was probably an understandable reaction.

'Your landline was cut off?' I suggested.

'Yes. And I'd got behind on my mobile phone payments too.'

'What did Wesley want?'

'I don't know. By the time Mr McDonald brought his phone down to me it had cut off.'

'He must have wanted to get hold of you quite desperately, calling the vicar at that hour.' Why did he even have the vicar's number? I wondered. Although perhaps it was a natural enough arrangement if he couldn't get his mum any other way, and hadn't Mrs Berkeley told me that Miss Westmacott worked part-time cleaning the church?

'I suppose he did,' she said. 'To be honest, I simply thought he was overwhelmed by the events of the day. Saying his final farewell to Kat and everything. I was tired out myself and thought I'd catch up with him in the morning, when he'd sobered up.'

'He did come home then?'

'Oh yes. I thought I heard him come in about 2 a.m. I took him up a cup of tea around eleven the next morning. That was when I found his bed had been slept in and some clothes and a bag were gone.'

'And he left a note? May I see it?'

I waited while she rummaged through drawers and in boxes, finally returning just as I was beginning to think she'd lost the note among the chaos. She handed the slip of paper to me while unconsciously pocketing another haphazard collection of objects that she'd picked up during her hunt – a spool of yarn, a reel of dental floss, a dried-up marker pen. By now her apron was bulging like a kangaroo's pouch.

The note read: 'Mum, I'm just heading off for a bit – too much going on right now. I've taken some money from the clown by the way, haha. Will call when I can.' I turned it over, somehow expecting more, but that was all.

'The clown?'

Miss Westmacott cupped her forehead with her palm. 'Oh yes, just a sec, I'll bring him down to meet you.'

'Absolute divhouse,' I muttered, as her slippered feet shuffled their way down the hall and up the stairs. What felt like half an hour later, she reappeared with a piece of ceramic, like a toby jug, but a version that had almost certainly been cast in the furnaces of hell. Moulded in the form of a Pierrot clown face with its characteristically pert lips, black diamond eye makeup, ruffed collaret and stark white skin, its pinprick pupils stared back at me.

'Charming.' I nodded.

She smiled. 'One of my lucky finds. I'm a little bit of a jumble sale addict, you know. Anyway, we've always used it as a kind of kitty jug. It had a hundred in notes and coins in it before Wesley left.'

'May I see?'

I ran my finger around the inside rim, perfectly smooth to the touch. 'Ah yes,' I said. 'We had one of these when I was a kid. Ours was a British bulldog. Where did you find the note, by the way?'

She cast her eyes upward. 'On the desk in his room.'

'And you've tried contacting him in the weeks since?'

She nodded. 'Constantly. His mobile has been off ever since that night.'

I held up the note. 'And you're sure this is your son's handwriting?'

'Absolutely. Look.' She ferreted in yet another drawer, bringing out handfuls of dog-eared birthday cards, showing me samples all signed 'Wesley' and, to my eye at least, corresponding with the handwriting on the note.

'But you still don't believe it,' I said. 'You think something's happened to him?'

'He wouldn't have just taken off like that.' She shook her head. 'Not for days and days without a word. He wouldn't do that to me.'

'Then how do you account for the note?'

'Maybe someone forged it. Or maybe it's genuine. Maybe he did intend to go away for a little while, but never this long and never without a quick call to tell me he's all right.'

'How much money did he take?'

'A hundred from the clown.'

'And the police have checked his bank accounts?'

'No activity, so they say. But he had some money stashed away, too. A couple of thousand hidden in the base of his bed. Enough to live off for a few months.'

'Then why didn't he reference that here in the note?' I wondered. 'Why only mention the money taken from the jug?'

'I can't say.' She witters on abstractedly, 'I was cooking him a special treat that night. Chocolate cake with Italian meringue buttercream. His favourite. I'd miscalculated the temperature and got it a bit soupy the last time I made it. Wes was so upset, and so I was taking special care with it that night. To cheer him up after the funeral. I was busy with some other work for one of the girls at the same time, but I wanted to do this for him. He wouldn't have just vanished, leaving me like this, Mr Jericho. He wouldn't.'

'All right. But then we have to ask the question: who would want to hurt your son? Did he have any enemies?'

'Not a soul.'

'And what was he like generally, as a person? I've heard some lovely things.'

'He was a kind boy. Very gentle.'

'No bad habits at all?'

'Well.' She smiled. 'He was a terror for cutting his toenails and leaving the parings all over his bedroom floor, forgetting to take the rubbish out, that sort of thing.' Taking the rubbish out? I looked around. Quite a herculean task. 'And the reward money went to his head a little bit. But we'd always been so poor, and it was quite a lot of money, so who could blame him really? And he wasn't clever in that way. Not with money and practical things. Not like Maddox Marsh with her fashion business and Ryan Marsh with the law, or even Stuart with his art and buildings. He had no ambition, his teachers always used to say that in his reports. But he had his own projects. And he was brave too, in ways most people aren't.'

'You mean like how he tried to save Jamie Allingham?'

'Exactly! He took risks when other people wouldn't.'

'And the reward. Where did that come from?'

'Mr Makepeace, of course.' She stared at me. 'Didn't you know?'

'The fairground owner?' I couldn't disguise my surprise. 'But why would he stump up reward money? Were they close?'

She shrugged. 'He's always been a community leader around here. A good man, likes setting an example for the town. And he's fond of children. Not in that way, before you say anything. Just because he is the way he is, people love to gossip. He employed lots of kids at the fair, always did. It gave them some pocket money and taught them the value of hard work.'

'How much was it?' I asked. 'The reward?'

'Fifteen thousand pounds.'

I whistled. Generous indeed. But perhaps not out of the way. Makepeace Funfair might now be a sad spectacle in decline but seaside amusements had enjoyed a mini boom a decade ago. In those days, such a sum for a local hero would not only have been affordable but could make a wonderful PR splash. Especially as a way to counteract any bad press attached to the fair as the last place Jamie Allingham had been seen prior to his death.

'What do you think has happened to your son, Miss Westmacott?' I asked gently.

'I don't know. I just feel he's not here anymore.'

'And if I find the person responsible, what then?'

For the first time a flash of colour suffused her cheeks. 'I want them punished,' she said, her lips turning white in her vehemence. And all at once it wasn't a timid, frail woman sitting opposite me but a mother, remorseless and terrible in her love. 'Not by the police and the courts, though. That's why I called Mr Noonan. I want them taken to *him*, Mr Jericho. I want them to suffer. Mark Noonan will know what to do with them.'

Chapter Thirteen

I ASKED IF I MIGHT SEE Wesley's room and Miss Westmacott folded her hands together as if in prayer. She asked to be excused showing me up. She couldn't face the emptiness of it, the void of her son not being there.

As I climbed the stairs, my hip groaning at me, I wondered: who writes a goodbye note these days? Wouldn't it have been more natural for a millennial like Wesley Sayers to text his mother? But then of course her mobile was out of action. That was why he'd phoned Mr McDonald the night of the funeral. They had all been drinking at the pub. In a sozzled state, the idea of going away, of tearing himself from the misery and grief of his friend's suicide and the town that had haunted them both since Jamie's death, might have felt urgent. But when the call to his mum via Reverend McDonald had cut off, perhaps Wesley's burning enthusiasm to communicate his plan had cooled. He still wanted to leave but telling her could wait until morning. And so, he stumbled home at 2 a.m., fell into bed, woke early, head thumping, packed his things and left the note. But where had he been in the intervening hours? And why not wait until his mother was up and about before leaving? Well, considering her possessiveness, I couldn't blame the boy avoiding that confrontation. He may even have feared his own compassionate nature. From all I'd heard, Wesley Sayers sacrificed much for those he loved. He knew he could easily crumble and stay if his mother made the right noises.

The bedroom proved to be tidier than the rest of the house, clothes neatly hanging in the wardrobe, good stuff too, brand names, but all a few years old and perhaps a little small for the figure in the funeral photo. They must have been bought with some of the reward money he received when he'd been a more slender sixteen.

On the desk below the window sat a laptop, its broken casing gaffer-taped together. I flipped the screen, plugged in the charger, tried a few obvious passwords and got nowhere. I was sure Harry would've been able to crack it in seconds. Beside the computer was a stack of payslips from the pub, a half-empty packet of chewing gum, a Bic lighter and a blank notebook that corresponded with the message he'd left behind. I held the pad up to the light, ran my finger across an impression of letters left from a sheet torn away. From what I could make out, it was a reminder of a shift change at the pub.

In the desk drawer, a pristine passport, issued when he was eighteen, no stamps; an old wallet without cards or money; a lanyard from a music festival from a couple of years back; a scuffed trophy from his debating club win at school; a swimming certificate; a few other mementos of childhood triumphs, nothing recent.

A collage of photos exclusively depicting the Sanctuarists was framed above his bed. I recognised more youthful versions of Stuart and Rowan. Then there were those I hadn't yet encountered – Indira, Lorelei and the Marsh twins. A variety of snapshots from their schooldays, striking poses in the hallway, competing at handstands on the sports field, in lab coats and safety goggles, tongues out and cross-eyed. Days out together: the beach, the woods, larking around among the tombstones and lounging across the pews inside the church. Stuart towering over the group with his good-natured grin; Rowan often sheepish, blushing and shying away from the camera; Indira with her arm looped protectively around Lorelei; the Marsh twins, impeccably dressed and somehow serious, even when smiling; and Wes and Kat, whatever the configuration of the others, always together, she hugging him about the waist, his hand resting on her shoulder.

Only one photo, placed at the centre of the collage and blown up a little larger than the rest, featured an additional figure. It's a joyous scene from the churchyard, the usual suspects sitting or standing on an above ground tomb while a little boy is nestled at their centre, his face screwed up with giggles as they all reach in to tickle him. Written in marker pen at the bottom in Wes's distinctive hand: 'In memory of Jamie, always and forever one of the gang. We'll miss you forever little dude.'

From the look of the boy, it can't have been too long after this photo was taken that Jamie drowned in the river. I focused my gaze on Wesley, grinning along with the rest. What does that do to a person, knowing that you almost saved a child's life? Do you believe the praise of your friends and the community, that you are a hero deserving of reward and adulation? That you tried your best and that your best was good enough? Or lying here alone in the dead of night, through the dark and doubting hours, would you always harbour a secret uncertainty as variations on what happened replayed inside your mind? Ones in which you swam a little harder, held your breath a little longer, pushed yourself that tiny bit more, and in so doing, the boy who died is now a man who sits with you in the pub as you both relive the story of the day he almost drowned. Is that why his image was hung like a curse above your bed, Wesley? To torment your wakeful mind, to torture you with what-ifs?

I checked under the pillows and mattress, nothing, then dropped to one knee. It hurt like hell, but I managed to get low enough so that I could look under the bed. Aside from dust devils, there was only a small plastic storage box pushed up against the wall. I used my stick like a hook-a-duck pole to pull it out. Then, virtually crawling onto the bed, I sat with the box in my lap and snapped open the lid.

Inside, a collection of keepsakes. The majority of these were held inside a pink cardboard folder marked in flowery lettering 'For Wes, to have always in memory of me. Please, don't ever forget me. I know you won't. Kat x'. The file contained a paper trail of the dead girl's life – an ultrasound scan labelled at the bottom in the same elaborate hand 'Me before I said hello to the world!'; a copy of her birth certificate; an ink print of her baby feet; a somewhat sinister crayon drawing of a mother, father and a little girl outside a lopsided house with a smoking chimney; school reports; a couple of birthday cards; her 11+ pass and a cycling proficiency certificate; a friendship bracelet woven with coloured twine; a concert ticket for some defunct boyband I'd vaguely heard of; a university acceptance letter; these and a dozen other such mementos and records charting her young life, right up until a final snapshot of Kat and Wes taken relatively recently.

They were standing at the bar of The Six Ravens, arms looped around each other, Wes grimacing comically as he plonked a HAPPY NEW YEAR party hat on her head. I felt an unexpected lump in my throat. A record not only of a life but of a loving platonic relationship. I wondered how Wes must have felt when he heard the news of her death. Despairing, bewildered, angry, guilty that he hadn't picked up the signs that might have saved her. After all, he had now failed both Kat and her little brother, ultimately unable to reach either of them in time. New what-ifs to add to those dark doubting hours. Perhaps this very personal bequest had been Kat's way of reassuring him that he'd always been the best of friends and that no fault lay at his door.

Beneath the file I found an even more curious item. Vacuum-sealed in a plastic bag, a rotted fragment of what looked like fruitcake. There was no smell to it, the bag was airtight. Had this also been gifted by Kat? And if so, what could it possibly signify?

There was one more treasure beneath the file. A poem printed on a piece of yellow card. As I read the lines, a memory stirred:

I fled Him, down the nights and down the days;
I fled Him, down the arches of the years;
I fled Him, down the labyrinthine ways
Of my own mind; and in the mist of tears
I hid from Him, and under running laughter.

The opening verse of 'The Hound of Heaven' by Francis Thompson. I'd studied this text during my brief time at Oxford, a devotional ode written in the late nineteenth century. An unusual and fairly obscure piece about a hound hunting a fleeing hare, symbolic of God's grace patiently pursuing the wayward human soul. What was it doing here, among Kat's treasures? Had the dead girl been fleeing someone? God himself in the sense of the poem – his forgiveness for what she'd done to her little brother, that one reckless, unintended push? Had she not wanted to be forgiven? Or was it the ghost of Jamie that hunted her, never letting her be until she had taken her life and silenced him forever? Or maybe the hound was a more corporeal type of hunter.

I turned the text over and on the reverse found a clue that might confirm my vague suspicions. In Wes's hand, scrawled on the back – 'Poor Katrina ran from that monster but he always found her. *Always.*' The last word underlined multiple times.

I looked back at the framed collage of photos over the bed, at the clusters and configurations of friends surrounding Kat and Wesley. One of those six? And if so, had Kat used this poem to communicate the fact of her persecution to her best friend? *I fled Him, down the nights and down the days.* Was that why Wes was now missing? Because he had confronted this 'monster' after the funeral and … what? Run away from Fenchurch, sickened by the now polluted memories the place held? Or had his fellow Sanctuarist silenced Wesley before he could share this newfound truth with the others? And what was that truth? That one of these childhood friends had perhaps gaslit the girl to her death, playing on her guilt? Was this poem in fact Kat's suicide note? After all, none had been found beside the body.

I shook my head. What did you know, Wesley?

I replaced everything in the box, tucked it under the bed and limped painfully back downstairs. Still in the kitchen, I found Miss Westmacott making an ineffectual attempt at the washing up.

'Was Wesley in love with Katrina?' I asked.

She turned to me, a little startled, those raw-knuckled hands dripping with foam. 'No, nothing like that. But they'd been very close ever since the accident. And Wesley? Girlfriends, boyfriends? He didn't have time for all that. He had his work, his projects, me.'

I nodded, picturing the somewhat empty bedroom upstairs. 'Did Wes ever suggest to you that someone was persecuting Kat?'

She turned back to the sink before answering. 'He was so angry after she died. I hardly ever saw him angry. Only a few times, like when Indira and Lorelei's relationship was exposed at school or when poor dear Rowan's aunt was taken into care. He was so protective of them all. He said it shouldn't have happened, Mr Jericho. That Katrina shouldn't have been taken from him.'

And perhaps he knew who by, I thought to myself.

Chapter Fourteen

'I'D LIKE YOU TO KEEP up the story that I'm Wes's cousin,' I told Miss Westmacott. 'It will help people open up to me.'

'Of course.' She wiped her eyes on the corner of a soiled tea towel, a little of that white gunge threading out like a spider web. 'Thank you, I'm so grateful. To you and Mr Noonan.'

The vengeful fury of a mother was gone and she appeared meek and fragile again.

The sound of the front door opening drew our attention. I glanced down the hall to see a fussy, plump little man shuffling into the house, his arms laden down with Christmas presents. He stopped when he saw us, blinking at me through a pair of steel-rimmed spectacles. One of the gifts dropped from the top of the pile and, in trying to rebalance his burden, he practically threw the rest down the corridor. He said nothing, only stared at them with a bland, baffled sort of expression while Miss Westmacott squeezed past me and started gathering them all up.

Running a finger under his dog collar, Reverend McDonald reminded me a little of George Smiley or Father Brown, awkward and owlish but, as with his fictional counterparts, probably not as stupid as he looked. Unless he was. Unlike in books, most people are exactly what they appear to be. There was a passing resemblance to Stuart too – the colouring, the receding hairline – but I guessed the Guinness-guzzling giant I'd met last night must have got his stature from another strand of the gene pool. The vicar gasped asthmatically and, searching his pocket, found an inhaler and took a grateful breath.

'Thank you, Stephanie dear,' he said, following her into the kitchen where I relieved Miss Westmacott of the gifts, finding space for them where I could. 'Presents donated by the community,' McDonald said and offered me a simpering smile. 'For the children of the families that use our food bank. So generous, my parishioners. Speaking of, I, uh, I wanted to talk about the church fundraiser.' He turned back to Miss Westmacott. 'I know you're not up to baking these days, but could you persuade Lorelei to donate a couple of arrangements? Some winter flowers perhaps?'

'Certainly, Richard. Oh, and this is Mr Jericho.' She touched my sleeve. 'He's come to look into Wesley's disappearance. He's a distant cousin of ours and has some experience in cases like these.'

Again, that finger running a half circuit of the dog collar. 'I see. Very good of you, I'm sure.'

'Lovely parish you have here, Vicar,' I said.

He blinked, more owlish than ever. 'Is it? Yes, I suppose.'

'And very spiritual, from what I've seen. Although maybe not orthodox. On my way into town, I ran into one of your community, almost literally. A lady called Muriel? She showed me some unusual decorations hanging in the trees in the wood. They looked a bit pagan, I suppose you'd say.'

'Bloody Muriel. Bloody woman.' He clasped his hands together, as if shocked by his outburst. 'I ... I don't blame her, of course. That would be unchristian of me. The poor woman hasn't been right in the head for years.'

'Since the tragedy?' I suggested. 'A young boy drowned in the river somewhere in the woods, didn't he? She called her creations "paper boys". I wondered if she'd left them in memory of him.'

'Oh no, she was ill long before that,' McDonald said. 'Years before. They tell me she was a talented mathematician once, went to university and everything. Interested in geometry and the like. But I hear this sort of thing runs in the family. Eccentricity, psychiatric degeneration, I don't know the medical terms. Personally, I don't subscribe to the belief that all such illnesses have a purely chemical or hereditary principle. Much of it can be put down to what you might call a spiritual decadence. Although she was a woman of science, she also delved into matters that are best left alone.'

'You mean superstition?'

He curled a clerical lip. 'There's a lot of such nonsense in towns like this. Tawdry, peasant beliefs, unworthy of serious thought and corrupting to the intellect. At least the classical mythology of the ancients had some elegance to it. A kind of spiritual heft. Of course, that too was all heresy but, in a way, those old gods and heroes anticipated the divine revelations to come. But these hackneyed local legends, grubby and debased? The making of paper images, the eating of sins, the bloody birds.' He visibly shuddered.

'Your Cain Ravens?' I said. 'But at least they nod to the Bible, don't they? And perhaps it's better to be safe than sorry. Isn't disaster supposed to visit the town if they ever leave the tower?'

'All I know is, they cost us a fortune in meat,' the vicar complained. 'Have their own exclusive freezer unit down in the crypt, running all year round. Fed twice a day. Biscuits soaked in blood, like some kind of perverse eucharist. But I'm told they must have it thus, and I suppose they've been here longer than any of us. The Cain Ravens of Fenchurch St Peter.'

'Your son told me last night that you were particular about such things,' I said. 'No working on a Sunday and so no summer job at the fair.'

'You've met Stuart?'

'He seemed upset,' I said.

'He's highly strung, always has been. It's his temperament. His mother was the same, my dear wife. He took her death very hard. He was only a boy, you see. I tried everything to save her – hospitals abroad, experimental treatments. Cancer, though, ravenous. Nothing worked. He, um.' McDonald shuffled in his chair, as if recalling himself to the room. 'He's an artist, you know, but not a pansy. He's actually a very practical boy, and strong as an ox. He wants to be an architect. He's saved us an absolute fortune on some repairs at the church this winter. It's been so bitterly cold, the frost has caused a spot of structural damage. He's our odd job man too, you see? Until he sorts himself out and earns enough to restart his studies. The university course on architecture is so long and expensive, he's taken a break to build up his funds. I had a word with the bishop last summer and got Stuart taken on as our caretaker here. And our Ravenmaster, as they call the role at the Tower. Of London, I mean. Not our poor turret.'

All good background on Stuart but I wanted to press on. 'Miss Westmacott tells me you had a call from Wesley on the night of the funeral?'

'Yes. I was in bed. Reading.'

'Poetry maybe?' I prompted. 'A religious work?'

The vicar blushed. 'P.G. Wodehouse. I'm an immense fan.'

I nodded. Of course you are, Reverend. Like dogs and their owners, I'd found that readers could often come to resemble the characters of their favourite authors. It was easy to picture this blustering country parson taking afternoon tea with Bertie Wooster's Aunt Agatha.

'It was near midnight,' McDonald continued. 'The line wasn't the best, very crackly and already cutting in and out. I honestly couldn't make out much of what he was saying. I tried to ask if I could do anything for him, but he insisted on talking to his mother.'

'How did he sound?' I asked.

'Sounded like he was in a tunnel. You know what these modern phones are like. Give me a good old-fashioned landline any day.'

'I meant emotionally?' I persisted. 'Was he angry, upset, distressed?'

'I couldn't really . . .' The vicar screwed up his face in an effort of remembrance. 'A little upset and distressed perhaps. He sounded drunk, if anything. They'd all been drinking after the funeral, Stuart too. He didn't come home that night.'

'Perhaps he stayed out with Wes?' I suggested. 'Miss Westmacott told me that Wesley was late back.'

'No, not with Wesley. I think he said he was with Indira Bakshi.'

'Stuart *was* with Indira that night,' Miss Westmacott said. 'They came here just before you arrived with the phone, Richard. They were looking for Wesley. Said he'd gone off by himself after leaving The Six Ravens and that they wanted to check he was all right.'

'I'm not saying getting sozzled after a funeral is a good idea,' McDonald continued as if following his own train of thought. 'But the flesh is weak, and it had been a very challenging day for all of them.'

'Lots of memories and emotions stirred up,' I agreed. 'One minute you're all crying, the next you're arguing.'

'They never argued, those children. They were the best of friends. Always had been.'

'So I've been told. But why do you think he called you?' I asked the vicar.

'I told you, my phone was off,' said Miss Westmacott.

'And I am their only near neighbour,' put in McDonald.

'But there are other cottages along the lane, aren't there? Other neighbours?'

'I'm the vicar, Mr Jericho. You might not know much about what we do, but calls at odd hours from distressed parishioners aren't all that unusual. We're like doctors in that sense. An A&E service for the soul. We never shut up shop.'

'So Wesley came to church? He was one of your flock?'

'Intermittently.'

'And Katrina too?'

'The same. Anyway, by the time I'd got out of bed, dressed myself and hurried down the lane, the call had unfortunately cut off.'

'But you brought your phone to Miss Westmacott anyway?'

'Naturally.'

'But it was the middle of the night. Wesley was drunk. It was most likely just overwrought nonsense, yet you still got dressed and came running over here?'

'I don't run,' the vicar said with some dignity. 'I was up and awake by then anyway. I thought I might as well bring the phone in case Miss Westmacott wished to call him back.'

'And did you?'

'I tried,' she said. 'But it said the phone wasn't available.'

'Network coverage in this town can be patchy,' the vicar informed me.

'How long did it take you to dress and make your way over?' I asked.

He considered for a moment, all the while blinking at me myopically. 'Fifteen minutes, perhaps.'

'And afterwards, did you remain here long or return straight home?'

'It was after midnight, I went home, of course.'

'And you didn't try calling Wesley back yourself? Why not?'

'I'm not Wesley's errand boy, Mr Jericho. I'd done my duty.'

'Of course you had,' I soothed, and turned to Miss Westmacott. 'I'll do my best to find out what happened to your son. As soon as I know anything, I'll be in touch. Thanks for the tea. And the cake.'

'I should be on my way too, Stephanie,' McDonald said, rising to his feet. 'If you could just take those up to the church hall when you have a moment?' He nodded towards the pile of Christmas presents. 'Much appreciated, my dear.'

I took my stick and coat from the hall and followed the reverend to the door. Chubb lock, I noticed in passing, and I'd heard the door click to when Miss Westmacott showed me in.

'Curious case, isn't it?' I said to the vicar as we walked together along the lane. 'A devoted son disappears after his best friend's funeral and not a word from him since.'

'Children these days have little thought for their parents, I'm afraid. I'm sure Wesley will turn up soon enough.'

'But he isn't a child, Mr McDonald. He's the same age as your son.'

'They're all children,' he said with a snap. 'Been brought up too soft, my own boy included. That little gang in particular never grew up.'

'The Sanctuarists? You gave them that name, I believe?'

He smiled what I thought might have been his first genuine smile since I'd met him. 'Mischievous little devils, the lot of 'em.'

'Can I ask, Mr McDonald, what did you think of Wesley yourself?'

He took a moment to consider. 'I thought he wasted himself here. He had a brain, if only he'd bothered to use it properly. But he was always good to his mother, I'll give him that.'

'And where do you think he's gone?'

'I haven't the faintest idea.'

'Miss Westmacott believes that someone has hurt him. And she wants them punished for it.'

'She's a frightened woman,' McDonald muttered. 'Always has been.'

'Frightened of what?'

'Of life, Mr Jericho. Her husband terrorised her for years before she divorced him. He was a bullying brute of a man, physically and psychologically. And so she sees life through that prism.'

'Of being a victim, you mean? Interesting, she thought Katrina Allingham was a victim too.'

He grunted. 'Don't the Freudians call that projection?'

'So what did you think of Katrina?' I asked.

'I can't really see what any of this has to do with Wesley's vanishing,' McDonald complained.

'Humour me.'

'She lived hard with her sin,' he sighed. 'That's what I think. Much too hard.'

'The push, you mean? But she was just a child.'

'So was her little brother, Mr Jericho. Childhood sins cast long shadows and very few of us ever truly escape them. Well, this is me. Good morning to you.'

I watched him wander up the path to his front door, stopping only to raise his hand to me before disappearing inside. The sturdy Victorian vicarage, clearly built to accommodate a large parson's family and their servants, now containing only the widowed Reverend McDonald and his son, stood just a few hundred yards from Miss Westmacott's cottage. And at the end of the lane next to the vicarage, the single-storey church hall. I frowned and my gaze moved on from the McDonald home, through the pretty little roofed lychgate, along a winding stone walkway to the fen church of St Peter. Buttoning my coat up to my chin, I stalked off in search of a certain grave.

Chapter Fifteen

THE PATH BEYOND THE LYCHGATE leading up to the church felt almost blasphemous; a collage in fact, like the one hanging over Wesley's bed, this time put together from bits of broken and discarded tombstones. I picked out names, phrases, dates as my stick tapped across them: 1789; 1803; 1826. Thomas Underhay, Who Departed This Life ...; *Requiescat in Pace*; Mary Openshaw, Taken to His Glory ...; Here Lies the Body of Samuel Snell, Who for Fifty Years Pulled the Tenor Bell ...; *Non Omnis Moriar*.

'I shall not altogether die,' I translated under my breath.

Reading that last inscription, I'd had a flash of Peter Garris standing over my hospital bed before the sepsis took me, speaking words I could no longer recall. Vital words, crucial, a message snatched up and scattered to the darkness of my coma. It was no good, the memory wouldn't come, and so I glanced again at the strange path.

I supposed the graves must have tumbled and shattered decades ago and that some long-dead predecessor of Reverend McDonald, in his thrifty puritanism, had repurposed them. Cheaper for the dead to pave the way to salvation than for new slabs to be commissioned and laid. Looking out over the wonky forest of tombstones surrounding the church, I could see gaps in their number, spaces to account for the fragmentary markers beneath my boots. My mind couldn't help burrowing under the frost-starred earth and into coffins whose dusty tenants must now remain unknown.

At the end of the path, I paused to catch my breath. Bustling up on three sides of the hilltop church lay Chattox Wood, winter-stripped trees swaying lazily in the breeze. Through those branches, I thought I could make out a glint of dark blue, shifting and sparkling. The thread of the Old Demdike river that had taken Jamie Allingham's young life. The site too of his sister's suicide a decade later. Both bodies reclaimed from pagan nature, from river and tree, from water and rope and delivered back here into the embrace of the church. I wondered if Mr McDonald appreciated that idea.

It took ten minutes of limping around the hill, cursing my weakened hip, to find the graves. A simple stone plaque laid flat on the ground marked the resting place of Katrina. No headstone and yet it had been six weeks since her burial. Surely enough time for the ground to settle and for the family to erect a permanent marker. Tributes had been left, however. I bent as best I could without falling over and read the card attached to a vivid display of preserved summer flowers – velvet-black iris, purple lily, a burst of yellow carnation, 'We're so sorry, dearest Kat. Your friends forever, the Sanctuarists.'

The grave next to Katrina's belonged to her little brother. This was an elaborate monument wrought in marble, a sepia photograph of the grinning seven-year-old at its head. 'Our darling son, taken from us.' Taken by the river or by their daughter's frustrated push? I glanced back at Katrina's plaque with its sterile name and dates. Did her parents still blame the girl for the accident? Even now, when she had sacrificed herself in the very place it happened, was there no forgiveness for her? And had Jamie's inscription been deliberately chosen so that, visiting her brother, she might always be reminded of what she had done? I felt a surge of anger and sorrow. But at least Katrina's friends had loved her and continued to do so, laying their tribute.

The sudden shriek of a bird drew my attention. Abandoning its tower, a single raven stood on the lychgate and watched me with its coal-black eye. Ringing through the freezing air, its complaint sounded offended and accusatory. The graveyard was its domain, the living were not welcome here.

'He passes by the gate of the hill and into the evil field beyond,' I murmured to myself. Was this Stuart McDonald's evil field, planted with corpses? And if so, was Wesley Sayers to be found here?

I made a couple of panting circuits of the churchyard but, aside from Katrina's, could see no evidence of any recent internment. And surely, as exposed as this place was, no one would risk digging here, in full view of the town. In any case, a new and unaccounted for grave would be bound to attract the attention of the fastidious vicar and his congregation. I entertained the idea for a moment that a murderer might have taken advantage of a fresh grave. That Wes might have been secretly placed alongside Katrina, to lie with his friend throughout eternity. But the church's gravedigger would certainly have noticed if the plot had been messed around with after the funeral. Anyway, something about the idea of Wesley being buried here did not chime with my instinct concerning that phrase of Stuart's.

It had stirred some deeper connection in my memory that I still couldn't quite grasp.

Only the image of myself as a boy kept returning to me, lying on my locker bed in our trailer, reading of long-extinct civilisations and their sacred rites.

My phone buzzed. A video call from Harry. I thumbed the screen and he grinned back at me. It appeared that he was standing outside some kind of grey municipal building. I could make out the colossal figure of Ben looming in the background, his very presence reassuring.

'You're a sight for sore eyes,' I sighed.

He frowned at me. 'Are you all right? You look so tired.'

'Thanks for the compliment.'

'Take it slowly,' he said. 'I keep telling you, you're still recovering.'

'Yes, Matron.'

He rolled his eyes. 'So how are you getting on down there?'

I took him through my conversations with Miss Westmacott and the reverend, as well as my discoveries in Wesley's bedroom.

'So you think someone might have been psychologically torturing Katrina about the death of her brother?' Harry asked. 'And what, she finally cracks? She doesn't write a suicide note but instead leaves Wesley the clue of the poem. A hound pursuing her. He knows who she's referring to and he confronts that person on the night of the funeral. I wonder, was that why he called his mum? To tell her what he'd discovered? The call cuts off when he's attacked. But even if one of the Sanctuarists had been secretly torturing her, could Wes ever have proved it? And even if he could, would it amount to a criminal act? They might have driven her to suicide, but wouldn't that be hard to stand up in a court of law?'

'Courts aren't the only way to punish the guilty,' I said. 'Maybe he threatened to expose them to the community, to their friends? This person might have a lot to lose.'

The only fresh development I left out of the summary was my possible sighting of Peter Garris. It must have been him, mustn't it? I didn't know anyone else with the same distinctive loose-limbed frame. Anyway, if that old psychopath really was dogging my footsteps, it was best that I kept his focus here in Fenchurch. Better for Harry too if he remained ignorant of Garris's presence. I didn't want him and Ben storming down here in an attempt to protect my now enfeebled backside.

'Oh, by the way, I haven't been able to turn up anything on that phrase,' Harry said. '"He passes by the gate of the hill and into the evil field beyond." No specific hits for anything historical or literary.'

'Thanks for looking. So how are you guys progressing?'

'Well, we're now firmly entrenched in Garris's boyhood hometown. Just spent an hour in the local library.' He threw a thumb over his shoulder to that nondescript grey building. 'But there's nothing I could find in their records on a "Peter Garris". Odd don't you think? A phenomenally successful detective coming from the area and not a trace of him in the archive.'

'But he never served up there,' I reminded Harry. 'He relocated from Bolesworth when he joined the army at around eighteen.'

Harry nodded. 'I get that. But still, local boy made good? There aren't that many success stories in this area. Believe me, I've trawled acres of microfiche and the only local celebrity I could find was a man who grew the UK's largest marrow. Plus there's the fact that Garris was from an established family hereabouts, so he was newsworthy without even trying. His great-grandfather founded the Methodist Hall on the high street; his granddad was a wealthy industrialist who made a small fortune in tyre rubber. It's odd that there's no mention of him. They have copies of the school newspaper on file here too; not even a best attendance or sporting trophy for our boy Peter.'

'I could have saved you time there,' I told him. 'Garris's dad stumped up for him to go to a minor public school just outside the town. He told me about it once in The Three Crowns. He hated every minute of it. The nonsensical rules and traditions, the snobbery.' The Three Crowns. I shook my head at the memory. All those chats during which we would analyse, take apart and rebuild our cases. Much as I hated to admit it, I could do with one of those boozy post-shift conflabs right about now. What would Peter Garris make of Wesley Sayers's vanishing?

'I'll check it out,' Harry said. 'We're going to finish here today and then visit the street where he was brought up tomorrow. He told you it was called Cable Street, right?'

'Right. But that was all, no name or number.'

'We'll figure it out.'

At those words an irrational chill ran through me and my gaze returned to the lychgate. The raven was back, its jealous eye trained on me, its beak plucking at some gleaming wet treasure. A hunter picking over the corpse of something foolish enough to wander across its path.

Chapter Sixteen

Ending the call, I decided to investigate the church itself. The long nave section ran out from the tower, its eroded stonework starred here and there with shocks of yellow lichen that made the body of St Peter's look like the hull of a sunken ship. The narrow Norman windows had also been battered by time, so they now arced and crumbled in the semblance of decaying ribs. It was an impressive hulk, but dominating the whole was the home of the ravens. Built from compacted flint and pebble, the circular tower loomed with a kind of entitled arrogance over the landscape. High above, the battlements sported what appeared to be a conclave of angels and demonic grotesques, each stone figure sitting in alternate gaps between the merlons.

I tried the great oak door but the iron ring wouldn't budge. And so, frustrated, I headed down to the forest. I needed to check out the location of Kat's suicide and I wondered if I might encounter Muriel again. She had seen something, I felt sure. What had she said last night? *The first wasn't a murder. Nor the second yet. But the third . . . ? Them Cain Ravens do kill killers, mister. Ain't I seen it?* And then something about a hex or a curse. Was it possible? Had she been there on the afternoon Jamie Allingham died? Seen Katrina's push and Wesley's attempted rescue of the boy? The first wasn't a murder but an accident. Afterwards, Muriel had tried to process the trauma with her paper boys, fashioned in his crude likeness and hung from the trees in his memory. Had this haunter of the woods then witnessed another tragedy ten years later? Not an accident this time but suicide? If so, Kat's hanging might have seemed a cruel mockery of Muriel's paper tributes. But what of the third, the only one she claimed was a murder? Wes confronting the tormentor of his late friend after her funeral, struck down and disposed of, and all of it addled in the mind of Muriel. If I could only speak to her without Rowan being present, perhaps I might make sense of her story.

I remembered the photo of the suicide location from Harry's file. The immense oak tree overhanging the river, its knotted and whorled surface quite distinctive. Chattox Wood wasn't all that large, it shouldn't be too hard to find. I pushed my way through the undergrowth, bracken scratching at the scarred skin of my hands.

It was as I stepped into what I recognised as the clearing Muriel had brought me to last night, that I realised I was being followed. I paused for a moment, as if wanting to examine the paper boys. There was hardly a breath of wind here, only that bone-aching cold that permeated the town, yet still the recreations of Jamie Allingham fluttered and clacked and whispered about me. Scraps of print, of different handwriting, some precise, some flowery, some flowing, some jagged, marked the pieces that Muriel had gathered together and refashioned. I wondered where she sourced them. Anywhere and everywhere, I supposed. All I knew was that it wasn't Rowan's aunt who stood behind me now, motionless among the trees.

I could hear their breath, thin and ragged, almost an echo of my own. Was it one of the Sanctuarists? Unlikely that any healthy twentysomething would suffer such laboured breathing. Perhaps the asthmatic vicar or Wesley's mother? Or the landlady of The Six Ravens, her browbeaten husband, or maybe someone I had yet to encounter.

Or was it *him*? My mentor emerging once again from his hiding place. Daylight flashed between the trees and strobed my shadow across the forest floor. I turned awkwardly on my heel just as the ravens screeched from their tower and the stark white disc of the sun silhouetted the figure on the bank above me. Garris. Who else could look so raggedy and lean, propped there with one hand against the nearest trunk for balance. I squinted in the glare, the sunlight made diamond-sharp by the pure freezing atmosphere. My breath smudged the air. The man was wearing a hood, his face lost in the bowl of it, features drowned in shadow. But I knew it was him. *I knew it.* The stance was his, the body language, that spare frame. I'd recognise it anywhere.

'Peter?' I called up to him. 'What are you doing here?'

It was silent in the clearing but for the bone-rattle of those bits of paper, hanging like suicides from their branches.

'What do you want?'

The white sun blazed and granted him a halo, the aura of a resurrected God.

He didn't move, not an inch.

'You told me something back in the hospital,' I said. 'Before you disappeared.'

I gripped my stick, tensed the depleted muscles in my thighs and calves. Readied myself.

'I can't remember what you said, but I think it was important. What was it, Peter? What did I need to know?'

'Scott Jericho ...'

It was his voice. That same raspy timbre from a forty-a-day habit, stretched and dried out like a piece of cured meat. I'd know it anywhere. And yet, not quite. Had he been ill since our last encounter? Perhaps it was a trick of the light, but he looked leaner than ever, a stick figure propped there against the tree.

'Peter ...' I breathed. 'What's happened to you?'

'Scott Jericho,' he croaked again. There was a kind of wonderment in the way he spoke my name, as if he couldn't quite believe it was me. 'I've found you.'

'You were looking for me? Well, I've been looking for you, too.'

'You and the boy.'

'Harry isn't here,' I said. 'He's back with my dad at the fair. I'm looking into my own case, nothing to do with you. I've no quarrel with you, Peter, not anymore. You go your way, I'll go mine.'

Keep him fixed on me, at all costs divert his mind from Harry.

'Scott Jericho. I've waited so long to find you.'

'I saw you six weeks ago,' I reminded him. 'At the hospital. Don't you remember? You told me that you regretted blackmailing Harry. You said we didn't have anything to fear from you anymore. You said something else, something I can't—'

'So long.'

The daylight dazzled around him. He was so insubstantial in its glare, like a fragment of a comet passing by the face of the sun. A strong wind might pick him up and chase him into the sea.

'Has someone got to you, Peter?' I asked. 'Hurt you? You don't sound like yourself.'

'So long,' he repeated. 'So long.'

Suddenly he turned and, with the light blinking behind him, lurched back into the trees. There was an oddness to the way he moved, a freakish spider-like quality, as if he had a few too many limbs. Had he been injured? Did that account for his complete vanishing these past weeks? Perhaps he'd been in hospital or nursing himself back to health after suffering some kind of assault or accident. Maybe an aggressive, fast-acting illness that had impacted his voice and mobility. I smiled grimly as I set off in pursuit. What a fine pair we made, me and my old mentor.

I struggled out of the clearing and up the bank, my stick sinking into the claggy earth. With each lunging step, I could feel the complaint of my coma-weakened legs and wasted hip. The stick kept anchoring me, slowing me down, but I didn't trust myself on this uneven ground without it. Still, flares of pain ripped through me every time I tore it from the mud, sending waves of nausea rolling up from my gut. I dry heaved as I reached the trees, trying my best to ignore a sudden slap of cold wind that set my senses reeling.

There, just up ahead, the dark flash of a coat-tail rounding one of the larger oaks. I set off again, stumbling, wheeling my left arm ridiculously to maintain balance. I was like an aged grandfather chasing a wayward child through the woods. But if I could catch him somehow, hold him here, then all might be well. Once I had him incapacitated, I could call my dad, get him to recruit some of the Eastern Counties Travellers. They could be here in minutes and help me subdue the monster.

There were places I knew, shipping containers in showmen's yards, the backs of unused lorries that might provide a temporary prison. Somewhere Garris could be kept neutralised until Harry and Ben dug up whatever evidence could be found to convict him. And if they didn't? If there was no evidence? If anything we produced was compromised by our imprisoning Garris against his will? Well, we could cross that bridge when we came to it. The important thing now was to keep the world safe from this sadistic killer. To keep Harry safe, most of all.

And so I ignored my pain and put on a fresh burst of speed. I rounded the oak, its trunk thick as a ship's mast, and ran directly into something hard and metallic. I saw a flash of silver – a long, cylindrical object, like my own stick – and heard the flat, dead smack of it against my face. A couple of months ago, the impact might have disorientated me for a moment. I would have cuffed the blood from my nose, shaken my wits back into place and set off again in pursuit, my temper raging. Now the blow felled me like a toddler running into a patio door. I was not angry, just stunned. Gasping, I reeled backwards, my knees unhinging, my legs flying out from under me.

At the same time, I heard Garris's own breathless gasp. It had taken a lot out of the old murderer to strike such a blow, but the effort was worth it. My walking stick flew from my hand as I tumbled down a raised bank, head over heels, the back of my skull seeming to find every stray rock. Chips of stone and straggled roots cut into my hands as I snatched for some kind of purchase, all in vain. I saw the ludicrous image of my feet framed against the sky; I'd lost a boot and my sock was caked in mud. Then I was somersaulting inelegantly off the bank and into a body of icy water.

Thankfully, the Old Demdike wasn't deep at that point and I flailed to the surface of the river like a half-drowned dog, coughing and spluttering. A little blood pinked the water around me. I pushed a curtain of soaking hair out of my eyes and scanned the rise. No sign of Garris. Ah well, at least I'd found the river and the spot where Katrina and Jamie Allingham had died.

Chapter Seventeen

'What happened to you?' Mrs Berkeley asked as I dragged myself over the threshold of The Six Ravens, still streaming from my unscheduled dip. She didn't seem overly surprised by my appearance. I guessed The Ravens was a rough enough joint that she'd seen far worse on a Saturday night.

I shrugged and poked my head back through the door, holding out an open palm. 'Isn't that always the way? Soon as you step inside it stops.'

You might have thought she'd let me haul my sopping sorry arse upstairs for a hot shower, but no. Despite dripping all over her hallway tiles, she stepped into my path.

'I've got a message for you. I should say, we don't run an answering service here. I'm not your secretary, Mr Jericho.'

'Who left the message?'

'I'll tell you, if you let me get a word in.' She drew herself up with one of her already clichéd sniffs. 'Old Tom Makepeace has been round. Heard you were in town and said he'd be grateful if you could pop by the fair at noon tomorrow.'

'Did Mr Makepeace ask for me by name?'

'"Mr Scott Jericho",' he said. 'That's you, isn't it?'

'I don't always get the "mister", and there's sometimes a fruity adjective slipped between my Christian and surname, but yes, that's me.'

I was halfway up the stairs when she called after me again. 'No drying wet clothes on the radiators.'

'You are all heart, Mrs B.'

Fortunately, my left boot wasn't the only thing to escape a ducking. Pulling myself out of the river, I'd found my phone sitting on the bank, screen cracked but still just about usable. Before stripping off and jumping into the shower, I fired off a message to my dad. 'Did you tell Tom Makepeace I was coming to Fenchurch?' The answer pings back as I'm about to step into the tea-coloured water that farts its way through the pub's pipework. 'No.' Curt and efficient, Old Man Jericho encapsulated in a single text. Then how does Makepeace know who I am? Another puzzle to add to my growing collection.

I took a quick glance at myself in the bathroom mirror before stepping under that uninspiring dribble. Harry would have a fit if he saw me like this. I looked worse than ever. The pills I was popping to help cope with the joint and muscle pain (popping sparingly, I hasten to add; I'd had issues with such tempting delights before and didn't want to return to my zombie days of last summer) had the unfortunate side effect of knocking the edge off my appetite. This combined with Mrs Berkeley's breakfast offering meant I hadn't eaten much in the past twenty-four hours. So yes, I looked more wasted than ever, cheekbones tenting my face, the line of my jaw sawing at my skin. Where was that stevedore-armed Scott Jericho, who had once cracked skulls for Mark Noonan and beaten the roid-addicted murderer Lenny Kerrigan to a bloody pulp? The man in the mirror looked like his ghost.

Submitting to the vague attentions of the shower, I thumbed a fresh gush of blood from my nose. The cuts across my face and hands were fairly shallow, I didn't expect any to leave a scar for Harry to fuss over. Still, I was certain a bruise or two would flower come morning. 'Fucking useless,' I muttered to myself, and thumped a masochistic fist against my hip. The spasm of pain almost made me weep, and I could hear Haz's admonishing voice in my head: *You'll be a big strong boy again soon enough. Just do your exercises and eat up all your dinner. And stop whining. You've got a case to solve.*

Two cases now, I corrected my inner Haz. What was Garris doing in Fenchurch? And what had happened to him since the last time we spoke? It was almost as if he too had spent a couple of weeks wasting away in a coma. And if he really was as ill as he appeared, did he in fact pose any kind of threat at all? I smiled to myself. Enough of a threat to knock you on your arse, mate. Sure, but the obvious conclusion was staring me in the face: the Big C. He had, after all, poisoned his lungs for decades. But could even the most virulent cancer be that aggressive? Perhaps. And maybe it accounted for the slight difference in his voice and his rambling, disordered conversation. Some mind-altering side effect of his treatment? If he was ill, even terminal, what then? Did we continue to pursue our investigation or should I call Harry off the scent? Just let the old demon wither away in peace. My instinct said no, that whatever his ultimate fate, the victims of Peter Garris deserved justice.

And what if it wasn't a terminal disease? Had some crim he'd put away caught up with the former DCI and given him a beating so severe he'd ended up in that debilitated state? Or perhaps a family member of some forgotten victim had cornered the serial killer and Garris had barely escaped with his life. Were we the only ones hunting him? If there was someone else out there with revenge in mind, why not step aside and let them finish the job? What was it Francis Bacon had said: that revenge is a kind of wild justice? I might once have sympathised with that sentiment, but Harry had shown me a different way. Garris must pay for his crimes and it must be done properly, in a court of law. In the meantime, I needed to be on my guard.

Stepping out of the shower, I wrapped a towel around my waist and stared again at my reflection, hazy now in the steamed mirror. We'd promised each other no more secrets. Had sworn that those days were behind us. I should call him now and tell him of my encounter in the woods. I limped slowly out of the bathroom, determined to do just that, when a knock sounded at the door. I opened it to find Mr Berkeley with Webster panting at his side.

'Old boy was pining for you. My good lady told me you'd taken a fall in a pond or somesuch. Here.' He glanced nervously over his shoulder. 'Give me your wet things and I'll chuck em in the washer-dryer with some of my fishing clobber. No charge.'

'You're too good for this place, Mr Berkeley.'

'Call me Stan. And yes, I know.'

I collected up my clothes and handed them over. Meanwhile Webster slunk into the room and went to rest his backside against the radiator.

'Tell me,' I said. 'I'm curious, what did you think of your former barman?'

'Wesley?' He chewed his bottom lip. 'A good enough worker,

though apt to gossip a bit. That's why *she* thought the world of him. Honestly though, I couldn't really fault the kid, and he did look out for that poor lass that died. I remember ...'

'Yes?'

He shook his head. 'I'm not like her, I don't like to flap my yap.'

'Please,' I coaxed. 'It might be important.'

'Well, they were all here that night of the funeral. The missus was fussing around Wesley like a ... well, clucking hen.' I wondered if this mild-mannered publican had pulled himself up short before choosing that particular adjective to describe his wife. 'They were pretty distraught, clubbed together on a table in the corner of the bar, singing songs from their young days and reminiscing, like you do at these things. Then Wesley suddenly stands up, his face all sullen and serious. Says it's time they were off. Said they had to do right by Kat, just as they had done right by her little brother.'

'Did you understand what he meant by that?' I asked.

The landlord shook his head. 'Not a Scooby.'

'What time was this?'

He hemmed and hawed a bit. 'Near closing. Maybe twenty to eleven.'

'Wesley's call to the vicar came at around midnight,' I murmured to myself. Mr Berkeley looked at me curiously. 'It's nothing. Please, go on.'

'Indira, she starts protesting, saying it's all nonsense,' the landlord continued. 'That they should have outgrown all that stupidity by now. Wes tried to shout her down but the others sort of backed her up.'

'Sort of?'

He shrugged. 'Well, they all seemed reluctant to head off with Wesley anyway. Only ... I don't know, it felt a bit like they wanted to go, too.'

'Do you mean Indira forced them to stay at the pub?'

'Not exactly. It's difficult to explain. It's like they were torn between staying and leaving. Anyway, Wes was furious about it, saying they were betraying Kat's memory by not going and out he stormed. That was the last time I saw him.'

'And the others?'

'They all trailed out in pairs about ten or twenty minutes later. I think so anyway, it's difficult to remember after all these weeks.'

'How did they seem?' I asked.

'Upset, like you'd expect. Only, maybe a bit excitable too. As if they were heading off to play a prank or lark about, like they did in the old days.'

'And Stuart, how was he?'

'What do you mean?'

'Was he like he is now?'

The landlord considered. 'Not with the drinking, if that's what you mean. It was only after that night that he properly started in on the booze.'

'After Wesley went to the woods ... Is there anything else you can remember about that night?' I pressed.

'I don't think ... Wait a bit, yes! There was something a mite strange. When I was tidying up the bar after last orders, I found this morsel of cake dropped by the fireplace. Right in the spot where those kids were all congregated.'

'What kind of cake?'

His brow corrugated. 'Bit of fruitcake by the look of it. Maybe a slice from the wake they had that afternoon up at the church hall. I don't know though, me and the missus'd popped along there earlier to pay our respects and I don't remember seeing no fruitcake among the spread. Plenty of nice treats there were, most made by Miss Westmacott. Great baker, that one. But no, I can't call to mind any fruitcake. And anyway, why would one of them kids be carrying such a thing around in their pocket?'

'I have no idea,' I said, my mind flying back to that portion of rotting cake I'd found in the vacuum-sealed bag under Wesley's bed. Had that been from the night of Katrina's funeral? I was no expert in such things, but it had seemed of an older vintage than a mere six weeks ago.

'Thank you, Mr Berkeley, you've been very helpful.'

'I'll send you up a sandwich.' He nodded. 'You look like you need it. Some chow for the mutt too. He's been a lovely bit of company for me downstairs, he has. Dogs don't never criticise, do they?' He stepped away then turned on his heel, tapping his forehead. 'Oh, by the by, I had someone in the bar earlier asking after you.'

'Did he give a name?'

'Name? I could barely hear him speak, his voice was that weak. Just said your own name and then limped off again. No message.'

I felt a chill trip along my spine. 'What did he look like?'

The landlord paused before answering, as if unwilling to recall the image of my recent visitor. 'Like something out of a nightmare, if I'm truthful,' he said at last. 'Thin as a whip and crooked somehow. Didn't see his face as he had this hood pulled low. Fair gave me the willies, I don't mind admitting.'

'What time was this?'

'Not long after you headed out this morning.'

So before I met him in the woods. What is your game, Peter?

'If he calls again, please come, and get me,' I said. 'He's an old friend and I'd very much like a word.'

Ten minutes later, my sandwich arrived together with a bowl of offcuts from the kitchen for Webster. I picked at my tuna melt while sitting at the window, my gaze lingering on the old phone box. *Yesterday upon the stair, I met a man who wasn't there; He wasn't there again today; I wish, I wish he'd go away.* Do I wish you would go away? Or would I like nothing better than for you to tap on my door right now and crawl your way back into my life? I can't deny it, you see? The urge to consult that cold, calculating intellect. To ask your opinion on the case of Wesley Sayers – another man who isn't there.

I laid down on the bed, my hand lolling over the side. I felt Webster licking at my fingers, the way he used to when he was a pup. My mum would scold me for letting him: *You'll teach that juk bad ways.* But I could never discipline John Webster . . .

And I'm not about to start now, Mum.

She stood at my bedside, her mask of disapproval cracking into a grin that lit up her whole face. 'You always were an obstinate little dinlo.' She threaded her finger through the chain of that glinting golden cross. 'Spent hours looking for this, didn't you? Days. In the mud and in the bushes. The Great Showman Detective but you never found a trace of it.'

'I tried,' I murmured. My voice sounded thick, ponderous, weighted with sleep. 'I tried so hard, Mum.'

'There he goes, there he goes.' She smiled. 'Solving every murder except mine. Just happy to let me rot like a morsel of old cake. Everybody pays the price except for that driver who ran me down and left me for dead.'

I whimpered and she hushed me. 'Now, now, it's all right, my darling boy. You'll get round to me one day, I know you will. In the meantime, sleep and dream of Harry Moorhouse, and of what your crooked friend will do to him when he finds out what that dear, sweet boy is up to. Oh, the horrors that await your darling Haz. Horrors beyond imagining ...'

Chapter Eighteen

I SAT AT THE BREAKFAST TABLE, waiting for the call to connect. My distorted image, glimpsed in the back of a cereal spoon, confirmed what I suspected might bloom overnight – a dusk-coloured bruise the shape of a lash running from cheek to jaw. It was rolling onto that tenderised side of my face that woke me with a jolt at 3 a.m. After my dunking in the river, I had slept solidly through the afternoon and into the early hours – my exhaustion another legacy of the coma that continued to sap my strength. Groaning into consciousness, I had blinked at the time on my phone. Too late to start tracking down any other members of Wesley's old gang, I'd lain there, scrolling through the internet in a vague sort of way.

I had already visited the fair, one locus of the Sanctuarists' backstory, now I felt like getting a virtual peek behind the locked door of the church. St Peter's had a rather antiquated website with a few murky snapshots of the interior, those narrow Norman windows spilling arrows of light onto semi-circular arches and a row of hefty cylindrical pillars. Typical of these Protestant fen churches, the inside was largely unadorned with little in the way of paintings or statues, the evidence of its Catholic past scrubbed clean away.

A potted history on the website confirmed this, stating that the bones of a local holy man, St Cuthbert the Hermit, had been smashed to dust by Henry VIII's agents during the Reformation and that 'the unusual resting place of his reliquary was then obscured for all time'. I'm sure Reverend McDonald approved. He probably also gave a clerical thumbs up to the persecution of a Fenchurch witch during the Civil War, a colourful character named Mother Godsole, who was said to have blighted the area's crops with her evil eye, consumed the sins of unbaptised children, and made a local publican 'unable to perform his husbandly duties to the satisfaction of his spouse'. These and other regional tales and superstition I found on a local history forum: stories of witches sabbaths in Chattox Wood; of duckings in the Old Demdike river where, centuries later, a little boy would drown; legends of a phantom coach haunting the streets 'every Christmastide'; a local variation on the common fenland tradition of Black Shuck, a demonic hound that plagued any traveller who dared to linger on the country roads after sundown. This particular image stuck with me as I battled to get back to sleep. A great black hound of heaven pursuing Katrina Allingham, down the nights and down the days until, at last, she had escaped it at the end of a rope.

Before finally drifting off to sleep, that scrawl of Wes's on the reverse of the poem came back to me: 'Poor Katrina ran from that monster but he always found her. *Always.*' Did the use of 'he' indicate an exclusively male monster – Stuart McDonald or Ryan Marsh of the Sanctuarists? Or perhaps the vicar or even old Tom Makepeace from the fair? Or was I narrowing my gaze too much? Had Wesley simply taken his cue from the poem with his reference to Kat's tormentor as a male figure? Maybe I shouldn't be so literal. Maybe Rowan or Indira or Lorelei fitted the bill. Or Muriel, who might once have been burned as a witch alongside good Mother Godsole. Could she, in all innocence, have pushed Katrina over the edge with the persistent creation of her paper boys? Well-meaning memorials from which the poor girl could not escape.

Before coming down to a very late breakfast (taking pity on his bruised and battered guest and ignoring his wife's objections about the hour, Mr Berkeley had rustled up a delicious sausage sandwich at the unheard-of time of 11 a.m.), I had looked again at that photo of the Sanctuarists from the funeral. Which of these friends, if any, fitted the role of monstrous persecutor? In their different ways, they all looked so desolate, especially Wesley as pallbearer, his tear-streaked face flat against the coffin. What had his anger and grief at the loss of his friend driven him to? And what fate had befallen him after the friends had left the pub?

Finally, on the third attempt, my call was answered. I'd checked in with Reverend McDonald that morning – one of the curses of being a vicar, he told me, was the necessity of having one's home number listed. After a little persuasion, he'd given me a contact for Mr and Mrs Allingham. They no longer lived in Fenchurch; hadn't since leaving Kat to fend for herself two years after Jamie's death. Now, as I sat over the crumbs of my sandwich, Katrina's father picked up.

'Yes, what is it?'

'Mr Allingham?'

'Speaking.'

'This is a friend of your daughter. Katrina.'

'I know my daughter's name,' he said. 'What do you want?'

I scratched my cheek. 'Well, I'm not sure if you're aware, but a good friend of Kat's has gone missing. After your daughter's funeral, in fact. Wesley Sayers.'

'Wesley is missing?' I detected a thaw in that icy tone. 'What's happened to him?'

'That's what I'm trying to find out.'

'And you're the police?'

'No, I'm a cousin of Wes.' I took Mr Allingham through the bare facts of the case. 'So you see, his mother's very worried.'

'Yes indeed. Poor Stephanie. It's a terrible thing to lose a son.'

I frowned. 'Has Aunt Steph been in touch with you? Did she tell you something had happened to Wesley? You said, "lose a son".'

'No, she hasn't. But it must be a concern, if he's been gone all this time without a word.'

'Did your daughter ever mention that there might be something worrying Wesley?'

'My wife and I didn't . . .' He cleared his throat. 'We weren't on those kind of terms with Katrina.'

'You mean you didn't talk?'

'Not for a long time.' That brittle defensiveness back again. 'So I'm sorry, we can't help you. We thought the absolute world of Wesley for what he tried to do for our boy. You know he risked his life to save our son?' I made as agreeable a noise as I could. 'He was a hero, not just to us but the entire community.'

'Even got a reward,' I said through gritted teeth. 'Did you and your wife contribute or was that all the doing of Tom Makepeace?'

'We made our gratitude known in ways that didn't involve a crass publicity stunt,' Mr Allingham snapped. 'You know what these showpeople are, all crude opportunism.'

'Uh-huh,' I grunted. 'So you said your thanks and patted the kid on the head. And what about the daughter you abandoned?'

'I don't have to justify our attitude to Katrina to a stranger. She did a terrible thing and the sweetest, purest little soul suffered for it.'

'So you rejected her.' I said. 'At sixteen. She was only a child herself; it was an accident. Did you even go to her funeral?' All I heard was the crackle of the line. 'No. You just paid for that sorry little slab up in the churchyard, you rank fucking joskin.'

'Fucking wh—?'

I cancelled the call and just about resisted the urge to throw my phone across the room. What kind of life had those self-pitying arseholes condemned their daughter to? I mentally compared it to my own family and community. In my shame and disgrace after my imprisonment, following years of rejecting them and keeping my distance, they had taken me back without question. That is what family does, or what it should do. The contrast between my dad, Sal, Jodie, Big Sam Urnshaw and the others and Mrs and Mrs Allingham couldn't have been more stark. My heart ached for the dead girl. It also made me ashamed of my own attitude to my people. Yes, I'd had my reasons for leaving the life, good reasons too. Ever since my mother's death, I had always accused them of failing to understand me. But had I made much effort to understand them? All I knew was, if I'd made a mistake like Katrina's, almost every showman in the land would have welcomed me back.

My phone pinged. A voice note from Harry. We had spoken a little over an hour ago; he and Ben had been on their way to the street Garris had grown up on: 'Hey, darling, so here's the latest from us. Peter Garris's family moved away from Cable

Street in the late 1980s. His father had a job opportunity across town – something to do with the gas board, according to a few hazy memories. Interestingly, none of the neighbours seem to recall a member of the Garris family matching Peter's description. Might not mean much. We could only offer them a vague idea of what he might have looked like as a boy, based on the earliest photos we could find of him during his days as a police constable. Obviously, he might have changed a lot in the years between leaving school, joining the army and then enrolling in the police. Also, the area has been recently redeveloped and many of the residents from that time have moved away. One old lady on the street did recall a boy roughly Garris's age living at the family home, number 29, though she thought his name was Paul. Easy enough mistake to make, but she did seem adamant. Paul, not Peter. Ben and I are now heading to the local council to check the electoral register. Apparently records before 2000 have yet to be digitised. If Peter was still here at eighteen, we should be able to find him.'

Another ping: 'Now on to your case. I couldn't sleep last night' (ditto, I groaned. If only I'd known, we might have kept each other company with a video call), 'so I did a bit more digging. Don't ask me how, but I found a backdoor into the coroner's records. Nothing new on Kat. Definitely suicide, no sign of foul play (God, I sound like Cluedo!). No defensive wounds, some bruising at her fingertips from where she struggled with the rope after pushing herself off a lower branch. Quite usual for a hanging, apparently (Jesus, this work is grim. How do you do it?). People often have second thoughts at the last minute or else their survival instinct kicks in. The coroner noted that it is virtually impossible to hang someone in such circumstances against their will, and then of course there's the fact that only Katrina's footprints were found in the wet ground around the tree. She might have been driven to take her own life, but it wasn't murder.

'The more interesting autopsy report was her brother's. Without question, Jamie died from drowning. Large amounts of froth around the throat and mouth and in the upper and lower airways were indicative. Again, there was no evidence of foul play and Katrina's push was in fact witnessed by a local farmer. He died two years ago but his evidence at the time was clear. From his vantage point in a field nearby, he saw a kid screaming at his sister and her shoving him into the river. She then appeared to freeze while Wesley jumped in and made "a valiant attempt to rescue the kid." Unfortunately, the current was too strong for him and Wesley didn't get anywhere near Jamie before the boy was swept downstream. In fact, the farmer had to throw in a rope as Wesley himself started to get into trouble.'

I nodded. So far it checked out with Muriel's ramblings. An accident and a suicide. I guessed that, if my suspicion was correct and she had also been a witness along with the farmer, her testimony had either been ignored or the authorities might never have been aware of her presence.

'One little detail, though,' Harry went on, 'the toxicology report did find a small amount of alcohol in Jamie's bloodstream. Not enough to make him lose his balance and fall in the river, but a trace amount nonetheless.'

I sat back, my mind going over this new piece of information. Was that part of the guilt Katrina experienced? Not only the shove but the fact that they had given the boy a drink? Was that why he was so hysterical at the waxworks, his natural fear intensified by the alcohol? And was this the reason the Sanctuarists had to get him away to the woods, because their prank had gone wrong and, as it was also their workplace, they needed to put some distance between Jamie and the fair? Perhaps he'd threatened to tell his parents what they'd done and Kat, frustrated and afraid, had shoved him. The other Sanctuarists had already gone home by this point, leaving Kat alone with her best friend, who had no doubt tried his hardest to calm the situation. Had one of the friends later played on the girl's guilt, perhaps because, showing off in front of them, she'd been the one to give Jamie the drink?

All I could picture was that storeroom at the waxworks, the two glasses containing the traces of bourbon. Had her tormentor taken Katrina there to relive the moment? And had that been the final straw for the poor girl?

I glanced at my watch. It was time to keep my appointment with Tom Makepeace.

Chapter Nineteen

I took Webster with me this time. The old mutt needed the exercise, and in all honesty, I felt better with the juk at my side. He might not be the menace of former days, but then neither was I, and there was always strength in numbers.

Before leaving The Six Ravens, I asked the landlord to do me a favour, slipping one of Mark Noonan's twenties into his pocket. Could he call around all the local hotels, B&Bs and campsites and ask if my hooded friend was putting up at any of them? I was much obliged.

And so Webster and I meandered at a pensionable pace down the high street and along the prom. It was another cheerful Fenchurch day, the sky black with rainclouds, the sea thrashing the shore. I kept my eye out for Stuart, Rowan or some other familiar figure from Harry's file, but the town appeared almost deserted.

The only movement came from behind the gate of the fairground. A handful of chaps were at work on the Winter Wonderland, throwing up decorations, stringing coloured lights around the rides, half-heartedly erecting a sad-looking Santa's grotto. I frowned as I threaded my fingers through the gate.

Something must be very wrong with old Tom Makepeace. This was not the attention to detail customary of a successful showman. The siting of a grotto outside the ghost train was a joskin's error. Too scary a location for the little 'uns, while teens who might want to try their courage in the spook house would be put off by the grotto's tweeness. It was the worst of all worlds.

I watched the lacklustre efforts of the chaps, my frustration mounting with every passing minute. My dad would have given them all a rocket.

'Fair's shut, mate. Come back at the weekend.' One of the workers – if I could call him that – came strolling over, a rollie hanging from his bottom lip. I took in the pristine overalls and soft, soap-scented hands. Pocketing the old showman's wages and giving nothing back in return. It made my temper flare.

The idle joskin stared in astonishment as I reached through the bars and snatched the fag right out of his mouth. I flicked the smouldering tip back at his chest where it burst like a mini firework.

'What's your fucking game?' he squealed, then stopped.

A murderous growl was rumbling at the back of Webster's throat. I followed the man's gaze to where the juk's teeth sat bared. Good old Webster, he still had it.

'Open the gate,' I said. 'I'm here at Mr Makepeace's invitation.'

Nervous fingers reached for the padlock, twirling the combination dial. 'You won't let him go for me, will you?' the chap bleated.

The heavy gate swung back on its hinges and I stepped through, my hand scruffing behind Webster's ear. 'Get back to work and put some effort in,' I said. 'I'll be watching and if I see you slack off? Well, my hound here hasn't had his breakfast yet.'

When I asked where I could find the boss, a tremulous finger was pointed to a flight of stairs riveted to the wall beside the gate. These zigzagged their way to a suspended structure, something like a shipping container, planted on columns forty feet up and situated directly behind those huge concrete letters that spelled out MAKEPEACE. I knew Webster wouldn't make the climb. I didn't much fancy it myself. So I left the juk tied to the gate where he could monitor the chap's work.

As I climbed, I considered that surveillance must once have been the purpose of the office to which I ascended. It sat overlooking the fair like a prison guard's watchtower. A handy vantage for a master showman to keep an eye on every clockwork intricacy of his empire. But those days were long gone, and I was soon to find out why.

Reaching the iron platform directly outside the suspended room, I took a moment to catch my breath. Not long ago, I might have raced up those steps like a gazelle. Now I clutched the railing in one hand, my stick in the other. This fairground wasn't the only ruin on Fenchurch's promenade. Recovered, I tapped a door marked 'THE BOSS – Enter if you dare.'

'In if you're coming,' a thin voice called out. 'And be quick about it.'

I stepped inside and shut the door behind me. Immediately, the roar of the sea was muted. Overlaying it was now the ponderous tick of a grandfather clock and the faint but persistent *shhhhh* of an oxygen tank. The office was so dimly lit it took a while to locate the old showman. He sat facing away from me in a low-back armchair, his head nodding in time to the pendulum voice of the clock. This handsome old timepiece, carved in glowing walnut, stood against the rear wall. Christ knew how they'd got it up here. Perhaps it had been assembled in the room decades ago, an idea that seemed to fit with the frail man in the chair.

'I saw you last night,' the showman wheezed. 'Trespassing on my ground.'

He raised claw-like fingers and beckoned me forward. As I obeyed the command, I took in some other features of the room. It was a shrine to the showman's way of life, every surface covered in photos and artefacts of our heritage. Here was a black and white photograph of a Victorian knife-throwing act, the stooge tethered to her rotating board, the thrower brandishing his Yakutian knives; there a beautiful hand-painted hoarding advertising 'Swanson's Hall of Wonders – Human Curiosities to Intrigue and Astound!'; a cast-iron fortune-telling machine with a mannequin soothsayer sleeping in its booth; framed gloves from a Regency-era boxing sideshow; even a vintage Stoehrer Brothers tin-built dodgem car from the twenties. My dad would adore these treasures. I was spellbound by them myself, so that it wasn't until I was level with the breathless figure in the chair that I again became conscious of his presence.

A watery eye peered up at me. 'You've been putting it around town that you're a relation of Wesley Sayers. No such thing. You're a showman, through and through.'

Tom Makepeace was clearly dying, most probably from cancer. He was wrung out limp like a rag and practically glowing with it. Skin so papery his veins ran visible in snaking blue rivers. But he had been a big man once, powerfully built like many Travellers. You could see the memory of it in the wiry biceps that poked out from his short-sleeved shirt.

He blinked at me, gaze narrowing. 'Yes, a showman. You have the swagger. You had it last night when I watched you from my perch up here, breaking into my ground. Any excuse for that liberty?'

I shrugged and he laughed, gasping against the oxygen mask. 'Bold as brass. I recognise you from off the telly, of course. That mullerdy business over in Aumbry. Dear old Tilda Urnshaw. I wish I could've gone to her funeral, but I didn't have the strength. She was a good woman, old Tils. Knew her from when I was a little chavvy. Did she suffer . . . ? Ah.' He waved that fleshless claw. 'Don't tell me, I don't want to know. Funny thing, getting old. You think when you're a young no-knowing that the years will harden you up, because surely by the time you make old bones, you'll have seen it all and felt it all. Nothing will be able to touch you. If only that was the way of it. The truth is, you get *more* sentimental with the passing years, not less. Yesterday I was up here looking over the sea and I watched a gull swoop down and pluck a fish out of the waves. And divvy joskin that I am, I sat and wept like a baby. Over a fucking fish.'

He laughed again, then choked and spluttered. I knelt as gracefully as I could beside him and touched his withered arm. 'Are you all right? Can I get you anything?'

He shook his head. Slowly his chest began to settle.

'Been in the wars yourself?' he murmured, raising his hand to my bruised face.

'No more than usual.'

He nodded. 'Always were a little rough-arse, weren't you, Scott? Right from when you was a toddler, you had a nose for trouble.' He smiled at my surprise. 'Go'an, take a seat in that there chair.'

I half-rose, half-staggered to my feet and moved across to the armchair facing Makepeace. A chair with its back to the huge panoramic window that commanded a stunning view of the fairground and the beach beyond.

'You don't remember me, do you?' the old man croaked as I took my seat.

'Not really. But I know you were a friend of my mum's. My dad told me so.'

'How is the boy Jericho?' Again, that odd tradition among elder showman, calling each other 'the boy'. Charming, if a little bizarre to outsiders.

'Dad never changes.'

'Jerichos don't,' he agreed. 'I've known enough of them over the years and that's something I can say with certainty. Pig-headed, stuck in their ways, unimaginative, fiercely loyal leaders of men. And kind-hearted to the core, under all the front. You're like that in some ways, I reckon. But more like her in others.'

I sat forward. 'Dad said you knew my mother very well.'

'You're the image of her.' He nodded. 'The very spit. She was dear to me, in the old days.'

I always loved hearing stories about my mother, especially now so many of the old timers like Aunt Tilda were gone. 'You were good friends?'

He closed his eyes and, quite suddenly, the lines of pain seemed to dissolve from his haggard features. 'Like brother and sister we were, back when we was chavvies. Rolling around the grounds together, exploring where we shouldn't, getting chased by the aunts when we pulled our tricks on them.' I smiled at him, thinking of my own childhood with Sal Myers. The twin bane of many a poor aunt's existence; Makepeace might've been describing our own chavvy years. 'But it was books we bonded over most,' he continued. 'Her mum, your grandmother and my own granny, they were close cousins, you see? And they both insisted that we had tutors. You have to remember, Scott, such a thing was virtually unheard of back in them days, when hardly any Traveller had much in the way of schooling. Most of our mates couldn't understand it, but me and your mum loved our books. It's what gelled us, a passion for stories.'

'She gave me that love too,' I said in a quiet voice.

'But all good things,' Makepeace sighed. 'When we got into our late teens, she started courting and soon fell for your father. Her relationship with your dad was stormy from the off, though I always had a lot of time for George Jericho. They was never really suited, anyone could see that, but you know how Travellers are. Till death do you part, for better or worse, row yourselves hoarse but never divorce. Still, when I was chucked out of the life, your dad sold me a few rides, helped me get this place set up.'

'Do you mind if I ask what happened?' I hesitated. 'You see, Mr Makepeace, I'm . . . I'm like you in that way.'

'None of that Mr Makepeace. Call me Uncle Tommy, if you like. And I know how you're made, Scott. Your mum told me.'

I sat back in my chair, thunderstruck. 'Mum knew I was—?'

'Bent as a nine-bob note?' He laughed. 'Course she did, mothers always know. Surely you're enough of a detective to have fathomed that one by now. No greater sleuth in the world than a showman mother. She knew right from when you were about eight years old, as I recall. Never let on to your dad, wasn't sure of how he'd take it. There was precedent, you see?'

My mind still reeling from his revelation, I gave the old man a polite bow of the head. 'Yourself?'

He nodded. 'I was caught out. Had some chap up my trailer at one of the backend fairs. I forget which.'

'Which fair or which chap?' I smiled.

But this time Uncle Tommy didn't return my grin. 'They beat me wicked when they found us. My brothers, my uncles, my old man. Beat the chap pretty bad too. Dragged us both out of the wagon and set about the pair of us like we were the worst kind of murderers. Your mum was there that night and, when she caught wind of what was going off, she came barrelling into the middle of it, fighting men like a tiger. Jumped on my brother's back and damn near clawed the bastard's eyes out, screaming at them to leave me alone. But the women came and took her away, saying it wasn't her business. I remember lying there on the ground, shaking and bleeding. I watched them pull the chap to his feet and drag him away. I heard later they'd dumped him behind a bus station and let their juks parney all over him.'

I closed my eyes. 'Did you ever see him again?'

'Didn't seem wise,' Uncle Tommy muttered. 'They chucked me off the ground the next day, all my belongings packed up in bin bags. My dad never spoke to me after that. When he died a few years later, a messenger was sent up here to make it clear: I wasn't welcome at the funeral. If I dared show my face, I'd get a second going-over, and that might be one I wouldn't recover from so easy.'

I could hardly speak for the lump in my throat. All I wanted to do right now was reach out and gather this poor old soul up in my arms. I would've too, if I hadn't thought he might break. But then I noticed him looking at me with a touch of amusement in his eyes.

'She was right about you,' he said. 'Your lovely mum. She said you'd turn out to be a soft sod.'

'I'm not sure many people would agree with her there.'

'Oh, you give it the hard man act, I'm sure. And I don't doubt that part of it ain't an act at all. But deep down, you're as soft as a Mr Whippy on a summer afternoon.'

'But was she OK with it?' I asked, heart in my mouth. 'With what I am?'

'She fought like a fucking lunatic for me, didn't she?' he chuckled. 'Course she was OK with it.'

I took an unsteady breath. 'My old man wasn't. Not at first.'

'Do you know that for sure? Did you even give him the chance?'

I thought back to how I'd left the life, abandoning my friends and family after I went off to Oxford, then cutting virtually all contact when I lost Harry and started working for mobsters like Mark Noonan.

'Your old man has his faults,' Makepeace continued. 'But I heard he rucked with my dad and uncles after they threw me out. Told them their rides weren't welcome anymore, not on his fair. And a dicky bird informed me that he took you back too, after your troubles.'

'That's true enough.'

'It was with his help that I managed to set up here,' Makepeace said. 'Not that he ever let on to the other Travellers. Had his reputation to consider, I suppose, but still he sold me my first rides and let me pay him off gradual over a couple of years.' He sighed. 'And I suppose I ostracised myself further with this place. I'm not sure Travellers are ever looked on as quite the same once they settle down.'

He shifted a little in his chair and fixed me with his eyes. 'Your mum, Scott. It nearly killed me when I heard about the accident. I came back for the funeral, stood outside the church. No one was gonna keep me away from that send-off. You know, I gave her a little something to remember me by when I was forced out of the life. Just a cheap gold cross, as a thank you for standing by me. I found it in a jeweller's up here and I thought it looked pretty.'

I stared at him. 'I didn't know you'd given that to her. After she was killed, it was the one thing they never managed to find. I searched for it myself, spent days hunting.'

'Trinkets are just trinkets.' He shrugged those painfully thin shoulders. 'It's memories that matter.'

He glanced at the old photos covering the walls. A life that had rejected him but which, in his exile, he'd clung to, despite everything.

'All I've got are memories now.'

Chapter Twenty

'So they tell me you're up here investigating the disappearance of Wesley Sayers?'

'Who told you?' I asked.

'Oh Scott, small towns are like fairgrounds,' Uncle Tommy said. 'Talk gets around soon enough. Thought you'd do a little snooping, eh?' He pointed a finger down to the main drag where the waxworks was situated. 'I watched you poking around and knew straight away what you were. Like I said, you move the way a showman moves. But why here?'

'I wanted to get a feel for the location,' I told him. 'The scene of a crime can often tell you how it was done, maybe even why.'

'Is there a crime here, then? I thought Wesley just took off after the funeral.'

I let his words hang for a moment, and he laughed. 'No, of course I don't believe that. We're natural sleuths, us showpeople.'

I nodded. 'Born detectives.'

'So you want to know about the day the boy died? Jamie Allingham. I suppose it might all go back to then. Bad day that. For the poor boy, for Katrina, for the town as a whole. Do you know, I think in a way we've all been dying ever since. As if that one tragedy cursed this place.'

'Like a hex,' I murmured, thinking of what Muriel had said in the woods.

'What was that?' He shrugged when I shook my head. 'I've been in this town a long time, Scott. Built this place up with my own hands, brick by brick, ride by ride. Oh, I'm not deluded, I know it's done and finished. But you should've seen it back in its pomp. Punters queuing round the block to get in, something like magic in the air. This Winter Wonderland is my last hurrah, you know? When it's done, I'll close the gates and let the sea roll in and wash it all away, me included.'

I sat forward. 'Tell me what you know, Uncle Tommy.'

He closed his eyes. 'That little gang used to come here all the time. Young Wesley, Katrina Allingham, Lorelei and Indira, the Marsh twins and the vicar's boy. The lure of the fair, it never truly loses its spell. I ended up giving them jobs when they were old enough. Told 'em, you might as well earn your rides if you're hanging around here all day. That old nark of a vicar thought they were mischief makers. He came up with some kind of nickname for them.'

'The Sanctuarists.' I nodded. 'Because they were always getting into trouble and seeking sanctuary. Stuart implied that their bolthole was here. The place where they kept their secrets.'

'Implied how?'

'A look.' I remembered how he had turned awkwardly on the bench outside the pub, his gaze fixed in the direction of the fair.

'It's funny,' Makepeace said at last, 'my memory isn't what it used to be. Bloody chemo fries your brain. But I wouldn't have called this place their sanctuary. Somewhere to enjoy themselves, yes, lark about and earn some pocket money. Then again, it all feels so long ago. They were good kids, in their different ways. Indira Bakshi and Ryan Marsh were natural leaders, Lorelei and Rowan the mothers of the group, Stuart the dreamer, Maddox the schemer, always coming up with some new plan.'

'And Wesley?'

'What was Wesley's role?' he pondered. 'A good question. Sometimes the shoulder to cry on, the listener, the rock. Other times the joker. He loved making fun of that old vicar. The good Reverend Arsy.'

'Why do you call him that?'

'A childish joke I heard Wes use. His initials, you see? R.C. McDonald. Funny really, that no one noticed that before, about the reverend's name. Often things can be staring you right in the face, but it takes someone to point out the obvious. But Wes? It shames me to admit it now, but I didn't take to him at first.'

'Why not?'

He shrugged. 'I thought he earwigged too much and spoke too little. But that was probably just Traveller prejudice. You know how we can be overly cautious about that sort of thing.'

Indeed I did. How many times had I heard an old uncle on the ground chastise a chavvy for loose talk? *Dickakai, the gavvers might be 'wiggin'.* Be careful, the police might be listening in. Sometimes showpeople have to live in the grey areas of society in order to make a living. I remember once police coming onto our ground with a noise complaint, ordering us to turn off our generators. No gennies, no way to run our rides, and therefore no way to feed ourselves. And so, after they left, cables had been run to the nearest public lampposts, a source of silent if illicit power. Showpeople do their best to live within the law, but when the law prevents them from feeding their children?

Well, desperate times. And in desperate times a delicate kind of existence can be threatened by loose lips.

'But Wes proved me wrong,' Uncle Tommy continued. 'That's why I gave him the reward money after the tragedy. I've been misjudged all my life, Scott. I didn't like to think I'd been guilty of misjudging someone else, especially a child.'

'You were very generous, I hear. Enough to provide Wes with a bit of an income for a time.'

'Well,' he sighed. 'I felt partly responsible.'

'What do you mean?'

'You might not be aware; it wasn't reported in the press. Delicacy shown to poor Kat, I suppose. But the kids had been drinking that day. Afterwards, I found an empty bottle of Jack Daniel's in the storeroom of the waxworks. If only I'd kept a better eye on my fairground, I might have caught them at it and made sure they all got home, safe and sound. But it was right in the middle of the school holidays and I was run off my feet. Still, what happens on a fair is always the responsibility of the showman in charge, no excuses.

'When I heard Jamie had drowned and Wes tried to save him? Such a bloody waste. I don't think any of them ever really got over it. Of course, poor Katrina was affected most. That nasty mother and father of hers, always piling on the guilt and then abandoning her as soon as she could fend for herself. Wes too. It seemed to fix him here.'

'Because he wanted to look after his friend?'

'I suppose that was it, yes.'

'And the others?'

'They went away. Stuart to study architecture, Indira and Lorelei got city jobs, Ryan and Maddox Marsh too. But this place – it's gradually pulling them all back. And now with Wes going missing ...' He clucked his tongue against the roof of his mouth. 'Course after it all happened, I offered them their jobs back, said I wouldn't tell anyone about the bottle of Jack.'

'The autopsy found alcohol in the boy's bloodstream anyway,' I said.

'Maybe,' Uncle Tommy agreed. 'But no one heard it from me.'

I nodded. This seemed to confirm my earlier conjecture – that it must have been one of the Sanctuarists who took Kat back to the waxworks just before her death, perhaps in a sick parody of the afternoon of the accident. Only they and the coroner knew about the alcohol. Unless, of course, one of them had told an outsider. Stuart in some quiet confessional moment to his priestly father?

'Naturally they never wanted to come back,' Makepeace continued. 'Can't say I blame them. That was when it all began to sour somehow in Fenchurch. The punters dropped off, the town started to look in on itself, like a kicked dog licking a wound that won't ever heal. I feel most for those kids, though. They were good people who didn't deserve to have their whole lives ruined by one tragic moment. Kat later told me that they even did their silly ritual after the boy died, to make sure his soul got to heaven.'

I stirred. 'What kind of ritual?'

'I don't know. She never went into details.' He looked vague for once, his face slackening. 'I really ... I can't remember.'

I reached out and touched that papery hand. 'Just one more question and then I'll leave you to get some rest. Up here in your watchtower, you saw me break into the ground. Have you seen anyone else do the same? Maybe Kat and one of her old friends? Or Kat and someone else you might have recognised from Fenchurch? You didn't kick up a stink because you always had a soft spot for them. It would probably have been in the days or weeks before she took her life. They might have brought a bottle of whisky with them?'

The old man stared at me. His eyes had glazed, and I wondered if some drug to help with the pain had kicked in. 'No one's been in that storeroom. Not since the boy died. I wouldn't allow it.'

There was a blast of cold air as the office door swung open and snapped shut. 'Who are you? What are you doing here?'

A strongly built man in his mid-fifties, dressed in oil-stained overalls and with an old tartan scarf cinched around his neck, came striding across the room. He had a face scored by the seasons, chipped at by winter, cooked by the summer sun. A showman's face, yet something about the gait was off. He didn't have the swagger, as Tom Makepeace might have said. He knelt beside the dying man, gently cupping a wasted shoulder. Uncle Tommy blinked up at him and smiled.

'How's my boy?' the newcomer asked.

'Not dead yet.'

'Don't say such things.' I heard the catch in his throat. 'Please Tommy, don't.'

Uncle Tommy turned to me. 'Do you have someone, Scott?'

'I do.'

'Mike here has been with me almost since I started up this place. The first chap I hired.' He bent his head slowly and kissed the wedding ring on Mike's finger. 'Do it before it's too late, that's my advice. You can waste a lot of time in the dance.'

'I'll let you get some rest.' Taking out my notebook, I scribbled my number on a sheet and left it on the arm of the chair. 'If you need anything, or you ever want to talk.'

I got up, took my stick, gave Mike a nod and headed towards the door. Just before I stepped back onto the iron stairway, I overheard the old showman whisper to his husband.

'He looks so much like her…'

Chapter Twenty-One

Located at the edge of town, Shady Lane Glamping Retreat was the kind of upmarket getaway you see on those reality TV shows, in which ferociously competitive B&B owners tear each other to pieces for the chance to win a laminated certificate. The retreat's swanky website, complete with black and white headshots of the proud owners – Lorelei Tey and Indira Bakshi – had guided me here.

As I steered along a white-pebbled drive, it struck me that you could never accuse their online presence of false advertising. Even out of season, the glamourous photos splashed across the website were a fair representation of what awaited the paying guest. A huge rolling field, dotted with high-end pods and luxury tents, swept down to the sea. Their layout was so stylishly haphazard it had probably taken months of careful planning. Every accommodation had its own outdoor decking, hot tub and barbecue, each boasting a breathtaking view of the windswept Norfolk coast.

I pulled up at the office – a large hut designed to look like a rustic logger's cabin – and groaned my way out of the car. My dip in the river and that climb up to Tom Makepeace's eyrie had taken its toll on my hip. Glancing into the back seat,

I almost envied the gently snoring Webster. No mysteries to trouble that juk's dreams.

Before making my way to the office, I stood for a moment at a lookout point set up to one side of the car park. It was a kind of raised concrete plinth complete with a coin-operated telescope to take in the view. I dropped my quid into the slot, put my eye to the lens and adjusted the sight. At first all I saw was the grey churning mass of the sea, a far-off curtain of rain dimpling its surface. I swung the scope on its axis and, shuffling around ninety degrees, looked south towards Fenchurch.

The town, the fair, the forest, the hill, St Peter's and its belltower. A host of ravens was sweeping about that old stone monolith like a dark cyclone, shrieking and laughing at the vanity of man. Eight hundred years was nothing to such creatures. Their descendants would be here long after the sea swept in and drowned both the tower and its church. I stood up, my hand massaging a twinge in my wasted thigh. For a millennia people had tried to make a home here, yet even in its current incarnation Fenchurch remained a desolate place. Beautiful in its desolation, no doubt, but not a habitat intended for humans. With its endless wetlands and sinking sands, its stark forest and immense skies, was it any wonder superstition had taken root here?

I stepped down from the lookout. Superstition. Rituals. Stuart had talked of a sacred rite practised by the original Fenchurchians to placate the dead. Muriel had told them of it when they were children. And just now, Tom Makepeace had mentioned Kat speaking of a ritual they'd all performed for her dead brother. What kind of ritual? Was it relevant to Stuart's odd words concerning Wesley and the gate of the hill and the evil field beyond? All I could be certain of was that the vicar would abhor his son's involvement in any such heresy.

A burst of laughter drew my focus. Hurtling across the field towards the car park, the yellow hood of her raincoat thrown back and her dark hair flowing in the breeze, came a little girl of about five years. A woman laden with some kind of transparent bag trudged in her wake, calling for the child to slow down. But there wasn't much of an order in her tone and the girl raced on regardless.

I began to make my way over to them. Ducking under the rail that bordered the car park, the child glanced over her shoulder before suddenly changing course. A warning shout from the woman, but it was too late. The kid crashed right into me.

I grasped my stick with one hand and grabbed the girl with the other, in an attempt to ensure neither of us hit the deck. I just about managed it but still the impact knocked the wind out of me. Jesus Christ, these days even a three-stone stripling could land me on my backside.

A shout from the field and the metallic clank of something in that plastic bag as the woman came running. 'Grace? Gracie, are you all right?'

The chavvy looked up at me and grinned. I grinned right back. She was a cute kid, big hazel eyes, a smudge of mud on her chin, a chipmunk nose not unlike Jodie's. Meanwhile, the woman had practically vaulted the rail and, approaching at a sprint, dropped to a crouch in front of the child. She gathered her into a hug before quickly checking for any mortal injury.

'I'm fine, Mum.' Grace squirmed under examination. 'Not even hurt. Not one little bit.'

There was no query as to how I might be doing. I guessed Indira Bakshi wasn't the public relations face of Shady Lane Glamping.

'When I say stop, you stop, young lady! Now, how can I help you?' she asked, standing up and drawing her daughter away from me. The contents of the bag clanked again with the motion. Through the plastic, I could see a trowel and a pair of secateurs, bundles of dirty tent pegs and a can of weedkiller. Tall, athletically built with strong features and piercing brown eyes, Indira looked something like a sixties flowerchild in her worn dungarees, yellow wellington boots, tie-dye shirt and straw sunhat. But I could tell the outfit was all for show. A uniform to fit in with the Shady Lane aesthetic, as carefully curated as the siting of the pods in the field. Underneath the happy camper facade, Indira was all business. It made me think of how Tom Makepeace had described her and Ryan Marsh as the Sanctuarists' natural leaders.

Suddenly her gaze narrowed. 'Wait a minute. You're the detective, aren't you? A cousin of Wes? Yes, Rowan said you'd probably drop by.' She glanced down at Grace, licked her thumb and wiped the smudge of mud from of the girl's chin. Then, her eyes back on me, she instructed, 'Gracie, I want you to come with us up to the shop.' When the kid started to whine, Indira snapped at the child, her gaze never leaving mine. 'You can play quietly in the back office, watch some of your programmes on the iPad. Me and your mum need to have a chat with this gentleman.'

Grace's little hand was taken and the child steered in the direction of the office. I raised an eyebrow and followed their lead.

Instead of the main office, with its Midwest-style porch complete with rustic rocking chair, Indira guided us around the side of the building and to the second string in her empire. I'd seen the clickable link on the website: 'LORELEI'S FLORAL BOUTIQUE – part of Shady Lane Enterprises.' On the steps outside the shop were baskets of fresh eggs and potatoes, creamy milk in old-fashioned glass bottles, as well as a host of other natural produce. The shop's quaint farmhouse-style windows were hung with gingham curtains and displayed a forest of artfully arranged dried flowers. When Indira opened the door, a bell trilled overhead. Honestly, it was almost too stage-managed.

Grace wrestled free of her mother's grip and scooted behind a counter overflowing with flowers waiting to be arranged. A door opened and slammed, and Indira sighed. 'She's lost to us now. Kids and their bloody screens.' I wasn't sure if she was talking to me or herself.

'That you, love?' A voice called from somewhere behind a heap of eucalyptus and bunny tail. 'Won't be a sec.'

'Hurry it up, Lor,' Indira said. 'We've a visitor.'

While we waited, I took a turn around this picture-perfect florist shop. The powdery, pungent, comingled scent of a hundred varieties of dried flower was almost overpowering. A collage of colours too – the pale pink protea, the purple-hued iris, a yellow haze of achillea. A poster on the wall identified each species with an explanation of their meaning according to 'the secret language of flowers'. Protea symbolised strength, courage and resilience; the iris meant faith, trust and wisdom; the achillea proclaimed everlasting love.

'It was developed during the early Victorian period,' said the voice behind me. 'Almost all well-to-do homes had a guidebook for deciphering the hidden language of flowers. It was used as a way to deliver messages in a time when appearances and discretion were everything. A rose signified devotion, the edelweiss courage, the blue hyacinth constancy, the yellow jasmine grace and elegance.'

I turned to the speaker. 'Fascinating.'

'Do you like flowers, Mr Jericho?' she asked.

'My partner does. I'm a bit of a philistine, I'm afraid.'

Lorelei Tey was sweaty and a little flushed from her battle with the sprigs of eucalyptus and bunny tail. Buck teeth hiding behind adult braces made her look younger than the other Sanctuarists I'd met so far.

'And what about any darker messages?' I asked.

She exchanged a glance with Indira. 'Sorry? I don't quite under—'

'I mean, if the Victorians wanted to send a nastier communication than love and devotion. If they fancied a bit of floral trolling, what was the equivalent of hate mail back then?'

'Oh I see! Yes, well, there were lots of options.' Her cheeks pinkened as she warmed to her subject. 'For example, the orange lily meant hatred and the yellow rose was jealousy. The tansy meant a declaration of war and the rhododendron signalled that the recipient must beware.'

'I'll be on my guard if my fella sends me any of those next Valentine's,' I said.

Lorelei used a long pearl-headed pin to fasten her arrangement into a foam base, then she came around the counter, removing her gardening gloves to shake hands. 'So nice to meet you.' Unlike Indira, Lorelei was softly spoken and I had to hang on her every word. A dusting of freckles bridged her cheeks while a small scar marked her chin, shaped like the blade of a scythe. She was dressed much like her partner, in an upper middle-class idea of a bucolic gardener's outfit, deliberately distressed dungarees and a red-check bandana around her neck. I doubted that the delicately smooth hand she offered had done much actual digging.

'The famed showman sleuth,' Indira said, looping a protective arm around her wife's shoulder. 'We read all about your last case online. Lor's quite the true crime nut, aren't you, my love?' She gave me what I thought must have been an uncharacteristic wink. 'Isn't it always the quiet ones?' Lorelei cut her gaze to the floor as Indira continued, 'We don't get many celebrities in these parts, I suppose we should be honoured.'

'I bet you'll be inundated with them soon enough.' I nodded towards the window and the campsite beyond. 'Lovely place you've built here. I'm sure it'll be trending in no time.'

'Thank you,' Indira said matter-of-factly. 'It's taken a lot of blood, sweat and tears to get the thing off the ground, but we're determined to do our bit, putting Fenchurch back on the map.'

'You bought the land yourself?' I asked.

Indira shook her head. 'It was already owned by my family. The first Bengali farmers in Norfolk. You can imagine the warm reception they received back in the day. But the sad truth is, farming has been a bit of a mug's game around these parts for a while now, and my parents weren't getting any younger. So we swept in, did our thing, and hey presto. It's not been an easy first year, but we're starting to turn a profit.'

'And you think you can turn around the town's fortunes too? Return Fenchurch to its glory days?'

'Decline isn't inevitable,' Indira insisted. 'Both Lor and I worked in finance in the city before coming back here, so we know how to shake things up.'

I looked at Lorelei. It was difficult to imagine her on a cut-throat trading room floor. Like picturing a newborn lamb trying its best to go unnoticed at a farmers' auction. I wondered then whether their move back to Fenchurch had been more for Lorelei's benefit than any great passion for hospitality on Indira's part.

'Tom Makepeace seems less optimistic about the town's future,' I told them. 'He says the place has been dying for a while now.'

For the first time, Indira's attitude appeared to soften. 'Poor Mr Makepeace. It's sad to see him now. He was always so vibrant, so full of life, bursting with energy and ideas.' She rallied herself. 'But fairs are old-fashioned attractions. Begging your pardon, Mr Jericho, but their day is done.'

'No, you're right,' I agreed. 'They are old-fashioned. And that's why people like them. They call to a trace memory in all of us. In some form or another, I think they'll always survive.' Perhaps I spoke with more hope than belief; the travelling fair was certainly an endangered species. 'But talking about the fairground, have you been back there since returning to Fenchurch? Maybe to call in on your old boss? Perhaps you even visited the waxworks?'

Indira's jaw set rigid and Lorelei stiffened. 'Why would we do that?' Lorelei asked. 'There'd be no reason—'

'Funny, but Wes never mentioned he had gypsy connections,' Indira interrupted.

'He didn't,' I said.

'So you're *not* related then?'

'You misunderstand me. It's just that Romani people and showpeople are different kinds of Traveller. It's a common mistake to lump us all together. There is some crossover occasionally, members of both communities marrying, having kids, working together, but culturally we're quite distinct.'

'I'm sorry,' Indira murmured, showing what I imagined was a rare trace of humility. 'I hope I haven't offended you. Growing up with my heritage in a place like this, I know what it's like when people make assumptions about your background.'

'No harm done,' I assured her.

'It's still a bit odd though,' she said. 'Wes not mentioning you. He always showed off about things like that. When we were kids, he boasted once about a gangster uncle down in London. We all ribbed him about it, do you remember, Lor?'

Again, a non-committal shrug from the woman at her side.

'And how did he take that?' I asked. 'Being teased?'

'He was pissed off,' Indira laughed. 'Stormed away in a right little strop.'

'But Wes never stayed angry for long, not about things like that,' Lorelei put in. 'He had wonderful self-control, even when we were kids, you could never really rile him.'

'That must have been frustrating for some.' I smiled at Indira. I got the feeling she would enjoy the challenge of riling the unflappable. 'So he was a show-off, was he? You know, that doesn't sound like the man I've been hearing about all over town.'

'But didn't you know him?' Indira almost snapped. 'As his cousin?'

'Distant cousin. We only ever met at weddings, christenings, big family occasions.'

'Wes had every reason to show off,' Lorelei said, her tone a little shrill. 'The things he did, the sacrifices he made. For Kat, for his mum. He was wonderful to them both. Isn't that right, Ind?'

'She's a scatterbrain,' Indira muttered. 'The mother, I mean. She couldn't have coped without him. I could never live under the same roof with someone like that. That kind of love, it's suffocating.' She glanced at Lorelei. 'I've no idea why you put up with her. You can never find a pen in this place because of Stephanie bloody Westmacott.'

'You mean she steals things?' I asked.

Lorelei looked appalled at the suggestion. 'No, never. She's just a bit lackadaisical, that's all.'

'Careless,' Indira corrected. 'Thoughtless.'

'How can you say that, Ind? She's one of the most thoughtful people you could ever meet.' Then, in a voice so quiet I had to lean in to hear, 'Wes took after her in that way. He always cared so much.' A brief pause followed, in which Lorelei fussed with her gardening gloves. 'Miss Westmacott forgets things,' she continued. 'She's a nervous person, always with a hundred jobs on the go, and sometimes she gets overwhelmed. She'll make arrangements and they'll slip her mind. She'll get halfway through telling you something important and her thoughts will wander off in a completely different direction. She'll pop things into her pocket and forget she has them. And then the next day, she'll come in with a whole box of new pens she's bought from Smiths, just because she's mortified that she took one of ours home without asking.' Indira rolled her eyes and Lorelei gave her wife a playful poke in the cheek. 'This one thinks I'm too soft. I give Miss Westmacott the odd bit of work when I feel she's hard up, is that a crime?'

'And the silly cow makes a pig's ear of it most of the time,' Indira sighed.

'Yet she's very supportive of you both,' I said. 'And she adores your little girl.'

Indira seemed to undergo a thaw. 'That's true, she loves Gracie.'

'She's adopted,' Lorelei put in, as if answering a question I hadn't posed. 'Gracie came to us from a very dysfunctional family. There was drinking and violence and things I don't like to think about. We go to family therapy once a week so that she can come to terms with it. And to help us understand her ways. Poor little thing's had a lot of stress and upset in her young life, but we'd do anything—'

Indira clasped her hand so tight I saw Lorelei wince. 'We love her very much.'

'She's lucky to have you,' I said. 'And Wes, he was a great supporter of yours too, wasn't he? Didn't he defend you both when you were outed against your will at school?'

'That was good of him,' Indira said. 'No one else stood up for us back then. Not Kat or Rowan, not the twins, not even Stu. Only Wes. God, I was raging about that. If I'd got my hands on that little sneak who saw us kissing in the woods.'

'Who was it?' I asked. 'Did you ever find out?'

They both shook their heads.

'Anyway, aren't we wandering from the point?' Indira asked. 'You're here because his batty mother thinks something has happened to Wes, correct?'

Chapter Twenty-Two

'H<small>E'S BEEN OUT OF TOUCH</small> for some time,' I said. 'Not a word from him since the funeral. Unless you've had any contact?'

'No, neither of us,' Indira said. 'But then *I'd* probably emigrate if that was my mother. Screen my calls, change my name, launch myself into bloody orbit.'

'Ind,' Lorelei murmured.

'But was Wesley like you in that way?' I asked. 'Would he take off and leave his mum to worry?'

'I wouldn't ...' Indira shook her head. 'No, I suppose not. But I'm not sure why our opinion matters.'

'Because he's missing. And the character of a missing person is always relevant. What their friends thought of them, any secrets they might have shared, anything troubling them.'

'I'm not sure we can tell you much you probably haven't already heard from Rowan and Stuart on that score. He was distressed by Kat's death, naturally.'

'But you don't think he might have done something stupid?' I asked. Again, heads shaken in unison. 'Grief can affect people in unexpected ways. For example, your friend Stuart seems very distraught.'

'He has a lot of pressure on his shoulders,' Indira said. 'Trying to earn enough to get back to uni and restart his course. And then there's his old man exploiting the situation.'

'Exploiting it how?'

'Ind, we shouldn't say anything,' Lorelei pleaded. 'Stu wouldn't like us gossiping about his business.'

'It's not gossip. We're standing up for a friend, that's all.' Indira looked back at me. 'Stu's father has always been a sanctimonious, penny-pinching old fraud. You know he called us the Sanctuarists? Well, that wasn't some cute nickname on his part. He disapproved of everything we did as children – our jokes, our games, the way some of us dressed and talked. For Christ's sake, anyone would think we were devil spawn, the way he went on. He called us the Sanctuarists because, according to him, we never learned from our "transgressions". We'd sin and then claim sanctuary when we got into trouble, trusting to God's forgiveness. The truth is, Mr Jericho, that bloody church of his is falling to pieces, but he won't go to the diocese for the money needed to repair it properly. All because of his pride and because he wants the bishop to think he's a steady hand. That he can manage the parish finances by himself. So Fenchurch is cursed with endless charity drives and bake sales, all with dwindling returns because the town is on its arse and you can only dip into the same well so many times. Everyone is drafted in to help – Miss Westmacott baking her cakes at all hours, Mr Makepeace putting on this Winter Wonderland bullshit when the poor man can barely take a breath, and Stuart acting as full-time handyman, architect and builder, patching the ruin up as best he can. And running himself into the ground in the process. All for Reverend Arsy McDonald and his ego.'

'Yes, I'd heard the vicar's nickname from Tom Makepeace. An invention of Wesley's, wasn't it? Based on his initials?'

Indira nodded.

'Because he didn't like bullies,' Lorelei said. 'So he'd use their vulnerabilities against them.'

'Going back to Wes and Kat. Can you tell me what happened after the funeral?'

'Of course,' Indira said. 'Well, I suppose we hung around the church hall for a bit, drank tea, made small talk with the locals who'd come along. The usual sort of thing. I remember that nasty old bitch of a landlady from The Ravens was there, looking like a bird of prey herself in her cheap black frock. Hanging around Wesley, practically ovulating whenever he brushed past her. God, straight people are a horror. And you know Kat's parents contributed nothing to the wake, so we all pitched in what we could. Anyway, afterwards Wes insisted we trot off to that God-awful pub where he worked.'

'Did the Berkeleys return with you?' I asked.

'The husband served us while she stood at the bar, laughing at Wes's jokes and looking desperate to join in,' Indira said. 'I told Wes, you invite her over and I won't be responsible for my actions.'

'How long did you all stay at The Six Ravens?'

'Until closing, wasn't it, Lor?' Lorelei nodded. 'We sang some stupid songs, told some stories, drank ourselves into a state of mild incomprehensibility. And that was that.'

'Who suggested it was time you wrapped things up?'

'I don't remember. Maybe Stu. Might have been Ryan or Maddox.'

'Not Wes?' I remembered what Mr Berkeley had told me about Wesley standing up and saying it was time they were off. That they had to 'do right by Kat, just as they had done right by her little brother'. I wanted to see if Indira or Lorelei would volunteer that bit of information.

'I can't say who it was,' Indira said. 'Probably too tipsy by then.'

'And after you left, what then?'

'I came back here with Stuart,' Indira said. 'We set up in one of the vacant pods, lit the wood burner, drank some more wine, compared notes on our career choices, got sentimental and fell asleep.'

'Nothing before that?'

'I don't think ...' She frowned. 'Oh yes, we popped into Wesley's on our way back. We wanted to see if he fancied coming here with us. But his mother said he hadn't come home yet.'

'Didn't that strike you as odd?'

'Not really. I thought he might have taken a walk in the woods or something, to clear his head, you know?'

'And you, Lorelei?'

'Me and Ryan Marsh went on a trip down memory lane. It wasn't a cold night for late October, so we walked along the prom and shared a bottle of vodka, talked about the old days. At some point we decided to walk right out to our old school. We must have been mad, it's at least three miles outside town. When we finally got there, we collapsed at the gate and waited till the sun came up. I think I passed out with my head on Ry's shoulder.'

'What about the others?' I asked. 'Rowan and Maddox? Were they together?'

Lorelei nodded. 'Yes. Row was worried about her Aunt Muriel.'

Indira sighed. 'What's new? I'm sorry, Mr Jericho, you must think me a heartless bitch. I didn't mean that to sound the way it did. The truth is, I admire Row for coming back here to look after Muriel.'

'She seems a very loving niece,' I said. 'Even when you were young, I understand she tried her best to look after her aunt. Until the poor woman was taken into care, of course.' A pause, filled by the screech of seabirds and the hammer of waves on the shore. 'But I'm sorry, you were saying.'

'Oh yes.' Lorelei blinked. 'Rowan and Maddox went back to Row's and stayed up playing board games and drinking hot chocolate, apparently. Muriel had a bad night, they told us. In and out of bed, up and down the stairs, trying to leave the house and go wandering in Chattox Wood, like she does. They had their hands full with her until the carer arrived in the morning.'

'So you didn't all stay together as one group. Was that a deliberate choice?'

Indira shook her head. 'I don't think any of us could bear being alone after burying Kat, but we couldn't stand being all together either. We'd tried it at the pub, telling stories, reliving old times, but it was too much. Like an overload of grief and memories. We had to parcel it out, if that makes sense? Dilute the misery a bit. So we each paired off and dealt with our own little portion between us.'

'And Wes, what happened to him?'

'He went off alone, afterwards,' Indira said.

'After what?'

She licked her lips. 'The funeral, of course.'

'You mean after the wake and your drinks at the pub?'

'Yes, yes,' she snapped impatiently. '"Funeral" is just a sort of umbrella term for the whole bloody thing, isn't it?'

'The wake, yes,' I said. 'These traditions and rituals are important, aren't they? A way to properly say goodbye, once all the formal religious stuff is over.'

I watched them both carefully. Indira looked out as a burst of rain rattled the window, Lorelei following her gaze.

'But didn't you feel that someone ought to look after Wes that night? Him being Kat's best friend and everything. After all, he stayed here in Fenchurch for her sake, didn't he? After you all up and left and went your separate ways. Didn't that deserve a bit of companionship on the night of her funeral?'

'I told you,' Indira said. 'Stu and I went to his cottage. His mother was being her typical self, the house an absolute state. She said she was baking some kind of cake for him as a treat.'

'What time was this?'

'I can't say exactly. Maybe half an hour after we left the pub.'

I nodded. Just before Mr McDonald received the phone call from Wesley at around midnight and then brought his mobile down the lane for Miss Westmacott.

'And that was it?' I said. 'You didn't search anywhere else? Just that one fleeting visit to his house? All right, let's talk about Kat for a moment.'

'She was a sweet thing,' Indira said softly. 'But not the most confident of people. She'd always be asking our opinions then parroting them back to us. She particularly loved Maddox, copying her haircuts and clothes. Katrina was a follower, poor love.'

'She was always vulnerable,' Lorelei murmured.

'Particularly after her little brother's death?' I suggested. 'Tell me about it.'

'Jamie was pestering Kat all that summer about going to the fair,' Lorelei continued quickly, the words spilling together. 'So in the end we agreed to give him a day out for his birthday.'

'That must have been annoying, though? To take some whiny brat to your workplace on your one day off?'

Indira shrugged. 'You know teens. Never the most patient when it comes to younger kids.'

'So you had a drink to take the edge off, didn't you?'

Lorelei stared at me. 'How did you—?'

'We had some cider,' Indira said. 'So what?'

'Cider?' I frowned. 'Not something stronger? Like bourbon, Jack Daniel's maybe?'

'It might have been,' she admitted. 'I don't remember.'

'Where did you get it?'

'Kat took it from her father's booze cabinet.'

'So not cider,' I said. 'And you gave Jamie some, yes?'

'No,' Indira insisted. 'He swiped it when we weren't looking. It wasn't a lot, but it made him giddy and he ran off into the waxworks and got himself overexcited—'

Lorelei burst in, 'He spooked himself, that was all. It was no one's fault. For Christ's sake, we were children. It wasn't *her* fault, despite what was said to her by her bloody parents.'

'And she stayed in Fenchurch ever since,' I said.

'She never had a chance to get away after that.' Indira spoke bitterly.

'Because her guilt kept her here.'

'Yes.'

'And you and Kat and the other Sanctuarists, you all did the ritual for Jamie, didn't you? After his funeral?'

'How did you … ?' Indira pulled herself up. 'That was all nonsense. Just something to make poor Kat feel better.'

'What kind of ritual was it?' I asked lightly.

'I forget,' Indira said. 'Some stupid hokum or other.'

'But who told you about it?'

'Rowan, I think. Or maybe it was her Aunt Muriel. An old family superstition of theirs. They could trace their roots in the town right back. A lot of ghost stories and hocus pocus.'

'She could trace her roots back to the old Fenchurchians?' I suggested. 'Those who were here before the seaside town was built, maybe even before the church itself?'

Indira shrugged. 'Who knows.'

'But Wesley. Did any of you see him again that night, after you all paired off into your individual groups?'

'No,' Indira said flatly. 'He just vanished.'

Vanished, yes. But where had Wesley gone in that crucial hour and twenty minutes between leaving his friends at The Six Ravens and his call coming through to Mr McDonald? The answer was obvious. Wes had insisted that the Sanctuarists honour Kat's memory the way they had honoured her brother's, most likely by performing the rite taught to them by Rowan or Muriel. A ritual that might have involved a piece of fruitcake, a morsel of which had been discovered by the landlord at The Ravens after the gang left. A mirror of the piece I'd found in the box under Wesley's bed, which had probably featured in the rite performed after Jamie's funeral. Wesley must have convinced one of the pairs of friends to accompany him to some secret place, most likely the suicide spot in Chattox Wood, and there they enacted the ritual. He had then phoned his mother before the call had been mysteriously cut short. The question was, what kind of rite had been performed?

'It was a lovely floral tribute you left at her grave, by the way,' I said, focusing again on Lorelei. 'Your work?'

The florist flinched as if I'd reached out and shaken her.

'Look, we have to get on,' Indira said. 'Gracie's been running a bit of a temperature and it's time we checked on her.' She left us and, rounding the counter, called to the little girl. Grace came bouncing out from the back office, grinning for England, her mouth covered in chocolate.

'Someone's got into the cake tin, little madam,' Indira chided indulgently. 'Now let's take a look at you.' From her inside pocket, she produced a small plastic thermometer, which Grace suffered to be placed inside her ear. The kid looked healthy enough to me, but considering her background, I supposed a little overparenting on Indira's part could be excused. 'Thirty-seven point eight,' she said, reading the digital display. 'It's going down. Good.'

Meanwhile I had tottered over to the door. Before stepping outside, I turned to them and smiled.

'He passes by the gate of the hill and into the evil field beyond.'

They stared at me. The child giggled. Indira shook her head.

'What's that mean?'

I shrugged. 'Something Stuart said last night. Well, thanks for all your help. Of course, I'll let you know when I find Wesley Sayers.'

Chapter Twenty-Three

BRANCHES CREAKED AROUND ME, LIKE ice on a lake about to crack. Through the trees, I caught glimpses of the church on its hill and of a large, heavy-set figure, head down, stalking along the gravestone path towards the great iron-banded door. Stuart McDonald. He wasn't swaying as much today but there was the glint of a bottle in his hand. Was Indira right when she said it was simply the pressure of earning enough to get back to uni, and of the workload placed on him by his penny-pinching father, that accounted for Stuart's behaviour? Or was something else haunting the man?

Much of my conversation with the two women troubled me, but all of it in a vague, shifting sort of way. Had Wesley really gone off alone that night while the others separated into their neat little pairings? Or had Katrina's final communication, in the form of 'The Hound of Heaven' poem, given Wes the clue he needed to identify her persecutor? Had he then used the excuse of the ritual to isolate and confront that person? If so, then according to the group's movements presented to me by Indira and Lorelei, at least one other must have been present at that confrontation. An innocent member of the Sanctuarists, who had witnessed what transpired and was now perhaps too frightened to tell what they knew.

I ran through the groupings in my head, figuring each individual in the role of persecutor and witness. First up, Stuart and Indira. It was easier to see the forthright businesswoman as aggressor and the now fretful Stuart as hapless bystander. Next, Lorelei and Ryan Marsh. I hadn't yet met the latter, but Tom Makepeace had described Ryan, along with Indira, as the leaders of the group. Someone thrusting and forthright. Again, it was natural to picture Ryan in the part of persecutor and the timid Lorelei as witness. Finally, Rowan and Maddox. As with her twin, for the moment Maddox Marsh remained an unknown quantity, but I knew she had a successful career in fashion, an industry that tended to favour the bold and decisive. And what of Rowan? Another potentially weaker character, more easily cowed by a dominant personality. Rowan and Stuart were upset, maybe even frightened, Lorelei too perhaps, but was that simply a normal reaction to the loss of one friend and the vanishing of another?

At last Webster and I came to the river. The poor juk was panting hard and, truth be told, I was doing a pretty good impression of him. This wasn't the same spot where I'd encountered Peter Garris yesterday. That area, together with the clearing containing Muriel's paper boys, lay a few hundred yards upstream. This place had taken a bit of finding again, but finally I'd limped into a setting that matched the photograph Harry sent over. The scene of Jamie Allingham's drowning a decade ago and of his sister's recent suicide.

There was an eerie tranquillity to it, the great oak overhanging the water, its yawning limbs reflected in the rush. Ice diamonded the flow nearest the bank, crystals detaching and floating downstream. In summer it must be a beautiful spot, and I could easily picture the Sanctuarists in happier times, swinging from that immense bough, squealing as they splashed into the river. Never imagining that one day a member of their company would swing out on a rope but never fall.

Was it only knowledge that lent a place its character? I wondered. Stumbling upon this scene without the history of its tragedies rattling around in my mind, would it enchant rather than unsettle. Or were the Romans right with their belief in the genius loci – that places held within them a spirit that made things happen there, for good or ill. Were Jamie and Kat destined to die in such a place, and had it perhaps taken other victims over the years? Even Wesley Sayers? The Romans ... *He passes by the gate of the hill and into the evil field beyond.* Why did I continue to associate that phrase of Stuart's with some vague memory of the ancients?

I shook my head. As Garris had once advised me, don't pick at a hunch. It will come when it's ready.

At the foot of the tree, cradled among the roots, sat a small but beautiful floral arrangement. Dried flowers, almost certainly from Lorelei's shop, as new as those at the graveside by the look of them. I took a photo and consulted a couple of websites. Blue hydrangea and purple hyacinth dominated the display. According to the language of flowers, the hydrangea symbolised regret and remorse while the hyacinth asked for forgiveness. I doubted the selection had been accidental and a note attached seemed to confirm this: 'We'll never forget. Sleep well now, darling Kat.'

It was signed in one hand on behalf of Stuart, Rowan, Ryan, Maddox and Lorelei. No Indira present. What did this tribute suggest? That the Sanctuarists had learned of Katrina's persecution, perhaps after Wesley had confronted her tormentor and paid the price of his outrage? And had that tormentor been Indira, whose name was missing from the card? If so, then Stuart fitted the bill as the second Sanctuarist who witnessed what happened to Wes that night. It would certainly explain his erratic behaviour ever since. But if so, were the others truly comfortable with allowing Indira to go unpunished? Was Lorelei? There had been a sense that the dominant Indira had somehow kept her wife in check during our conversation.

My gaze tracked along the bank. A little way off there was a mark in the ground, a depression about the size of my fist, the earth here a deeper brown than the area immediately surrounding it. I knelt, my hip predictably shrieking at me, and placed my palm flat against the spot.

Then suddenly Webster was barking and I struggled back to my feet.

'Hush, that juk,' I barked back at him, and he obeyed readily enough.

Rowan had paused on the path between the trees, a hand to her mouth. She was dressed in the same thick winter coat as yesterday, her face more drawn than ever. She dropped her hand and tried out a smile that didn't quite take.

'You startled me.'

'Sorry,' I said. 'But he's a gentle giant really. A bit like your friend Stuart, all bark and no bite.'

She appeared to come forward reluctantly, her gaze sweeping towards the river.

'Lovely flowers,' I said, nodding towards the tribute.

'Yes. Lorelei arranged them and I brought them down here.'

'Did you write the card? I think you left someone out.'

She walked slowly over to the tree, as if some invisible force was dragging her there. 'Oh gosh, I did. Poor Ind, I feel awful. How could I have missed her off?'

'Easily done. How's your aunt doing today?' I asked.

'She's at the church hall. Respite care. They're making Christmas cards and baking, I think.'

'With Miss Westmacott?'

'No. Wes's mum doesn't bake anymore. She was making something special for Wes the night of the funeral and I think . . .' She sighed. 'I don't know, it's almost like she's made some sort of pact. She won't bake again until he comes home, does that make sense?'

'Of course,' I said. 'It's how we bargain with God, isn't it? Or with fate. We make a ritual out of ordinary things on the basis that, if we keep our promise, perform the rites, make the correct sacrifices, we'll get what we want.'

'I suppose it's how we stay sane sometimes,' she agreed. 'Counting magpies and avoiding cracks in the pavement. An attempt to make the world feel a bit less chaotic and frightening.'

'I've been talking to your friends Indira and Lorelei,' I said. 'I spoke with Stuart's father too. They both happened to mention an actual ritual. Something your aunt taught you when you were children.'

She laughed a high, piping sort of laugh. 'Oh, Muriel told us all kinds of nonsense. We never took a lot of notice of her.'

'Didn't you? But I heard Wes was quite invested in one particular ritual. You performed it in memory or in tribute to Jamie? On the night of Kat's funeral, when you were all together at the pub, before you paired off, didn't he want to—'

'I saw a man, up there on the ridge,' Rowan blurted out. 'A funny-looking man. He reminded me of that old nursery rhyme. You know the one? *There was a crooked man and he walked a crooked mile*. He was very thin and wearing a sort of hood, I couldn't see his face. He stood there for a little while looking back at me and then, when I called up to see if he was all right, he turned and limped away. I think he had a stick of some kind, or maybe a pair of sticks, I don't know.'

'Did he say anything?'

She shook her head. There was a timorous smile on her lips, like a child who thought they'd got away with a prank but who wasn't yet entirely certain of their safety. 'He didn't say a word. He gave me the creeps, though.'

'Yes, he can have that effect on people,' I said.

'Is he a friend of yours?'

'He used to be. Listen, if you see him again, don't try to approach him or talk to him. He isn't a very nice man.'

I looked back the way I'd come, through the path in the trees. What do you want, Peter? And what has happened to you since that night in the hospital. I saw him again in my mind's eye, looming over my sickbed, peering down at me, some devastating revelation on his lips ... Again, best not to prod the memory. It will come in time. Or it won't.

'I thought I saw Stuart earlier,' I said.

Rowan nodded. 'He's probably in his studio at the church. He works there most days in between his repair jobs.'

'Great,' I said. 'I'd love to see his work.'

I whistled for Webster and we set off back along the path, Rowan following a step or two behind.

Chapter Twenty-Four

Webster wouldn't move an inch. The juk sat at the church door, whining and whimpering, big sad eyes staring into the darkened vestibule. I called his name, patted my thigh, but it was no good, and so I limped back and lifted his jaw so that our eyes met. This was the beast of Jericho Fairs, a guard dog that had faced down rats the size of puppies and made rioting skinheads piss their boxers with sheer terror, yet here he sat, quivering like a man on the scaffold.

'What is it, boy? Something in there you don't like?'

The juk's whole attention remained fixed on the space beyond the doorway. His nostrils flared and he whimpered again.

'It's all right,' I told him. 'You stay here and keep watch. I won't be long, I promise.'

Webster seemed happy enough with this suggestion and allowed me to tie his leash to the iron door handle. Then, with Rowan at my elbow, we stepped inside the great fen church.

The report of my stick echoed down the vast shadowy nave. Beyond the vestibule screen, I got the impression of immense cylindrical pillars running along the aisles and bearing the weight of arches that swept up into the gloom of a traceried ceiling. Illuminated by the weak winter sun, panels of soot-smeared stained glass cast a murky light across vacant pews. The church smelled of guttering candles and moth-eaten hassocks, of faded incense and damp Bibles.

'This way,' Rowan said. She guided me to a small door inlaid into the wall of the narthex. At first, I thought she was going to take me up to the tower. I could hear the ravens calling, their chorus the only sound in the silent womb of the church. Steps worn shiny by eight hundred years of passing feet wound their way towards the turret. But instead, Rowan took me down into the crypt. I had to grasp a frayed rope attached to the wall as we descended, the ball of my hip grinding with every downward step.

'Are you all right?' she asked, glancing over her shoulder. 'You look very pale.'

'I'm fine,' I said, cursing myself for having forgotten to take my pain pill.

'Good. It's not far now.'

The subterranean space we entered was deeper than I would have thought likely. The fine-grained sand and saltmarsh clay that makes up fenland earth is notoriously unstable, always shrinking and shifting, undermining foundations and knocking buildings askew. Knowing this, I wouldn't have thought the original architects of St Peter would have delved so deeply for their crypt. And yet their ingenuity was proved by its survival. Not a single crack in those stone ribs holding up the low vaulted ceiling.

There might once have been tombs here but if so, they must have been cleared out long ago. Flat unmarked slabs paved the crypt while a vine of electric cable hanging from hoops in the wall provided power to a couple of builders' work lights and a humming chest freezer set up in the far corner. Canvases were stacked here and there, one painting in progress perched on an easel directly in front of a buzzing lamp. The air was chillier even than the forest and our breath billowed. Yet the giant hunched over the open freezer unit seemed immune to the cold. He was dressed only in a paint-smattered vest and jeans, his fisherman's jumper and winter coat discarded on a stool beside the easel.

'Stuart, I've brought Mr Jericho to see your paintings,' Rowan called out. 'We met down by the river and he ... Stu, what are you doing?'

Rowan stopped dead. I believe we both saw it at the same moment. We were only a step or two inside the long, low crypt, a space that must have run at least half the length of the nave above. Stuart was standing at the far end, his features underlit by the freezer's internal lamp. Yet even from this distance we could make out the weapon clasped in his fist and the gore staining his hand. Watery streaks of it slipping in threads down his bare arm and dripping from his elbow.

At first, I wondered if it might be paint. The red looked very much like the rusty hue that clothed one of the figures in his painting. Figures I couldn't quite make out from this distance. But no, the smell was unmistakable. It was the only smell, I now realised, to penetrate the lifeless odour of damp earth and mouldering brickwork. The distinctive metallic insistence of blood. Stuart looked from the ice-pick in his hand to his childhood friend and smiled.

'You've caught me,' he said. 'I was just preparing dinner.'

He leaned back over the freezer, swearing and hacking away at something inside. Then he brought up a fresh fistful of frozen meat and threw it into a bowl that had been lying at his feet.

The metal tray chinged and almost overbalanced. It was already stuffed with slowly defrosting chunks.

Laying down the pick, Stuart came forward, wiping his hands on a grubby towel.

'I'd shake,' he said, 'but I'm not sure you'd appreciate it.'

I smiled and stepped around him. The echo of my stick bouncing from wall to wall, I had to crouch a little as I crossed the crypt, making my awkward way to the far wall. The freezer lid still yawned wide, the unit chattering away and throwing out dragonish snorts of condensation. My gaze tracked reluctantly from the bowl of hacked-up meat on the floor to the contents of the unit.

I let out a relieved sigh. It was about a quarter filled with the preserved corpses of mice, rats, baby chicks and other assorted wildlife. In death, they had all been unified into one frozen mass of closed eyes and frigid limbs.

'The ravens' mealtime?' I asked, glancing over my shoulder.

Stuart shrugged. 'What else?'

'Nothing else,' I murmured to myself.

There was no evidence that anything more substantial than a moderately large rodent had ever lain there. The bodies in situ were compacted together, scratches from the ice-pick on the topmost surface showing where Stuart had chipped away every time the ravens required a feed. The stock of birds and mammals, which must naturally have once occupied much more space, had clearly been here for months. Even now, with the unit only partly full, there would be no room to store a human body.

Wesley Sayers had never been coffined here.

'The sodding thing keeps over-freezing, if that's a word,' Stuart complained to Rowan. 'I'll break a wrist one day, hacking away at the bloody thing. I keep telling Dad but he's too tight to splash the cash on a new unit for those "heathen birds". He resents feeding them as it is.'

I turned from the freezer to take in the rest of the crypt. No sign that any of the heavy floor slabs had been moved, not in the past few centuries anyway, and the walls were made up of the church's original foundations. Solid stone, utterly impregnable.

And yet I was now more convinced than ever that the church had been the children's original sanctuary. I believed that Stuart had tried to confuse me with that pointed look towards the fairground, but this place made more sense. If his father's spare key had once been stolen, maybe even copied, then the young Sanctuarists would've enjoyed unfettered access to a lair all their own. The same wouldn't have been true of the fairground with its security and CCTV. Maybe this very crypt provided their bolthole, a den to share and hold their secrets. The question was, did it now hold a clue to a secret that seemed to have shattered the mind of Stuart McDonald? And if not, why had he been so keen to misdirect me?

I watched Stuart pick up his coat from the stool beside the easel, pull out the bottle I'd seen him carrying earlier from its inside pocket, and spin the cap. On a table nearby stood a small heap of pill packets; many I recognised from my own hazy days of misuse – uppers, downers, benzos and zopiclone sleeping tablets, most of which I guessed Stuart had bought himself illegally over the net.

'One good thing about this fucking place, it keeps the vodka cold.' He held the bottle out to me. 'Wet your whistle?'

I shook my head. The pain in my hip cried out for a numbing

throatful, but if I started, I wasn't sure I'd be able to stop. It had taken Harry coming back into my life to wean me off my old appetites, and I was determined not to let him down. Stuart shrugged and, throwing back his head, sucked on the bottle like it was mother's milk.

'Stu, please . . .' When she reached for him, Stuart elbowed Rowan's arm aside. It wasn't a deliberate gesture, and I was sure she hadn't been hurt, still he pulled the bottle from his lips with a gasp. It sounded almost anguished.

'Row, I'm sorry. I didn't . . . I'm so sorry.'

'It's all right,' Rowan soothed. 'I know you didn't mean it. You just have to be careful, that's all. Understand?'

He nodded like a chastened child.

'What a striking piece of work,' I said, moving over to the painting perched on the easel.

It wasn't an idle compliment. The scene depicted the monstrous minotaur of Greek myth, lying dead at the mouth of its labyrinth. The human half of the creature's prone body stretched back into the shadowed entrance of the maze while the bestial bullhead lolled out into a shaft of Aegean daylight. One black eye, fixed and lustrous like a raven's, glinted in the sun. In the foreground of the picture strode the victorious Theseus, bloodied sword in hand. Gore dripped from the weapon as it had recently dripped from Stuart's elbow, staining the hero's sandalled feet. Circling the image were seven shining stars.

'What do these represent?' I asked.

Stuart's shadow loomed against the canvas. 'They symbolise the seven maids and the seven youths that were sacrificed each year to the minotaur,' he said, his hot vodka breath against the side of my face. 'And for the gate to the seventh circle of hell – the zone of violence – that, in Dante's *Inferno*, was guarded by the monster. You know another name for the minotaur was Asterion, meaning "star"?'

'I didn't,' I said. 'Fascinating.'

My eyes played over that entrance to the maze and the felled monster. Was this slain guardian of a hellish gateway in some way related to Stuart's words regarding Wesley? *He passes by the gate of the hill and into the evil field beyond.* But then that phrase had struck something in my memory related to Roman rites and religion. Although the Romans later co-opted many Greek beliefs into their own mythos, the minotaur felt separate from the association that continued to niggle at me. But there was another association here too. The poem entrusted by Kat to Wesley's keeping.

I fled Him, down the labyrinthine ways of my own mind. What did this painting actually represent? The slain but misunderstood monster that some might picture Katrina Allingham to have been, accidental destroyer of her innocent brother? Who then was the heroic Theseus that had killed her? Did Stuart sympathise with the tormentor that had driven his old friend to her death? Or was it the other way about? The persecutor was the justly felled monster that, in life, had fed on the soul of the guilt-ridden girl. Had Stuart painted a fate he wished to see enacted? A fantasy in which Wesley as Theseus had been successful in his confrontation of the persecuting Sanctuarist and in which justice had been served? If reality had played out differently, and an outraged Wes had been killed for his trouble, then this alternate version, in which good triumphs and monsters die, might be a comfort to Stuart, the troubled witness to his friend's murder.

A witness who dared not tell what he knew. Or was I reading too much into a talented, but clearly disturbed, artist's work?

'My father taught me all the classical legends from antiquity,' Stuart said. 'It was the one blasphemy he'd allow, the one trespass against his faith. The old gods and monsters are fine as literature, as entertainment. Just so long as you don't take them too seriously.'

I nodded, unconvinced. A puritanical fanatic like Reverend McDonald couldn't allow himself a single lapse. If he did, then more must come in its wake. And, in my experience, those that followed would be ever more intense and transgressive.

I remembered a case Garris and I had investigated back in the day. A dusty little by-the-book accountant who'd spent his entire working life obeying the rules of his profession, never so much as stealing a paperclip from the supply cupboard. Then one day he had pointed out an unguarded back door in a client's financial security system. The client dismissed the accountant's concerns, saying any money stolen via that route would be so much chickenfeed, and therefore hardly worth the investment in any extra safeguards. And so, almost as an academic exercise, the accountant had siphoned off a thousand pounds, covering his tracks so expertly no one would ever suspect. The first transgression of his sacred law. But the ease of the thing, coupled with the original contempt shown for his expertise, proved a heady mix. In the end, that fussy little stickler for the rules had embezzled millions and, when his fraud was eventually uncovered, had panicked, kidnapping and then murdering the client who had once laughed at him.

I recalled Garris's words as we wrapped up the investigation: if he'd stolen that paperclip, maybe even dipped his beak in the petty cash occasionally, none of this would have happened. Denial isn't good for the soul. So be wary of the petty fanatic, Scott, they almost always end up destroying themselves, as well as anyone unlucky enough to be close to them.

Chapter Twenty-Five

'Your dad must appreciate your talent,' I said to Stuart. 'This really is incredible work.'

He grunted out a laugh. 'You've met the old bastard, right?'

'Stu, don't ...' Rowan began.

'You'd wait around till doomsday before you got a word of praise out of him. All his holiness wants is a minimum wage lacky to keep his precious church from collapsing around his ears. It's amazing, you know, how he can talk us all into supporting this edifice he's built up. Poor Miss Westmacott running his charity drives, old Tom Makepeace dragged out of his sickbed to open the fair in the dead of winter, me here, papering over the cracks. All to keep the great illusion from falling apart. And what does he do while we slave away for him? Ponce around the town like his sacred shit don't stink.'

'Stuart, that's enough,' Rowan said, her tone sharper than I'd heard it before.

'Well, I for one think you're very talented. Little details here I hadn't noticed before.' I looked more closely at the picture. 'Like that final shred of flesh hanging from the minotaur's mouth. Although it looks more like a beak than a mouth.

Maybe you took inspiration from the ravens? And the seventh star here. Is it meant to be slightly smudged out?'

'The side of my hand rubbed up against it while the paint was still wet,' Stuart mumbled. 'Blame the voddie, I guess.'

'Do you mind?' I asked, moving away to examine the other canvases stacked against the wall.

'Knock yourself out,' Stuart said, and planted his lips back around the bottle.

I hunted for a short time among the paintings. All landscapes and architectural studies of historical buildings and churches.

'I'm open to offers if you want to buy one,' Stuart laughed. 'A tenner or two should do it.'

'You're trying something new with the minotaur?' I said, straightening up. 'I can't see anything like it here. Perhaps it's allegorical in some way? Representing something you've seen or felt recently?'

Stuart took a final swig and placed the vodka bottle unsteadily on the floor. 'It's a story my dad told me when I was a kid. A story of monsters. Don't get all Freudian about it. Anyway, enough chat. If you don't want an original Stuart McDonald for the price of a drink, why don't you help me feed those rowdy bastards upstairs?'

I felt like asking him again about Wesley 'passing by the gate of the hill and into the evil field beyond', but Stuart's attitude warned me against it. There would be time later perhaps.

As all three of us climbed the stairway to the tower, me having to drag myself up by the rope handrail, I said to Stuart, 'So this work you do for your dad. Aside from being the Ravenmaster, what does it actually involve?'

He swung around mid-stride, the metal bowl in his hand

spilling some of its gruesome content onto Rowan's shoes. He gave her an offhand apology while his bleary gaze bored into me. 'Nothing too grand. I wouldn't be qualified to interfere with the work of the old master builders.' He said this with a touch of reverence, his free hand almost caressing the stonework of the tower. 'But I did a summer skivvying on a building site before I started my architecture course, so I know the basics.'

'And it saves your dad and the diocese a few bob?'

'I mainly work here,' he said. 'A bit of superficial repair to the mouldings on the tower windows. Just here really, nowhere else much.' He made a show of indicating the spot where he'd built up a crumbling arch. It was neat enough work but hardly worth the trouble he took displaying it. He seemed to sense my unspoken comment.

'Come on,' he muttered. 'The vultures are hungry.'

By the time we reached the top of the tower, my fists were gripped tight against the pain of my hip. When Stuart opened the tiny door that led onto the rooftop, the sunlight dazzled through the haze of my unspilled tears.

'All right, all right,' he bellowed at the birds squalling overhead. 'I'm here, ain't I?'

'Are you all right, Mr Jericho?' Rowan asked. 'You really do look very ...'

I took a deep breath and nodded. 'I'll be fine, thanks. So, I heard there was a legend about these ravens? That if they ever left the tower, disaster would follow. And something else your aunt told me as well, Rowan. The Cain Ravens – they kill killers.'

I pictured the old woman on the night I'd met her, speaking those cryptic words.

'Dad hates it,' Stuart muttered. He was throwing the chunks of still-thawing meat haphazardly across the rooftop, pieces landing on the battlements and the shoulders of the angels and grotesques that squatted there. His lack of attention might have had something to do with the fact his eyes were fixed on Rowan, even when addressing me. 'Like I was telling you, Mr Jericho, Dad despises all heresy and superstition, other than his precious gods of antiquity. He loathes the fact he can't get rid of the ravens. That the locals won't hear of it and that the bishop sides with the townspeople. I honestly think they drive him mad, you know? Their shrieks and their shadows constantly falling over him. Their voices like laughter.'

'And amid tears and under running laughter, I fled Him,' I murmured to myself.

If either Stuart or Rowan heard my words, they didn't react. Stuart simply continued to dish out the meat to the birds who floated above us, diving in at intervals to fight over a morsel of vole or a scrap of mouse. I went to stand at the battlements, my hand resting against one of the demonic grotesques. Alternating gaps between the merlons sported a figure, weather-beaten, nibbled by time, their finer features worn to smooth obscurity.

'Your father certainly seems set in his ways,' I said.

'He's an arsehole.' Stuart grinned. It looked awful, like a rictus. 'That's what Wes used to call him, you know? Reverend Arsy, right to his face sometimes. Had other nicknames for him too, when he found out the truth. But yeah, he's always been a right sanctimonious old sod. When that rumour got out about me smoking weed at school, boy did I cop it then! Remember, Row?'

Rowan didn't answer. Only flinched as one of the ravens swooped close to her face.

'Whispers can be dangerous,' Stuart said.

'Yes, they can.' I glanced at Rowan who flinched again. Was the person Wesley confronted – the one who persecuted Kat to her death – the same malignant whisperer who'd once watched Indira and Lorelei kissing in the woods and then revealed their secret? The same sneak who told Stuart's dad about the weed and who informed social services about Rowan's aunt? Had Katrina's hound been with these friends ever since childhood, sowing doubt and division, until finally their whispers had gone too far and Kat had died?

'Wes had something similar,' Rowan said, her eyes also fixed on Stuart. 'Don't you remember? Someone told the headmaster that he hadn't given in all the sponsorship money for that charity swim for spina bifida. It was bullshit, of course. Wes not only raised the most out of anyone, he was the only one of us to complete the swim in under an hour. And you know something else, even if he had taken a tenner from the thousand-odd quid he raised, I for one wouldn't have begrudged him. His dad had died when he was a little kid, his mum worked all hours to keep a roof over their heads, they were poor as church mice. He might not have been a saint, but he was as near to one as any of us knew.'

Stuart nodded. 'Amen to that anyway.'

'But why do you think someone would have targeted your group like that?' I asked. 'Spreading gossip about you all?'

Rowan shrugged. 'Who knows? Except kids are sociopathic little demons at the best of times. I should know, we have them mucking about in the library often enough. Maybe someone at school was jealous of not being included in our gang?'

'Or perhaps it wasn't one of your contemporaries at all.'

'What do you mean?' Stuart asked sharply.

'Nothing, just thinking out loud.' But a figure had sprung into my mind – a fussy little vicar who saw sin everywhere and wished more than anything for it to be punished.

'I think these beauties have had enough,' Stuart said. 'Shall we go down?'

He locked the tower door behind us and I took a breath, anticipating the agony of the descent. To take my mind off it, I said, 'So how was Wesley the last time you saw him?'

I noticed Rowan's shoulders stiffen and Stuart, leading the way, bowed his head a little.

'Mad with grief,' he said, his voice hollow in the stairway. 'Raving about how unjust it all was. Saying how Kat ought to be with him now, not rotting away in the ground.'

'And that was just before you left the pub? Didn't he also say something about doing "right by Kat, just as you'd done right by her little brother"? What did he mean by that?'

'I don't remember him saying anything like that.'

'No? The landlord remembers it.'

'Him?' Stuart laughed, turning back to me. 'That poor bastard's drunk off his tits half the time, or else freezing his bollocks off fishing on some riverbank. Not that I blame him, having a wife like that, but you can't rely on anything Stan Berkeley says.'

'Do either of you remember someone carrying a piece of fruitcake in their pocket that night?' I expected laughter at the absurdity of the question, but all they did was shake their heads. 'So Wes was mad with grief and yet none of you stayed with him. You just all paired off into your own little groups. Who did you go off with again, Rowan?'

'Maddox Marsh. She came back with me to help look after Muriel.'

'And you, Stuart?'

'I went to the glamping site with Indira,' he said. 'We popped into Wes's cottage on the way, saw his mum, but she told us he hadn't come home yet.'

'I see.' But I wasn't certain that I did. These pairings felt wrong somehow. Could I really imagine the sensitive, artistic Stuart McDonald whiling away the wee small hours with the all-business Indira Bakshi? Wouldn't he feel more succour from Lorelei or Rowan?

We reached the bottom of the stairs and re-entered the echoing nave. I started to hobble away between the pews, making for the altar, when Stuart called after me, 'Hey, where are you going? I need to be locking up soon.'

'Won't be a minute,' I called over my shoulder. 'I love nosing around old churches.'

It wasn't a lie either. Harry has described me as something of a high church atheist. A non-believer who appreciates the grandeur and beauty of religious art, music and architecture. As my words died in the belly of the nave, I glanced up into that vaulted ceiling, ribbed and fluted with stone. My voice rebounded in the soaring vastness and I thought of how Harry would love to conduct his choir in a place like this.

My shadow loomed and stretched across the unadorned pillars, each so wide that two grown men with outstretched arms would have difficulty encircling them. Pews of cherrywood gleamed darkly while, beneath my feet, markers untouched in centuries paved the way to the heart of the church. To the left of the altar stood a Christmas tree pushed up against the final pillar before the nave opened out into the crossing. I wondered if this concession to the season had had to be wrung out of Reverend McDonald. Did he see even plastic baubles and a paper angel as idolatry? Perhaps that was why the artificial tree had been shoved behind a pillar and not placed centre stage at the altar.

On the wall opposite the final pillar hung a huge painting that must surely once have been an altarpiece. A depiction of The Raising of Lazarus, a haloed Christ standing with arms outstretched as he commanded his dead friend to live again. At his feet, the shrouded corpse had begun to stir. These details were all I could make out because the picture was so dirty, decades of grime obscuring all but the central figures. Another example of the miserly vicar neglecting his church's treasures.

My eye didn't stay on the painting, however. Framed below it and facing the last pillar was a print of 'The Hound of Heaven'. I moved over to examine it, my reflection cast dimly in the glass.

I fled Him, down the nights and down the days . . .

Footsteps echoed behind me. Stuart and Rowan. I turned and saw their hands reaching, as if wishing to grasp one another for comfort and support.

'Was this a favourite poem of Kat's?'

Rowan swallowed. 'I don't think so. Why do you ask?'

'I found a copy among Wes's things, in among some keepsakes belonging to Katrina. Why would she have left him this poem, do you think?'

They didn't answer and so I stalked back down the nave towards them.

'Was someone persecuting your friend? Stuart? Rowan? Is that why she died?'

'No.'

'No.'

'Then why? She left no note.'

'We don't know,' Rowan said, wiping away a tear. 'Honestly, we don't. I wish we—'

'What?'

'I wish we did. That's all.'

'I really need to lock up now,' Stuart said quietly.

Outside, I untied Webster from the brass ring and the old mutt whined, his wet-eyed gaze still fixed on something beyond the door. I crouched beside him. 'What do you see, old juk? Oh, I know.' I scratched behind a tattered ear. 'You'd tell me if you could.'

I was starting down that path of broken gravestones again when Stuart called to me. He was holding the big brass key of the church in his hand. 'Mr Jericho?'

'Yes, how can I help?'

He licked his lips and glanced at Rowan, who was heading down the hill towards the woods. 'He passes by the gate of the hill and into the evil field beyond. You see, don't you? It's what they used to do, the ancients. My dad told me the story, and we ...' He shook his head. 'I can't.'

I took out my notebook, scribbled my number and handed it to him. 'You can call me anytime, if you need to talk'.

Stuart gripped the piece of paper. 'He hides in the dark place. He's waiting behind the paper figure in the tree. Do you see? Do you—'

'Stuart?' Rowan, calling up to him. 'Are you coming?'

He placed the key in the lock and stared back at me, unmoving. I watched him until Rowan called again, and then I turned and headed back towards The Six Ravens.

Chapter Twenty-Six

HIP ACHING LIKE HELL, I trudged down the lane, Stuart's words resounding in my head. *He hides in the dark place. He's waiting behind the paper figure in the tree.* Did that mean Chattox Wood was the 'evil field', perhaps beyond the church gate? The paper figure being Muriel's paper boys? Was Wesley buried there, maybe near the spot where Kat had killed herself? But the ground thereabouts didn't look as if it had been disturbed, and surely whoever might have killed Wesley would have been taking a colossal risk, burying him in such a public space. I shook my head. None of it felt right.

As I passed the vicarage, I noticed the twitch of a curtain in a downstairs window. Reverend McDonald, looking up at his church, something like concern in his eyes. Was his gaze on the ravens? That black cloud that hung almost incessantly over the tower, the birds that his son claimed tormented the clergyman. Or was it the sight of Stuart himself? I looked back now as the two friends joined hands, Rowan almost proprietorially claiming the vicar's son and guiding him as though he were a little child.

Back at the pub, I found the landlord waiting for me. He appeared delighted to see Webster, feeding the old juk a handful of bacon from the kitchen while glancing warily over his shoulder.

'I saw her emptying ashtrays on the forecourt,' I told him. 'You're safe for now.'

He gave me a pathetically grateful smile. 'I've checked with all the local hotels and B&Bs,' he said. 'No sign of your friend, I'm afraid. The only other place I can think of is Lorelei and Indira's glamping pods, though it seems unlikely. Your fella looked a bit shabby for a place like that. If it was the old days, I'd have suggested trying Indira's dad's campsite. That's how Mr and Mrs Bakshi used to earn a few extra quid when the farming was going through a lean patch, but their site's been closed for years now. Oh, by the way.' He leaned in as if sharing a delicate secret. 'This poor old chap had a bit of an accident in the downstairs lounge this morning. The missus didn't notice, thank God, but I thought I'd let you know.'

Five minutes later, the juk and I were settled in our room. I gave the phone box in the street a cursory glance before collapsing onto the bed; there was no sign of Garris. Meanwhile, Webster dropped to his haunches and I noticed how his back legs quivered, a spasm that ran the length of his spine. He looked up at me with those huge sad eyes and I reached down to cup his jaw.

'Don't abandon me now, boy,' I murmured. 'I need you.'

My phone chirruped. A call from Harry. As ever, my heart jolted in my chest.

'Are you OK?' I asked before he even had chance to say hello. 'What's happened?'

'Nothing,' he said. 'Well, not nothing, quite a lot, in fact. But I'm OK and Ben's OK and there's no need for you to worry.'

I let out a breath. He asked about my day and I rattled through everything I'd discovered since the last time we spoke. He started to pose a few questions, but I cut him short. I was keen to hear his news. I could hear the excitement in his voice – something else too, a kind of jittery anxiety, a little like dread.

'I didn't want to phone until we'd confirmed it,' he said. 'You see, there was no Peter Garris on the electoral register at number 29 Cable Street.'

'He might not have been old enough,' I said. 'He could've left home as soon he hit eighteen and before he was required to register.'

'Possibly.' But I could hear his doubt. 'Did Garris ever tell you he had a brother called Paul?'

'A brother?' I almost laughed. The idea of Garris existing in any kind of family unit seemed ridiculous. It was almost as if he'd sprung fully formed into the world, parented by nothing but a sly kind of darkness.

'No,' I said. 'He never mentioned any blood relatives at all.'

'That's interesting,' Harry said. 'You see, Paul was the Garris child that the neighbour remembered living at the house during the 1960s and '70s. She said that Paul left home in his early twenties and went on to become a postman in the local area. He died last year, complications from heart failure. According to the electoral register, Paul Edward Garris and his mother and father were the only residents to have ever lived at that address during the period we're interested in.'

'So what are you saying?'

'I thought we'd check on the deaths of Paul's father and mother,' Harry continued. 'Quick dash through the obituaries at the library gave us their funeral arrangements. One passed away in the late nineties, the other in the mid-noughties, both buried in the municipal cemetery. We took a drive over there hoping to locate their graves and, Scott, we found something.' He took a long breath. 'I'm sending you a picture of the parents' tombstone. They're all buried in the same spot.'

'All?'

'Scott, you need to prepare yourself.'

A pause. I could hear fingers tapping at a screen and Harry's frustrated sigh. 'Sorry, my coverage isn't great here. It's taking a while to ... Ah, that's it, you should have it now.'

My phone finally pinged. A photograph of a simple granite tombstone, lightly splattered with bird shit, the gold lettering on the inscriptions a little worn but easily readable. The full names and dates for the mother and father and, at the bottom of the stone: 'Peter Michael Garris. Resting Now with the Angels. Died at 3 weeks old.'

I felt the room tilt around me and my heart lodge in my throat. I tried hard to focus on Harry's voice.

'I looked it up after we found the grave,' he said. 'There *was* a fourth resident of the house, Paul's younger brother. But he died in infancy. Cot death. You see, Scott, *Peter Garris doesn't exist.*'

My mouth felt like a dustbowl. 'But that must mean—'

Harry cut in, 'The man you know as "Peter Garris" is someone else entirely. He took the dead child's name to make himself a new identity.'

I nodded slowly. It had happened before. Undercover cops and secret service operatives adopting the names of dead children in order to build themselves a false cover so they might infiltrate organisations that the state deemed dangerous or transgressive. Sometimes these might have been legitimate targets – terrorist cells and violent far right parties – but there was a record of infamy too with these people targeting peaceful action groups.

'But I don't understand,' Harry said. 'Wouldn't the police have checked his background when he joined up? Surely he wouldn't have got away with faking who he was in such a security-sensitive profession?'

I shook my head. 'Garris – God, it feels sick even to use that name – he joined the force in the 1980s, after his stint in the army. Back then, other than birth and death records, there was no real data trail for anyone to follow. Even the army wouldn't have delved very deeply into his past. All he needed was a name and a forged birth certificate. He might even have had a copy of the real thing; I think you could simply apply for one back then and it would be sent to you through the post. He'd present the certificate after a successful interview and the application would be rubber-stamped. No one even thought about identity theft in those days, and of course there was no online trail to follow.'

'But why would he bother to disguise who he really was?' Harry asked.

'Possibly because he'd killed already,' I said. 'Or he was on the brink of it. Maybe in his teenage years, maybe just after he joined the army. And perhaps someone suspected his tendencies, a relative or even the police. He's always been a careful, cautious man. And so to start again, he simply vanished, abandoned his old life and his true name and crafted this new personality for himself.'

'Then who is he?'

'That's a difficult question,' I said. 'I wonder if he knows himself anymore.'

'Well, it makes trying to track his background more difficult,' Harry said. 'If we don't have his real birth name.'

'For those years before he joined the army, yes,' I agreed. 'But from the point he adopted this dead child's name, he officially became Peter Garris. That's the thread you need to follow, the one he constructed himself. It's an artificial thread for the most part, but he lived it and so there might be vulnerabilities there. Places where he made mistakes, slipped up. And maybe the backstory he invented is one of those places. Back then, when he took that child's name, he was young and inexperienced. He would have looked for solutions that were close at hand. His world was smaller in those days, his horizons more limited. He might not have actually lived in Bolesworth where this kid died, but my guess is that he wouldn't have been too far away. The knowledge of this tragedy would've been familiar to him as a child. A boy who died around the time he himself was born – remember, the dates of his birth and the real Peter Garris would need to line up fairly closely.'

'OK, so what do we do next?' Harry asked. 'Stay here in town and ask around for people familiar with the Garris family? The older brother Paul is dead, but maybe he had relatives?'

'No. You could waste days, maybe even weeks on that track,' I said. 'It might be a worthwhile line of investigation at some later point, but the avenue with more potential is Garris's life *after* he took the child's name. Try to trace him from his army days and his early police career onwards. Maybe start in Colchester, that's where he underwent training as a new recruit, or so he told me.'

'OK. Let's talk tomorrow, yeah? I love you.'

'I love you too. And, Harry—'

'I know. Be careful.'

'And if you want to, stop,' I told him. 'There's no shame in it. I'd rather you were safe and sound back at the fair than out there digging up the past, even with Ben at your side.'

After I hung up, I went to the window that looked out onto the old telephone box. It was empty, the street likewise. My reflection stared back at me from the glass, a gaunt face stamped with a new kind of fear.

'I met a man who wasn't there,' I murmured to myself. 'Were you ever truly there, you old bastard? Who exactly are you? And what are you doing here in Fenchurch?'

Chapter Twenty-Seven

I FELL BACK ONTO THE BED. Hunger gnawed at me, but I was too tired to limp my way downstairs in search of a sandwich. Instead, I reached over to the bedside table and popped the cap on my pain pills. Two white tablets sat in my palm, full of the pale promise of oblivion. A tempting treat to swallow down dry and ease the persistent throb of my hip, but I needed my wits about me. I tossed the pills back onto the table and let my heavy-lidded gaze wander around the room.

An icy mist pressed at the window, leaving dripping trails on the pane. Pulsing inside that grey vapour, a host of multi-coloured lights. Makepeace must be testing the illuminations at his fair before the big opening. One last defiant blaze from the old showman.

I dozed.

I drifted.

I dreamed ...

Harry stood in the nave of the church, his back turned to me, staring up at the painting of Lazarus raised from the dead. He lifted his arms like the saviour in the picture, commanding the shrouded figure to throw off the shackles of the grave and come forth from his tomb. The image appeared as frozen as the painting itself and so, when Harry suddenly turned to face me, his mouth gaping, I sensed my dream-self recoil. Eyes fixed and staring, Harry's lips didn't move yet still the song projected in one long ululation from the back of his throat: *Und hier der Stein, Der solche zugedeckt. Wo aber wird mein Heiland sein? Er ist vom Tode auferweckt!* By some dream magic, the lyrics translated as they hit my ear: *And here is the stone which covered it; But where will my saviour be? He has risen from the dead!*

As if responding to this incantation, the painting of Lazarus loomed ever larger behind Harry. Layer by layer, brushstroke by brushstroke, it then began to peel away from the canvas, and I saw that another scene had been hidden beneath the surface image. Now a great Roman gate dominated the frame, a sombre procession passing in front of its arched entry point. Six figures in a kind of mourning dress and a woman in the whitest robe, her hands bound with cord. She screamed to the heavens for mercy and her face, masked lightly behind a veil, in an instant transformed into the agonised features of Wesley Sayers.

The party passed on, their cries of admonishment for the doomed figure ringing out and finding their echo in the nave of the church. Before vanishing from view through the gateway, Wesley turned and looked over his shoulder, his wild gaze trained on me as he intoned: *I fled Him, down the nights and down the days; I fled Him, down the arches of the years; I fled Him, down the labyrinthine ways of my own mind . . .*

The painting changed again, colour and shade running together, coalescing and transforming into Stuart McDonald's striking depiction of the mythological minotaur. Slain by Theseus and entombed within the labyrinth, the great beast lay still, only its blinking raven eye still clinging to a semblance of life. As I watched, paper bodies floated down from a pallid winter sky. The cut-out forms drifted across the corpse of the monster, burying him as if under a fall of snow. And then I heard Stuart's words again, spoken outside the church: *He hides in the dark place. He's waiting behind the paper figure in the tree. Do you see?*

I woke with a cry and Webster nuzzled my palm, anxious to comfort. I sat up, cuffed the sleep from my eyes, and searched around in the bedclothes for my phone. A single bar of battery, enough to make an online search and confirm a memory that had, until now, eluded me. I'd read about it in some book of Roman history, stolen from a library in my childhood.

While I searched, I went over in my mind a myth of even more ancient origin that chimed with the theme I now pursued. After Theseus killed the minotaur, he had presumably left the creature's body inside the labyrinth. Entombed within that fortress maze, hidden for all time. A monstrous secret kept from the view of mortal man.

I looked down at the result of my online search.

It concerned a certain religious rite of Ancient Rome, a subject Reverend McDonald knew well. Yes, here it was: if they ever betrayed their vow of celibacy, the vestal virgins who guarded Rome's sacred fire would be punished by living entombment. Buried alive at a site by the Porta Collina, a now lost gateway to one of the seven hills of the immortal city. The exact location of the unfortunate virgins' horrific fate was a place known in those antique days as the Campus Sceleratus, or 'the evil field'.

An innocent soul, walled up and forgotten.

'He passes by the gate of the hill and into the evil field beyond.'

I wrenched back the bedsheets and stood shakily, telling Webster to stay put. He grunted only mild defiance while I continued pulling on my coat and boots. Finally, I snatched up my stick, clattered down the stairs and stepped out into the night.

A bone-aching gale roared off the sea, shredding the mist and making skipping ropes of the Christmas lights that hung across the high street. Beyond the empty promenade, sprays of foam leapt against the seawall and slicked the road. I pulled up my collar and turned towards St Peter's.

The church waited on its hill, the tower like a beckoning finger.

Come, Scott Jericho, discover the secret I have kept.

The secret of a Sanctuarist perhaps.

As I stumbled along the lane, through the lychgate and up the gravestone path, I heard again the vicar's words concerning his son: *He wants to be an architect. He's saved us an absolute fortune on some repairs at the church this winter. It's been so bitterly cold, the frost has caused a spot of structural damage.* But those windows inside the tower to which Stuart had drawn my attention earlier in the day were surely not structural repairs so much as cosmetic. Why had he been so keen to focus my attention on that spot? Another memory stirred as I reached the church door: how on the night we'd met, Stuart had pointedly looked away from this place when discussing the friends' childhood sanctuary. An attempt to make me believe that it was the fair and not the church that had been special to them.

But I was now convinced that the holder of their secrets – the sanctuary from which they had taken their name – was this church. Just as I was convinced that Stuart, tormented and conflicted, knew what lay hidden here.

I gripped the brass ring of the door and pictured Webster cowering at this threshold, refusing to enter. Even his senses, dulled by age, had picked up on the horror within. I thought of Stuart standing at the door with the key in his hand, unmoving as he returned my gaze. Had he ever turned it, locked it, secured its secret?

I twisted the handle and the door swung open. There was a war going on inside that boy. Loyalty to someone, or fear, pulling him in different directions, plaguing his conscience until he sought the oblivion of the bottle. What had Mr Berkeley said? That Stuart only started drinking heavily after the funeral? The vicar's son wanted to distract me, to point me down misleading paths, and yet at the same time was desperate to tell what he knew. To unburden himself.

I entered the pitch-black throat of the church. My bootsteps echoed hollowly down the nave while the gale probed every crack and fissure of the building, whistling among the rafters and chuckling like a demon in the belltower. The great pillars passed in silent procession, the windows held the night. On the wall beside the altar, the reborn Lazarus looked down on me, his painted eyes full of a mad kind of wonder. As I remembered, the Gospels made no mention of him after his unrequested resurrection. Had he even wanted to return? I wondered. And what sights might he have recalled from his time among the dead? What truths, what miracles, what terrors?

I turned to the last pillar on the left and pulled away the Christmas tree from where it had been so awkwardly, and deliberately, positioned. A handful of baubles fell to the floor, one cracking on the flagstones, others bouncing merrily into shadow. The paper angel crowning it was jostled to a jaunty angle. Why had the tree been placed here, tucked away behind this pillar and not, as is more traditional, nearer the altar or in the vestibule? The answer was quickly revealed.

There was new plasterwork here. A large patch of it covering a third of the pillar's width and rising up to the level of my head. I laid my hand flat against it and thought of what I'd read online: the bones of St Cuthbert the Hermit, sacred to this fen church, had been smashed to dust by King Henry's agents during the Reformation and 'the unusual resting place of his reliquary obscured for all time'.

A resting place rediscovered during the recent renovation works carried out by Stuart McDonald. A fissure in this pillar perhaps, requiring deeper investigation, which in turn had revealed a treasure long buried. What would his father have made of such a discovery? Even smashed and forgotten, such popish idolatry as the hermit's remains would not only have offended the good reverend, it might have meant expensive official renovations being required. Works that would have exploded the church's carefully managed finances, and all for what? So that superstitious locals, who didn't even attend weekly services, could come and gawp at a few old bones? And so, had the vicar ordered for this secret place to be hidden away again? And in doing so, had he unwittingly offered a killer an opportunity?

I moved to the next pillar along and, reaching back, cracked my walking stick hard against the stone. The insistent reverberation shuddered along my arm. The pillar was solid throughout. I returned to the last column and repeated the action. A less insistent shudder this time, and the echo of hollowness within.

I threw my stick onto one of the nearby pews and limped back down the aisle to the tower stairway. Again, an unlocked door, ready and waiting for me. I gasped my way down the winding stairs to the crypt, using my phone torch to illuminate the shadowy extent of the chamber. I knew I shouldn't be doing this. I ought to call the police, no question. But I told myself that it was only a hunch, and anyway, that old fever was burning under my skin again. The desire for the mystery to take on a new and darker aspect. I couldn't stop myself, not now.

In the cellar, the freezer unit containing the raven's sustenance hummed away like a hungry god. I gave Stuart's painting of the minotaur a fleeting glance, that beady black eye appearing to wink at me in the dimness: *On, Scott Jericho, race now into your own labyrinthine way.* I snatched up the ice-pick from beside the freezer and turned back to the stairway.

Chapter Twenty-Eight

BACK IN THE NAVE, I drew the pick over my shoulder. One last moment of hesitation, one heartbeat in which to reconsider that phone call to the gavvers.

And then I made my swing.

It didn't take long for the plasterwork to start coming away. I pounded and hacked, an avalanche of dusty white fragments falling across the flagstones at my feet. And all the while the thought persisted: *Stuart knew. He must have.* But did that mean he was responsible? Or had a stronger personality cajoled, convinced, bullied or blackmailed him into this?

More particles of plaster gave way, then jagged chunks, puzzle pieces that would never be put back together, each revealing the ancient brickwork beneath. Irregular-sized slabs, red clay blackened at the edges, the scorch mark of a kiln that must have fired its last brick half a millennia ago. Small blocks densely packed, medieval in all likelihood, and certainly not strong enough to support St Peter's vast vaulted ceiling. They were never intended to. This pillar originally had quite a different purpose.

Under the plasterwork, fresh modern mortar held the original bricks together. They had been removed and then replaced, all quite recently.

I dropped the ice-pick, its clang fading among the untenanted pews, and placed my palm against the brickwork. The cold they held was almost unbearable to the touch. I moved my face nearer the column and took a tentative sniff. Not a hint of anything suspicious. As perfect a storage space as the freezer unit in the crypt. Close up, just level with my chin, I noticed a couple of marks on the bricks. Upward strokes, fresh chips in the skin of clay, each one shallow, a few no more than scratches. They matched some of my own marks made by the ice-pick. Stuart's work, must be. And yet something about this idea struck me as wrong.

I shook my head. I could go over any inconsistencies later, for now I needed to reveal the secret this pillar had been concealing.

I abandoned hacking and began to prise away with the business end of the pick, slotting it between the bricks, using the tool like a lever. The new mortar gave way without too much effort, and all at once, three or four bricks sputtered out from the column and dropped to the flags. In the space they'd occupied, an envelope of untextured darkness opened up. Pausing a moment, I heard what I thought might be a sigh or exhalation, a final breath. The gale no doubt, finding fresh fissures through which to sing. I pulled away another brick, then another, pushing at some that wouldn't budge so that they dropped into the black void beyond. I dragged the last couple out with my bare hands, my heart hammering.

Then, in the half-light that struggled through the stained glass behind me, I saw the horror that had been entombed here and the breath caught in my throat. I swallowed, licked my lips, thumbed my phone torch. I was desperate to make out the figure and at the same time repelled, both by the reality I was facing and my own morbid compulsion.

Here, tucked away within a narrow cavity inside the pillar, stood a man. Or what had once been a man. His head was bowed like a penitent monk, the brow resting on the inside surface of the hollow column. He wore a black funeral suit strung with cobwebs and smattered here and there with mud. It was a cramped space and his hands were laid flat against the inner wall of brick. Stepping sideways, I noticed that the fingers weren't bloodied and the nails remained smooth and intact. No sign of any desperate attempt to free himself from this prison. He must have been dead when placed here, not immured alive like the vestal virgins of antiquity. That was a mercy at least.

Using the ice-pick, I gingerly lifted his chin. And almost dropped the tool. His lips were withered and drawn back over a set of shining teeth, the partially decomposed mouth pulled into a rictus. The nose had been nibbled, by bacteria or insects or both. There was a queasy shininess to the cheeks, as if the bones beneath might be ready to cleave their way through that finely marbled flesh. The most awful sight though was the missing eye.

The left orb stared back at me, gaping and utterly vacant. Just a tag of torn lid still adhering, like the beady eye of the minotaur in Stuart's painting. When the head dropped again, I noticed a small wound at the back of the skull, the hair around it matted with a dark crust of blood. I couldn't see any other injuries and, if there were none, then it looked as if Wesley met his end by this blunt force trauma and by that stabbing wound to the eye. Possibly struck first to disable him, followed by the killing blow penetrating the ocular socket and maybe the brain.

Which indicated what? Two killers? One attack from behind and a second frontal assault? It would almost certainly take two people to manoeuvre a man of Wesley's size into this cramped space and then to wall him up. I stepped back, wiping the horror of the thing from my mind. I needed to focus on details.

After six weeks, I was surprised at so little decomposition, but the recent long spell of cold weather had done a wonderful job, not only of preserving Wesley Sayers but keeping the smell to a minimum. I stepped forward again and craned my head further into the gap, making sure my skin didn't brush against that fungus-furred cheek. At Wesley's feet sat a small collection of white debris, not unlike the remnants of plaster on the flagstones. I focused my light, and it took a moment to realise what I was looking at: the last earthly remains of St Cuthbert, smashed by the hammers of the king's agents. This pillar was the location of his reliquary, which must originally have been partially open for parishioners and pilgrims to pass by and pay homage. A shrine now desecrated for a second time.

Two further details caught my attention before I turned my light away from the corpse. A ghostly autumn leaf snagged in his hair and, adhering to the collar of Wesley's funeral suit, a crumb woven inside the heart of a sagging spider web. It looked like a morsel of fruitcake. The same kind sealed inside the plastic bag back in Wes's bedroom. The same kind picked up by the landlord of The Six Ravens after the Sanctuarists had drunk there on the night of Kat's funeral. Did this suggest that, despite everyone's denial, one of their party had indeed met with Wesley later that evening? Perhaps on the pretext of performing the ritual in honour of Kat, as he'd suggested. Her persecutor, who had then been confronted by Wes and who had ensured his silence by killing him and placing him here. If so, the question remained: had there been a second Sanctuarist present at that fateful encounter, and was that person Stuart McDonald?

I turned away from the false pillar and looked to the wall opposite, the place beside the altar on which hung both the painting of Lazarus and the framed poem, 'The Hound of Heaven'. A poem that had so clearly obsessed Katrina Allingham during her short life. Was this burial site for her best friend chosen merely for its utility or did the killer want her champion to lie entombed here, his head bowed forever within sight of those lines? Was this the persecutor's final mocking insult of both Katrina and Wesley Sayers?

'I fled Him, down the nights and down the days,' I murmured.

Then I switched off the torch and made two calls.

The first was to Mark Noonan. The ageing mobster picked up on the third ring.

'I've found him,' I said.

'And?'

I gave Noonan the details, sparing him nothing. He'd seen worse in his career, or at least just as bad. Still, it took a little persuasion to stop him descending on the town mob-handed in his search of vengeance. As he admitted, he barely knew the kid. But still, family is family and bloody recompense was what Nana Noonan would have expected. I told Mark to stay put, that I hadn't finished my investigation and that I would decide how best to handle the murderer when found. He might have argued with me once, demanded I deliver up the killer to his own special attentions. Instead, all I heard was a muttered 'Keep me informed', then the line went dead. The mobster was losing his grip. I wondered if he would survive long into the new year.

My second call was to a more recent friend. It was past midnight, yet I was not surprised at the alert, youthful voice that answered.

'Scott Jericho. What trouble are you in this time?'

I allowed myself a small smile. 'Hello, Inspector Tallis.'

Chapter Twenty-Nine

CHIEF INSPECTOR THOMAS TALLIS STOOD at the battlements, his hand planted on the folded wing of a stone angel, his gaze playing over the slow-waking town and the buzz of forensic activity in the churchyard below. A white tent had been erected inside the doorway. Men and women in Tyvek suits passed in and out, clipboards and sample cases held in nitrile-gloved hands. The gale of last night had blown itself out and a fiery winter sun, blazing but heatless, dazzled against those sterile forensic uniforms. Meanwhile, above our heads the ravens called to both the living and the dead.

Tallis was dressed in a creaseless suit and immaculate woollen overcoat, a yellow check scarf tied around his smooth neck. Short, tousle-headed, all teeth and pink-cheeked, he looked much too young to have reached his rank, and yet I knew that guileless outer shell disguised formidable ambition and shrewdness. We'd met during my last case in the fenland city of Aumbry. An investigation that might have ended in a whole mess of legal trouble for me if Tallis hadn't smoothed over an awkward detail or two. He now stepped back from the statue and dusted off his hands.

'Are you still trying to grow that thing?' I asked, gesturing to the bumfluff adorning his upper lip.

'It does the job,' he said.

It did indeed. Along with that slightly infantile Rupert Bear scarf, the moustache was another feature of Tallis's disguise. A blind to lull both rivals and prey into the belief that he was as callow and inexperienced as he looked.

'How are you, Scott?' he asked. There was no pity in his tone, only concern. 'You won't remember, of course, but I came to see you during your coma. It looked a bit dicey there for a while. I'm glad you pulled through.'

'More or less,' I said, holding up my walking stick.

'I'm sure that's only temporary,' he said. 'And I'm sorry by the way, that your involvement in the Aumbry case leaked to the press. No anonymity now for the Great Showman Detective.'

'It hasn't been all bad.' I shrugged. 'I even got a couple of flirtatious fan letters. But I think that was in response to some old photos online and in the papers. I'm not sure I'd get the same response if they saw me now.'

He didn't stroke my ego, simply said, 'You'll heal. Anyway.' He gestured at the activity below. 'You summoned and I dutifully arrived with the cavalry and all their toys. Although I think, if you could get away with it, you'd keep us out of an investigation altogether. So tell me, how exactly did that young man end up inside a church pillar?'

I took Tallis through the case step by step. The disappearance of Wesley Sayers following Katrina's funeral on Friday 30th October; how her dearest friends had all gathered at The Six Ravens after the wake; how, according to the landlord, Wesley had proposed they should leave at around 10.40 p.m., so that they could 'do right by Kat as they had done right by her brother'; how the others appeared to have rejected the idea and so Wesley had left the pub alone.

'What do you mean, "do right by her as they did right by her brother?",' Tallis asked.

'I'll come to that,' I promised. 'There's something odd you need to see in his bedroom that I think might be connected to what Wesley got up to after leaving the pub. But going back to that night – Wes leaves alone while the six old school friends all paired up for the evening. Paired up platonically, before you ask. Stuart McDonald spent the night with Indira Bakshi, Rowan Chesterton with Maddox Marsh and Lorelei Tey with Maddox's twin, Ryan Marsh.' I gave him a brief character sketch of each of the Sanctuarists I'd met so far, saying that I'd yet to encounter the Marsh twins. 'They are all able to alibi each other from that point on. As far as they tell it, no one was alone until the following morning.'

I moved on, informing Tallis how, following his departure from the pub at around 10.40, there'd been over an hour of Wesley's movements unaccounted for until Reverend McDonald received a call from him at close to midnight. I explained that Wes had wanted to speak to his mother and that, due to her phone having been disconnected, the vicar had walked his own mobile down the lane to the Sayers' cottage, but that the call had cut off before Miss Westmacott had been able to speak to her son.

'Helpful vicar,' Tallis said. 'Did Wesley say anything to him during the call?'

'Nothing apparently, just insisted on talking to his mum. That's the last anyone heard of him, although Miss Westmacott said his bed had been slept in and that he left a note. Here, I have a photo of it, the original's still at the house.'

'"Mum, I'm just heading off for a bit – too much going on right now. I've taken some money from the clown by the way, haha. Will call when I can",' Tallis read aloud. 'OK, so what do we make of this?'

'I've got a theory,' I said. 'But again, there's something you need to see in the lad's bedroom. I can best explain it there.'

Tallis rolled his eyes. 'You do like to make a production of things. All right, so from the fact that he's still in his funeral suit, this note can't be what it appears. He must have been killed either that same night or in the early hours of Saturday morning. The recent cold snap has kept him pretty well preserved inside that reliquary thing.'

'Feretory,' I corrected him. 'A reliquary was a portable container, usually a highly decorated box or casket, that protected the saint's relics. The feretory was the small chapel or area of a church that housed the reliquary. In this case, I'm guessing the hollow pillar was once open to public view, the bones possibly displayed behind some sort of barred gate. Then when the Reformation came about, the king's men smashed up the saint's remains and tossed them back inside the false pillar, simply bricking it up. In the centuries since, the location of the feretory was forgotten.'

Ever a man for detail, Tallis made a note. 'A useful little nook, almost airtight,' the DCI mused. 'He'd have started to stink up the place eventually, but possibly not until late into the new year when the weather improved. Whoever killed him may have had a plan to move him again at that point. Good.' He nodded. 'So tell me, how did you know he was there?'

'I didn't. Not for certain. But a few ideas started to come together suggesting that's where a killer might have placed the body.'

I ran the inspector through the clues and hints: Stuart's cryptic reference to Wesley having passed 'by the gate of the hill and into the evil field beyond', a classical allusion to the fate of the faithless vestal virgins probably picked up from his father's love of the ancients; his parting comment yesterday regarding Wesley hiding in the 'dark place' and 'waiting behind the paper figure in the tree', referring to the paper angel topping the Christmas tree and the peculiar placing of the tree itself behind the pillar.

'All right,' Tallis said. 'But you should have called us rather than acting on your own initiative. I suppose I'll be able to square it all with the chief constable, but honestly, Scott, what a bloody liability you are.'

I held up my hands. There was no arguing with that.

'So give me a picture of our victim,' Tallis said. 'Why would anyone want to kill Wesley Sayers?'

'That's the million-dollar question,' I said. 'According to everyone I've spoken to in Fenchurch, he seemed to be very popular. Friend to all, fiercely defensive of those he loved, a good son, a reliable worker, not an enemy in the world. My bet is you won't even find an unpaid parking ticket in his glove box.'

'Come on,' Tallis laughed. 'I know that look. What aren't you telling me?'

'The girl whose funeral they were all attending. She was a friend from their school days, Katrina Allingham. She had a brother called Jamie who drowned in an accident about a decade ago. On the day he died, they'd all had an outing to the fair to celebrate Jamie's birthday. They were all there, Wesley, Stuart McDonald, Rowan Chesterton and the rest. It seems Kat wasn't thrilled about the idea of having to entertain her little brother when what she really wanted was just to hang out with her friends. But the gang pitched in and they made the best of it. Then it seems that the kid got into some of the booze they'd swiped from Kat's dad's liquor cabinet and insisted on visiting the fair's old waxworks exhibition. Creepy places at the best of times, and what with the boy having taken a slug or two of whisky, he started freaking out. So the friends took him into the forest to calm him down.'

I pointed towards Chattox Wood and a space in the trees where a spark of blue glimmered. 'Right about there. Apart from Wesley, the others all drifted off back home while Kat, infuriated with how her brother had shown her up, pushed the boy into the river. A farmer saw the whole thing. Wes tried to save Jamie, but it was no good and the kid drowned. The girl never forgave herself and, ten years later, she takes her own life at the very same spot.'

'Tragic,' Tallis said. 'But what does it have to do with this case?'

'Perhaps nothing. But it appears that, around the same time as the accident, someone had been targeting members of this little gang with malicious gossip. Each had stories told about them. Romances exposed, some minor drug taking revealed, family circumstances reported to the authorities. Suffice to say, it almost ruined their summer.'

'And this happened to all of them?' Tallis asked.

'I believe so.' I took him through each instance. 'I haven't spoken to Ryan and Maddox Marsh yet, so I don't have the details of their persecution, but I've been told they were also targeted.'

'Some spiteful kid at school?' Tallis suggested. 'Jealous because they weren't a member of the gang?'

'Possibly. But here's the thing: it appears that Kat was targeted most viciously after the drowning. And her persecution didn't last for that summer only. I think it went on for an entire decade, until the point where she couldn't take it anymore and ended her life. She didn't leave a suicide note, but I found a poem in Wesley's bedroom among a load of other keepsakes of Kat's. It seems she bequeathed him the most important treasures of her life. One of them was a copy of 'The Hound of Heaven', a religious poem that would have been familiar to all of them from their days messing about in the church. There's actually a framed copy on the wall opposite the pillar where Wesley was buried. The theme of the text can be read as a soul being relentlessly hunted by another. That's certainly how Wesley saw it. On the back of the copy Kat left him, he wrote something. Here, look.' I flicked through the pictures on my phone again and showed Tallis the scrawl left by Wes, that final word furiously underlined: 'Poor Katrina ran from that monster but he always found her. *Always.*'

'By the way, I'm not sure we should take that "he" literally,' I said, explaining my idea that Wesley could have simply been following the gender of the hunter from the poem. '"He" might still refer to a "she" in the context of the "monster" who was persecuting Kat. But it certainly sounds like Wes knew who it was, doesn't it? I've heard other reports in town about how protective he could be of Katrina. There was an incident in the pub where some drunks were teasing her about the death of her brother, and Wes lost his temper. And then this girl he loves so much kills herself, leaving him the poem as a clue to what had been happening to her. I think it's possible Wes waited until after he'd left the pub and then arranged to meet the persecutor, a confrontation ensued, and Wes was killed.'

Tallis nodded. 'We'll need to check his phone records, see if he called anyone else that night other than the vicar.'

The inspector's gaze swung around, across the town to the promenade and the fair. He pointed. 'Are you familiar with the people who own it?'

I nodded. 'Tom Makepeace. He was an old friend of my mum's.'

'The kids all went there the day that Katrina's brother died,' Tallis mused.

'They worked there too,' I said. 'Summer jobs. All except Stuart. By the way, if you decide to interview Tom Makepeace, please go steady. He's a very sick man. I don't think he has much time left.'

Tallis tapped two fingers to his forehead. 'Scout's honour.'

'Yes,' I said. 'I can see you as a scout. Five years back?'

'Cheeky sod. So which of them did it, do you think?' he asked.

'I don't know for sure that it was any of them,' I said. 'There could well be others at play here.'

Chapter Thirty

I TOLD TALLIS ABOUT THE PURITANICAL vicar of Fenchurch, the frustrated landlady of The Six Ravens and her browbeaten husband. But honestly, it was difficult to picture any of them in the role of an active killer. The landlord and his wife could just about manage it, I supposed, though they were neither of them in the first flush of youth. And what would be the motive? It was obvious that Mrs Berkeley had an unrequited crush on Wesley. I'd heard that she'd tried it on with him before and had been rebuffed. Maybe she lashed out after a second rejection, smashed the lad over the head with a beer bottle and then asked her dogsbody husband to help conceal the crime, but how would they get access to the church in the middle of the night? And the vicar? Wesley occasionally made fun of him, apparently, but murder over a cheeky nickname felt a bit extreme.

'What about the mother?' Tallis asked.

I shook my head. 'I can't see it. She was the one who insisted something had happened to Wes and asked for me to be called in. If it hadn't been for her belief that something was wrong, the body might never have been discovered. And what's her motive? She relied on Wesley emotionally and, in part at least, financially. Also, she's a bit ditzy. I can't see her murdering her son and then having the wit to cover it up. And who would be her accomplice? It would take at least two people to put the boy's body in the pillar and brick the thing back up again. The vicar helping her out? She's built like a fresh-hatched bird and he's a gasping asthmatic. No. This feels like a crime only a young and reasonably fit person could execute.'

'So we're back to the old school friends?'

'The Sanctuarists.'

Tallis gave me a questioning look.

'That's what they call themselves, a nickname given to them by the vicar back in the day. But as I said, they all have an alibi for the night of the killing. Of course, one of those alibis could easily be false – a pair of them murdering Wes then concocting a story to account for their movements. A story that it would be difficult to disprove.'

I sighed. 'The only thing I feel certain of is that Stuart McDonald *must* be involved somehow. He'd been working on repairs at the church for his father. He'd have noticed if anyone had mucked around with the pillar without his knowledge. And he's obviously been labouring under some extreme pressure ever since the funeral, drinking himself into a haze virtually every day. He's been trying to tell me what he knows since I got here, but either fear or loyalty or both has kept pulling him back. I think at the very least he helped conceal the body. That's why the Christmas tree was placed so awkwardly in front of the pillar, so he didn't have to face it every day.'

'And he went off with Indira Bakshi that night, am I right?' Tallis asked, glancing at his notes.

'Yes. Apart from a brief visit to Wesley's cottage to check if he'd returned there, they claim to have spent the entire night at the glamping site, drinking.'

Tallis nodded. 'Can you see Indira killing Wesley Sayers?'

I considered. 'Not for any purely emotional reason. She's much too cool and self-controlled for that. But to protect herself, her family? If she had been the one persecuting Kat and Wes threatened to expose her? Absolutely. But that's the role that doesn't fit her – persecutor. I think she'd find such a thing silly. But I can certainly see her intimidating Stuart into compliance.'

'I think you're right that it would take two people,' Tallis said. 'Even if he was killed inside the church, to manoeuvre the body into that gap, to hold it up while the other walled him in? Not an easy business. And if the murder occurred elsewhere, harder still to carry the body up that hill and into the nave.'

'And the wounds,' I said. 'They're indicative, aren't they? A blow to the back of the head and stabbed through the eye. It suggests one assailant standing behind the victim and another in front. I suppose it's possible that someone might hit him and then roll him over in order to stab him after he fell, but that feels like overkill, and I couldn't see any other rage-inflicted wounds on the body.'

Tallis agreed, 'Prelim examination suggests there are none.'

'But why the eye?' I frowned. 'They strike the back of the head to disable him but if that didn't kill him outright, why not just go on hitting him? Why that single blow followed by such a sickening and awkward killing wound? It seems so vicious, so unnecessary . . .' I paused, collecting my thoughts. 'There's something else you should know. We might have an eyewitness to the murder. Muriel Chesterton, Rowan's aunt.' I told Tallis of her strange words the night I'd met her in the woods: *The first wasn't a murder. Nor the second yet. But the third ... ?* 'I think the first she was referring to was Jamie's death, an accidental drowning. The second would be Kat's suicide in the same location. Then the third. She would only be able to identify that as a murder for certain if she'd seen it herself, or possibly if she'd overheard someone speaking about it in those terms. But my instinct is that she was out in Chattox Wood that night. She haunts it almost constantly from what I can gather, placing these little paper figures in the trees as a tribute to Jamie.'

Tallis raised an eyebrow but said nothing.

'It would be good if you could try to interview her without Rowan being present,' I said. 'And there's something else too. She made a gesture when I met her, slapping the back of her head like this.'

'Right at the spot where Wesley was hit?'

I nodded. 'It might mean nothing. She was confused and rambling, mixing up what she may have seen with talk about the ravens and their legend.'

As if hearing their name, the birds wheeling above us cried out in unison. Tallis followed my gaze. 'What legend?'

'They're called the Cain Ravens, after the first murderer from the Bible,' I said. 'The story goes that they take revenge on killers and that, if they ever leave their tower, the town of Fenchurch will fall. The vicar's not a fan. He seems to hate any kind of superstition associated with his church.'

Tallis made a note. 'I'll get one of our family liaisons to come with me and see if we can talk to Muriel.'

'Good. Have you spoken to the reverend, by the way?'

'I have.'

'How did he take the news?'

'Shellshocked, I'd say. And not just about the fact there's a month-old corpse walled up in his church. His son Stuart hasn't been home since you saw him yesterday afternoon.'

'What?' I stared at Tallis.

'Bed not slept in,' the DCI confirmed. 'Phone switched off, some clothes missing, wallet and cards gone. I hear his usual routine was to come up to the church early to do some painting before starting work for the day. I guess he might have seen us arrive, got the wind up and done a vanishing act himself. Which suggests you're right about his involvement in the murder. And you don't look happy about it.'

'I'm not,' I muttered. 'Truth is, I like the man and I'm worried about him. As I told you, I think he must have taken some part in the burial and cover up, but I just can't see him as a cold-blooded killer.'

'Come off it,' Tallis said. 'You're experienced enough to know that not every villain walks around in a top hat, twirling his curly moustache and cackling. Your experience in Aumbry alone should have taught you that.'

'You're right,' I admitted. 'But I still see him more as an accessory than anything else. He wanted me to know about the body, Tallis, I swear.'

'Which means he could be at risk. All right, I'll do the rounds of the local friends, ask if they know where he might be hiding.'

I looked at this keen, insightful man. He had once made me reflect on my time as an official detective. Not an entirely successful career, I'd always been too abrasive a loner for that, but there had been moments when I'd enjoyed being part of an investigative team. I felt it again now, the collaborative thrill of unpicking a mystery, of sparking ideas and theories off another curious mind. Thomas Tallis as a replacement for Peter Garris perhaps?

And here was the temptation: to tell Tallis everything regarding Peter and to recruit him in the search into the monster's past. But this young DCI played by the rules, he'd surely never condone such a private investigation. Or would he? Tallis had broken the rules once before, at the end of our case in Aumbry when he'd followed my lead to secure a killer's confession. One thing I'd learned was not to make any assumptions where Thomas Tallis was concerned.

As if reading my mind, he said, 'You weren't upfront with me the last time we worked together. Not about everything.'

'In the end I was,' I objected.

'That's a matter of opinion.'

'Of interpretation, maybe.'

He laughed. 'You're an obstinate bugger. So, Scott Jericho, tell me: why are you really here in Fenchurch? And don't give me that distant cousin bullshit. You're no more related to Wesley Sayers than I am.'

'His uncle is an old friend of mine,' I said. 'He was contacted by Miss Westmacott. She was in a bit of a state, asking for his help tracing Wes, so I said I'd come up and look into it for him. Pretending I was a cousin gave me an in with these people.'

'And who is this uncle?'

'An old friend, like I said.'

'Uh-huh. Well, I'll allow that to slide. For now.'

In the end, we decided to work together although, as far as

any official record was concerned, deniable collusion would be the order of the day. I had perfect cover established as Wesley's cousin, which Tallis admitted had already proved useful. As we headed back down the tower stairway, Tallis asked me once again to go over the clues that led me to Wesley's burial place. He rolled his eyes when I reached the part about the vestal virgins and a misplaced Christmas tree.

'God knows how I'll explain all of that in a report,' he said. 'Were you like this during your time on the force? How on earth did your old DCI explain these hunches to his superiors?'

'He fudged it,' I said. 'Like you will.'

'Christ. You know, I feel like I need some kind of debrief with the man. He's retired now, right? What was his name again?'

'Garris.'

'Ah yes, the legendary Peter Garris. Well, you learned from the best, I'll give you that. So, is there anything else you'd advise us to do in this case?' Tallis asked as we reached the bottom of the tower. 'I'm all ears.'

'Only to keep something back from the press and public,' I said. 'The eye injury maybe. It'll help flush out any false confessions. But you've already thought of that.'

'It might have crossed my mind.' Tallis smiled.

'All right, so what's next for you?' I asked.

'I'm meeting the mother and the vicar at the Sayers' cottage.'

'McDonald will be there?'

'For spiritual support, so he claims.' Tallis clapped me on the shoulder. 'Care to come along for the ride, Cousin Scott?'

Chapter Thirty-One

WE LEFT THE CHURCH TOGETHER, Tallis signing us both out of the scene log, and moved down the hill towards the lychgate. As we walked, I scanned the faces of the people crowded into the narrow lane. A host of journos and TV hacks, their trucks blocking the path. If the fourth estate had caught wind of the story this early, someone in Tallis's team must have loose lips.

The DCI was adept at keeping his expression neutral, but I could see a line of irritation crease his brow. We met the surge of reporters, all being kept back by a couple of uniformed officers, and began pushing our way through the throng.

'Inspector Tallis, any initial statement on the case?'

Tallis nudged aside the microphone that had been shoved under his nose. 'Nothing yet, you'll have to wait for an official statement later today.'

Another mic bobbed out from the crowd. 'Is it true that the body of a young man was found walled up alive inside the church? The rumour around town is that this person has been missing for months, and that the police didn't take the concerns of the family seriously. Any comment on that, Inspector?'

Tallis shook his head and shouldered on.

'Locals are talking about a girl whose suicide might be linked to the murder.'

'And some old legend regarding the ravens that are kept here at the church.'

'Be serious,' Tallis muttered. 'Surely you're not going to put nonsense like that on the six o'clock news?'

Then a flurry of excited chatter broke through the mass.

'Wait a minute, is that the guy?'

'Dunno, looks a bit like him, I suppose.'

'Jesus, though, what happened to the poor bastard?'

A dozen mics sprouted from the pack.

'Scott Jericho, isn't it? Can we ask, what are you doing here, sir?'

'Have the police called you in to consult on the case, Mr Jericho?'

'Scott, Scott, over here. Have you come up with any theories as to how this man died and who put him in the wall?'

'What do you think of the legend about the ravens? You've been involved in some weird cases in the past, is this another of them?'

'Inspector Tallis, do you think the showman detective will solve this one for you, like he did with the Aumbry serial killer?'

But I was no longer listening. Over the heads of the scrum, I had seen a figure, thin and hooded, lurking inside the doorway of the church hall at the end of the lane. Peter Garris, his face obscured in shadow, but close enough that I could read the posters tacked to the door beside him: LECTURE NEXT WEDNESDAY – THE IDEA OF SIN IN MEDIEVAL THEOLOGY WITH DR ALICE ROPER; PLEASE NOTE – THE WI CHRISTMAS BAKE SALE HAS BEEN

CANCELLED; a cartoon devil sitting on a plump lady's shoulder as she tucked into a huge cake, DON'T LISTEN TO TEMPTATION! JOIN THE FENCHURCH FIT CLUB TODAY! Again, something scratched at the back of my mind, but my attention remained fixed on the spectre in the doorway. Before I could even begin to think about fighting a path towards him, the man raised a gloved hand in salute and, in the next instant, a paparazzi flash went off and I was blinded. When I blinked the scene back into focus, the figure had vanished.

We finally emerged from the pack, more uniformed officers swarming in to help clear the lane between the vicarage and Miss Westmacott's cottage.

'Your fame precedes you.' Tallis smiled. 'Jericho, are you all right?'

'Huh?'

He followed my gaze back towards the church hall. 'Looking for anyone in particular?'

'No. No, I . . .' I shook my head. 'Sorry, it's nothing.'

He gave me a long appraising look. 'What's worrying you?'

'Nothing, like I said. Nothing to do with the case, anyway. Come on, let's go and see Wesley's mother.'

He held me with his eyes for a moment longer, then shrugged and we continued along the lane. Nothing gets past this man. I needed to remember that.

When we reached the cottage door, Tallis placed his palm against my chest. 'I want to know all your ideas, Scott. When you're ready, of course. But *all* of them, understand? No holding back on me this time.'

That said, he rang the bell.

Reverend McDonald opened the door and showed us into the sitting room. The vicar looked like he hadn't slept in a week, his hair dishevelled, food stains spotting his black jacket, his dog collar askew. He went to sit on the couch next to Miss Westmacott. Meanwhile, Tallis took in the interior of the cottage, his eyes moving over surfaces cluttered with a jumble sale's worth of bric-a-brac. Miss Westmacott seemed to sense some unspoken judgement and absently picked a few items from the table, slipping them into the voluminous pocket of her apron.

'Mr Jericho,' she said, rubbing a red-rimmed eye. 'Mr Jericho, I told you, didn't I? I told you he was gone. My Wesley, my dear good boy. No one wanted to listen, but I *knew*. Have you spoken to Mr Noonan yet? What's he said? Is he coming up here? It would be wonderful if he could sort things out for us.'

'He knows and he sends his condolences,' I said. 'He's happy for me to keep looking into the case, as long as you agree?'

She nodded. 'Absolutely. If that's what Mr Noonan thinks is best.'

I noticed a sharp look from Tallis.

'I've come along with DCI Tallis,' I said. 'We just want you to run through what happened again on the night of the funeral, would that be all right?'

She did so, adding no fresh details. Coming home from Kat's wake at the church hall, she had set about baking a treat for her son to cheer him up. The Italian meringue buttercream required careful monitoring, and so she hadn't noticed the passing hours. She expected Wesley to be out with his friends most of the night anyway. Indira and Stuart had popped in sometime after eleven looking for him, saying he had left the pub alone, but reassuring Miss Westmacott that, by that time, Wesley had probably met up again with the others. It wasn't until Mr McDonald came down with his mobile, saying Wes wished to speak to her, that she realised it was near midnight.

'But the call cut off before you could talk to him?' Tallis looked up from his notebook.

McDonald nodded. 'And then I pottered off home.'

'And that's the last you heard from Wesley?'

'He didn't even get to try his treat.' Miss Westmacott blinked at the sorry-looking slab of Battenberg on the coffee table in front of her. 'I'm so sorry, I meant to ask if you'd like a piece? Only from the local shop, I'm afraid. I can't face baking right now.'

'Of course not,' I said, thinking of the posters I'd seen on the door of the church hall. 'Do you organise the WI bake sale, Miss Westmacott?'

The reverend and Tallis looked at me as if I'd lost my mind. Even I wasn't sure why I'd posed the question. But Miss Westmacott appeared not to have heard me.

'I told the police,' she said. 'The note wasn't right, not at all. And then there's the fact he never would have abandoned me without a word, not for weeks on end. But no one would listen and so I got in touch with Mr Noonan. He has a reputation, you see? He can organise things.'

'Yes, so I've heard,' Tallis said. There was no pointedness in his tone but still I shuffled a little in my chair.

'Mr McDonald.' Tallis flicked a page of his notebook and glanced blandly at the vicar. 'Where is your son?'

McDonald jumped up, his cheeks flushing red. 'I've already told you people when you came barging into the vicarage this morning, I've no idea where Stuart might be.'

'He didn't come home last night. Bed not slept in. Correct?'

'Yes, I informed your sergeant—'

'You've tried calling him?'

'Once or twice.'

'Once or twice.' Tallis tapped his pad. 'We've just found the body of one of your son's best friends entombed inside a pillar of your church. Don't you think you ought to be making more of an effort to locate Stuart? Perhaps stay at home and wait for him there?'

'It's very good of you to keep Miss Westmacott company,' I said, slotting neatly into the good cop role. 'But if Stuart did want to get away, somewhere he could be alone and not be recognised, where might he go?'

An Adam's apple throbbed above that clerical collar. 'I've no idea.'

'University friends?' I suggested. 'A girlfriend who lives away? Perhaps he's gone to visit Ryan and Maddox Marsh? Maybe you could give the inspector a list?'

'Of course I'll do that. Most happily.'

'Did you know about the hollow pillar, Reverend?' Tallis asked. 'The feretory containing the saint's remains? There's new plaster there, you must have noticed it. Didn't you ask your son what repairs he'd been doing in that part of the church?'

'I let Stuart get on with it, Inspector. He's a good craftsman, I didn't think it worth my while supervising his every move.'

'And cheap too, so I'm told,' Tallis observed.

McDonald bristled. 'I knew nothing. I know nothing.'

'But didn't you wonder about the placement of the Christmas tree?' I asked. 'Isn't it more usual to put them near the altar or in the entrance?'

'I don't concern myself with frivolous decorations,' the vicar muttered. 'The parishioners expect such vulgar nonsense, and they kick up a fuss with the bishop if we don't have one. Personally, I think the church ought to be a place of serious reflection and worship, not some gaudy children's playground. So I may have asked Stuart to situate it out of sight, I don't recall.'

I sat forward, my hands pressed together. 'I don't want to distress you, Mr McDonald, I honestly don't. But you must see that Wesley's body being discovered in a place to which Stuart had almost exclusive access is highly—'

'I'm as anxious as we all are for this awful accident to be cleared up,' the vicar snapped. Then in a softer tone, 'It must be an accident. It *must*.' He looked lost for a moment before drawing himself up again. 'One thing I can tell you gentlemen – my son is blameless. He's a child in many ways, an innocent. Too innocent if anything. He would never hurt anyone; Miss Westmacott agrees with me there.'

Wesley's mother pocketed yet another stray item from the table and nodded obediently.

Chapter Thirty-Two

I took Tallis up to the murdered man's bedroom and showed him the things left to Wesley by Katrina Allingham. He glanced over the file with its paper trail of her life – the ultrasound scan, the copy of her birth certificate, her school reports, the friendship bracelet, the university acceptance letter and other mementos. He then focused on 'The Hound of Heaven' poem and Wes's inscription on the back before holding up the vacuum-sealed bag with its fragment of fruitcake.

'What the hell's this?'

'I think it might be connected to a ritual,' I said. 'I don't know the full details, not yet. But ever since I arrived here, there've been hints about some kind of rite performed by the Sanctuarists. Stuart mentioned it first, a sacred ceremony linked to the ancient people who used to live in the wetlands. Rowan's Aunt Muriel told them about it when they were kids. And you know how teenagers latch onto anything ritualistic and bizarre. Apparently, Katrina told old Tom Makepeace that they did "a silly ritual" after her brother died to make sure his soul went to heaven. When I asked Indira and Lorelei about it, Indira claimed that it was all nonsense, but her objection felt a little forced, if you know what I mean? When I raised it with Rowan, she diverted onto another subject.'

'What subject?' Tallis asked.

She mentioned seeing a figure in the woods that I believe to be Peter Garris, I thought. The same figure I'd just seen outside the church hall. But that wasn't a conversation I wanted to have with Thomas Tallis.

'I can't really remember.'

He raised a sceptical eyebrow. 'All right, go on.'

'I think Wesley wanted to perform the ritual again the night of Kat's funeral. Whether because he really believed it would give her peace or out of some sense of nostalgia, I'm not sure. In any case, the others appeared reluctant. Say he went off by himself into the woods, determined to perform the rite. He meets the persecutor there, perhaps by arrangement, perhaps accidentally, and they get into it. Wesley throwing around accusations, saying he'll reveal the truth about how this person drove Kat to her death. The end result, he's killed and his body sealed away inside the pillar.'

'All right.' Tallis nodded, holding up the vacuum-sealed bag. 'I'll go along with that, but what exactly was this ritual?'

'I don't know. They all seem very reluctant to tell me.'

'Odd if it was just some childish nonsense, as Indira claimed.' Tallis wandered over to the desk by the window and picked up the note I'd left there. 'And then there's this little mystery.'

'Something about it struck me as off, right from the start,' I said, joining him.

Tallis nodded. 'It feels too informal. Not emotionally charged enough for a young man who needed to get away after the loss of his best friend.'

'And then there's this,' I said, showing him the pad from which the note had originally been torn. 'If you check the watermark on the notepaper, you'll see it matches the rest of the sheets here. But look, the indentations on the topmost blank page show that the last note written on this pad was about a shift at the pub. It wasn't the farewell note at all. Therefore, this note must have been written at some point *before* the funeral. Perhaps even weeks or months before.'

'So you think, what?' Tallis asked. 'That the killer came back here after Miss Westmacott went to bed, found the farewell note, and planted it for her to discover in the morning, giving the impression that Wesley had gone away of his own accord. But wouldn't she have recognised it as an old note?'

'Not necessarily,' I said. 'Say he wrote it ages ago with some vague plan to take off for a while but that, for whatever reason, he never ended up going through with it.'

'A lucky find for the killer,' Tallis said. 'But it's possible, I suppose. Only, why would the murderer come here at all after the crime?'

'Perhaps to see if there was any direct evidence in Wesley's possession linking them to their persecution of Kat.'

Tallis shook his head. 'I'm not sure I buy this motive. Even if someone had tormented the girl all those years, prosecution for crimes like harassment are tricky at best, especially if there's no living victim. Even with Wesley's suspicions about them, would the persecutor really have murdered him to avoid the chance of an official investigation? Why not just deny it or laugh the whole thing off?'

'Maybe in the moment of being confronted they were scared or angry and they lashed out?' I suggested. 'Also, they might not have known that it would be hard to prove a case against them for driving Kat to suicide. Not everyone has the knowledge we do about how difficult these things are to prosecute. Or there might be more direct evidence that Wesley threatened them with and of which we know nothing. If so, they might have thought coming back here was worth the risk.'

'That's true.' Tallis paused, reading over the note again. 'But what's this stuff about a clown?' He pointed to that section of the message.

'Apparently, it's an allusion to a porcelain figure that Wes and his mother used to keep bits and bobs of spare cash in. We had a similar thing at home, a kind of loose change pot.'

'You don't sound satisfied with that. Another idea niggling away at you?' Tallis sighed. 'All right, I'll leave it to niggle.'

'Wesley took other money as well, according to Miss Westmacott,' I said. 'A few thousand he had stowed away. Although I suppose we must now suspect his killer of taking that too, to reinforce the illusion Wes vanished of his own free will.'

'Must have been a close friend to know where the money was kept,' Tallis said. 'Another indication our murderer is one of the Sanctuarists. All right, but going back to your idea that the killer or killers came here that night and discovered the note. How did they get in?'

'There're a few possibilities, as far as I can see,' I said. 'They take the key from Wes's body before bricking him up inside the pillar. Your guys will have to check if he had his house key on him. Or perhaps they simply broke in, this place isn't exactly Fort Knox.' I showed him how the bedroom window was secured with a simple catch, easily lifted from the outside with the blade of a penknife or a wire coat hanger.

'Doesn't look like it's been forced though,' Tallis observed.

'No,' I admitted, 'and there's no sign of the front or back door being tampered with recently either. I checked on my first visit.'

'Miss Westmacott told us that one of the pairs came here sometime after Wesley left the pub,' Tallis said.

'Indira and Stuart, yes. They claimed they were looking in to check that Wes was all right.'

'But at that time Wesley must have still been alive,' Tallis observed. 'His call to his mother via Mr McDonald came *after* their visit, correct? They'd hardly have come here to search for incriminating evidence against themselves before he'd confronted them with what he knew. Unless they'd already killed him and the call to the vicar was a blind. Perhaps one of them impersonated Wesley, or Mr McDonald agreed to cover for his son. He brings the phone down the lane and then claims the call has cut off just as he hands it over to Miss Westmacott, thereby giving Stuart and Indira a sort of alibi.'

I shook my head. It didn't feel right. 'I'm not sure McDonald would ever agree to such a thing, even to save his son. And I doubt either Stuart or Indira in the heat of the moment would pull off an impersonation convincing enough to get the vicar out of bed at midnight and trotting down the lane. I think it *was* Wesley calling to speak to his mother. But as you say, if they were involved, how do we account for Stuart and Indira's visit here before the murder could have happened?' I closed my eyes, frustrated. 'They are our natural prime suspects. Stuart must have at least known about the burial in the pillar.'

The secrets of the room explored, we were back on the landing when Tallis stopped me in my tracks. 'Noonan?' he said. 'Mark Noonan? I know that name, don't I?'

'An old associate,' I said.

He raised that inquisitorial eyebrow. 'Interesting company you keep, Mr Jericho.'

We left Miss Westmacott, Tallis saying he would need to return at some point to take a formal statement. While the inspector checked in with his team, I headed back to The Six Ravens where the landlady, bristling with excitement, tried to corner me in the corridor.

'Please don't tell me it's true,' she said, rushing out of the kitchen and wringing her hands through a stained tea towel. 'Not poor darling Wesley. It's all over the town; people around here are such vultures. Can't wait to pick over the bones of any tragedy.'

'I'm sure they are,' I said, trying to sidestep her. We continued this complicated dance all the way up the stairs.

'They're saying it was you who discovered the body. That you're actually a private detective of some sort. Like …' She struggled for a fictional equivalent, flapping the tea towel at me before blurting out: 'Poirot!'

'Six foot three, dressed in yesterday's polo neck and the only time I ever grew a moustache was when I was in a coma. You're right,' I agreed, 'we could be twins.'

'Tell me, had he really been bricked up inside a wall?' She pressed herself between me and the bedroom door. 'Who would ever do such a thing?'

'A jilted admirer perhaps?' I suggested. 'Someone who wouldn't take no for an answer? Or a cuckolded husband? Now, I best go and feed my dog.'

She sniffed and drew away, as if someone had just wafted one of her own pub lunches under her nose. 'Well, I don't want to take up your time, I'm sure.'

Back in my room, I made a fuss of Webster, feeding him some chews from the pocket of my coat before trying Harry's mobile. It went straight to voicemail. I gave him my news and asked him to ring me back as soon as possible. Then I headed to the bathroom, stripped and stood under a scalding shower. Feeling a little fresher, I pulled on a fresh vest, socks, briefs, polo neck and jeans and grabbed one of the cheap biscuits from the tea tray.

Webster seemed a little friskier this morning and, although I'd been up all night, one look from the hound guilt-tripped me into clipping the leash to his collar. It struck me as we both hobbled into town that all detectives should have a Webster as their companion. An elderly juk with the grand gift of silence made excellent ruminative company.

Now mid-morning, swags of cloud rolled in from the sea and blotted out the sun. As we wandered down the high street and turned onto the prom, I could almost feel eyes swivelling in our direction, conversations held in suspension. Little knots of Fenchurchians stood in shop doorways, open-mouthed pensioners huddled under the bus shelter, a cluster of men vaping outside a tired-looking amusement arcade.

'They all know,' said a cracked voice at my side. 'And they're desperate for you to tell them – just how did poor Wesley Sayers die?'

Chapter Thirty-Three

'That's the curse of a place like this. Gossip is passed around quicker than a dose of clap in a Soho bathhouse.'

I looked down to find Tom Makepeace slouched slightly lopsided in his wheelchair. His wasted frame, covered in layers of clothing and blankets, reminded me a little of the emaciated figure of Peter Garris. Uncle Tommy's husband Mike released the handles of the chair and came round to the front, helping me rearrange the old showman more comfortably.

'There you go.' Mike smiled, and ran his fingers through Tommy's gossamer silver hair. 'Got to have my boy looking presentable.'

Uncle Tommy gripped that strong workman's hand and smiled back. 'He's taking me for my daily constitutional. Got to get some colour in these cheeks, apparently.'

I smiled too. I couldn't help but picture the absurdity of these two in the role of Wesley's murderers, the dying showman and his burly, weatherbeaten beau, taking the young man unawares. Mike striking from behind with some blunt object and then holding Wesley down as Uncle Tommy creaked out of his chair to perform the coup de grâce, perhaps using a candyfloss stick to stab his victim through the eye. And then Mike coasting the corpse over to the church in his lover's wheelchair, industriously bricking up the body while Tommy sat in a nearby pew, eating fairground popcorn and providing a running commentary. And what would be their motive? The showman, incensed at how the reward money he had once bestowed on the boy had been frittered away, now out for revenge.

'What are you grinning at?' Tommy asked. Then his gaze narrowed. 'Ah, I see. You now have a body, don't you, Mr Jericho? And so everyone is in play as a suspect. Are you casting me in the role of calculating killer? Mike too perhaps, as my reluctant accomplice. Two embittered old queens, insanely jealous of the boy's youthful vigour and beauty, hand him a poisoned toffee apple and, once the prince has breathed his last, wheel him over to the church in the dead of night, the strapping corpse thrown across my bony knees, Mike panting like a showground steam engine as he shunts us up the gravestone path and plants our boy behind the bricks. Snow White in his stony tomb.'

I shook my head, amused. 'I sometimes forget that all showpeople are detectives, to a greater or lesser degree.'

He cracked his own crooked smile in response. 'Your mother certainly was. You must get at least a little of your talent from her, I think.'

My smile faltered. 'You and Mike did cross my mind, fleetingly,' I admitted. 'I'm sorry.'

'No need to apologise.' Uncle Tommy waved my words away. 'You wouldn't be doing your job if you didn't at least consider the possibility. After all, I had known those kids very well back when they used to work for me. They were at my fair on the day of Jamie Allingham's drowning, larking about in my waxworks. I am very much part of their story.

'And so the question arises: is there some guilty secret from my past reaching out to darken my final days? Is that why I really gave Wesley Sayers the reward money? To silence him, or perhaps as payment for some private service he'd performed for me? Or maybe it was blackmail money. Was Wesley holding something over me, a perversion that would see me tarred and feathered and run out of town? And in the end, did I need to stop his wagging tongue for good?'

'Don't talk rubbish, Tommy,' Mike muttered, casting his gaze along the prom.

The old man shrugged. 'No need to look so uncomfortable, Scott. You're a gay man, you know as well as I do that these absurd stories will spread whenever one of us shows even the smallest kindness towards a child. It's the age-old libel, isn't it? That we're all predators and therefore our every action must be suspect. But I didn't kill Wesley Sayers. I didn't hurt him or Jamie Allingham or any other child. I've been hurt myself, as I told you, very badly. I know what it feels like to be beaten and abused, and so I would never ...'

He trailed off. When he spoke again it was with trembling emphasis. 'I would *never*.'

'So who do you think might have done it?' Though my hip bawled at me, I knelt down so that I could be eye-level with the showman. 'Like I said, we're all detectives to a greater or lesser degree. You must have some idea.'

'Oh, I do,' he murmured. 'I have a very definite idea ...'

His eyes appeared to glaze, and I wondered if his pain medication might be kicking in. I straightened up and turned to the ever-stoical Mike, back in his position at the handles of the chair.

'What about you? Any theories?'

'My guess would be the vicar,' he answered without hesitation. 'Wes often used to get a rise out of him. Arsy McDonald and stuff like that. It was all in good humour, but some people can't take a joke. That old buzzard certainly can't.'

'But you don't think he'd kill Wesley over something as petty as that, surely?'

The chap shrugged. 'People lash out in temper sometimes, even over things that don't matter all that much. They regret it later, of course, but maybe none of this was intentional.'

'No,' I conceded. 'I think maybe you're right. I'm not sure that any of it was.'

It was an idea that had started to form in my head ever since my discovery of Wesley in the pillar: that, unlike some of my more recent cases, there was no great malignant intellect behind this murder. Instead, it felt as if an air of desperation and panic hung over the mystery. A deep sense of sadness too – of lives shattered and derailed by tragedies beyond anyone's control.

'Do you have any idea where Stuart might have disappeared to?' I asked Mike.

'The boy's done a runner, has he? Hmm. That does look sus.'

'He seems to have,' I said. 'Hasn't been seen since yesterday afternoon anyway. Did he have any particular friends that you can think of? Anywhere he could lie low for a while?'

'I honestly don't know him all that well,' Mike said. 'I was already full-time on the fair when they were all youngsters, during that summer when Tommy took them on as hired help. But I worked the big rides and so didn't have too much to do with them. Teens were only ever given cleaning jobs or else ticket-takers on the juveniles back then. After they all left school, most of the gang went off to university and the like. All except Wes and Kat, of course. They never left. Stuart went away too, right up until his money ran out and he had to come back here to earn a few quid doing the renovations at the church.'

'What about you, Uncle Tommy?' I asked. 'Any ideas where Stuart might be?'

I looked back at the old man in the chair. He seemed not have been listening to our conversation. Instead, his eyes were trained on a point further down the prom.

'Yes,' he repeated, as much to himself as to us. 'I have a very definite idea about who it might be . . .'

He stopped himself mid-sentence, withered lips pursing tight together. Then, shaking his head at me, he said, 'You'll come to the opening of the Winter Wonderland tomorrow, won't you? Mike, give him one of the fliers.'

While Mike searched his inside pocket, I turned and looked along the prom to the point where Tom Makepeace's gaze had focused. A pair of young people, arm in arm and stylishly dressed, were bracing themselves against the wind that had started to whip up along the front. I recognised them at once from the funeral photograph. Here were Ryan and Maddox Marsh at last, the final members of Sanctuarists, the last of the set of eight.

As I watched, a figure emerged from a side street and hurried over to join them. Rowan, bundled up in her thick winter coat, a bulging string bag slung over her shoulder. She was greeted warmly by her old friends, their arms thrown protectively around her. Even from this distance you could feel the reassurance Rowan took from them. The way she seemed to fall into their embrace, surrendering to their confidence. I glanced back at Tom Makepeace. Which of the twins had he been looking at when he spoke those words – *I have a very definite idea of who it might be* – or had he possibly been referring to both?

'Here you go,' Mike said, handing me the flier: MAKEPEACE FUNFAIR PRESENTS: A WINTER WONDERLAND CHARITY EXTRAVAGANZA! ALL THE FUN OF THE FAIR, IN AID OF THE RESTORATION OF ST PETER'S CHURCH. FINAL DAY OF RIDES AND ATTRACTIONS BEFORE THE LEGENDARY MAKEPEACE FUNFAIR CLOSES FOR GOOD! DON'T MISS OUT! I folded the paper and put it in my pocket.

'So it's still going ahead?' I asked. 'Even after what's happened?'

'I didn't like to,' Uncle Tommy admitted, 'not under current circumstances. But the vicar called up this morning and insisted we push on. Said St Peter's was relying on us.'

'His son is missing and a young man he's known all his life is found dead inside his church,' I murmured. 'And he immediately thinks of the fundraiser.'

'Interesting man.' Uncle Tommy nodded. 'But I'd given him my word months ago that we'd open up one last time in aid of the restoration. And as you know, a showman's word is his bond.'

I thanked the two men for their time and hurried down the prom, Webster panting at my side, keen to intercept the Marsh twins and Rowan Chesterton. I was just within earshot of their conversation, a few stray words from Rowan were delivered to me on the breeze – *No one's seen him. Guys, I'm worried. What if he does something stupid like Kat?* – when Maddox Marsh hushed her friend, and she and Ryan turned towards me.

'Hello,' they said almost in unison. 'And who are you?'

Chapter Thirty-Four

MADDOX WAS, LIKE HER BROTHER, stunningly beautiful. They shared the same high cheekbones and piercing blue eyes, identical strong jawline and full lips, the same flawless skin. Maddox's rich brown hair was gathered up into a luxuriant bun on her head, speared into place with a ruby-studded pin, while Ryan's was swept away from his brow and trimmed tight at the sides. They both possessed a powerful physicality, Maddox broad-shouldered and clearly toned under her cashmere cardigan, Ryan's gym-sculpted physique perfectly complemented by his Brunello Cucinelli blazer. They treated me to identical welcoming smiles. It was almost eerie.

'Hello,' I said. 'My name's Scott Jericho.'

Maddox's smile spread like a scar across her mouth, so full and red. The exact shade of lipstick I'd seen on the glass in the storeroom at the waxworks. Had she gone there with someone after Kat's funeral, perhaps to toast the memory of the dead girl and her little brother? And if so, was that person her twin? Or had it been the member of the Sanctuarists that Indira and Lorelei claimed Maddox had paired off with after they'd all left The Six Ravens? The same girl who now clung to Maddox's arm, as if terrified that I might snatch her friend away.

'Mr Jericho is a cousin of Wesley's,' Rowan said. 'Miss Westmacott asked him to come down a few days ago to see if he could find any trace of—'

'And now you have, or so we hear,' Ryan interjected. He had a smooth, honeyed sort of voice, the only point of difference with his sister's more brittle tone.

I glanced up at the sky, now teemed with cloud. 'Why don't we grab a coffee or something? It looks like it's going to pour.'

'I don't know.' Rowan dragged again at Maddox's wrist. 'We really ought to—'

'No, we must, Rowan dear,' Maddox insisted. 'Mr Jericho has lost his cousin, we've lost one of our closest friends. It's only polite. What about The Bluebird? They're fine with dogs, I think.' An eyebrow pruned as precisely as any bonsai was cocked at the sight of Webster. 'What a dear old doggo. Come on, if the place is still standing, it's this way.'

She didn't wait for our consent, simply pulled Rowan across the prom with her, like a battleship tugging a toy boat in its wake. There was something of the forthrightness of Indira Bakshi about Maddox Marsh, yet she possessed her own force, perhaps tempered by a more natural sense of ease within herself. Ryan meanwhile gave me a swift up-and-down appraisal before following his twin. As I hobbled after them, Webster panting on his lead, I watched the flame red of Maddox's scarf, almost an exact match for her lipstick, fly out on the breeze like the stamen of some poisonous flower.

Not quite breakfast, not quite lunchtime, The Bluebird tea-shop was less than a quarter full when we stepped inside. It had a prim, faded fussiness about it. A relic of genteel seaside holidays gone by, all doilies and fake Spode teacups and placemats decorated with hunting scenes. We took a table in the window, the view of the prom discreetly veiled by yellowing lace.

At the sight of us, a bored-looking waiter immediately perked up and came galloping over, laminated menus clamped under his arm. Passing one to Ryan, the spotty twentysomething practically licked his lips, an appreciative gaze roving over those Olympian features. Honestly, I couldn't help feeling a little left out. We ordered coffee and a selection of cakes and the waiter reluctantly cantered away.

'Pretty thing, I might look him up on Grindr while I'm in town,' Ryan smirked. Then his eye fell on the easy-wipe plastic tablecloth in front of him and his expression soured. 'The ghost of Terence Conran preserve us. How on earth are places like this still operating? Stuck in the seventies with all the charm of white dog turds baking on the pavement.' He waved a manicured hand; I wasn't entirely sure if his criticism was restricted to the tearoom itself or the entirety of Fenchurch. 'Speaking of, the mutt is housetrained, yes?'

I gave Webster a pat under the table. 'If you can manage to contain yourself for half an hour, Mr Marsh, I'm sure Webster can do the same.'

'Don't worry, my brother only indulges in verbal diarrhoea,' Maddox assured me. 'He'd find the other kind far too plebeian.'

'Both of you, please just stop,' Rowan murmured.

She gave me an apologetic smile. The poor girl looked even more tired today than when I'd first met her in the woods. I wondered if Aunt Muriel had been having many sleepless nights, wandering around the forest, displaying yet more of her paper boy tributes. Ryan reached carefully across the table, making sure the sleeve of his designer jacket didn't make contact with the despised tablecloth, and took her hand.

'I'm sorry, Row. I sometimes forget that you and the others have been sucked back into this hellish vortex of a nowhere.'

'Don't be a snob, Ryan,' his sister scolded. 'It never did us any good at school and it won't with Mr Jericho, I'm sure.'

'Scott,' I said.

'Jericho.' Ryan picked up a teaspoon and waved it at me. 'I know that name, don't I? Where have I heard of this guy, Mads? No, no, don't tell me, I've got it! All those psychic crackpots getting killed a couple of months back. You solved it, didn't you? Like Miss Marple or Jack fucking Reacher or something. Good for you.'

'Stop throwing around the fucks, darling,' Maddox said. 'You're not at a Westminster drinks party now. This place aspires to higher manners.'

Ryan mimed zipping his lips, immediately unzipping them again when our order arrived. Maddox rolled her eyes as the waiter leaned over the table, taking his time to lay out the plates and coffee pots, Ryan ogling the pert little backside so pointedly presented for his inspection.

'Thank you, sweetness,' Ryan purred, and the waiter disappeared again with a grin and a tenner smoothly slipped into his back pocket. 'Such a pretty thing.'

'You don't seem hugely cut up about your friend,' I said, pouring milk into my coffee and stirring. 'Was it a surprise, that Wesley's corpse was found walled up inside a pillar?'

They stared at me. Even Ryan seemed at a loss.

'Sorry,' I said. 'I thought we were all being fashionably callous.'

'We came back as soon as Rowan phoned and told us what had happened,' Maddox said, inclining her head towards her friend. 'Don't pay any attention to my idiot brother, Mr Jericho. He masks his emotions with a general aura of dickheadedness.'

'You must admit, I do it very well,' Ryan put in, though his tone had dropped an octave.

'If he prays to the blue fairy then one day he might even become a real boy,' Maddox confided. 'With proper human emotions and everything.'

'So you both just up and left work this morning and came straight here?' I asked. 'Well, that's real friendship. But then I'd expect nothing less of the Sanctuarists. Where is home for you, by the way?'

'We share a flat in Pinner,' Maddox said. 'Only way we can make London-living affordable, tolerating each other in a tiny two-bed that backs onto the Underground line. I work in fashion, designing jewellery for a couple of the smaller boutiques up West. Ryan's at one of the big legal firms in the city.'

'Commercial law?' I suggested. 'Hedge funds?'

'How ever did you guess?' Ryan smiled.

I smiled right back, wondering if this glib little grifter worked for one of the partnerships currently putting fairgrounds out of business up and down the country. 'Important jobs to drop at a moment's notice,' I said. 'You must really have been close to Wesley. Tell me, what do you think happened to him?'

'I can't believe it, honestly I can't,' Maddox said. 'We left him alive and well at the pub that night after the funeral tea. When we heard he'd vanished, I thought he'd just gone off by himself for a few weeks. His mother can be a bit much, and poor Wes took Kat's death very hard.'

'*He* left you alive and well, you mean,' I corrected her.

'I'm sorry?'

'It was his suggestion, wasn't it, that you leave the pub and go off together to honour Kat's memory, as you had honoured her brother's all those years before? But you refused. And so Wesley went off alone while the rest of you remained at The Ravens.'

'You have been busy, Mr Wesley's cousin,' said Ryan smoothly. 'Funny, he never once mentioned you to me. What about you girls? Ever heard of Wes's famous detective relation?'

I glanced at Rowan who was nibbling like a mouse at her slice of sponge cake. 'How is it?' I asked.

'Oh, it's delicious, thank you,' she said.

I picked up my own piece of cake and took a bite. 'This is good too. Am I the only one having the fruitcake?'

Silence around the table. Glancing towards the till, I saw another copy of the Fenchurch Fit Club poster tacked to a noticeboard, the same cartoon devil perched on the same plump lady's shoulder that I'd seen outside the church hall. It was at that moment that a series of ideas and images began to coalesce inside my mind: another poster from outside the hall – THE IDEA OF SIN IN MEDIEVAL THEOLOGY WITH DR ALICE ROPER; the history of Mother Godsole that I had read about online, a local witch who was said to have 'consumed the sins of unbaptised children'; Stuart's talk of the old Fenchurchians performing 'sacred rites to placate the dead'; Tom Makepeace telling me that Kat and her friends had enacted 'a silly ritual to make sure her brother's soul got to heaven'; and Indira's reference to an old rite that Rowan or Muriel had told them about when they were kids. A ritual that Rowan herself had mentioned. I thought of the piece of fruitcake vacuum-sealed in its plastic bag under Wesley's bed, left to him as a keepsake by Katrina; of the fragment of cake found by the landlord of The Six Ravens after the Sanctuarists had all finally left the pub, and of the crumb I'd seen inside Wesley's makeshift tomb, woven into a web that silvered his funeral jacket.

'Would you excuse me a moment?' I asked them.

Taking out my phone, I typed into a search engine 'sins consumption ritual'. The results came back, 'Sin-eater', with the following article topmost:

> A sin-eater is someone who consumes a ritual meal in order to spiritually take on the sins of a deceased loved one. The dead person is thereby cleansed of all wrongdoing and may pass unchallenged into heaven. Examples of sin-eating were witnessed as recently as the late nineteenth century in the English counties of Norfolk and Lincolnshire. After a funeral service, mourners would gather in the churchyard or in woodland close to the burial site, intone some arcane prayer or catechism in memory of the deceased and then between them consume a 'funeral biscuit' or 'corpse cake'. This strange rite is said to persist in certain quarters of the country, its adherents sworn to secrecy lest the power of the magic be compromised. The eating of sins is believed to be especially necessary in cases of sudden death, suicide or murder.

I put away my phone and looked up. Three questioning faces stared back at me.

'So tell me,' I said, 'why did you all refuse to consume Katrina Allingham's sin?'

Chapter Thirty-Five

'You ...' Maddox took a quick sip of her coffee. 'You know about the ritual? Who told you?'

'Not Rowan,' I said, catching the twins' accusatory glance. 'It was Wesley and Kat who told me.'

'But ... but that's impossible,' Ryan started.

'What do you mean?' asked his sister.

I shrugged. 'I found a fragment of the fruitcake you used as teenagers among Wesley's belongings. The corpse cake, you might have called it. I think Kat had kept a piece preserved in memory of her brother, and possibly of the bond you all shared back then. A morsel of her part of the cake, which you all ate after Jamie's funeral to absorb his sins and ease his passage to the afterlife. She left it, along with some other mementos and treasures, to Wesley. Your Aunt Muriel told you about the ritual?'

Rowan nodded slowly. 'Kat was so distraught after Jamie died. Her parents—'

'Her parents were monsters,' Ryan said, his flippant mask slipping and a glimpse of the true friend showing beneath.

'*Are* monsters,' Maddox corrected. 'You know they continued to blame Kat for the accident, all these years later? They never let her forget it. Wouldn't pay for a proper headstone and didn't even come to the funeral.'

'Yes, I've spoken to them,' I said. 'And I agree, they are monsters.'

'Kat was in such a state,' Rowan said. 'She didn't seem able to forgive herself for what happened. It wasn't her fault that Jamie got into the drink and then started freaking out in the waxworks. It was just one of those things.'

'Kat had snuck the whisky from her father's liquor cabinet?'

'She thought it would make up for us having to spend our day off with the little shite,' Ryan muttered.

'Ryan,' Maddox snapped. 'Show some respect.'

'Jesus Christ, all right,' Ryan snapped back. 'I'm sorry the kid died, we were all sorry, but let's not pretend he wasn't anything other than a selfish, whiny little brat. Just because he happened to be the apple of his parents' eye, that doesn't mean we have to sit here like hypocrites and pretend we liked the kid. God, if I'd still been there in the woods that afternoon, I might have pushed him into that fucking river myself.'

'He *was* a kid,' Rowan said pointedly. 'He never got the chance to grow up and be any better.'

'That's true, I suppose,' Ryan admitted. Then, reaching across the table, he grabbed a slice of fruitcake from my plate and took an almost absurdly savage bite out of it. His mouth full, he grinned at us all, 'Sorry. Ryan Marsh upsets everyone again. Mea culpa.'

'So Katrina was devastated and you were looking for a way to make her feel better,' I said, turning back to the others.

Rowan nodded. 'Aunt Muriel had always been interested in the history and superstitions of the town and of our family.

We go back a long way in these parts. Some even say we were related to a witch who was burned here during the civil war.'

'How does it feel to be such an inbred hick, Rowan?' Ryan asked, and received a warning glare from his twin.

'Mother Godsole?' I said. 'Yes, I've read about her.'

'That's right,' Rowan confirmed. 'Some of the old legends say that the Cain Ravens up at the church are all descended from her original familiar. A demon imp called Lucky Wilt who kept her company and who would pluck out the eyes of any thief or murderer it came across. You can see how that legend gradually became connected with the six ravens kept at St Peter's and the superstition that they take revenge for any murder committed within their bounds. Anyway, even before Aunt Muriel's mind started to wander, she was fascinated by all those old tales. Right among her books on mathematics and geometry, she'd have volumes about the history and myths of the fen country.'

'And she'd scare us silly with them too,' Maddox said with a nostalgic smile. 'Phantom coaches haunting country lanes, demonic dogs stalking lost travellers.'

'So you learned the ritual of the sin-eaters from Muriel,' I said. 'A way to comfort a grieving, guilt-ridden sister.'

'It made her happy,' Ryan sighed. 'For a time, anyway.'

'But what possible sins could Jamie have?' I asked. 'He was only seven years old.'

'None, of course,' Rowan said. 'I mean yes, he'd swiped some of the drink from us, and as Ryan said, Jamie could be a bit of a brat, but it was really just to set Kat's mind at ease. You know what teenagers are like with nonsense like witchcraft and magic. Don't we all have a romantic period in our childhood where we believe impossible things might be true? I think we all . . .' She tailed off, blushed and lowered her head.

'We got a bit of a kick out of it,' Ryan said. 'It felt naughty, you know? Rebellious. Parading down into the woods at midnight, dressed in white sheets and making up bullshit phrases to speak over bits of bloody cake, then eating it all up like we were solemn practitioners of the dark arts. There was a kind of thrill to it.'

'Perhaps especially for the Sanctuarists?' I suggested. 'A ritual performed within sight of the church where Stuart's father preached as vicar. A man who would hate anything so pagan and sacrilegious happening on his doorstep.'

'Exactly,' Ryan said. 'Stu in particular loved that idea. It felt like flipping that prissy old fucker the middle finger.'

'And when Kat died, Wesley wanted you all to repeat the ritual. He brought along a piece of fruitcake to the pub after the wake?' They all nodded. 'A piece for each of you. But you didn't want to take part, why?'

'It was mostly Indira,' Maddox said. Absently, she took out that beautiful ruby-studded pin from her hair and let the tresses fall down her back, placing the pin – perhaps her own design – into her purse. 'Ind wouldn't hear of it. Said it was childish rubbish and that we'd only indulged Kat because she was so upset about Jamie. Wes was furious. He said we weren't doing it because of any belief of our own but in memory of Kat and what she might've wanted.'

'But none of you went along with him?'

'It was bloody freezing,' Ryan muttered. 'It had been a long, miserable day and the rest of us were happy where we were, sitting by the fire, sharing jokes and getting royally pissed.

Indira was right, it was a stupid idea. But, yes, I suppose we felt bad about it afterwards. We should have gone with him. One of us should have, anyway.'

I nodded. 'And not long after Wesley left, you all went your separate ways. Ryan, you went off with Lorelei Tey, Maddox with Rowan, Stuart with Indira. Tell me, did you all pair off naturally or was there some discussion about who fancied doing what?'

I wanted to see if any one of the pairings – the persecutor and their accomplice – had been particularly keen to stay together that night.

'It just sort of happened, didn't it?' Ryan said, his brow furrowed. 'I think we were all too squiffy by that point to plan anything properly. Before I knew what was happening, me and Lor were toddling off towards the town. Ended up walking all the way out to our old school.'

'And no one bothered to check in with Wesley, who'd just lost his best friend?'

'That's not fair,' Maddox said. 'I think Indira and Stuart went down to his mum's to see if he'd gone back there.'

'So they did,' I said. 'Approximately an hour after he left you all at the pub. And there was no sign of him at the cottage.'

I let the implication hang for a moment. That wherever Wes had disappeared to, he had most likely met his fate not long after he'd departed The Six Ravens, abandoned and alone.

'Tell me about your childhoods,' I said, leaning back in my chair. 'It seemed like a very close bond you all developed.'

'You must have heard it from the others.' Maddox shrugged.

'I'd like to hear it from you.'

'Mr Jericho seems to enjoy a good story, sis. It'd be rude not to indulge him. After all, he is poor Wesley's "cousin".' Ryan planted his elbows carelessly on that same plastic tablecloth for which he had shown such disdain. 'Looking back, I guess we hit it off right from our first meeting at Liz Fry Grammar. Me and Mads joined after our private school closed down. Some scandal involving a PE master and the hockey team from which the perverted soul of St Ignatius never recovered. But then, if Mr Harrington hadn't indulged his predilection for sniffing the girls' training bras after practice, Maddox and I would never have met these awful plebs.'

'Rein it in, Ryan,' Maddox muttered.

'But we really gelled that summer,' Ryan went on as if he hadn't heard. 'All working at Makepeace's together.'

'You two don't seem much like the summer job types,' I said.

'No, well, I didn't expect we'd take to it like we did either,' Maddox said. 'In fact, neither of us were supposed to be on the fair at all that summer. Ryan had been due to start work experience at a solicitor's firm in Norwich, but that didn't exactly pan out as planned.'

'Why not?'

'Talk started flying around about me getting into a fight in the woods,' Ryan said airily. 'They said I'd broken some kid's jaw because he called me a faggot.'

'And did you?'

'I did, as it happens.' He sat up, looking particularly proud. 'Some little shit-for-brains from school followed me home one afternoon, throwing stones and going through the usual homophobic handbook of stock phrases. He seemed to imagine that, as I wasn't shy about my sexuality, I'd be an easy target. One smack on the chin taught him differently. It was so delicious, how he went down, screaming like the little bitch he was. Our pa thought he'd hushed it all up. Paid the kid's family a grand or two to keep their mouths shut, but you can't keep anything quiet in a place like this. Someone sent an anonymous email to the solicitors' firm telling them all about it, so that was me out on my ear.'

'And you, Maddox?'

'I was lined up for an internship with a fashion designer in London. I'd worked incredibly hard on the application, flew through the interview and assessments, and ended up nailing the gig. It was a big deal. I was to be chaperoned and everything. Then I posted some stupid comment online, fat-shaming a young model who worked for the company. I realised it was a dumb thing to do almost immediately and deleted it straight away, but some arsehole screen-grabbed the post and sent it over to the company. Like Ryan, after that I was screwed.'

'Our parents were furious and said we had to work summer jobs, not lie around on our lazy arses all break,' Ryan said.

Maddox nodded. 'I think it was supposed to be punishment or character-building, having to work with the riffraff of Fenchurch. But we both ended up loving it, which of course made our folks even more furious. We cemented our friendship with the best people we'd ever known.' She smiled what I thought might be a genuine smile. 'Still the best.'

'But even so, it sounds like you all had some bad luck that summer,' I said. 'Stuart caught out smoking weed and his father told; Rowan having the authorities informed about her aunt and Muriel taken away by social services; Indira and Lorelei outed against their will and Wes with the story about him stealing from his sponsored swim.'

'That made me so angry,' Ryan seethed. 'For someone to accuse Wes of anything like that, it was a fucking scandal. You know he gave away a lot of the reward money that old Makepeace handed to him for trying to save Jamie? Thousands of it donated to charities. That's why he continued living like a pauper with his mother in that hovel of a cottage.'

'It does sound as if someone was deliberately targeting you all.' I looked carefully at each of them. 'All except Kat. She doesn't appear to have been persecuted, does she?'

'No,' Maddox admitted slowly. 'Except by her parents, I suppose. They never let her forget that stupid push.'

'But that was different,' I said. 'It doesn't fit the pattern of hounding that the rest of you experienced that summer.'

I continued to observe the trio of friends, half of the remaining Sanctuarists. Would one of them bite? Did they know about the legacy of torment inflicted on Kat over the past decade? When none of them responded, I tried another tack.

'Katrina Allingham kills herself on the same spot where her brother died a decade ago. She leaves no note, but it is suicide beyond any doubt. So why did she do it?'

Ryan threw up his hands. 'Because she was depressed. And still grieving. And her fucking parents would never let her forget it. Not everyone leaves a note before they tie a rope around their neck, don't you know that?'

'I know it very well.' I pushed on, 'Two weeks later, Kat is buried and Wesley goes missing. How was his mood that night, would you say?'

'I can't remember,' Ryan said with a petulant shrug. 'I was pissed out of my skull. Row? Maddox? The great detective wants to know: how was Wesley the night some mad fucker slit his throat, or whatever they did to him, then chucked him inside a wall? Or maybe they stole one of Row's lethal knitting needles and plunged it into his heart.'

Illustrating the suggestion, Ryan thrust his hand into Rowan's string bag and brandished a wooden needle like a dagger. Rowan took it back with a muttered, 'That's not mine. It's from my knit and natter group at the library. We've just had a meeting and one of the ladies left it behind.'

'Knit and natter. God save us,' Ryan sighed, giving his friend a pitying look.

'Wesley was sad and angry,' Maddox said. 'He loved Kat, and he couldn't understand what had happened to her.'

'And he wanted you all to perform the sin-eating ritual, perhaps to help him make sense of it. But you refused.'

'Right,' Ryan said. 'And we're terrible people. Is that what you want to hear?'

'But I think that maybe one of you *did* indulge him,' I said slowly. 'After the pub, one of you wandered away from the rest of the group, met Wesley in the woods, and then that person killed him.'

'You don't know it was one of us,' Rowan objected.

Ryan leaned across the table. 'No, let him speak. Tell us more, oh great detective. What do you think happened to Wes that night?'

'I think it's possible that you already know, or that you've guessed. Stuart *must* have been involved.'

'No! Stuart is kind, gentle,' Rowan insisted. 'He would never—'

'But he's right,' Ryan interrupted her. 'Think it through, it must've been Stu. He was the only one who could have put

Wes in the wall or whatever it was. Working up there, the way he did, who else could it have been? And after all, they were fairly argumentative, Row, you have to admit that. When Stu came back here, he was pissed off that he couldn't fund himself straight through uni without having to work up at the church. Burying himself away in this dead-end town again. And there was Wes, like some ghost of the past, always teasing his dad, always content with his own lot. No wonder they had a barny or two.'

'Is that what you think, Maddox?' I asked. 'That Stuart battered your friend to death and bricked him up inside a pillar?'

'I suppose . . .' she hesitated. 'I mean, I suppose it's the only thing that makes sense.'

'But?'

'I'm sorry?'

'It felt like there was a "but" coming there.'

'No.' She squared those broad shoulders. 'No but.'

'He wouldn't,' said Rowan. *'He wouldn't.'*

'The thing is, if it was him, the police don't think that Stuart could have acted alone,' I told them. 'So who was his accomplice? Stuart spent the entire evening with Indira, if your testimonies regarding how you all paired off are accurate. So what do you think of Indira as a killer?'

'Never,' Ryan said without hesitation.

'No,' Rowan agreed.

'Not a chance,' Maddox said. 'Ind is many things, but she could never kill anyone. Not in cold blood.'

'It's funny, you all being so adamant about Indira's innocence and yet so certain of Stuart's guilt. At least two of you seem certain.' I looked at Maddox and Ryan before turning to Rowan.

'But if Stuart did it, then Indira must be at least an accessory to the murder. According to Indira herself, they spent the whole night together.' I took a long breath. 'Where is Stuart McDonald?'

They all blinked back at me, silent as the grave.

'You don't know. You have no idea. One of your dearest friends and ... not a word.'

I gave Webster a gentle tug and he emerged slowly from under the table. Before heading for the door, I laid down two twenties on the table.

'Coffee and cake on me. You know, you really should try the fruitcake, it's a revelation.'

Chapter Thirty-Six

THE LATE MORNING DRONE OF The Bluebird was immediately muted by the wind as I stepped back onto the prom. No sign of Tom Makepeace and his husband Mike. In fact, it was as if the light December drizzle had scrubbed the seafront of all life.

I turned my face to the high street, intending to brave the elements and take another look at that spot in Chattox Wood where two members of the Allingham family, and perhaps Wesley Sayers himself, had died. But it was no good. After a step or two, I knew I was done. A sleepless night, coupled with constant pain from my hip, had finally taken its toll. And so I trudged back through town in the direction of the pub, my brain blurred by the fog of exhaustion. I noticed things only in fleeting glimpses; chaps at work behind the huge gate of the fair, testing rides and stalls before tomorrow's opening, silent lights running like coloured water down their rain-slick ponchos.

What did I make of the Marsh twins? Was Ryan's heartlessness just a little too arch? Was Maddox's weary outrage at his antics just a little too staged? It was as if I'd witnessed a rehearsed two-hander in which Rowan had failed to find her own role. But still, the story remained as clear as ever. The Sanctuarists had stayed at the pub while Wesley vanished into the night, angry that no one would follow his lead and perform the ritual that had meant so much to their dead friend. Only he had stood by her to the end, Kat's champion and defender even in death.

Yet one of the three pairs must have peeled away and gone to meet him. Had it been an arranged rendezvous or a chance encounter? If the former, then it must have been set up after Wes left the pub or else why would he have invited the entire group? Unless he'd wanted to expose Kat's persecutor in front of them all. If it had been a chance encounter, however, then did that suggest an impromptu, unpremeditated killing, as I had already imagined it? The murderers stumble across Wes in the forest, he confronts one of them, the killing is done and a handy burial site settled on.

In either case, I kept coming back to the same thought: Stuart had to be involved in at least the burial and, therefore, Indira must be firmly in the frame. It was then that another possibility struck me: what if Wesley's phone call to his mother that night was nothing of the kind. Perhaps he had contacted Reverend McDonald because *he was the person he wished to speak to*, not Miss Westmacott. The vicar only makes a show of taking the mobile down to the Sayers' cottage to provide himself with a cover story for the call. Wesley arranges to meet McDonald in the privacy of the woods, there challenging him with what he knows: the vicar of St Peter's hounded Katrina Allingham to her death. After all, who better than a clergyman, with visions of damnation and hellfire, to play on a tormented girl's conscience?

McDonald strikes out and kills Wesley, but he isn't strong enough to carry the corpse up the hill and conceal it himself.

But he has a strapping young son on hand. Did this explain the animosity Stuart bore his father? That he had been made complicit in the murder of one of his dearest friends? But the question then arose, why would McDonald persecute the girl at all? What would he get out of it? Unless the man's well-attested puritanism had become a mania, and he saw himself as an instrument of some divine justice.

Before I knew it, I'd reached the back door of the pub, hauled myself upstairs and fallen gratefully into bed. I sensed Webster snuffling around the room until he finally took my lead and collapsed beside me. At first, my sleep was deep and dreamless, no shadows to parade across the unlit stage of my conscience. Just the same kind of merciful blankness that I had experienced during my weeks in a coma.

A blissful oblivion.

I eventually stirred to the tap of what sounded like long, sharpened fingernails at the window. An insistent and irregular *tat-tat – a-tat-tat – tat-a-tat*, like the ticking of a broken clock. In my mind's eye, I saw nicotine-stained talons scratching the glass.

Blinking the room into focus, I caught the glint of a bird's beak hit the pane. A hoarse cawing echoed in the street outside and Webster lifted his heavy head and barked back at the raven. Startled, the guardian of St Peter's spread its wings and, in the next instant, was gone. I watched the bird float to the heights of its tower, moonlight gleaming like oil on its feathers. Then it was lost again among the stone angels and grotesques.

I pulled my phone from the bedside table and checked the time. 5.47 p.m. and already dark outside. I'd managed almost six uninterrupted hours and felt refreshed enough to take a stroll. Out for the count again, I left Webster snoring away to his heart's content and limped my way downstairs.

I met the landlord in the hall, newspaper and sticks cradled in his arms. 'Fire in the main bar is going out,' he muttered. 'She who must be obeyed is on the warpath. She took the news this morning very hard. Wesley was always a great favourite of the missus.' He spoke without any obvious sign of jealousy and I wondered if he very much cared what Mrs Berkeley got up to, as long as it provided him with a quiet afternoon of fishing. He looked disappointed when I told him Webster was taking a nap. 'With your permission, I'll look in later and maybe bring him a bowl of something. Poor old fella. Our Maisie passed away this summer and she had that same look about her. I reckon they know the end's coming long before we like to admit it, and their sorrow's more for us than themselves. They wonder how we'll ever cope without them.'

His words might have annoyed me. I had seen the look he mentioned, as well as the way the old juk's hind legs trembled at the slightest effort, but Mr Berkeley had spoken with such sadness I couldn't hold it against him. Instead, I asked a question that had been scratching away at the back of my mind.

'Do you do much fishing in the Old Demdike?'

'Of course,' he said, his expression brightening. 'Get a nice bit of perch and roach down there. I can show you some of the best spots, if you like?'

'What kind of river is it?' I asked. He looked at me blankly. 'I mean, does it have particular currents and eddies or whatever they're called.'

His smile became a little patronising. 'Can tell you're not an angling man, Mr Jericho. One look at the Demdike should tell you it's a tidal river, and so the main run of it is dictated by the sea. High and low tides, you get me? And then there's the slack tide which in general comes after the high in the early afternoon. That's when it's safest to get right in and do a bit of angling in your waders and waterproofs.'

'I see, very interesting, thank you.' He blinked dumbly at me as I put my next question. 'I don't suppose you could lend me a torch?'

The weather had cleared and a bright, cloudless evening capped the seaside town. As I made my way around the foot of the hill, I saw that the journalists and news crews from earlier had all packed up and abandoned their spot at the lychgate. Now only a handful of police remained outside the church, locking the great door and strapping blue and white tape across the entrance. I guessed that the body had been removed hours ago and the forensic teams were now at work in their labs. There was no sign of Tallis among the uniformed officers who strolled wearily down the hill towards their waiting cars.

Something had been bothering me throughout the day. A half-realised discovery I felt I might have made during my first visit to the scene of the Allingham tragedies. And so, I now retraced my steps into the wood. As the last streetlight faded among the trees, I pulled the landlord's torch from my pocket and clicked the switch. As I'd hoped, it was a much stronger beam than the measly illumination my phone could muster.

It pierced a path through dense shadow thrown by oak and alder. As I walked, my gaze swept those spaces between the trunks, expecting at any moment the hooded man might make his appearance. It struck me then that I was being hunted as surely as the figure from Katrina's poem, perhaps even as surely as the victims of the minotaur from Stuart McDonald's painting. But was I fleeing Peter Garris, down the nights and down the days, or rushing on to meet him?

It was not the livid face of my old mentor that glanced at me from among the shivering branches, however, but Muriel's paper boys. Those two-dimensional representations of the drowned Jamie Allingham, which must have haunted Kat as much as her persecutor. I walked beneath a host of them now, each snipped and shaped from pamphlets and fliers, birthday cards and old letters, every pale body tattooed with faded ink.

The chuckle of the river told me that I'd reached the spot. I could see that it was still high tide, or perhaps 'slack tide' as my friend the landlord described it, the crystal-clear water running sluggish and almost overflowing the bank. Still at the foot of the suicide oak sat the floral tribute to Kat left by the Sanctuarists, blue hydrangea and purple hyacinth and the card reading, 'We'll never forget. Sleep well now, darling Kat.' Signed on behalf of all, except Indira.

My gaze moved on, skating along the bank until, yes, there it was – a mark in the ground, a shallow depression about the size of my fist.

I turned and trained my torch on the river, leaning out as far as I could. It took a minute or two to be certain, even with water this clear the flow and eddy could easily deceive the eye, proportions of objects on the riverbed distorted and magnified. But finally I felt sure of what I'd found. And so, taking out my phone, I put in a call to Thomas Tallis.

Chapter Thirty-Seven

'You'll need to retrieve it, of course,' I said. 'But as you can see, it's the only stone of that size on the riverbed. My guess is that it will match perfectly with the depression here.'

I pointed to the mark left in the earth, a stone's throw, fittingly enough, from the bank. 'See how the rough oval of ground at this spot is a deeper, richer brown than the area immediately surrounding it? The stone rested here until at least or month or two ago.' I trained my torch into the depths of the river. 'And look at the other rocks at the bottom there, all covered and furred with moss and lichen. That would take some time. Our stone is practically clean.'

Tallis nodded, shining his own torch around the glade. 'So you think Wesley was killed here, hit with a rock that was then disposed of by chucking it in the river?'

'In a panic, yes. Which suggests it wasn't a premeditated murder. No weapon was brought with the killer, they made use of what they found. There was also the forest leaf caught up in Wesley's hair, remember? Killed here and then carried up to the church.'

'Hit from behind,' Tallis said. 'But not only hit. Some implement was used to stab him through the eye.'

'Perhaps something as simple as a stick or the end of a branch?' I suggested.

'Well, I have some news for you on that score. Early forensic results, all very rough and preliminary, but interesting nonetheless.' Tallis took out his phone, scrolled for a while and then began reading highlights from the report. 'There was some minor bruising to his upper arms and chest but no defensive wounds to the hands. Perhaps indicating a tussle but not an attack with any sharp object, at least not initially.'

'Wesley confronts the persecutor, tells them he knows the truth about how they tormented Kat, there's a fight and the persecutor's accomplice strikes him from behind,' I said. 'Or the accomplice says something, distracting Wesley, and the persecutor picks up the rock and strikes him himself. But what about the eye?'

'The head wound was caused by a blunt object, "roughly fist-sized",' Tallis told me, glancing up from his phone. 'And I suppose we now have a prime candidate for that particular weapon, though I doubt there'll be any useful forensics we can pull from it, after so long in the water.' He returned his attention to the report. 'A stunning blow to the occipital bone but not fatal in itself. The eye was punctured by something long and sharp that penetrated right through the ocular socket, glancing against the inferior frontal gyrus. Some kind of long thin dagger, they suggest, not serrated. That was the killing wound. Death caused by trauma to the frontal part of the brain and resultant blood loss. There were some traces of brick dust inside the ocular socket, but the pathologist thinks that was post-mortem penetration. Basically, particles of stone from inside the pillar wafting into the wound after death. But here's the interesting bit. Right at the back where the eye had been stabbed through, they found a fragment of a petal.'

I stared at him. 'Do they know what kind of flower it came from?'

Tallis glanced again at his phone. 'They think a petunia. Does that mean anything?'

'It could,' I said, consulting my own mobile. After a brief online search, I pointed to the floral tribute at the foot of the suicide tree. 'Blue hydrangea and purple hyacinth. According to the language of flowers, the hydrangea symbolises regret and remorse while the hyacinth means forgiveness.' I explained to him the poster I'd seen on the wall of Lorelei's florist shop and her explanation of the Victorian pastime of giving secret meaning to flowers. 'From what I can find online, the petunia signifies "anger and resentment". The question is, was it placed inside the wound deliberately?'

'Surely,' Tallis said. 'How could it possibly have got there accidentally?'

I shook my head. 'I don't know. But if it was deliberate then the implication is clear. It suggests that we're wrong. That the killing *was* premediated, the flower petal a prearranged artefact to be left with the body. A message being sent, at least to Wesley Sayers himself. Anger and resentment. Maybe the persecutor was enraged that he had been found out. Or perhaps resentful that his victim had removed herself from his power by taking her own life.'

'You don't look satisfied with that,' Tallis observed.

'I'm not. You see, I still can't shake the idea that this *wasn't* a planned killing but something more impromptu. The hiding of the body feels panicked and clumsy, doesn't it? And the use of a stone found here at the murder site is suggestive of that, too. But then the petunia points in the other direction. It also guides us back towards the pairing of Indira and Stuart as the killers. Apart from Lorelei, Indira was most familiar with the language of flowers from her co-ownership of the florist. And she and Stuart admitted visiting the Sayers' cottage that night, perhaps to search for any incriminating evidence left by Kat that Indira was her persecutor.' But I was still dissatisfied. 'What about Wesley's phone? Any joy with that?'

'Our tech guys got into it easily enough,' Tallis said. 'The last call was placed by Wesley at 11.56 to Mr McDonald, just as the reverend told us. It lasted around thirteen minutes and was cancelled by Wesley himself. No calls after that time, so he doesn't appear to have phoned any of the group to meet him here in the woods.'

I nodded. 'Which fits with the vicar's account. He receives the call, gets out of bed, dresses and takes the phone down the road to Miss Westmacott while Wes is still on the line. That would probably have taken all of thirteen minutes. It also means Indira and Stuart couldn't have killed him before they visited the cottage at around 11.40. Yet if we think that visit was to search for incriminating evidence against them, the timings make no sense. The confrontation and murder obviously couldn't have happened until after midnight and Wesley's call to McDonald.'

'And why did Wesley cancel the call himself before speaking to his mother?' Tallis asked.

'Perhaps because someone had arrived to meet him here, and whatever he wanted to say to his mum could wait. This was his priority now, to confront the persecutor.'

'But what was it that he wanted to tell her so urgently?'

'Maybe the identity of the person who'd just arrived,' I suggested. 'Perhaps he was worried that they might be a threat to himself or to others he cared about. He wanted their identity known but before he could tell Miss Westmacott, the confrontation begins. Let's imagine Indira and Stuart suspected that Wesley knew something about their persecution of Kat. He leaves the pub alone and they team up to search for him. They naturally visit his cottage first, but he's not there. Then they stumble across him in the woods during the call to his mum; they argue, and they kill him. But why not then return to the cottage to make a search for any evidence that could implicate them?'

'Perhaps they did,' Tallis said. 'You showed me how those locks on his bedroom window weren't all that secure.'

'I suppose that makes sense,' I admitted. 'What about any calls earlier in the day?'

'None since first thing that morning,' Tallis said. 'And that was just to rearrange a dentist appointment, nothing significant. The phone battery died about fourteen hours after the last call to McDonald.'

'While he was dead and buried inside the pillar. Yes. In their panic, the killers must have forgotten about the phone. Then, once they realised, I can easily imagine a traumatised Stuart refusing to disinter his old friend to retrieve it. Anyway, it was a Friday, and so no one apart from Stuart would likely be in the church until early Sunday morning. The killers would bank on the battery dying long before then.' I suppressed a shudder. 'Imagine if they'd been wrong? A phone call coming through for the dead man, possibly from his distressed mother, during morning hymns or the vicar's Sunday sermon. Heads turning this way and that, the reverend outraged, and the phone chirruping merrily away inside the pillar.' I looked at Tallis. 'Has there been any sign of Stuart?'

'None. We've got a watch on his bank accounts and mobile activity, but there've been no flags as yet. The town itself is forested with CCTV; I've got a small team going through most of it. No sign of him so far, but there's not much surveillance on the roads leading out of Fenchurch and this forest stretches a little inland. He could have trekked that way and we wouldn't necessarily pick him up.'

As we wandered together out of the woods, Tallis put through a call to get forensics back to retrieve the stone from the river and make a sweep for any physical evidence and possible blood splatter.

'It has to be done, but I don't imagine they'll turn up much of anything,' he said. 'After almost two months of autumn rain and winter sleet, wild animals picking over the site, dog walkers and hikers, you could douse that riverbank with a truckload of luminol and be lucky to pick up a single spot of blood.'

Before parting, I filled Tallis in on my own discoveries. My meeting with Mike and old Tom Makepeace, my conversation in The Bluebird tea-shop with Rowan and the Marsh twins, my theory that Wesley's phone call might not have been to his mother but to Reverend McDonald and that the vicar could be our killer.

'Not that I have any evidence for such an idea,' I told him. 'It's just a possibility. That's the trouble with this case — it's all theories, nothing concrete. You take a step in one direction and the ground falls away from under you, like the sinking sands that used to drown the old fen fishermen before the land here was drained. Nothing feels real or solid in Fenchurch.'

Tallis nodded. 'I know what you mean. Rites and rituals, corpses in pillars, a girl tormented to her death and ravens guarding a tower.'

'Have you managed to speak to the others yet?' I asked.

'Only Lorelei and Indira.'

'What did you think of them?'

'Indira is formidable, Lorelei a little vague. They're committed to this new business venture of theirs, and they both adore their daughter, no question about that. I don't usually give my opinion on potential suspects, but I liked them.'

I nodded. 'Me too. I like all of them. Even Ryan Marsh has a certain dickish charm.'

'By the way, she mentioned that floral tribute down there by the tree,' Tallis said.

'You mean Lorelei?'

'No.' He surprised me. 'Indira. She said she'd asked Rowan to leave her name off the card because she thought such things were silly, even though her wife had arranged the bouquet. She said it quite casually as I was leaving. Perhaps too casually, like she'd been saving it up to slip into the conversation when she could. "The dead don't care whether we leave them tokens," those were her words.'

'Interesting. I wonder why she decided to volunteer that information.'

Tallis shrugged. 'She might be worried that we would notice something like that. Her name so obviously missing from the card. It doesn't mean that she did anything necessarily, but she'd realised it might look bad. Probably just wanted to get her explanation in. She also said that the same belief motivated her objection to Wesley's suggestion they go off that night and perform the ritual. She said that it was the most absurd nonsense and that they oughtn't to tarnish Kat's memory with such stupidity.'

'Did she tell you what the ritual involved?' I asked.

'She did. The rite of the sin-eater. I looked up the bare bones of it online afterwards.'

'She's become very forthcoming all of a sudden,' I said. 'When did you interview her?'

'Early this afternoon. Is that significant?'

'I'm not sure. Possibly. What about Muriel?'

He shook his head. 'Rowan is her legal guardian and she objected in the strongest terms to an interview. Said that it would upset her aunt and possibly put frightening ideas in her head. I did manage a very brief talk with the poor lady, and I'm inclined to agree. Unless we've got some concrete evidence that she witnessed Wesley's murder, then I can't see us being given carte blanche to interview her.

'By the way, that stuff about the language of flowers? If the killer used the petunia to indicate rage and resentment, what does the floral tribute left at the tree mean? Regret and remorse? They felt bad for what had happened to Katrina, they're upset and grieving, sure. But those words suggest to me that they might've blamed themselves for what happened to her.'

'Maybe.' I nodded. 'Oh, and before I discreetly vanish and leave you to your forensic buddies, I should say: Tom Makepeace seems to think he knows who's behind all this.'

Tallis raised an eyebrow. 'He told you?'

'Not exactly. But he sort of hinted that either or both of the Marsh twins might be involved. Not that I think you'll get him to give a statement to that effect. Showpeople aren't exactly talkative around gavvers.'

'Aren't they?' Tallis smiled. 'I know at least one exception to that rule.'

Chapter Thirty-Eight

I LEFT TALLIS AT THE EDGE of the woods and plodded back to The Six Ravens. It was now early evening and the bar was full of locals, all feverishly speculating on the day's events. Mrs Berkeley looked to be in her element, buzzing from table to table, dispensing crumbs of dismay and lurid speculation. I placed the landlord's torch onto the bar and slipped away unnoticed.

Upstairs, I found Webster happily tucking in to the bowl of chow promised by the landlord; a cold club sandwich, a can of Coke and a packet of crisps left for me on the bedside table, together with a scribbled note: 'Thought you might fancy something away from the crowds.' I sat on the edge of the bed and sighed gratefully.

'You're a good man, Mr B.'

Ignored by a preoccupied Webster, I slid a slightly greasy cocktail stick from the centre of the club, and then spent the next minute staring at that little wooden prong.

'Some kind of long thin dagger, not serrated,' I whispered to myself. A weapon like the rock, not deliberately brought to the scene but handy nonetheless, if the killing was unpremeditated. A parade of macabre possibilities passed through my mind, each unlikely but nonetheless feasible.

Rowan is our killer. Her accomplice, Maddox Marsh, strikes Wesley with the rock, the man falls and begins to spasm on the ground. Rowan is appalled, frightened, she wants it to stop. She reaches into her string bag and brings out a stray needle from her knit and natter group. It only takes a little courage and effort, and her childhood friend lies still and dead. Or what of Maddox herself? Rowan is now the accomplice who strikes with the stone, but Wesley isn't killed outright. Rowan is scared; it was too feeble a blow. And so Maddox calmly removes the jewelled pin from her hair, a thing of beauty, her own design, and plunges it into her friend's eye. Next up, Indira Bakshi. Wesley confronts her with the truth of her persecution of Kat, they begin to struggle, and Stuart fells him from behind with the rock. Wesley isn't killed outright and so Indira reaches into her pocket and finds a stray tent peg from the glamping site. She drives the sharpened prong home and all is still. Onto Stuart. The roles are reversed again. Stuart struggles with Wesley, Indira strikes the back of his head and Stuart then brings out the fateful ice-pick he uses to chop away at the ravens' frozen meat, a handy tool and just right to puncture his friend's ocular socket, grazing the brain beneath. And what of Lorelei? I picture the florist's needle she had used in my presence to keep her arrangements in place, thin and sharp, perfect for the job at hand. Her accomplice in this scenario is Ryan Marsh, and what suitable stiletto-like implement might he have on his person? A letter opener from his office, perhaps?

I shook my head and threw the cocktail stick back onto the plate. They had been at the funeral all day; apart from Maddox and her hair pin, was it likely that any of them would have such bizarre weapons on their person? And what of the fragment of petunia found inside Wesley's eye? Would the Sanctuarists have been carrying around something like that, if the killing was in the heat of the moment?

I groaned and fell back onto the bed, my appetite gone. I needed to stop thinking about the case. It was a sage piece of wisdom given to me by Garris half a lifetime ago. If you keep worrying at the threads of a mystery, they will only become increasingly entangled. Best leave them be and take a step away. Think about something else.

Fortunately, a distraction presented itself almost immediately. My phone rang. Again, that familiar twist of anxiety as I clocked the caller ID.

'Hello stranger,' I sighed. 'How're things?'

'How are *you*, darling?' Harry asked. I could hear the concern in his voice. 'Listen, are you near a TV? Better switch on, Scott Jericho, you're national news.'

I sat up, scrabbling around for the remote. It took an eternity for the prehistoric television to blink into life. After a bit of surfing through disorganised channels, I finally found the right station and the scrum of reporters from earlier today crowded the screen.

A sea of heads and bobbing microphones all gathered around the church gate. And then the youthful Thomas Tallis and my own coma-ravaged features hove into view. The questions rang out again, this time through crackling speakers: 'Is it true that the body of a young man was found walled up alive inside the church?' The babble continued as before, and I saw my expression darken as the reporters recognised me: 'Scott Jericho, isn't it? Can we ask, what are you doing here, sir?' 'Have the police called you in to consult on the case, Mr Jericho?'

The scene switched to a calmer shot of St Peter's later in the day. Forensics milling around the tent outside the church doorway, a body bag carried down the gravestone path and deposited in the back of a refrigerated truck. Then the camera focused on a sombre-looking journalist.

'The victim has now been formally identified as twenty-five-year-old resident of Fenchurch, Wesley Sayers. No definite cause of death has been released to the press, although it appears the victim suffered a blow to the back of the head. This took place sometime after a funeral attended by the deceased and a number of old school friends. The body then appears to have been concealed within the structure of the church behind me.' The journo turned and pointed unnecessarily to the tower, at that moment haloed by a circle of ravens. 'Police are keen to interview one Stuart McDonald, friend of the dead man and son of the local vicar.' A downward glance to consult his notes. 'Reverend R.C. McDonald. Mr Stuart McDonald has not been seen since yesterday and, while the police advise that he is not yet a suspect in the case, the public should approach him with caution.'

A beaming photograph of Stuart appeared momentarily on screen. It really was difficult to picture that gentle giant as a threat to anyone, and yet it was right to advise caution. There was, after all, no getting away from the fact that Stuart remained the prime suspect in a vicious and violent murder.

'It has also come to the media's attention that Mr Scott Jericho has taken an interest in the case,' the journalist continued. 'Viewers might remember Mr Jericho in connection with the "psychic serial killer mystery" that baffled the authorities only a few months ago. Mr Jericho, a disgraced former

CID detective, was able to help the police solve that case, and so the question must now be posed: what is the so-called "showman detective" doing in Fenchurch-on-Sea, and will he be able to capture the killer before the police?'

I muted the TV and closed my eyes. 'Fuck.'

'I'm sorry, my love. And I hate to tell you, but the story's already blowing up online. I know you don't follow all that bullshit, and I'm glad you don't.' Harry was right; I'd never had so much as a Facebook account. 'Predictably, half the world is rooting for you while the other half think you should be arrested for interfering with a police investigation. Anyway, ignore the noise. How're you doing?'

'I'm fine,' I said.

And maybe that ought to have worried me. Was it normal to be fine after discovering a month-old corpse bricked up inside a church? Not just fine either but exhilarated by the discovery. When Harry tried to interrogate me further, I diverted the conversation.

'What about you and Ben? How are you getting on? I tried calling earlier.'

'I know, I'm sorry. We've had a hellish day. I was driving when you called and then we hit a big wall of nothing in Colchester. Despite our best efforts, no one from his old army barracks would talk to us about Garris. We were even escorted off the premises by the military police.'

'Good lad.' I grinned.

'We tried asking around the town, but even the regulars in the squaddie pubs here don't remember Garris ever popping in for a pint. Which is apparently very unusual. There was one old landlord at a place called The Battle of the Nile, used to be an infantryman himself and takes pride in his memory for all the recruits who've passed through Colchester over the years. Even the few teetotallers from the barracks go to the Nile once or twice. It's like a rite of passage, he told us. There's a helmet on the bar from the Battle of the Somme that the soldiers tap three times for luck. "We're a superstitious breed," the landlord said, "and there aren't many that don't poke their head in the Nile to give that battle bowler a tap." But he couldn't remember anyone by the name of Peter Garris.'

'Despite the fact that Garris definitely trained there,' I said.

'Definitely,' Harry confirmed. 'It wasn't him stealing someone else's identity this time. I found a picture of Garris and his squad taken for the *Colchester Evening Standard* after they did a charity run for a local hospice. Wait a sec, I'll send it through.'

My phone pinged and I opened the attachment. The black and white shot was a little blurry and it took me a second or two to pick out the youthful, raw-boned Garris among his fellow recruits. As ever, he stood somewhat apart from the rest, a smile that I now recognised as an early rehearsal at humanity creasing his features.

'So he kept a low profile while training,' I said. 'Of course he did. If he was already killing back then, he would've made sure his activities were always well away from the barracks. Any violent deaths in an army town, the police inevitably focus on the local squaddies, whether that's fair or not. So what next?'

'We're moving on,' Harry said. 'Looking into his first official posting as a uniformed constable after he left the forces. I've already made contact with his old landlady in Hampstead, we're going to interview her tomorrow.'

'Hampstead.' I smiled. 'We wintered there often when I was a kid. All right, well you know what I'm going to say.'

'Be careful. We will.'

'And give my regards to Ben. Is he coping all right?'

'I'm fine, Scott!' A voice called as if from across a room. 'And I'm looking after him, so don't you worry none.'

We said our goodnights and I stretched back onto the bed, the image Harry had sent over ghosting the darkness behind my closed lids. Garris as a young man. Again, the idea of him having any life before I'd met him seemed strange.

A knock at the door, so polite that at first I hardly noticed it. I groaned onto my side and called out, 'Cheers for the sandwich and crisps, Mr B. Just pop it all on my tab. I don't need anything else, thank you.'

Again, that feeble *rat-tat-tat*, a little like the raven's beak at the window.

'I said I'm fine, thanks. I really don't need anything else. I'll probably just hit the hay and—'

Rat-a-tat-tat.

'Is that you, Mrs Berkeley? Is there something I can help you with?'

I stared up at the ceiling, listened to the throb of conversation from the bar downstairs. Up on the hill, the church clock tolled the quarter hour. Nine fifteen and all is well, or as well as it can be right now in Fenchurch-on-Sea. I looked back at the door. Maybe my hosts had been called away. Finally, I pulled myself upright and started towards the bathroom. A wash, a shave and an early night were called for. Perhaps the answers I was seeking would come to me, unjumbled by my dreams.

It was around fifteen minutes later, as I was stepping out of the bathroom, that I noticed the paper pushed under my door. A full sheet torn from an exercise book, I could see the letters scratched into the page from here. I limped across the room and snatched it up, unfolding and reading. Just my name printed in shaky characters: *SCOTT JERICHO*. In my mind, I could hear the echo of Garris's weakened rasp struggling over those syllables. I threw open the door, already knowing that I'd find the hallway empty.

'What do you want, Pete?' I whispered to the shadows and looked down again at the note in my hand. The letters so clumsily formed, like an infant's scrawl, it was impossible to tell whether he had written them or not. But it *must* be him, mustn't it? The gaunt, hooded scarecrow that dogged me.

'Handwriting,' I murmured to myself, hardly understanding why. 'Notes left behind, waiting to be found …'

Chapter Thirty-Nine

I WOKE IN THE WOODS, THE shape of a huge tree yawning overhead. Shafts of winter sunlight shivered through skeletal branches and framed that swaying bough. The river's hollow laughter came to me gradually, defining itself against the creak of the forest and the sough of the wind.

I rolled onto my side and took a gasp of freezing air, my hand moving automatically to the back of my head. I raised it to the light, fingers splayed like the twigs of the oak, and saw my blood almost black against the glare. I wondered at first if I was dreaming. And then a playing deck of memories shuffled in my mind. The first that I drew from the pack was of waking at around eight o'clock this morning, Garris's note still clasped in my hand. I'd showered and dressed and took a lumbering Webster for a stroll through town.

I'd met the vicar at the church lychgate, McDonald trembling inside his thin tweed jacket. His words came to me, fragmented and thickened by the pain that now pulsed through my skull.

'Still no sign of Stuart. I'm worried sick. I'm being looked after by Miss Westmacott. United in our grief and troubles.'

All at once, the memory sharpened like a blade and I winced against it: my hand clasped tight around Webster's lead, the juk shying away from the vicar's caress.

'That's very generous of Miss Westmacott,' I said. 'She must know the police suspect Stuart of being involved in Wesley's death.'

'She doesn't believe it,' McDonald said, drawing himself up. 'No one who knew my boy would ever believe such a wicked lie. Stuart was the gentlest of souls.'

I nodded. 'Rowan said the same thing.'

'And what do you believe, Mr Jericho?' he asked, his tone half hopeful, half derisory. 'I hear that you're actually some kind of fairground detective, whatever that means.'

I smiled at him. 'I hardly know myself most of the time. But as to your son, I've known dozens of killers, Mr McDonald, and while it's true that some of their disguises are brilliant, I don't believe Stuart is one of them.'

'Thank you,' he murmured. 'Thank you.'

Another memory drawn from the pack. Lying there beneath the oak, I couldn't be sure if it came before or after my conversation with the vicar. It's a morsel, an inconsequential crumb. A group of women waiting for the bus, shrewd eyes watching us as Webster and I lingered around a particularly fascinating lamppost.

'I've agreed to help out Lorelei Tey up at her shop,' one of them said in a preening sort of voice. 'Miss Westmacott can't be expected to, not with everything that's going on.'

Another of the harridans agreed, 'Poor lamb doesn't even bake these days. Bide my words, that woman is heading for a breakdown.'

They all tutted and clucked.

'Anyway, did you know that the Marsh twins are back in town? Swanning around like they're on a catwalk. Indecent,

I call it. And they aren't the only indecent ones in the place. Old Tom Makepeace might well be dying, but that doesn't mean we have to watch that husband of his pushing him up and down the prom, kissing him in broad daylight.'

Another card is pulled from the deck, this memory plucked from a point contemporary with the delightful harridans' gossip. Tom Makepeace trundling up to the bus stop, Mike piloting him with an assured grip.

'Ladies,' he croaked, and three wagging tongues were stilled. A flier was graciously accepted by each, together with a promise to attend the opening of the Winter Wonderland that afternoon.

'Anything to help with the church restoration, of course,' one purred. 'How kind of you, dear Tom.'

Then Uncle Tommy was wheeled over to Webster's lamppost – the juk had claimed it with a proprietorial cock of the leg.

'Nasty old crones.' Tommy smiled. 'But their posh is as good as anyone's. We'll see you later, Scott?'

I'd nodded. 'Sure thing.'

Another card pulled seemingly at random: I am in Wesley's bedroom, sometime today but no notion of exactly when and with no clear memory of Miss Westmacott letting me into the house. I stood in the centre of the room, something clawing at my mind. In my hand, the pink cardboard folder left to Wes by the dead girl, flowery words inscribed on the front: 'For Wes, to have always in memory of me. Please, don't ever forget me. I know you won't. Kat x'

Notes, letters.

I had seen this handwriting somewhere before ...

Another shift, another card drawn. Lorelei, Indira and their daughter walking along the beach. Waves hushing against the shingle shore, the little girl playing chicken with the tide. A joyous Webster dashing with her as fast as his quaky hind legs would carry him.

Lorelei mid-sentence: 'Yes, we feel very lucky to have been blessed with her. Gracie is our life.'

Indira, allowing herself an indulgent smile.

The light changed, a cloud passing over the sun.

'So you've no idea where Stuart might be?' I asked them. Heads were shaken. 'The police think he could be involved in covering up the murder. But he was with you all night, wasn't he, Indira?'

'Not *all* night,' she corrected me. 'I fell asleep around 3 a.m., didn't wake again until dawn. He could've gone off then to meet Wes.'

'So you think it's possible that Stuart killed him?'

A shrug from Indira; Lorelei examined the bounty of shells in the bucket hanging from her wrist. Treasure collected by their daughter.

'Such a pretty name, Grace,' I said. 'What with her being adopted, I suppose you couldn't have changed it, even if you wanted to?'

'What do you mean?' Indira asked.

'Nothing. Only that you're so fond of flowers, Lorelei. Maybe you'd have liked something more floral. Like Rose or Hyacinth or Petunia.'

'Petunia?' Indira almost laughed. 'Are people still calling children that?'

A final card: I am back in Chattox Wood, some sense that this was immediately after my visit to the Sayers' cottage. Webster is no longer at my side. I feel sure that I'd returned him to The Six Ravens, that Mr Berkeley had ushered the hungry juk into the kitchen.

'The wife's napping upstairs, so we should be safe enough. You go off and do what you need to, Mr Jericho.'

And so I was alone as I traipsed through the forest, heading once again to the glade and the site where three young lives had been cut short. Would a superstition grow up around them, I'd wondered, as the legend of the Cain Ravens had taken root over the centuries? Perhaps in future times children would claim to have seen spectres down by Old Demdike river. A trio of innocent souls – one accidentally drowned, one killed by her own hand, one murdered – just as Muriel told me on my first night in Fenchurch. That she witnessed Wesley's murder, I was now convinced. If only she could tell us what she saw.

It was as this thought occurred to me that I heard the rush of approaching feet and, before I could turn, felt a blow across the back of my head. My hand spasmed in response and I dropped my stick. A follow-up push, as infantile as a playground shove, sent me reeling to the ground. Face planted sideways in the frozen dirt, I'd seen two sets of feet shuffle around me in a hesitating, uncertain circuit.

Scuffed Nike trainers and a pair of nondescript black hiking boots. A dull ache pulsated somewhere near the base of my skull, and I could already sense the shadows of the forest thicken at the edges of my vision. Black Boots stepped back far enough so that I could make out a powerful, compact body, the face hidden beneath a balaclava. Possibly Ryan Marsh, possibly Maddox, perhaps even Mike the chap. They were looking down at me, something shiny clasped in their fist. Not a stone like the one that had felled Wesley Sayers, a piece of hollow metal piping.

A shrug, a panicked gesture shared with their companion who remained out of my line of sight, what next? I didn't think this assault had been thought through. It was an on-the-fly plan prompted by fear. I could see it in the tense, jerky body language, a mind caught between action and flight. And then Black Boots turned sharply, as if at some unexpected sound, and beyond the masked figure I saw another standing on the rise above us. Hooded, skeletal, his own face obscured.

He too had something shining in his hand, an object which was trained on both my assailants. And then my name was spoken in that old rasping tone.

'Scott Jericho. Mine.'

In the next instant, Black Boots and Nike Trainers dashed across my field of view and were gone. My world narrowed by degrees until only the hooded man remained. My mentor, my saviour. A fixed point staring down at me as the darkness claimed us both.

Now I sat up, my hand returning to the back of my head. A persistent ache continued to pulse there. How long had I been out? I wrestled my phone from my pocket – 2.43 p.m. A couple of hours maybe, but with my memory of the morning so fragmented it was difficult to be sure.

I searched among the bed of leaves for my stick and, claiming it, rose unsteadily to my feet. The question throbbed along with the pain: which of them, and why? The latter was surely no mystery. Whichever pair had killed Wesley Sayers were panicked and, whether or not they meant to kill me, at the very least their intention had been to scare me away. A desperate course of action that reinforced the idea that there was no great calculating intellect behind this case.

I rolled my head from shoulder to shoulder and muttered a curse under my breath. Taken unawares by a couple of amateurs and knocked unconscious with a single blow. I could just imagine Mark Noonan laughing his fat tits off over that, my dad merely shaking his head in disappointment.

'What's happened to you, Scott Jericho?' I muttered to myself.

But there wasn't time to give the attack and my rescue by Peter Garris any further thought. I was limping back towards the town, dreaming of a hot shower and a cold compress, when my phone bleeped with a message: 'Mr Jericho. I need to talk to you. I can't take it anymore. I killed Wesley. Smashed in the back of his skull and put him in the pillar. I acted alone. I left Indira after she fell asleep and met Wes in the woods. He knew that I'd been torturing Kat for years. But the memory of what I did is eating me alive. I've come back to town and I need to see you. Then you can speak to the police for me. I'll be waiting at the bench outside the church. Please come as soon as you receive this. Stuart.'

I stared at the message. In all the varieties and combinations of killers and persecutors, I had never once pictured gentle Stuart McDonald in the role of Kat's tormentor. Had I misread him as badly as that? I might be off my game, but it seemed almost impossible. Then again, could I imagine a young man forced to return to his childhood home, to labour away at his father's behest, toiling towards escape while at the same time taking out his frustrations on a silly girl who couldn't forgive herself? Perhaps.

But there was something amiss with this message. Not only the unidentified number it bore, but the substance of the text itself. Everything about it shouted that, far from being a killer, Stuart McDonald himself was now in grave and immediate danger.

Chapter Forty

I THRUST THE PHONE INTO MY pocket and hurried as fast as I could through the forest. Whatever idea had originally drawn me back here could be checked later. The identity of my attackers and the reason for Garris's rescue I'd also fret away at once I had time to think. For now, I needed to get to the church.

As I emerged breathless from the treeline and rounded the foot of the hill, I kept glancing up at that soaring tower. The ravens crowned it in a furious blizzard, screaming like I'd never heard them before, swooping and diving among the battlements. The shoulder-high wall that encircled the churchyard would once have posed no challenge for me. Now, as desperate as I was to reach Stuart, I knew I didn't have a hope of scaling it. Not with my weakened hip ready to sweep the legs from under me. A small secondary gate connecting the churchyard to Chattox Wood was chained and padlocked, and so I staggered on, occasionally grasping at the wall for support, my heart hammering with every step.

Was he already dead? Had the pair of Sanctuarists that attacked me in the woods, keeping me out of the way for those precious few hours, already silenced their friend? Or were they nothing to do with the message I'd received? Surely the two things couldn't be a coincidence.

As I reached the last stretch of wall and the lane of cottages that led to the lychgate, I ran directly into the solid form of Ryan Marsh.

'Whoa, steady there,' he said, righting me. 'I mean, I enjoy handsome men throwing themselves at my feet as much as anyone, but there are limits.'

'Are you all right, Mr Jericho? You look very pale.'

I glanced around the circle of concerned faces. Pretty much all my suspects, present and correct – Ryan and Maddox, Rowan, Indira and Lorelei, Miss Westmacott and the reverend. Rowan came forward and rubbed my arm, like a concerned parent consoling a child.

'I'm fine,' I said. 'I just need to check something up at the church.'

'You won't have much joy there,' Mr McDonald said sourly. 'The police still have it locked and cordoned off. Even I'm not allowed inside until I get the say-so from Inspector Tallis.'

'Rowan's right, Mr Jericho,' said Maddox Marsh. 'You really don't look well. We're all just on our way to the fair, but if there's anything we can do?'

'I'd rather stay at the vicarage,' Mr McDonald said. 'I shouldn't be gallivanting about when Stuart is still missing. But then Indira pointed out that this Winter Wonderland is for the church's benefit, so I really ought to show my face.'

I nodded, my shoulders still heaving as I caught my breath. 'And you've been persuaded too, Miss Westmacott?'

She blinked at me as if coming out of a dream. 'Oh yes, I didn't want to. Not really. But these dear friends of Wesley insisted.' She gave the remaining Sanctuarists a vague smile. 'Said I needed some fresh air, a distraction. I suppose they're right. By the way, did you find what you were looking for earlier? Up in Wesley's room?'

'Yes I ...' Another volley of shrieks from the ravens. My eyes swept beyond the lychgate to the looming tower. 'Yes, I think so.'

Lorelei glanced at her watch. 'We should be on our way. Mr Makepeace said to be there by three o'clock.'

I watched them for a moment, the preacher and the grieving mother, the old school friends ushering them on. And at the junction where the lane met the road, Mr and Mrs Berkeley, waving at the crowds from the courtyard of The Six Ravens. The publicans then joined the throng that bustled down the high street, the burble of excited chatter almost a challenge to the chorus of the ravens. It seemed that the whole of Fenchurch was off to the fair.

All except me and Stuart McDonald.

I wrenched open the lychgate and started up the gravestone path.

The figure on the bench came slowly into view as I mounted the hill. Stuart sat just as arranged, directly beneath the great tower of Fenchurch St Peter. I saw his head first, listing a little onto his right shoulder. And then, limping on and gaining higher ground, his entire body was revealed. He was propped slovenly against the bench's elbow rest, one arm dangling to the ground where a bottle of vodka lay discarded. It must have been dropped recently because some of the alcohol was still dribbling from its neck.

Stuart was dribbling too. Even from this distance, I could see the untidy beard around his lips wet with drink. He was dressed in the same rough workman's clothes as the last time I'd seen him, although his overalls appeared even more stained with food and paint. His eyes were closed, his legs extended in front of him, toes turned out like an absurd imitation of a ballerina. He grunted and muttered in his sleep, and I felt my heart steady a little.

He's still alive, thank God.

And then the shadow fell over him. A winged monstrosity tipping forward, as if keen to inspect the fragile insect that slept beneath its tower. Stuart stirred and blinked against the sudden darkness. The shadow elongated, the horns that sprouted from its head spreading out across the churchyard, the shape of its hunched shoulders and taloned hands slipping over tombstones like spilled ink. Stuart's mouth dropped open at the sight. A stupid expression, halfway between confusion and dread. He raised his arm as if to shield himself – a powerful arm, a labourer's muscled limb – yet feeble as a reed against the force that meant to claim him.

'Oh,' he murmured.

Just that. No surprise, no terror, only a sad sort of acceptance.

From the battlements, the scrape of stone upon stone, the shadow lengthening to its limit and then drawing back again as, in one headlong rush, the granite guardian of St Peter's took flight for the first and last time. The ravens' shriek muffled my own scream. I stood there, rooted to the gravestone path, unable to move, incapable of looking away.

The plummet, the fall, the breath of air displaced, the gentlest breeze buffeting against my face. And in almost the same moment, a sound I'll never forget. One that will echo in my dreams until my own darkness rushes in to claim me. Hard and wet, resistant and yielding, a blow like the fist of God. The demonic grotesque that had sat upon its plinths for centuries now lay broken among the splintered ruins of the bench. Something else was lying there too. Something red and pale and equally unmade.

I covered my mouth at the horror of the thing, breathed through my fingers. And then a flame of rage ignited inside me. At this desecration, at this contempt. I forced my eyes from the ground, swung my gaze up to the tower. There was no figure silhouetted in that space so recently occupied by the fallen statue, but the murderer must still be there.

He *must*.

I threw my stick aside and stalked across to a small door inlaid into the side of the south transept. From my earlier explorations, I knew this to be the only other access point to the building. I found it locked and covered in police tape. I moved on to the main entrance and tried the brass ring. Again, locked. There was one non-stained-glass window on the other side of the church, the vestry window, but it was small and barred. No way out there. The tower itself had a drainpipe running top to bottom but I wouldn't trust a child's weight to those rusted bolts.

The killer must have locked themselves inside, which meant that they were now trapped. I gripped the mobile in my pocket. I should call Tallis, I should wait. But the anger burning through me would permit no delay. It was an old rage, birthed in the days after my mother's death and undimmed by the passing years. It called out for justice.

There was no way I could break down this main door. Once I might have been able, but not now. And so I forced myself to return to the body, to look upon the devastation, to search among the pockets. I blinked back tears as my fingers traced the shape of a wallet, a phone, a few stray coins and finally the big brass key. I made Stuart McDonald a promise as I slid it free – *I'll find who did this to you* – and returned to the door.

The lock clicked, the oak panel slackened in the frame. I pushed it open, tore away the police tape and stepped inside. The nave was silent and empty. I made quick work of checking among the pews, searching the vestry and behind the pillars, ensuring that the killer hadn't already descended the tower and was hiding somewhere, patiently waiting for me to ascend so that he could make good his escape. But there was no one.

Next, I staggered as fast as I could down to the crypt, even checking inside the humming freezer in case a desperate man might have concealed himself there. It was empty, of course. Returning to the nave, I pulled open the main door and glanced outside again. If someone had been waiting further up the stairs and made his dash while I was in the crypt, I'd still be in time to see him racing down the hill. Again, there was no one.

And so, to the tower.

The stairway wound ahead of me, an icy breeze swirling from above. The tower door must be standing open. I took huge gulps of that freezing downdraught, allowed the cold to shock me out of my horror. I had to think. Who would I meet up on the rooftop? Which of them could it be? I realised even before I made the final step that there was only one possible answer.

None of them.

I'd seen all my suspects only minutes ago in the lane, the remaining Sanctuarists, the vicar, Miss Westmacott, the publicans of The Six Ravens. None could possibly have passed me on the hillside, gained entry to the church, climbed the tower and pushed the grotesque from its plinth. There was neither the time nor any access to the building that was out of my sight. I supposed that Tom Makepeace could have sent his husband on the fateful mission but, in the event of the body being discovered, his absence from the fair that afternoon would be so suspicious I doubted Uncle Tommy would risk such a thing.

So who could be waiting at the top of the tower? Some person unaccounted for? A murderer as yet unimagined? My brain ran through every possibility, however unlikely. In the end, however, nothing could have prepared me for the truth I found beyond the doorway.

Chapter Forty-One

THERE WAS NO ONE THERE.

I staggered out onto the flat roof as the ravens screamed about me, their beaks dripping with fresh meat. I didn't want to imagine the source of their contentment. Food from the freezer in the crypt or some fresher supply at the base of the tower. I moved across to the battlements and the place where the grotesque had stood.

My gaze swept the hillside, though I already knew what I'd see. Nothing and no one. Just the empty churchyard stretching down to the woods and, away to the east, the town and the prom and the fair, buzzing and alive with light. I placed my shaking hands on the crenellation before me. The grotesque had rested on four cuboid plinths roughly five inches square. I leaned out, over the parapet. From my position, I could make out where the front set of stone cubes had fallen as the statue was pushed from its placement. They lay scattered at the feet of Stuart McDonald, or what was left of him.

But pushed by who?

It was impossible.

The ravens cackled, contempt in their tone. I stared up at them as they wheeled away from the scene of the crime.

'What did you see?' I murmured. 'You punish killers, don't you? Did you punish him?' I shook my head and took out my phone.

Tallis backed away from the battlement.

'That gargoyle sits up here ever since God was a boy and only falls when someone is sitting under it?'

'Grotesque,' I said. He looked at me curiously. 'Technically gargoyles are carved waterspouts shaped in animal or demonic form. The statues are called grotesques.'

Ever one for precise detail, he made a note.

'Anyway, you're right,' I said, turning my phone screen towards him. 'It wasn't an accident. Here, look at what I was sent just before he was killed.'

'I've already seen it,' Tallis said. 'We've retrieved the phone from his pocket. A brand-new burner, no other calls or texts on it. I guess he must have bought it sometime after he disappeared. Didn't want to use his own phone in case we used it to track him.'

I shook my head. 'Stuart wasn't some kind of criminal mastermind. Would he even know enough about police investigations to buy a burner?'

'Doesn't everyone know everything these days?' Tallis asked. 'Bloody CSI.'

'Did you find his old phone on him too?' I asked.

'No. Although he might have disposed of that as soon as he went on the run. Chucked it in the river or dumped it in a public bin somewhere. We're checking local phone shops, hopefully we'll get lucky and find the place he bought the pay-as-you-go.'

'Or someone else bought it,' I said. 'Then sent me the text before planting it on him.' I winced, my hand going to the back of my head. The adrenaline was wearing off and my wound from the forest was making itself felt again.

'You should get that looked at,' said Tallis, then sighed when I told him I was fine. 'So you were attacked in the wood before receiving the text? Why?'

'To warn me off, perhaps?'

'Do you get attacked often?'

'It can be an occupational hazard.'

'So who do you think did it? Tallis asked.

'I didn't get a clear look at the both of them,' I told him. 'One was physically strong. Might have been Ryan or Maddox, possibly Indira. The other? No idea.'

'I wonder why they stopped,' Tallis said. 'I mean, if we're saying they wanted to scare you off. And why then send you the text pretending to be Stuart?'

'To have me at the scene, I suppose.'

'Obviously,' Tallis said. 'But why? They push the statue, they escape somehow, why would they want a witness?'

'And they can't have done it anyway,' I said. 'Not a single one of them. I saw them all heading off to the fair with the reverend and Miss Westmacott only minutes before the statue was pushed.'

'So how was it done?'

I shook my head. 'It's a kind of locked room mystery, only this time the locked room just happens to be outside.'

'All right, for the sake of argument, let's say there's something we're missing here,' Tallis said. 'A point of entry and exit we haven't thought of yet. But the murder itself, what do you think of that?'

'It's a heavy statue,' I said. 'I think it might need two people to dislodge it.'

'So we're back to the groups who paired off on the night of Wesley's killing?'

'Maybe. Oh, and there's another thing: in your toxicology report on the body, I think you'll find that he had both alcohol and sleeping tablets in his bloodstream, probably prescription zopiclone. They're a strong hypnotic. Believe me, I speak from experience. I saw that Stuart had some downstairs in the crypt, and the state he was in just before the statue fell? Looked like he'd been dosed with something.'

'Do you think he took them himself or were they administered to him? Possibly force-fed the pills while he was drunk?'

'It all looked so staged,' I frowned. 'Say he was positioned there on the bench, the killers then get into the church and lock the door behind them. They must have had a duplicate key, perhaps a spare taken from Stuart. Then they race up to the tower, push the grotesque and promptly vanish into thin air. They'd need Stuart at least partially drugged so that he didn't move in the time between them placing him on the bench and pushing the statue. But if the pills were forced down him, that would certainly require two or more people. He was a strong lad even when drunk.'

'All right, so *why* was he killed?'

'I don't believe that text,' I said. 'Stuart wasn't responsible for Wesley's death. At least, not solely responsible. But some sense of guilt was definitely eating away at him, hence the drinking. Did he directly threaten the killer? Perhaps saying he would tell me what had happened, who was involved, or was it the mere danger of him being a loose cannon? Whatever the truth, the mention of Indira in the message looks suspicious.'

Tallis nodded. 'But in a way to exonerate her or implicate her? The true killer pointedly referring to her to focus our suspicions?'

'I don't know. But can I ask a favour? I'd like to take another look at something inside the crypt.'

We descended together, down the spiral stairs all the way to Stuart's subterranean studio. As ever, the freezer chattered away in the gloom. I moved with Tallis over to the easel that still sported the portrait of the mythical minotaur.

'There's something here,' I said. 'Something we're not seeing.'

'Well, when you do see it, let me know,' Tallis sighed. 'I'm away to inform the vicar what's happened. Would you like to come along?'

I shook my head. 'I'm not sure I can face that.'

'All right, but I'll need a full statement from you later.'

'Come and meet me at The Six Ravens,' I said. 'Room four. Right now, I need to get some air.'

'Oh, just one other thing,' Tallis called after me. 'Wesley Sayers had five thousand quid deposited in his bank account a month before he died. Paid in cash to a branch in Norwich. No name attached to the deposit. What do you think it means?'

'I don't know,' I said, my gaze playing around the low vaulted ceiling. 'But this has to stop. There's a darkness in Fenchurch and I don't want it corrupting anyone else.'

I walked slowly around the church's boundary wall, ignoring the buzz of activity on the hillside. It was now late afternoon. I hadn't eaten since breakfast. At least I didn't think I had, the memories of that morning were still a little fractured by the blow to the back of my skull. I'd spent some time in Wesley's bedroom, looking through the things Kat had left him, and then gone to the forest. Why? What had I seen among those keepsakes and mementos that sent me hurrying to Chattox Wood?

I paced back around the foot of the hill and re-entered the embrace of the trees. Before long, I was once again in the clearing where I'd been attacked. The same clearing where I had first met Rowan and Muriel. I wandered under a gentle sway of branches, each leafed with Muriel's paper boys. A memory stirred, tricky and elusive: *Sometimes them six bring white treasure in them talons for old Muriel, though they don't know I keeps it. Make my boys with it. They leaves it to rot in the hollow place, but it makes good boys to remember him by.*

She had been speaking of the ravens, at least that's what I'd thought. But what if, in her confused interpretation of what she'd seen, she had associated the birds with something else? And the white treasure they had brought . . . I looked up into the branches, to the paper figures that danced and whispered there, pale bodies covered in print and scrawls. And yes ... there and there, a distinctive, flowery hand. The same handwriting I'd seen on the cover of the file left in Wesley's safekeeping.

Katrina's handwriting.

'She did leave a note,' I murmured to myself.

A suicide note. Entrusted, like the rest of her keepsakes, to her best friend Wesley Sayers. I pictured it in my mind's eye: Wesley summons the killer and confronts them with the dead girl's final message. A testament to condemn her persecutor. A revelation that strips away a smiling mask and reveals the monstrous reality beneath. The face of a hunter, as vicious as the mythical minotaur from Stuart McDonald's painting. A petty, vindictive and relentless pursuer who stalked Katrina down the nights and down the days.

Wesley is angry, outraged, throwing around threats and accusations. He holds up the suicide note, flourishing it as proof. He might not be able to persuade the police to prosecute, but he'll try nonetheless. And, in so doing, he will expose the persecutor for what they really are. I imagined two figures dumbstruck by this onslaught. One the target, the other a witness, or accomplice or innocent bystander. Whatever the nature of the second, they will soon be drawn into a crime from which they cannot escape. Wesley Sayers must be silenced.

The stone is snatched up from the riverbank and brought down on his head, his eye is then pierced to seal his lips forever. He is carried away and entombed in the pillar. But what happens to the incriminating suicide note? In his haste, the murderer tears it from Wesley's dead hand and rips it to pieces, placing the fragments in the hollow of a tree, intending to return and collect them later. Only Muriel has been watching the whole thing.

She sees the funeral-clad murderer and their accomplice as akin to the Cain Ravens. I recalled the way she slapped the back of her head and then looked at me so imploringly – *You must listen. They pecks hard. They bring treasure. Understand?* When the conspirators have left, hauling the body up the hill to the church, Muriel emerges from her hiding place and claims the white treasure, refashioning it into her paper boys. Later, the killers return but the note is missing from the hollow. Do they realise what has happened? Or is it possible—

Is the note that will unmask Wesley and Stuart's murderer still here, floating above me?

Chapter Forty-Two

It took an age to collect all the fragments together. They were spread throughout the wood, a piece here, a piece there, paper boys sharing their secret among a hundred irrelevant scraps of letter, Christmas card and flier. I used the handle of my stick to bend the boughs, drawing the cut-out figures to me, freeing string from branch. It was awkward work. I tried to be as respectful as I could, untying Muriel's complicated knots, but at times I was forced to wrench the offering roughly from the tree.

My heart ached every time. It felt like kicking over flowers left beside a grave. But with the light failing, I eventually believed I'd collected them all and so hurried back to my room at The Six Ravens.

Some of the crowds had tired of the fair and were back at the pub. I saw a few familiar faces as I passed by. Rowan and Lorelei warming their hands at the fire, sharing a joke; Ryan Marsh standing with Indira and his sister at the bar, chatting with Mrs Berkeley; the old ladies from the bus stop gossiping over glasses of sherry. There was no anxiety on their faces, no grief. I guessed that the news of Stuart's death hadn't yet leaked. It would soon enough, and then the place would be abuzz with fresh excitement and horror.

My hand stole to the back of my head as Ryan glanced over and caught my eye. The careless expression dropped for a moment and he blinked and looked away. Was it you? I wondered. Did you and your pretty sister ambush me in the forest? Did you send a text implicating your friend and then, somehow, push the statue that stopped his wagging tongue?

I dragged myself up the stairs and locked the bedroom door behind me. Webster plodded over, licking the back of my hand in greeting.

'Good juk, bide for a while,' I said softly, and he obeyed, returning to his spot beneath the window.

I pulled off my coat, taking the dozens of paper boys from my pocket, and flicked the light switch on the wall. Then I spread my treasure across the bed. It took perhaps ten minutes to assemble Katrina Allingham's suicide note. Some fragments were interchangeable, others slotted naturally into a certain rhythm and structure, a few fell more awkwardly into place, perhaps because connecting passages from the original had been lost. Muriel might have overlooked them, or they may have been claimed by foraging birds seeking out scraps for their nests. In any case, I believed I had enough to read the meaning of the note.

And what it told me turned the entire case on its head.

I stood back from the bed, my mind reeling.

'Idiot,' I muttered to myself. 'Oh, you divvy, joskin-brained dinlo. How could you have got it so wrong?'

The fragments of the reconstructed note ran:

'Wesley tormented me – Wesley persecuted me – tortured me – tormented me – All my life – For the past ten years – decade of mental torment – Since Jamie – Ever since Jamie died, he – You didn't know what he was really like – none of you – Wes has killed me – Driven me to this – I can't live anymore with his constant persecution – He isn't who you think he is – He kept saying I'd pushed Jamie deliberately and that was why he drowned. I didn't, I promise – It was an accident. It was – But Wes never let me forget what I'd done. Not once in ten years – Every day, reminding me. Every minute – He kept me here, with him. Under his control. His power – said I didn't deserve a life – Wesley was always sick in the head, but we didn't see it. His disguise – loving friend was too good. But it wasn't just me – You might not have guessed but Wes hounded us all when we were kids – hounded you too, secretively. He hated us. His friends – because we were cleverer or more successful – He hated you so, so much – He told me everything he'd done to you – pleased with himself – happy he'd ruined your perfect life – Wesley said he was doing you a favour anyway and that you had too much – he'd seen you after school that day and how you got physical with – that boy and that he was hurt and bleeding – said that afterwards you looked scared and excited – He laughed when he said he'd contacted the so – firm, and that they then kicked you off your work experience – Said that now he could call the – shots and you'd be heartbroken – and he could expose you for the hypocrite – If you hadn't broken that stupid boy's jaw – if he hadn't seen that, then he'd have had nothing on you, and so he said that you were a joke of a clown just like – and that you deserved everything you got. Like I deserved everything I got – I'm sorry I didn't tell you what he was like. What he was doing to me – I don't blame you, but you must be careful of him – Wesley Sayers is pure evil – Goodbye, my dear friend. All my love, Kat xxx'

I sat back on the bed, head in my hands. I'd been wrong. Wrong from the very beginning. I'd imagined Wesley as the dead girl's friend and defender. Instead, he was cruel, controlling and manipulative and, in this last note before she took her own life, Katrina had revealed the hell he'd put her through. Wesley was the hound who persecuted her, not one of the other Sanctuarists. Tom Makepeace with his old Traveller's instinct had been right all along about the boy.

I thought of the treasures Kat had bequeathed him. All the most precious things of her life, not because he had loved her but as a prick to whatever conscience he might have possessed. I pictured her note attached to the file: 'For Wes, to have always in memory of me. Please, don't ever forget me. I know you won't. Kat x'. The file with its paper trail of her life – the ultrasound scan; the copy of her birth certificate; the child's drawing of her family; school reports; a friendship bracelet; a concert ticket and the university acceptance letter, of course. It had been her way out of Fenchurch, an escape from her past and the boy who tormented her. For whatever reason, she hadn't taken that escape. Perhaps because he, the hero who had tried to save her little brother after the push, would not allow it.

I remembered how Mrs Berkeley had spoken of that moment in the bar when a local bully had tried to pick at the open wound of Katrina's guilt. She'd thought Wesley was standing up for his friend. 'She's my girl,' he'd shouted as he pummelled Katrina's tormentor. 'No one says a word about her.' And then he'd grabbed Kat and held her tight, like his life depended on it. Or held her as *his possession*.

No one says a word about her ... except me.

Another thought occurred. Kat had left Wesley a copy of 'The Hound of Heaven' poem. They were all familiar with it from their childhood at the church, and the image of Wes as that faceless hunter must have felt powerfully apt. But the note he had made on the reverse, the anger I'd misinterpreted as his outrage on discovering that Kat had been tormented by one of their childhood friends: 'Poor Katrina ran from that monster but he always found her. *Always.*' He had in fact been proud to identify himself as the pursuing monster, and his inscription was no more than the petulant fury of a sadistic mind finally robbed of its victim.

Wesley was behind it all. And yet, although Kat had been his primary and most long-suffering target, he had once victimised all the Sanctuarists. From the letter, it now seemed beyond doubt that he had been the one to out Indira and Lorelei against their will; to reveal Stuart's drug taking; to inform the authorities about Rowan's aunt; to send anonymous messages to Ryan Marsh's solicitors' firm and to Maddox's fashion design company, scuppering their work experience placements. And as for the allegation made against himself, that he had stolen money from the sponsored swim? I had to admit, right at that moment, that particular element of the story didn't quite fit.

But one fact did scream out from the suicide note.

The identity of the killer.

I ran over the indicative phrases again, filling in gaps and smoothing out the meaning:

'He'd seen you after school that day, and how you got physical with that boy, and that he was hurt and bleeding. He said that afterwards you looked scared and excited. He laughed when he said he'd contacted the solicitors' firm, and that they then kicked you off the work experience. Said that now he could call the shots and you'd be heartbroken, and he could expose you for the hypocrite you were. If you hadn't broken that stupid boy's jaw, if he hadn't seen that, then he'd have had nothing on you.'

Ryan Marsh. Surely there was no doubt. Kat commits suicide, hanging herself from the tree that overlooks the site of her brother's death. She cannot escape her persecutor, but she can expose him, finally. She leaves a letter for Ryan. He is appalled, enraged. He decides to bide his time throughout the funeral, waiting for a moment to get Wesley alone. But when? And who was his accomplice? According to his alibi, it must have been Lorelei, but then why go on to kill Stuart?

A possible scenario: Ryan realises he might need backup confronting Wesley. He makes some excuse to leave Lorelei and calls Stuart. Maybe he's already told his friend about the revelation in Kat's note or perhaps he unmasks Wesley during this phone call. Whichever way it happened, Stuart meets him in the woods and together they get into a tussle with Wesley. One of them strikes him with the rock, the other stabs him in the eye and Wesley is placed in the pillar. Afterwards, they somehow convince Lorelei and Indira to uphold their alibis. But Stuart begins to fall apart after the murder and must be dealt with, especially when I arrive in town and start nosing around. Ryan convinces him to disappear for a short time, possibly using the Marshes' flat in London. Then Stuart is brought back to Fenchurch, plied with whisky laced with his own sleeping tablets, and ...

And here's the hitch. Ryan couldn't have pushed the statue from the tower. I saw him only moments before in the lane with the others. Still, I'm as certain as I can be that one of my assailants in the woods today was Ryan Marsh. If the second turned out to be Maddox, could he have involved his twin at some later stage after Wesley's murder? I shook my head. I still came up against the fact that Maddox had also been in the lane just before Stuart's death, and so couldn't have been at the top of the tower only minutes later.

I scanned the reconstituted suicide note again and cupped my brow with my palm. My head was pounding. I needed some air.

With Webster still slumbering beneath the window, I picked up my coat from where I'd thrown it and headed back downstairs. The place was empty, the Sanctuarists gone. Mrs Berkeley stood behind the bar, idly leafing through a magazine and yawning. Clearly the news of Stuart's death still hadn't leaked to the town. I guessed that anyone seeing the renewed police activity up at the church must have assumed the gavvers had returned to reinspect the scene of Wesley's burial.

'Evening, Mr Jericho.'

The landlord appeared from the kitchen. He had a tray of old toby jugs in his hand, each sparkling and steaming in the gloom of the hall. I recognised them from the main saloon where they adorned a shelf above the bar. He caught my gaze and pressed a finger to his lips.

'Don't let on to the wife. I stick 'em in the dishwasher every couple of months. She thinks they're worth a few bob and that they should be cleaned by hand. But they're so chipped and knocked about, I doubt you'd get more than pennies for 'em on a car boot.'

At his words, I shook my head, cursing myself again for my blindness.

'The clown,' I murmured. 'Of course ...'

Chapter Forty-Three

I LEFT THE LANDLORD STARING AFTER me and ducked out into the courtyard. It was a fine night, the sky dusted with stars, not a shred of cloud. As I walked down the lane, past the church hall and a line of cop cars still parked up beside the wall, I tapped a quick search into my phone. It confirmed what I suspected and, before I knew it, I was at the vicarage door.

The man who answered my knock looked utterly broken. Gone was the fastidious, self-righteous preacher I'd first met at Miss Westmacott's cottage. In his place stood a man psychologically and spiritually undone. He looked at me with desolate eyes, his dog collar absent, shirt unbuttoned to his midriff, the hairy bulge of his stomach on display for any parishioner who cared to call. In his hand was a bottle of gin, already half empty.

'What do you want?' he demanded, some of the old fire and brimstone resurgent in his tone. Then, in a quieter, more doubtful voice, he repeated, 'For God's sake, what do you want?'

'I'm sorry for your loss,' I said. 'Truly. But I need to speak with you.'

'The shop's shut,' he laughed. 'No confessions taken this evening, Mr Jericho.'

'But I think that's just what you need,' I said. 'A confessor. Can I come in?'

He stumbled a little, falling back from the door, his eyes wide and staring. I followed him into a small front parlour, undecorated apart from a few religious paintings and a single black cross on the wall. He dropped into an armchair and gestured for me to take the sofa opposite.

'Wesley Sayers wasn't the person this town thought he was,' I began. 'The kind, sweet-natured, neighbourly young man who cared so deeply for his friends and family. That was all an act, as hollow as the pillar in which he would be buried. In reality, something very dark existed under that carefully constructed mask. A soul that delighted in the persecution, the torment and the ultimate destruction of others. I don't mean that he was a murderer, he would have been too cowardly for something as bold as that. No, it was in the manipulation of others that he delighted. He would be the piper playing the tune and his victims would all dance whenever he commanded it. Perhaps he'd always been that way, ever since early childhood. He certainly enjoyed ruining the lives of his school friends, though always working anonymously and behind the scenes. But I think with you, he decided to show his face.'

There was no fight left in the vicar of St Peter's. He merely nodded at my words.

'Wesley found out the truth soon after we came to Fenchurch,' he said. 'I don't know if Stuart told him. Maybe I'd been going on at the boy, disciplining him too harshly. He might have wanted to punish me in turn.'

I nodded. 'Wesley learned your name.'

The vicar took a thirsty swig from the bottle and then laughed, throwing his face to the ceiling. 'Yes, my name. How pathetic. How utterly banal. And I let it get to me.'

'Reverend R.C. McDonald. He'd make fun of you, call you Reverend Arsy,' I said. 'But that wasn't the extent of it. I remember something Stuart told me. That Wesley had "other nicknames for you, when he found out the truth". And then I thought of the note he supposedly left for his mother after he vanished. An old note that might have been planted by his murderer to make us believe he'd gone away of his own free will, but genuine nonetheless. "Mum, I'm just heading off for a bit – too much going on right now. I've taken some money from the clown by the way, haha." Miss Westmacott tried her best to shield you. She said the clown referred to a sort of toby jug in which they kept odds and ends of money. Spare change, that sort of thing. We had something similar at home when I was a kid, but here's the thing. You keep chucking coins into a porcelain jug like that, it will inevitably become chipped and knocked about. There's no avoiding it. Yet Miss Westmacott's jug was completely smooth to the touch.'

I shook my head at the clergyman. '"The clown" was his nickname for you, wasn't it? Inspired by your real name. Not Reverend Richard McDonald, as you claimed to the whole town when you arrived here. I looked you up in Crockfords on the way over, the directory of all Church of England clergy. Your real first name—'

'Ronald,' he laughed hysterically, and raised his bottle in a toast. 'Here's to good old Reverend Ronald fucking McDonald. The clown vicar. Laugh it up, Mr Jericho. Laugh it up.'

'I've taken some money from the clown.' I sighed. 'Wes found out about your name and he blackmailed you.'

'My pride, my pomposity.' McDonald laughed again. 'My Achilles heel. It always has been.'

'I guess it started small,' I said. 'Bits and pieces of pocket money here and there. But once he knew you would pay to maintain your facade of sober respectability, the floodgates opened. And his blackmail only intensified when he discovered your affair with his mother.'

'You know about that too,' the vicar sighed.

I nodded. 'You entered her house without knocking on the day I met you. Even the most solicitous vicar wouldn't have his own key to a parishioner's cottage. And there you were, labouring under all those Christmas gifts which you'd apparently brought along for her to sort out and take to the church hall. But why lug them all the way down the lane, simply for Miss Westmacott to take them back up again? The church hall sits right next door to the vicarage. You brought them to Miss Westmacott's because that was your second home.'

'We were lonely,' he said simply. 'We took comfort from each other. I was weak.'

'No,' I said softly. 'You were human. But back to Wesley. The money from the reward old Tom Makepeace had given him for trying to save Jamie Allingham had finally started to run out. He was a lazy, indolent young man, happy to stay in Fenchurch and sponge off his mother. He had no particular ambition and had been frugal with that reward money. But now, with only his part-time work at the pub, poverty stared him in the face. He tried a job with his uncle in London, but it didn't go to plan. He was too soft. And so he returned here, tail between his legs, angry and embittered.

'The only project he'd ever shown any real commitment to was the persecution of his victims. His successful friends had flown far from his grasp and only Katrina Allingham remained, fixed as if in amber by her guilt and by Wesley's hold over her. His constant psychological torment of the girl—'

'What?' McDonald looked up, appalled. 'He was torturing poor Katrina too?'

'She had no money to pay him,' I went on. 'And in any case, his persecution of her was purely to satisfy his own vindictiveness. But you were a different story. He had your real name, he had your moral hypocrisy, your affair with his mother, but there must have been something else. A month before he died, you placed five thousand pounds in cash in his bank account. That suggests more than the mere threat of an affair exposed.'

'He overheard me telling his mother one night about my late wife,' McDonald said, defeated. 'How I'd embezzled from church funds to pay for private treatment abroad when our options here had run out. We had no idea he was even in the house.'

'And so to pay him off you had to return to that original sin. That's why you had Stuart come home from university to work on the repairs to the church. Stuart needed a short-term job to continue funding his studies and you needed a way out of your predicament. You're a by the book sort of man, Mr McDonald, and so you must have been desperate to take such a risk. If it was ever found out, then the works wouldn't have been insured, as I'm guessing Stuart had no official qualifications to perform them. You could pay your son a small wage yourself while forging invoices from reputable builders who, of course, would have charged much more for their time and labour. The difference went to Wesley.

'But when Stuart's repairs uncovered the saint's reliquary inside the pillar, you knew you were in trouble. If it was reported to the bishop, then all works would have to stop and a proper archaeological investigation instituted. It was now a site of historical significance. How the saintly bones inside the pillar were uncovered would obviously be a focus of such an investigation, and in turn, your own secret would inevitably be exposed. And so you had Stuart cover it back up. How long before Wesley's disappearance was the reliquary found?'

'A matter of days,' the vicar said. 'I had the church closed while Stuart attended to the work, sealing the pillar back up again. It had to be completed by the day of Kat's funeral, of course.'

'And on that day, the bricks had been replaced but the pillar hadn't yet been replastered?'

McDonald nodded. 'We stacked some chairs in front of it, just to be extra safe.'

And later the Christmas tree, I thought to myself. Placed there by Stuart who, by that time, knew that the pillar contained a new and much more terrible secret. One which he couldn't bring himself to face.

'And your puritanism was the obvious blind for this extraordinary concealment?' I said, refocusing on the vicar. 'You told Stuart that such idolatry as the saint's bones was an affront to God and he went along with it.'

'I don't think he was fooled,' McDonald sighed. 'I think he guessed that Wesley had been blackmailing me and that I was skimming off the church accounts to pay him. That's why I had to push old Tom Makepeace to keep the Winter Wonderland running today, as distasteful as it seemed after the discovery of Wesley's body. Wes was dead but I now had to replace as much of the money I'd taken as possible.'

'So you think Stuart knew about the blackmail? And is that why Wesley died?' I asked. 'Your son killed him as revenge for what he'd done to you?'

'Mr Jericho, what I say next, I swear before the God that I have loved and served all my life.' He suddenly seemed to have sobered up, his gaze clear and focused, no slur in his speech. 'My son would never have hurt a hair on Wesley Sayers's head. No matter the insult, no matter the provocation. He was the kindest, gentlest soul I've ever known. I only wish I'd told him so.'

I sat back in my chair. 'I believe you, Mr McDonald. But in that case, I must ask: did you kill Wesley yourself?'

'I did not. He was bad, Mr Jericho. The only truly evil person I've ever met. Have you encountered real evil before? Not damaged, not traumatised, but evil in its purest form?'

'Yes,' I said slowly. 'Yes, I think I have.'

'Wesley was like that. There was a cruelty inside him that would have made even our Saviour shudder and turn away.'

'So who do you think killed him?' I asked.

'Whoever it was, they may have been the instrument of a power greater than any of us. God's eye is always watching, Mr Jericho. You should remember that.'

'His eye is always watching,' I repeated to myself.

And at that moment, a glimmer broke into a darkness that had, until now, seemed impenetrable. A glimmer that made my heart sick with the reality it revealed. Was it possible? Surely not. *Surely not.* I felt my hands tighten into fists, felt my soul shrink from the horror of it. Because if it *was* possible, then how would they ever live with the truth?

Chapter Forty-Four

'Thank you, Mr McDonald.' I said, getting to my feet. 'Thank you.'

'Mr Jericho?' He looked at me, concerned. 'Are you all right?'

I almost laughed. This man had lost his son in the most violent and, as I now believed, unnecessary of murders, and here he was, asking if *I* was all right.

'I will be,' I said. 'And I promise, unless it becomes unavoidable, I won't betray your secret. But I think it's possible that I might have news for Miss Westmacott later this evening. Would you mind sitting with her until I'm ready? It might not be until the early hours.'

'I was on my way down there anyway,' he said. 'She's a good woman. God knows what she did to deserve a son like that.'

He walked with me to the door and, on the threshold, took me by the wrist.

'Do you know who killed my boy?' he asked.

'Yes, I think so.'

'And how they did it?'

'That too. And I'm sorry, Mr McDonald. I truly am.'

*

I walked slowly down the lane, plagued by visions as spectral as dreams. Dark birds, Cain Ravens, flocking jealously around their tower. *Them kill killers, mister.* A grotesque statue sprouting living wings and enveloping Stuart McDonald in its fatal embrace.

And all for nothing.

My phone buzzed in my pocket. It was Harry. Harry, thank God. I needed him now as my mind recoiled from the truth of what had been happening here in Fenchurch-on-Sea. His voice alone would soothe me. I thumbed the screen and he broke in excitedly before I could even say hello.

'Scott, are you there? Listen, we've spoken to Garris's landlady in Hampstead. I think she had the hots for Ben, so she spent ages talking to us in her little kitchen downstairs. Gave us homemade biscuits and squeezed his knee. If only she knew, eh?' he laughed. 'Anyway, she remembered Garris very well, even after all these years. Said he was the best tenant she ever had, so quiet and respectful and tidy in his habits. Always kept himself to himself, though he'd sometimes come in at odd hours. But that didn't make her suspicious because he was a young police officer. Though she said she'd had coppers lodge with her before, and that she never knew any of them get lumbered with as many night shifts as "poor Mr Garris".

'Anyway, it was such a small flat, he didn't have much room for his stuff, and so she remembered him renting a storage space nearby. She couldn't recall the name but thought it might have sounded something like a big shop or department store. After we left her, I went through some old listings from the local newspaper and, after a bit of trial and error, we found it. Stoller and Debenham's Storage Units. It was on the outskirts of Hampstead and has been closed for years, but we were in luck. The library had the answer, as it always does.

'There was a security guard who'd worked at Stoller and Debenham's around the time Garris rented his unit. I found a piece on him in the *Hampstead Gazette* from when he'd foiled a burglary. Through that article, we tracked him to an address in St Albans. He'd retired up that way. Long story short, after handing over fifty quid, he remembered a man answering to Garris's description who'd kicked up a stink when Stoller and Debenham's shut down. He seemed a bit panicky, so the guard told us, fretting over what he would do with all his belongings. Then he returned about an hour later, overly polite and tipping the man a large amount if he could bring a truck right up to the gate after hours. Said he didn't need any help loading his things, that he'd see to all that himself. Our guard remembered the rental company from the side of the truck because it was one that lots of customers used when moving their bits and pieces. Manderville and Son of Ealing.

'Ben and I headed straight over and found the manager still in his office. We said Garris was an elderly uncle of ours, that he'd suffered a stroke and that he wanted us to check his unit for him. That the thought was preying on his mind and making him sick and anxious. The manager went on about client confidentiality, saying we needed authorisations and paperwork, but Ben said that "Uncle Pete" was too ill for all that. He couldn't even sign his name, let alone tell us where any paperwork might be. He said that we needed to put his mind at rest, and we weren't budging until we got access to the unit. Even I was a bit intimidated!

'Anyway, the man's finding the key for us right now. It has to mean something, doesn't it? Garris panicking about the old storage space shutting down and shifting his stuff across town to this new place in the dead of night? He had a hideaway, just like you thought, Scott. His trophies, perhaps even his true identity, might be waiting in there. We can put it all together, get a real view of who he is . . .'

'Scott? Scott, are you still there?'

'I am, my love,' I said. 'That's excellent work. I just need . . .'

I struggled to find the words. Silence filled up the space.

'Scott, you're frightening me,' Harry said. 'What is it? What's happened?'

'I'll tell you all about it soon, I promise. Right now, I need to sit and think for a bit. But it's been good to hear your voice. I love you very much, Harry. Very much.'

'I love you too.' I could hear his concern. 'We'll call as soon as we know anything. And, Scott?'

'Yes?'

'Be careful.'

I smiled as I ended the call. The old sign off, but now with our roles reversed.

I had barely walked another step before my phone buzzed again. I answered straight away, not even glancing at the caller ID.

'Harry, I—'

That cold, impersonal, familiar voice cut in.

'Call him off, Scott. Call Harry off. I won't ask again.'

The phone went dead. I stared at the screen – Unknown Caller – but there was no doubt about his identity. It was Garris. Yet not the Garris I had so recently encountered, stalking the woods and streets of Fenchurch. The voice had none of that cracked, dried-out weakness. Instead, he sounded exactly like he had on that last night in the hospital back in Aumbry, when he had confronted me with a revelation I still could not bring to mind. What did it mean? I shook my head. I could fret at that mystery later, for now I needed to contact Harry.

Heart pounding, I brought up his number and hit dial.

'It has not been possible to connect your call, please try again later or leave a message after the tone.'

'Fuck, fuck, fuck,' I muttered, and brought up Ben's number. Again, the same automated message: 'It has not been possible ...' I gripped my stick, took a breath. They must be inside the warren of storage units, their phones out of reach. I called Harry back and left a message. I didn't mince my words.

'Harry, listen to me *very* carefully. Somehow, Garris has learned what you're up to. If you love me, you'll do exactly as I tell you. Get back in your car and drive straight to my dad's yard. Tell him that you're in danger. If all goes to plan, I'll be able to leave Fenchurch sometime in the early hours. Then we can put our heads together and work out what to do next about Garris. But I'm deadly serious, Harry. You get home and you wait for me. I should never have let you start this thing in the first place.'

My mind whirring, I was soon back in my room at The Six Ravens. Picking up on my mood, Webster plodded over and laid his great head against the back of my hand.

'He'll be all right,' I said to the juk. 'We'll keep him safe.'

But first I needed to tie up the mystery of Fenchurch. I stood in front of the bed, the reconstituted suicide note laid out before me.

And all at once I saw it – the final thread unravelling before my eyes. It was the 'clown' again that showed me the way. I snatched up my phone and put a call through to Tallis.

'Hello, Inspector.'

'You know, don't you?' he said without preamble. 'I can tell from your voice. You know what's been happening here?'

'I think so, yes.'

'You know who killed them both, Wesley and Stuart? And was it two killers, like you thought?'

I almost smiled. 'In a sense. Only not in any configuration we imagined.'

'Well, you don't sound too happy about it.'

'I'm not,' I said. 'Not at all. Because you see, if I'm right, then one of these men has died for no reason at all.'

'All right,' Tallis said. 'So what next?'

'It's difficult,' I told him. 'There's no direct proof as far as I can see ... Do you trust me, Thomas?'

He took a breath. 'I think I'll probably have to, won't I? What's your plan?'

'One of them I'll bring to you through their own guilt,' I said. 'The other through fear. But it's a risk. The question is, are you willing to take it?'

Chapter Forty-Five

I WALKED BACK FOR THE FINAL time to the scene of the Allingham tragedies, Chattox Wood murmuring around me as if eager to share its secrets. My phone pinged as I reached the riverbank. A voicemail from Harry, at last. It must have come through while I'd been on the call with Tallis. I hit play. Harry, sounding weary and nervous, not entirely himself. 'Hello, my love, I got your message while we were inside taking a look at the storage unit. Understood. We're going straight back to the yard. There was nothing much in the unit anyway. See you at home tomorrow, darling. I've missed you. Be careful.'

His tone troubled me – no arguing with my instructions, no fight, no defiance. Looking back, that ought to have alerted me that something was amiss. But at that moment, I reassured myself that I'd be seeing Harry soon enough, and that he still had Ben by his side. Anyway, right at that moment, I needed to find somewhere to hide.

In the end, a screen of bracken on the elevation just behind the suicide oak gave me a good vantage point. I settled myself into as comfortable a position as possible, my wasted hip supported against an eruption of tree root, turned my phone to silent and waited. It was possible, of course, that I was wrong. That recent events had blasted apart those old childhood bonds and customs that had held the Sanctuarists together across the years. That the ritual itself had become polluted by the violence that had overtaken them. Was I wasting my time here?

An hour passed, then another and not a hint of movement among the sleeping trees. No human movement at any rate. Occasionally some nocturnal bird or wakeful creature might stir the shadows before folding itself back into the night. But for long stretches of time my only companion was the moon, tracing a frosty path across the starless dark.

And then, close to midnight, a scrap of white flitting between the shapeless mass of trees, like one of Muriel's paper boys grown life-size and venturing down to the river to play. I watched them as they gathered, one by one beneath the oak, each Sanctuarist with their gaze fixed on the bough from which their friend had swung. Five of the original eight – Maddox and Ryan Marsh, Lorelei Tey and Indira Bakshi and lonely Rowan Chesterton, her face long with grief and wet with tears.

Rowan could not bring herself to look at the others and they seemed unable to look at her. All dressed in various costumes of white, they appeared like pristine statues come to life, angels that would disdain the crude battlements of the tower that loomed above us.

Rowan reached into the string bag she had brought along and, taking out a large round cake, broke off a portion for each. She passed it to them wordlessly, snatching back her hand each time as if fearing contamination. Then she lifted her own portion over her head and spoke the words taught to the Sanctuarists by her aunt half a lifetime ago.

'We gather here, in this sacred place, in memory of our dear lost brother, Stuart. Who was taken from us ...' She swallowed hard and the bitter tears fell again. '*Taken* from us before his time. We who loved him absolve our brother of all his earthly sins. We welcome them into our own hearts and souls and carry the burden for him, willingly and without regret. In the name of kindness and of sacrifice, in the presence of Father River and of Mother Tree, we free you and let you pass unhindered into your reward. We do this gladly and for your own dear sake.'

They each lifted their portion of the corpse cake to their lips and consumed it.

A pause followed, filled only by the ever-present chuckle of the stream, indifferent and immortal, mocking the platitudes of the Sanctuarists. And then Lorelei broke the circle and attempted to put her arm around Rowan's shoulder.

'Don't touch me,' Rowan cried, flinching away from her. 'Don't you fucking dare touch me. Not any of you, understand? Never again. Just leave me alone, all right? It's done now, so just go and leave me.'

'Row,' Ryan murmured, and she thrust an accusing finger at him.

'Go. Or I swear to God, I'll ...' And then she buckled over, hugging herself and screaming in her agony and despair. 'Go. For Christ's sake, go!'

They exchanged a miserable glance. Indira closed her eyes, Maddox folded his arms, Lorelei clutched at her own throat as if wanting to choke the words forming there. Ryan shook his head. 'We had no choice, Row. What else could we have done?'

'Go,' Rowan repeated quietly. And that whisper was somehow more terrible than her scream.

They obeyed, leaving one by one, Lorelei shrugging off Indira's attempted embrace, the Marsh twins walking apart. When I was sure that they had all departed the wood, I rose to my feet and called out to the remaining Sanctuarist.

'You loved him, didn't you, Rowan?' She turned to me, startled. 'It's OK,' I assured her, limping down the rise, my hands held up. 'There's no need to speak. Let me tell you a story and you can say if I go wrong, all right?' I joined her on the riverbank overlooking the inky run of Old Demdike. '*I fled Him, down the nights and down the days; I fled Him, down the arches of the years; I fled Him, down the labyrinthine ways of my own mind; and in the mist of tears, I hid from him* . . . That poem haunted Katrina so much that she left a copy of it, along with all the other treasures of her life, to the man who had tortured her conscience for over a decade. It was her final condemnation of Wesley Sayers, that pursuing monster who had never let her forget what she'd done. A single push.

'The irony was, of course, that Wesley himself made no attempt to save Jamie's life. I think that day went something like this: as you all told me, Kat was annoyed at having to babysit her little brother on his birthday. Her friends rallied round, making the best of a bad situation. Kat had brought some drink along from her father's booze cabinet, probably in an attempt to impress you all. But where to drink it discreetly? I don't think Jamie had any enthusiasm to go to the old waxworks exhibit. I think you headed there because the back storeroom offered a handy place away from prying eyes. You started sharing around the bottle, got a little merry, not realising that Jamie had also been taking the odd shot.'

'He wandered off while we were still mucking about in the storeroom,' Rowan said dully. 'The drink went to his head and he started freaking out. The waxwork figures, their eyes. It was always an eerie place but what with the alcohol …'

'You were scared you'd be discovered,' I said. 'What would your parents say if they found out you'd been drinking and had got the little boy intoxicated too? You'd certainly lose your jobs at the fair. And so you took him into the woods to calm him down. But by that point, you'd all started to tire of the kid.'

Rowan shook her head. 'Ryan and Indira had. But Lorelei was feeling sick too. So we all wandered off home, leaving Jamie with Kat and Wesley.'

'Then came the push.' I nodded. 'Her stupid little brother had ruined everything, embarrassing Kat in front of her friends. She'd sneaked the booze to show off and it had all gone wrong. The farmer on the far bank reported later what he saw. Or thought he saw. Wesley bravely diving in, a heroic attempt to save the kid. I wonder if even then the possibility was in his mind. He'd had fun that summer, persecuting you all, holding you in his power, though none of you had ever guessed. But he knew that could only be a fleeting triumph. You were growing up – clever, talented young people ready to stretch your wings and fly far away from Fenchurch. I think Wesley was self-aware enough to realise that he had neither the brains nor the commitment to follow in your wake. But if he could hold one of you here, under his thumb always? Imagine the power of that idea.'

'It could just as easily have been me,' Rowan said. 'Both me and Kat were vulnerable in our own ways. Me with Aunt Muriel, Kat because of the dominance of her parents and their preference for Jamie. But it was the circumstances that afternoon that condemned her.'

I nodded. 'Wesley jumped in, miming some sort of rescue attempt. But if he'd been serious then the task would've been an easy one. He was already in training with the RNLI, he'd competed in a sponsored swim. He was strong in the water. The river here is tidal, and at the time of Jamie's death it would have been just after high tide, also known as "slack tide". The time when the current is at its most sluggish. Too much for a drunk seven-year-old, perhaps, but not for Wesley Sayers.

'I don't think there was any deliberate attempt to harm the kid. Wesley was a coward, a blackmailer, not a killer. He jumps in and flails around, making a good show of it for the farmer and for Kat. Does the thought occur to him as he is swimming out that a valiant attempt ending in heroic failure might make him look all the more sympathetic, and place Kat even more securely within his power? In any case, the boy dies and Wesley's ascendancy over Katrina begins.

'His mother told me that he had no ambition but that he had "his projects", Kat being his primary obsession. But I think that recently he'd begun to tire of her. A bully will only torture an ant under a magnifying glass for so long before the thrill starts to wane. Then his reward money ran out and he tried to go and work for his uncle in London, a venture that met with abject failure. So he returned to Fenchurch, bitter and disappointed, his attention refocused on the one success in his life. He had probably always been jealous of your individual achievements. Well, he would flourish now in what he was good at. His persecution of Kat intensified. I think he even took her back to the waxworks in the weeks before she died. Made her share a glass or two of the same bourbon you'd all drunk that day. I found two glasses in the storeroom, one with lipstick that matched Maddox's shade.'

'Kat always hero-worshipped Mads,' Rowan murmured. 'Copied her clothes, her style.'

'Yes, I remember Indira telling me so.' I sighed. 'Katrina fled Wesley until she couldn't flee him anymore. But after her death, she left her treasures to her persecutor, so that he would never forget what he'd done to her.'

'It's evil,' Rowan said, despairing. 'If only we'd seen it.'

'She could never tell you in life what he was really like, perhaps because she believed his whispers,' I said. 'That she was to blame for Jamie's death. But before she took her life, here on this very spot, she wrote each of you a letter.'

I smiled bitterly to myself. 'At first, I didn't see that letter for what it was. I was so focused on a pair of conspirators that I imagined it was written to only one of you. Ryan Marsh. But if you take the fragments apart and look at them again, the truth becomes clear. It was not a single letter but *six*, one for each of the Sanctuarists to open on the night of her funeral. Why else that repeated insistence at the beginning on Wesley as her tormentor?' I took out the fragments from my pocket, reading each opening passage: '*Wesley tormented me. Wesley persecuted me. Tortured me. Tormented me. All my life. For the past ten years. A decade of mental torment. Since Jamie. Ever since Jamie died.*' I shook my head. 'It feels repetitive to the point of mania, but if it was in fact the opening to six *different* letters, each specific to the recipient?

'I'd originally imagined that the letter referred only to Ryan, to his beating up of the boy who'd tried to bully him and the resulting loss of his work experience at the solicitors' firm. But what if those pieces could be read in another way? *He told me everything he'd done to you. So pleased with himself. Happy he'd ruined your perfect life.* That of course could refer to either Ryan or Maddox Marsh, with their background of comfort and wealth. *Wesley said he was doing you a favour anyway and that you had too much . . .* Again "too much" might refer to the Marshes, but what if it was addressed to you, Rowan? Wesley saying to Kat that he was doing you a favour by reporting your situation with Muriel to the social services because you had "too much to deal with by yourself"?'

She closed her eyes as I continued.

'*He'd seen you after school that day and how you got physical with – that boy and he was hurt and bleeding.*' I glanced up from the scraps. 'Obviously, the last part referred to Ryan, but the preceding section? *How you got physical with?* Could that actually be from Kat's letter to Lorelei or Indira, revealing how Wesley saw them in the woods kissing, getting "physical with each other"? Moving on: *He laughed when he said he'd contacted the so— firm and that they then kicked you off the work experience.* Again, the second part refers to Ryan, but the first? What if that sentence had ended "social services" rather than "solicitors' firm"? Was that part of your letter, Rowan? Revealing how Wesley had informed the authorities about Muriel? The next part probably ran on from this: *Said that now he could call the – shots and you'd be heartbroken, and he could expose you for the hypocrite.* A reference to a "hypocrite" surely suited what he thought of Maddox more than her brother, the girl who wanted to work in fashion but had posted an ill-advised comment online, fat-shaming a model. Now back to Ryan: *If you hadn't broken that stupid boy's jaw – If he hadn't seen that then he'd have had nothing on you and so he said that you were a joke of a clown just like* ... Again, the first part is from Ryan's letter, but the second probably came from Stuart's, with a reference to "the clown", Wesley's cruel nickname for Stuart's father. As I say, six letters that might be misread as one.

'You all received something in the post after Kat's death?'

Rowan nodded dumbly.

'An envelope with a covering note inside, asking you to open the enclosed letters together on the night of her funeral? Perhaps when you would gather for the sin-eating ritual, down here by the river, but stating that Wesley should not be included in your number.'

'We thought it was strange,' Rowan said. 'Her instruction to deliberately exclude Wes and not tell him anything about the letters. He was her dearest friend. Jesus Christ.' She stared at me miserably. 'If only we knew. He was the devil.'

Chapter Forty-Six

'But you went along with Kat's wishes?' I said. 'Wes remained ignorant of what was going on that night?'

She nodded.

'You were all so insistent that the sin-eating ritual was nonsense,' I continued. 'A relic of your childhood left in the past. But the sentiment was too uniform to be credible. Just as the Wesley Sayers you all presented to me was too good to be true. No group of friends ever has so unified a view of one of their own. There'll always be variations of opinion, even for the most giving and selfless of people. But your opinions of Wes were such a consistent hagiography: he was the best of you, a saint, a hero. There had to be collusion to present a character that none of you had any reason to kill.

'Likewise, you decided that you would claim the ritual was a forgotten game from childhood. To disguise the fact, of course, that you intended to go through with it the night of the funeral. But *not* with Wesley in attendance.'

'We were confused, couldn't make any sense of it,' Rowan said.

'But you followed Katrina's instructions.'

'It was her last wish. We had to honour it.'

'When he got angry at the pub, insisting that you all go down to the woods, Indira pushed back against the idea and so he left alone.'

'He wanted to do the ritual,' Rowan said quietly. 'Was desperate to. I think it was his way of keeping some control over poor Kat, even in death.'

I nodded. 'You all left the pub and hurried down here almost immediately after Wesley's departure. But you found him waiting for you?'

'No,' she said. 'He came later. We did the ritual for Kat, just like you said. Then opened our letters.'

'I should have known,' I said. 'Your Aunt Muriel told me what happened. "*Them spoiled my birds that night. Them didn't want them's dinner afterwards. Not after they ate their fill. My seeds and berries weren't good enough for them then.*" You did the ritual with the pieces of fruitcake, as I saw you perform it just now, throwing the uneaten crumbs aside. Later, Muriel's robins ate their fill of the discarded pieces and so didn't want their dinner.

'But if the murder site was ever located, it was important to maintain the fiction that none of you had performed the rite. That you disdained it as childish nonsense. To build up this picture, you omitted Indira's name from the floral tribute left by the tree, lending weight to your version of events – that you followed Indira's lead that night and did not perform the ritual.'

Rowan sighed. 'We'd all been standing around for a while afterwards, discussing the letters and working ourselves up. Ryan was livid, Indira and Maddox too. Me and Lorelei were trying to calm them down, saying we should report everything to the police. Stuart just stood there, stunned. I know we told you that Wesley was the best of us, but I think in our hearts we were picturing Stu when we said that. He couldn't believe anyone could be so cruel. And that's when Wesley showed up. Came strolling through the trees, not a care in the world. "You sneaky little rats," he said. "What are you all doing here without me?"'

'And you confronted him?'

'He laughed,' Rowan said. 'Can you believe it? He stood there and laughed at us. Didn't even try to deny it. Then he stared at each of us and his face … Mr Jericho, there was nothing there. No expression, no emotion. "Prove it," he said. "Prove that I tormented the silly bitch. It's my word against hers. You know, I'm so tired of playing the saint. It's been fun but this is even better. The look on all your stupid faces."'

'And so?'

'He tried to leave,' Rowan said. 'Threw insults at us over his shoulder and said he was going home. But then Ryan caught him by the arm and pulled him back to the riverbank. I don't really know how to describe what happened next. It's a bit of a blur. I think we each grabbed hold of him at some point, even me and Lorelei. We were screaming in his face, shoving him. All this rage and grief spilling out of us.'

'Even Stuart?' I asked.

'No.' Her expression cracked and she began to sob. 'No, not Stuart. He really was the best of us.'

'And in the end, one of you picked up the stone and struck Wesley on the back of the head.'

'No,' Rowan cried out. 'No, I swear we didn't.'

I sighed. This felt even worse than if they had struck him down. 'He fell, didn't he? Hit his head on the stone and—'

'He wasn't breathing,' Rowan said. 'And we all started to panic. Stuart tried CPR but it was no good. We'd killed him.'

'Let me guess. One of you, Ryan or Maddox, maybe Indira, started talking consequences. Who knew if Kat had written to anyone else, revealing Wesley's true nature and how he'd victimised you all that summer long ago. You were the last to be seen with him at the pub. Even if you said it was an accident, there would be evidence of a fight, both on the body and possibly at the site of the murder itself.'

'Not murder,' she insisted. 'An accident.'

'But could you convince the police of that?'

'Ryan said that there might be microscopic blood splatters on our clothes. Tiny particles of evidence we'd leave behind us. He knew about such cases from his friends who worked in criminal law.'

'And you all had much to lose.'

She nodded. 'Ryan and Maddox had their careers, Stuart his future as an architect, Indira and Lorelei might lose their little girl.'

'And you might lose your Aunt Muriel again.'

'Even if we could convince the police it was an accident, Ryan said the rumours alone would be enough to destroy our lives. We'd never escape them.'

'And so you threw the rock in the river and then you all carried the body between you up to the church.'

'Stuart had told us about it earlier that night at the pub,' Rowan said. 'He'd had a few too many and it all came rushing out of him. His dad forcing him to work for peanuts and asking him to cover up the hollow pillar with the saint's remains. Ryan thought of it later when we were discussing what to do with the body.'

'A perfect place to conceal Welsey until you could think of somewhere better. And after all, the church had always been your sanctuary. The keeper of your secrets.'

'Only afterwards Stuart couldn't bring himself to open it back up again,' Rowan confirmed. 'And then you discovered the body.'

'But someone else knew your secret. You were seen by Muriel that night. She must have slipped out, hunting for her white treasure to make her paper boy tributes to Jamie. I believe she witnessed that first accident, and perhaps even looked on as Kat hanged herself from the oak. Now she witnessed a third death. In her addled mind, she told me what she'd seen. When I first met her, I thought she'd said the word "hex", possibly referring to a curse and her interest in superstition, but she'd once been a mathematician, yes? A geometrist? So I wondered if she had in fact been trying to say the word "hexad", as in a group of six. She also associated you all with the six Cain Ravens of the tower, who punished murderers. I'm guessing that's what you accused him of and so that's how she thought of Wesley too?'

'Kat's killer, in all meaningful senses of the word.' Rowan nodded.

'Muriel said that these ravens, all dressed in funeral black, had pecked him here.' I laid my palm against the back of my head. 'Tell me, what happened after Stuart sealed Wesley inside the pillar?'

'Poor Stuart,' Rowan said. 'We tried to help him, all of us, but he pushed us away. I don't think he ever forgave us. But afterwards, he and Indira visited Miss Westmacott on the pretext that they were worried about Wes. Stuart kept her talking downstairs while Indira checked his bedroom.'

'In case there was anything Kat had left him that might suggest you had a reason to hate Wesley. The keepsakes under the bed wouldn't constitute any direct clue. Instead, Indira found something useful – the unused note.'

'In the pocket of one of his suits,' Rowan confirmed. 'Ind didn't know if Miss Westmacott had seen it before, but she thought it was worth a try. She left it on the desk and ruffled up the bedclothes, so that it looked like Wes had come back and slept there.'

'Then I suppose you all went off together to concoct your alibis? If couples like Indira and Lorelei alibied each other, they would be worthless, the same went for the twins. But if you paired off in a particular way – a strong personality coupled with a weaker – then it would seem less likely that any of you had something to do with Wesley's disappearance. But then later, things started to go wrong.

'Stuart became increasingly unstable. He couldn't cope with what you had done. He might crack. Wes inside the pillar haunted him. That first night I met him, Stuart tried to tell me the location of the body, his classical allusion to Wesley "passing by the gate of the hill and into the evil field beyond". He painted a metaphorical Wesley as the minotaur, a devourer of innocent humans, slain and bricked up inside his labyrinth. I should have known the seven stars that encircled the image pointed to something more personal than the symbolism he claimed. Not the seven youths and seven maids sacrificed to the minotaur's destructive appetites, but the seven Sanctuarists that Wesley had persecuted. With one star faded out to represent the dead Katrina. Though I believe his reference to the seventh circle of hell that the mythical beast was said to guard – the zone of violence – did reflect Stuart's true artistic intent. The violence that Wes's persecution of Kat inspired, his own bloody destruction. Stuart was trying to tell me what he knew, the guilt that burdened him, but he couldn't betray you. Not directly.'

I looked at the woman before me, twisting her hands together, trapped inside the labyrinthine agony of her grief and remorse.

'But then you decided to betray him,' I said. 'By murdering him.'

Chapter Forty-Seven

ROWAN SHOOK HER HEAD MISERABLY. 'I didn't know, I swear. Neither me nor Lorelei. We would never have let them—'

'The risk was too great,' I pressed on. 'There was a detective in town asking questions and Stuart was a loose cannon. The dangers to you all that Ryan outlined after Wesley's death remained very real. But how to silence Stuart and keep your secret? You had to devise an impossible murder. A locked room mystery executed out of doors.

'Somehow Stuart was got out of the way for a night so that the plot might be hatched and agreed on. Did Ryan spirit him away to the twins' empty flat in London?'

'No,' Rowan said. 'Indira put him up in one of her family's old caravans outside town.'

'Of course,' I said, remembering Mr Berkeley's talk of the Bakshis' defunct caravan site. 'And there he was kept, drunk and drugged until you were ready for him. You bought a burner phone to send the message that would ensure I was in place as your unimpeachable witness. But you didn't want me on the scene too early, messing up your carefully laid plans. My memory of that morning is a bit fractured, I must admit. But I think

I'd probably been busy all around the town, poking my nose into things, as I do. And you couldn't risk me arriving at the church while you were setting the scene.

'And so, two of you arranged to attack me in the woods. I'm not sure you had a very clear plan, that part was probably executed on the hoof after you saw me buzzing around Fenchurch that day. But the idea was to incapacitate me for a short time before the message summoning me to the church was sent. Only I think Ryan overplayed his hand, hitting me a little too hard. Down I went, and he and his accomplice – I'm guessing Indira or his sister – panicked. Only then an old friend of mine intervened, scaring them off.'

'They told me he had a gun,' Rowan said. 'Whoever it was. They didn't get a clear look at his face. He wore some kind of hood.'

I nodded. 'What did he say to them? My memory's hazy.'

'Just your name and that you were his. They told me there was something off about his voice. Like he was ill.'

And yet that tone had been so clear in his phone call to me earlier this evening. I pushed the thought away. I'd have to deal with Garris later.

'I came round after being hit and my phone pings. Stuart supposedly messaging me, ready to confess, to unburden his conscience. I'm guessing one of you was watching me from the trees, primed to alert the others when I regained consciousness? I receive the text and hurry off to meet Stuart. And I must admit, this next piece of theatre was timed to perfection. You not only wanted to provide an alibi for yourselves but for any innocent person who might be suspected of Stuart's murder, and so you cajoled Miss Westmacott and the reverend to accompany you to the fair. I passed you all in the lane, a cast-iron witness to your alibis, and then I marched on up the hillside. There to witness an impossible murder.'

I closed my eyes as the memory played again inside my mind.

'Sometime earlier, you had positioned a heavily drugged Stuart on the bench beneath the tower, taking his key from his pocket so that you could access the church. Then it was down into the crypt to collect one vital ingredient for the crime. Then up into the tower where it would have taken at least two Sanctuarists to lift the statue from its plinths and to drop the two frontmost supports over the side, where they landed at Stuart's feet. All to appear as if they had fallen when the grotesque was pushed. I think Maddox must have been one of the people up in the tower; I found a thread from her scarf caught in the door. But now to replace the plinths with what you had brought with you from the crypt . . .'

I opened my eyes and gave Rowan a sad smile.

'I'd be impressed with the ingenuity of the thing if it wasn't so horrific.'

'Mr Jericho, please. I didn't know . . .'

'I wondered later why the ravens were screaming around the tower before I got there. Something was exciting them more than usual. And then I realised that they probably hadn't been fed since Stuart's disappearance the day before. You removed the frontmost plinths and replaced them with chunks of frozen meat from the freezer in the crypt. It was a very cold day, they wouldn't defrost quickly. It would all take some time. You raced back down the tower, relocked the door and placed the key back in Stuart's pocket. Then you sent me the text, supposedly from Stuart confessing to Wesley's murder and exonerating Indira, and planted the burner phone on him.

'Meanwhile the birds are plucking away at the frozen meat, ravenous beaks destabilising the statue's makeshift support. I get the message and race to the church, just as the final strand of flesh is plucked away and the statue falls. By the time I gained access to the church and the tower, any remaining meat on the ledge had been consumed and so it appeared that an invisible hand must have pushed the statue onto the man below. I only wish ...'

I took a breath. Tried to push away the memory of that desecrated body.

'I only wish you hadn't made me your witness, Rowan. I won't ever be able to forget what I saw that day.'

'Mr Jericho, I swear I didn't know what they were planning,' she sobbed. 'I would never have let them go through with it. I swear. I swear.'

'I believe you,' I said. 'But now you have a choice, Rowan. Inspector Tallis will probably trace who bought the burner phone, but there's no guarantee that he will. And so the truth about what happened to your friend rests with you. Don't you owe it to Stuart – the best of you – to tell what you know? To give his father some sense of peace?'

She clasped her hands together. 'I can't. I can't betray them.'

'All right,' I sighed. 'But there's one thing you should know. Your friends murdered Stuart McDonald, they plotted his destruction and obliterated him from the world ...'

'Yes,' she said. 'Yes, I—'

'And it was all for nothing.'

She stared at me. 'What do you mean?'

'I'm so sorry, Rowan. But you *didn't* kill Wesley Sayers. Not you, nor Ryan, nor Indira nor Maddox. None of you. You weren't murderers then, only later. There was no reason to kill to Stuart, to silence him. He died for nothing.'

Rowan threw her hands over her face. 'What do you mean?' She screamed at me. 'Please tell me, *what do you mean?*'

'I mean his eye,' I said, and felt the sting of my own tears. 'Oh Rowan, you don't know what I'm talking about, do you? Of course you don't, otherwise Ryan would never have suggested your knitting needle as a weapon that might have killed Wesley, even as a joke. But they *would* have put the detail of his eye in the message they sent me, the one claiming it came from Stuart. But all it said was that he had "smashed Wesley's skull in". You poor fools, you didn't know about his eye . . .' I placed a gentle hand on her shoulder. 'Call Inspector Tallis, tell him everything. That's your only sanctuary now.'

She looked up at me, such desolation in her gaze. 'But where are you going?'

I turned back to her, my heart heavy with the hopeless horror of the thing.

'To speak with Wesley's murderer.'

Chapter Forty-Eight

The vicar opened the cottage door.

'Hello again, Mr McDonald,' I said wearily. 'May I come in?'

He ushered me through the house and into that cluttered kitchen where Miss Westmacott sat in her ubiquitous apron, nursing a cup of tea and staring into the milky liquid as if it held some unfathomable truth. The reverend sat beside her while I remained standing.

'How are you, Mr McDonald?' I asked.

'Devastated,' said Miss Westmacott without looking up. 'The poor dear man. Losing a son is very hard.'

'It must be,' I nodded. 'So tell me, Miss Westmacott, why did you kill yours?'

She answered hollowly, defeated. 'I didn't, I swear. How can you even ...'

'Your insistence that something had happened to him was an insurance policy in case he was ever found, wasn't it?' I said. 'Inside that pillar, where his friends had bricked him up. You hoped that, by insisting he had come to harm and not just gone away of his own accord after the funeral, you wouldn't be believed. A scatty, worried, overly affectionate mother, lonely and abandoned. You thought the note so thoughtfully left by Indira on his desk would be taken as the police took it, at face value. But that note always bothered me. Too brief, too informal for someone apparently traumatised by his friend's death. It was an old one, of course. It might even have been left behind when he went to try his luck working for Mark Noonan.'

She said nothing, just continued to stare into her tea.

'You were with Mr McDonald the night of the funeral, here at your cottage,' I said. 'Your landline was disconnected, your mobile not in use, and so it was Ronald who received the phone call from Wesley. When I first came here, you said, "By the time Mr McDonald brought his mobile *down to me*, it had cut off." I didn't know then about your relationship. I took it to mean that he had brought the mobile down the lane from the vicarage. But wouldn't those words sound more natural if you meant he'd brought it down to you from upstairs? Isn't that how people usually use the phrase?' I turned to the vicar, his face ashen. 'Mr McDonald, when you answered the call, you said that it "sounded like Wes was in a tunnel".'

'Something like that, yes.'

'In fact, it was the echo of the hollow pillar in which he had been entombed.'

I switched back to Miss Westmacott. 'Wesley had woken inside the pillar after being attacked at the riverbank. His friends thought the blow had killed him and, in their panic, they'd unwittingly buried him alive. It always bugged me, why did Stuart and Indira make their visit to you here *before* the murder could have been committed? The answer: because at that point they believed Wesley was already dead. But when they buried him, they forgot that he still had his mobile on his person. I can only imagine his terror and confusion on waking. He must have been both frightened and exhilarated by what had happened to him. He fumbles around in the dark, taking out his phone and using its screen to illuminate his situation. The truth gradually dawns on him. He remembers the story of the saint's reliquary told by Stuart in the pub that night, of the vicar persuading his son to cover it up. So what does he do?

'He might have called the police, of course, but instead Wesley sees an opportunity. If he can only hold his nerve and escape the pillar, then he will have them all in his power, just as he had held Kat for so many years. Only this would be so much better. Six souls to play with, making them dance to his tune. And so he calls the one person on whom he can thoroughly rely.

'A thirteen-minute phone call,' I said. 'But if Mr McDonald was here rather than at home in bed when he received it, as he originally told us, then why did the call take so long? Ronald, you take the call, Wesley telling you nothing but knowing that you will do anything he commands. You head downstairs to find Miss Westmacott here in the kitchen, busy baking a treat for her son while also doing a bit of extra work for Lorelei's florist shop. I was told how you'd sometimes bring bits and pieces home to work on, Miss Westmacott. Ronald hands you the phone and, I'm guessing, returns to bed and falls asleep. Meanwhile, Wesley tells you what has happened. His friends thought they'd killed him and now he needs your help. You leave your stove and your flower arranging and head up to the church, taking the vicar's keys and his phone with you.'

She didn't respond, but absently plucked a spoon from the table and slipped it into her apron pocket. Mr McDonald sighed and placed his hand on her arm.

'You found the spot quickly enough,' I said. 'Was he screaming at you through the phone the whole way up the hill? Why wouldn't he? It must have been terrifying for him. But I doubt he pleaded, that wasn't Wesley's style, was it? Thirteen minutes to explain the situation and for you to make your way to the church and reach the pillar. Once you're there, he ends the call himself. And then?'

'He called me a useless bitch,' she said quietly, her gaze still fixed on her tea. 'Said that was why his father had drunk himself to death. Because he couldn't stand my fucking uselessness and stupidity.'

'Stephanie.' McDonald looped his arm around her shoulder. 'Oh Steph.'

'He said he felt like he was suffocating and had to get out of there,' she continued, oblivious. 'He kept screaming and screaming at me through that stone. "I've been buried alive, you stupid fucking cunt. Get me out, you ugly, stupid, fuck of a woman."'

'You panicked?' I suggested.

'I didn't have any way to free him,' she said with a careless shrug. 'Not on my own. There were no tools around, nothing I could use. I said I'd go back to the house and get Ronald to call the police.'

'But Wesley didn't want that?'

'No. He wanted to get out and to keep what had happened to him a secret. To find his friends and to hold what they'd done over their heads. For the rest of their lives. Torture and twist and bleed them dry with the truth.'

'He'd blackmail them?'

'Yes, I suppose. But money was never his main motivation. He never took a penny from Katrina, you know. It was the joy of working out all his little projects, the intricacy of how he would torment them.'

'Yes,' I murmured. 'You told me he was clever.'

'"Just wait until I see their dumb-fuck faces," he crowed. "Their resurrected friend back from the dead, like Lazarus." And all the while he went on cursing me and cursing me.'

'And you continued searching around for something to hack away at the bricks,' I said. 'To free him. In your distress, you forgot about the ice-pick downstairs, used by Stuart to chop up the ravens' meat. And so what could you do?'

I watched now as she found a stray pin on the tabletop and squirrelled it away thoughtlessly in her pocket.

'You began searching your apron. The place where you so often absent-mindedly place odd items. You'd been baking that night, something special to cheer Wesley up after the funeral.'

'Chocolate cake with Italian meringue buttercream. His favourite. I'd got it wrong before and he'd been so furious with me. It was always very frightening, whenever he got mad. Such a tricky cake to get just right, too. You need to be very careful or it will turn soupy.'

'Careful with the temperature,' I said.

Shrugging off the vicar's embrace, she rose from her chair and turned to the dresser beside the sink. Her shoulders hunched, she searched among the contents of the drawers, all the while muttering under her breath, 'Now where did I put it? It must be here somewhere. Ah yes!' Victorious, she brought out her find and showed it to us, her gaze fixed with a grim kind of wonder on the long, slender prong of the cooking thermometer, its sharpened point now blunted and grey with brick dust.

'You pocketed it in your apron when Mr McDonald brought down the phone,' I said. 'Then rediscovered it in the church. You used it to hack away at the pillar.' I recalled the upward-slanted dents in the brickwork, made by a small woman hacking overarm. 'Chipping until a peephole had been made in the mortar. It always puzzled me: why would a killer strike Wesley from behind and then inflict such a different and precise death blow? Malice perhaps, but there were no other injuries indicative of hatred on his body. It was you who gave me the clue, Reverend. The eye of God is always watching.

'Wesley is now desperate to be freed from his living entombment. He's screaming at you, berating you, tearing your character to pieces, all the while gloating over the agonies he will inflict on his friends, and in that moment—'

'I knew what he was,' she said. 'I'd always known, right from when he was a little child. Spiteful and manipulative and deceitful. And such an excellent disguise, too. He would always share his toys, always be the first to console a friend, the ideal shoulder to cry on. And forever listening, storing away secrets and confidences and those little slips we all make when we're talking to someone we trust. Even before he became the hero of the town, saying he tried to save the Allingham boy, it was a perfect mask.'

'You knew he never really intended to save Jamie?' I asked.

'Oh, of course,' she said, blinking at me as if I was stating the obvious. 'But from that moment on, no one ever doubted him again. Even those suspicions about him stealing from his sponsored swim money evaporated.'

'He was guilty of that too.' I shook my head, remembering how the Sanctuarists had tried to weave that particular story into their picture of a saintly and maligned Wesley Sayers.

'Only me and his victims knew what he was really like,' Miss Westmacott continued. 'When you live with a monster they can't hide their true face.'

I nodded. 'Wesley is inside the pillar. He's desperate, frightened, excited. He wants to see what's happening. He places his eye to the peephole you've made, curious as to why you're hesitating. Those medieval bricks are small and narrow. And so you ...'

She held up the blunted prong, allowed the kitchen light to play along its length, a gleam momentarily dazzling on the lethal tip.

'I didn't even think before I did it. I just thrust it into the gap. I felt it slide through his eye, smooth as jelly. Hardly any resistance at all. And he didn't make a sound, Mr Jericho. Just a sigh, perhaps, although that might have been the wind. And you know, I was glad to have done it.'

I took a breath. 'You had been testing your recipe all evening, anxious that the temperature should be just right. The end of the thermometer was sticky with the sugar syrup from the butter cream. As you snatched it up from the table where you'd been working on Lorelei's flowers, a petal from a dried petunia adhered to the prong. You left a fragment of that petal behind after you stabbed him. A curiously appropriate red herring. In the language of flowers, the petunia represents anger and resentment. The same emotions that had ultimately ended your son's life.'

She didn't respond, only continued to stare at the makeshift weapon in her hand.

'You took a little of the mortar and thumbed it back into the hole,' I said. 'Then you returned home, found the note left by Indira on the desk, noticed the rumpled bedclothes, understood what the Sanctuarists had tried to do and accepted it as part of your own deception. The following day, suspecting nothing, Stuart begins to plaster over the wall. That same day, you started calling Mark Noonan, playing the role of worried mother. Right from when I first agreed to investigate this case, my partner Harry wondered why you had pestered Noonan rather than the police. It was because you knew that, if the body was ever found and if Noonan suspected you of the crime, he wouldn't hesitate. To your late husband's relatives, that is their code. Family is family and must be avenged. But who would suspect the mother who'd always insisted that something terrible had happened to her son?'

'Yes.' She nodded. 'My husband used to tell me the most nightmarish things about his cousin. The beatings, the torture. Wesley had been down there recently and, although he'd made a mess of things, I knew that Noonan wouldn't take his murder lying down. I was scared, Mr Jericho. I'm still scared. Not of dying but of what might come before death.'

'It preyed on your mind,' I said. 'And so did the murder itself. You said you were glad to have killed Wesley? In the moment, I think that was true. But the memory of what you did began to trouble you. Did you see it in your dreams, Miss Westmacott? Your makeshift weapon thrusting into that peephole again and again, the prong emerging from the pillar, slick with his blood?'

'Mr Jericho, please,' the reverend objected.

'The association with the weapon and what you were doing with it before the murder,' I continued. 'You couldn't bring yourself to bake again, hence the store-bought cake when we first met.'

'He was like the ravens up in the tower,' Miss Westmacott said in a sing-song voice. 'Pecking at all our souls.'

I let out a breath. 'I'm going now, Miss Westmacott. I won't tell Mark Noonan what I know, not immediately. If you want to stay safe from him, you will pick up the phone after I've left, call Mr Tallis and tell him everything. He'll be able to protect you, I promise.'

McDonald rose from the table, showing me to the door.

'I didn't know,' he said as I made to step out into the lane.

'Not for certain,' I agreed. 'But you guessed at least some of it?'

He looked away. 'All I'm certain of is that Stephanie didn't kill my son. Do you know who did?'

'I do,' I told him, glancing up at a starless sky. 'And you will too. Very soon, I think.'

Chapter Forty-Nine

I WANDERED BACK ALONG THE LANE, the Cain Ravens silent for once in the tower. Satiated perhaps. The killers are all discovered in Fenchurch, no need now for their legendary vengeance.

It took only a few minutes to pack up my belongings, pay my bill and help an exhausted Webster into the back of the Merc. The old juk mumbled a little in his sleep as I carried him across the courtyard and placed him onto the back seat. Mr Berkeley stepped out to wave me off while his wife watched from an upstairs window.

'We heard just before closing that poor Stuart has died,' the landlord said. 'Whenever will it end, Mr Jericho? It's as if this town is cursed.'

I couldn't find any words to reassure him, and so I simply wished him goodnight and drove out along the prom.

The funfair stood swaddled in darkness, its show finally over, its lights extinguished for good. I gripped the steering wheel tight. I should have known what kind of man Wesley Sayers really was. Old Tom Makepeace had told me. His first instinct about the boy had been right all along. Travellers know human nature, you see? They always *know*.

*

I arrived back at our winter yard just as my phone pinged. I parked up next to our trailer, under the pre-dawn shadows, and glanced down at the screen. A message from Tallis: *Two confessions in the bag. One through guilt, one through fear, just as you promised. Thank you, Jericho. I'll be in touch.*

'You're welcome,' I murmured, but I felt no triumph or exhilaration from my meddling in Fenchurch. Instead, my soul was sick with what I'd uncovered and I longed to hold Harry again in my arms. To find the solace and absolution he always brought me. I hobbled out of the car and took in the silent scene.

The yard was still and peaceful, trailers and static chalets cloaked in shadow. Yet I knew within a couple of hours, Travellers would be out and about, cleaning their lorries and making ongoing repairs to their rides, ready to roll out again for another day at the Winter Wonderland. A chance to earn a few quid before the lean months set in. Apart from a car turning round in the lane behind me – some joskin no doubt lost and doubling back on himself – nothing disturbed the stillness. I let out a long sigh.

I was home.

The stranger's headlights spilled over me as I let Webster out of the back seat. The juk struggled to the ground, his inquisitorial gaze narrowing in the glare. He let loose a single bark and then plodded dutifully behind me as I guided him to his box outside my dad's trailer. Then I turned and limped across to our own small home, unlocking the door and lumbering up the steps.

Harry was tucked up in bed, snoring away gently. I let go of a breath I hadn't realised I'd been holding. He was safe, for now at least. I pulled off my clothes as quietly as I could and slipped in beside him, hugging him to my chest.

'We need to tell him what we found, Harry. He has a right to know.' Ben's voice, muffled as it came through the thin wall of the trailer.

'Yes, of course he does. But let him have a moment of happiness first, all right? Before we drag him back into the dark again?'

I moaned and turned onto my side in the empty bed, the exhaustion of the past few days clinging to me like an eel, its teeth sunk deep into my flesh. After a second or two, sleep reclaimed me.

I looked down at the note on the table beside the locker settee. Harry's delicate hand: 'Morning, sleepyhead, come and meet us all at the Winter Wonderland when you're up and ready. We have a little surprise for you, so make an effort. All my love, Haz x'

I glanced back at the wardrobe where my best suit hung from the door, freshly laundered and encased in a plastic dry-cleaning bag. 'What are you up to?' I murmured to myself, before pouring a bowl of fresh washing water from the canister and starting to dress.

It was a crisp clear morning, the sun almost blindingly bright. The yard appeared to be deserted, my dad's truck already gone and Webster absent from his box. All along the avenues, Travellers' homes were bedecked with outdoor Christmas decorations, pedestal postboxes garlanded with tinsel, the areas in front of chalets a crowd of festive tableaux.

I yawned and stretched, my suit swamping my still emaciated frame. Then I wandered over to the Merc and set out for the Winter Wonderland. Tallis would arrive soon to take my statement and collect the evidence of the paper boy letters, but until then I tried my best to put the shadows of Fenchurch in my rearview. In this, I wasn't entirely successful. Now and then a little slice of horror would intrude – the rotting cadaver bricked up inside the pillar, his gaping eye boring into me; the obliterated corpse of Stuart McDonald, his blood splashed against the wall of the tower; the shriek of the ravens circling inside the confines of my head. I wondered if they would soon join the company of my recent cases and continue to plague me, just like the ghosts of the Malinowski children, the victims of Peter Garris from Bradbury End, the slaughtered psychics of Aumbry, and the dying spectre of the fascist killer Lenny Kerrigan.

I shook myself, as if to dislodge that last persistent shadow.

Twenty minutes later, I pulled into the vast car park that served the Winter Wonderland. Beyond the fence surrounding the fair, all the familiar silhouettes of my childhood rose up, stark against the pale morning sky. The soundtrack of my youth too, dance beats from the Waltzer and the galloper's jangled calliope.

Big Sam Urnshaw greeted me at the gate, a grin as generous as his heart plastered across his face.

'What's going on, Sam?' I asked.

He touched an oil-stained finger to his nose. 'Just get on over to your dad's Waltzer,' he said. 'Some folks are waiting for you there.'

I passed through the turnstile with all the other early-bird punters, cutting between the crowds with the practised ease of a born showman. Eyes followed me, whispers exchanged behind hands, familiar faces alight with excitement. Detective that I was, I still didn't guess what awaited me around the next bend in the drag.

Sal, Jodie, Old Man Jericho, Ben Halliday and a host of other showpeople were gathered together at the footboards of the Waltzer. Even Webster stood proudly among them, his threadbare coat freshly brushed. The ride had been temporarily closed and cordoned off, though the lights continued to flash as if in mute celebration. And at the centre of the gathering, perched on the third step, Harry Moorhouse, resplendent in his own best suit. Those gentle jade eyes brimming with tears, as beautiful as the day I had first met him at that university pub back in Oxford.

He waved me over and I passed through the crowd, Travellers smiling and slapping me on the back. Jodie hugged me around the waist, her impish features scrunched up with a secret she could barely hold on to. She was dressed in her prettiest frock and even Sal had made an effort, swapping her work overalls for a gorgeous ivory dress. My dad stopped me, straightening my tie and leaning in to whisper: 'All right, son. Your mum would be very proud.'

'Dad,' I frowned at him. 'What's going on?'

Ben stepped in, placing his huge hand on my shoulder. 'Happy for you, mate,' he said. 'So bloody happy.'

'Thanks for looking after him,' I said with a shake of my head. 'So, listen, did you find anything in that lock-up back in Ealing?'

His smile faltered a little. 'Nothing much. Anyway, Harry's waiting. On you go.'

It didn't really take a detective to work out what was going on here. Even my sleep-deprived brain had finally made the inevitable deduction. Still, I couldn't quite believe it. Harry beamed and glanced at Jodie, who came forward, all excitable solemnity, and handed him a small black box. The pixie then retreated, taking her mother's hand. Sal blew me a kiss, wiped away a tear. I felt my own tears start as Harry dropped to one knee, that sweet face smiling up at me.

'My love,' he said. 'My Scott. My big, clever, brooding idiot. I've got something to ask you.'

I stared at him, dumbfounded.

'Ever since you found me again, I've been waiting to speak these words.'

'Harry...'

He laughed. 'Don't start, or I won't be able to get through this.' He lifted the little box, unclasped the lid. I saw a spark of silver inside. 'You are the love of my life. My best friend. You rescued me when I needed rescuing, and so now, will you do me the honour of—'

'Scott Jericho. Look at me. I'm here. *I'm back.*'

We all turned our heads to the punter who stood in the middle of the crowd. Garris, hooded and skeletal, as he had been throughout my encounters with him in Fenchurch, his voice back to that dried-out rasp. He had something in his hand.

Webster let loose a single outraged bark. And in the next instant, the crowd was screaming and I was pulling Harry to his feet, instinctively hugging him to me. The gun was raised and, with his free hand, Garris pulled back the hood covering his face.

And it wasn't Garris at all.

The memory crashed in on me at last: I am back in my hospital bed in Aumbry, and the real Peter Garris is standing over me, speaking his revelation: 'Lenny Kerrigan is alive and well and sends his compliments. Well, you never actually saw him die, now, did you?'

Lenny Kerrigan, fascist thug and child killer, resurrected in this shambling broken form. He leaned on his walking frame as he trained the gun on me.

'You left me to die,' he croaked. 'Back in that library in Bradbury End. But *he* saved me. He brought me back to life. And now he has freed me. Fuck you, Scott Jericho. Fuck you to hell!'

Kerrigan squeezed the trigger.

A deafening explosion.

And Harry jerked in my arms.

'Scott.' He blinked up at me, and I heard Kerrigan shriek in pain and frustration. From the corner of my eye, I saw Ben and half a dozen Travellers drag the killer to the ground, burying his fragile body beneath theirs. 'Scott, something's wrong ...'

And there was. Desperately wrong. Harry's eyes rolled white in their sockets, his mouth dropped open, slack and full of blood. Somewhere little Jodie was screaming and my dad was shouting orders and, above it all, I could hear the slow dead hammer of my heart.

'My love,' I said. 'My love.'

But Harry wasn't moving anymore.

Epilogue

I REACHED INTO MY JACKET POCKET, took out the hip flask and half a dozen pills and swilled down that numbing delight with a mouthful of vodka. The man beside me started to say something but a glance stopped him dead. And so, we sat in silence in the mobster's parlour, where Harry and I had once sat not all that long ago.

Ben shuffled in his seat, his huge hands folded together. He'd been a good friend these past few days. His only crime: when I gently relinquished Harry to the care of the paramedics, he had stopped me tearing my way through a cordon of police, wrenching Lenny Kerrigan from their protection and beating the sadistic fuck to death.

I love Ben, but I might never forgive him that.

Later, he told me what he and Harry had found inside Garris's storage unit in Ealing. And of course, hearing those details, it had made perfect sense that the monster had sent his broken lapdog to kill me. Somehow, Garris had kept Kerrigan alive after their encounter in Bradbury End, for what reason, God only knew. But in those months of caring for him, a docile obedience and dependency must have been nurtured. A kind of Stockholm syndrome hardwired into the fascist's shattered mind.

Perhaps for his own amusement, Garris had then sent his plaything to dog my footsteps in Fenchurch. A man who had lost his own identity and taken on the mannerisms and even the speech patterns of someone he saw, not as his tormentor and mutilator, but rather his protector and saviour. And then, when Harry and Ben's investigation had touched close to Peter Garris's most treasured secret, the dog had been let off his leash.

The only question was, where had Garris squirrelled Kerrigan away all this time? After all, following the business in Bradbury End, I'd had my former mentor under surveillance for months. And then Ben had reminded me: back when we were en route to Garris's empty house, ready to dig up the marigold patch that I'd thought contained Kerrigan's corpse, Harry had suggested that maybe Garris had some long-term confederate. A disciple who'd followed his lead from the very beginning. He was, after all, always good at attracting devoted followers. I myself was proof of that. Whoever this mystery accomplice might be, I would hunt him down eventually, just as I would now hunt Garris, whatever the cost.

Sitting in the hospital corridor, waiting for news on Harry, I had made a vow to Ben. We'll find Peter, but first I must pay Mark Noonan a visit. I needed a favour. Ben had caught my meaning and tried to dissuade me. But here we are, paying court to the bloated mobster sitting opposite us.

'I've decided not to take any action against Wesley's mother,' he told me with a bored wave of those chubby fingers. 'I hardly knew the kid anyway, and I don't like hurting women if I can help it.'

I nodded. 'If only she'd known that, it might have saved a lot of heartache and bloodshed in Fenchurch.'

'Well, you can't blame me for that,' he grunted, taking a sip of the festive eggnog at his elbow. 'It was your job to go up there and sort things out. If you made a pig's ear of it, that's your lookout. Anyway, I'm a busy man, Scott, so let's cut to the chase. What are you after?'

'It's about Harry,' I said.

'Oh yes, the pretty boy.' For once, there was no mockery in Noonan's voice; there might even have been a trace of pity, if you listened hard enough. 'I was sorry to hear what happened to the kid. Some crazy fuck who bore a grudge against you, wasn't it? Well, you mustn't blame yourself, Scotty. Collateral damage is an occupational hazard for men like us.'

He leaned over and placed a brotherly hand on my knee. He had fancied me once, but I thought those days were over. I glanced at myself in the reflection of the glass cabinet that housed Nana Noonan's collection of porcelain piggy banks. The longs hours of Harry's coma had taken their toll on me. I now looked closer to sixty than thirty.

'How's the boy doing anyway?' Noonan asked.

'They're not sure if he's suffered any brain damage,' I said. 'They won't until he wakes up. But he's very weak and the doctors are concerned that something like a chest infection or pneumonia will probably kill him before the new year.'

'Scott,' Ben murmured.

'Sad Christmas for you,' Noonan sighed. 'But what can I do to help?'

I sat back in my chair. It was time to barter with the devil. To sell my soul.

I would, and gladly.

'Lenny Kerrigan is on remand at HMP Hazelhurst,' I said. 'I can't get to him, but you can. You'll have people you know inside. You take care of him, Mark. You kill him for me, but I want you to make him suffer first.'

A beat. The sonorous tick of Nana's cuckoo clock.

'And what do I get out of this arrangement?'

'Me.' I fixed him with my gaze. 'I come back and work for you. I do anything you ask. Anything. As long you take care of Lenny Kerrigan.'

'Anything?' Noonan echoed, a faint smile on his lips. 'And what will be left then of Scott Jericho?'

I looked down at the golden crucifix in my hand. The single item that Harry had retrieved from Garris's lock-up, a place that Ben told me had been stuffed with earrings and purses and rings and odd shoes, all the manifold trophies of old kills. And this one relic, once given to my mother by Tom Makepeace before he left the travelling life for good. Taken by Peter Garris after he killed her and then staged my mother's body on the road to look like she'd been the victim of a car accident. Now I understood, finally. He had been in my life longer than I had ever imagined, a dark shadow tracking my footsteps.

I turned the cross over and looked at the inscription on the back: *For my darling friend Marian. All my love, Tommy.*

'Scott Jericho is dead,' I said, looking up at the mobster. 'Dead and buried. It's time for a new chapter to begin.'

Glossary of Traveller Slang

Chap: a worker on the fairground who is not himself a showperson.
Chavvy: a Traveller child.
Chor: to steal.
Dinlo: an idiot; a moron.
Dukker/dukkerin: fortune telling.
Gavvers: the police.
Ground: abbreviation for 'fairground'.
Jel: to go/to leave.
Joskin: a non-Traveller. NB 'rank joskin' can be used as an insult akin to a 'proper idiot'.
Juk: a fairground dog; usually a watchdog.
Juvenile: a child's ride.
Minder: a showman or a chap looking after a ride or attraction.
Mooie: face.
Moosh: a man.
Muller: to die or murder.
Mullerdy: haunted/creepy.
Parney: urine or to urinate.
Posh: earnings, wages, profit.
Rokker: to speak.
Ruk: a fight.
Scran: food.

Acknowledgements

THANKS, AS EVER, TO MY brilliant agent Veronique Baxter, my TV/film rights agent Clare Israel, Jem Dryer, Sara Langham, Deirdre Power, and everyone at David Higham Associates. To my editor Ben Willis, who never fails to encourage and re-energise me, especially when I'm flagging mid-draft, all my gratitude. Thanks also to the fabulous team at Zaffre – Isabella Boyne, Sarah Benton, Georgia Marshall, Melissa Cox, Holly Milnes, Justine Taylor, Beth Whitelaw, Chelsea Graham, and Jenny Richards.

Special thanks to Hannah Campbell, Suzanne Mackie, Sophie Loizou and Seth Sinclair for their enthusiasm and support for the Jericho books.

Once again, I am indebted to DC David Bettison of Lincolnshire Police CID and the brilliant author and advisor on all things police procedural, Graham Bartlett (check out Graham's spellbinding books and his advice for crime novelists, established and aspiring, at www.policeadvisor.co.uk). Thanks also to Jane Mitchell for her expert views on Fenland churches and ecclesiastical architecture. Naturally, all mistakes are my own! Thanks as well to all the booksellers and bloggers who have taken Scott Jericho to their hearts – I am very grateful.

The past year has been a delightful whirlwind with KILLING JERICHO winning the Genre-Busting Book of the Year Fingerprint Award at Capital Crime, being shortlisted for the Theakston Old Peculier Crime Novel of the Year, and the Polari Prize. I'd like to thank all the judges and those organising these wonderful awards and festivals for their hard work and passion for books.

My heartfelt thanks, as ever, to my family – Georgia, Carly, Jon, Jamie, Johnny, Lyla, Jackson and Charly. And to my partner and soon-to-be husband, Christopher White. I love you, darling.

Finally, a quick favour. If you have enjoyed BURYING JERICHO, I'd very much appreciate you taking a moment to leave a review on the site from which you purchased the book or the usual review places online. Just a few words will do. It will help readers like you find the book and encourages word-of-mouth support so that Scott can continue solving cases!

Until next time, farewell Travellers and joskins alike! We hope to welcome you again to Jericho Fair very, very soon ...

SCOTT JERICHO
CRIME FICTION'S FIRST TRAVELLER DETECTIVE

AND YOU HAVEN'T SEEN THE LAST OF JERICHO YET...

Can't get enough?
Visit *www.williamhussey.co.uk*
to find out more about
Scott Jericho and other books
from William Hussey.